Turn of the Tide
The Return of Nathaniel Brookes

By

Elizabeth Revill

For Andrew

1

The return of Nathaniel Brookes

THE RIDER GALLOPED FURIOUSLY along the battered coastline, buffeted by storms and winter rain. His black cloak streamed behind him in the attacking wind resembling a pursuing shadow of a terrifying creature of the night. The cape flapped and tugged at its fastenings and billowed behind the horseman, who was now drenched in both sweat and rain with the urgency of his mission.

He pulled up his steed, whose nostrils flared and streamed with smoke-like vapour as he looked down on the scene below. A sleepy village shivered next to the bustling town, which sheltered against the hillside that fed down to the golden sand and the voracious sea that boiled and churned on this the filthiest of days.

The rider took off once more almost losing his distinctive Tricorne hat in the continuing blustering wind. Young Samuel Reeves picked his way down the sodden cliff path littered with stones swept by cascading water, which escaped from the fields, and ran in rivulets down the track onto the road below. From there he cantered outside the village of Mumbles to a large smartly elegant and pretty property dressed in newly flowering climbing wisteria gleaming with raindrops. He tied up his stallion, Hunter, whose back was steaming with heat from the journey. He opened the small wooden gate, hurried down the path and pounded on the door.

The answer was slow in coming so he hammered again. Dainty footsteps were heard approaching and the door opened. Fine featured, dark eyed beauty, Jenny Brookes, wife of Nathaniel, looked enquiringly at the visitor who stood six feet tall. He swept off his sopping wet hat in a shower of water droplets and his ebony curls soaked by the rain hung in ringlets around his face. He was a handsome man with chiselled features and his eyes were a deeply piercing blue.

"Sorry to disturb you... Ma'am," he added as a boy darted to her side and hid behind her skirts. "I'm seeking Nathaniel Brookes. Is this his residence?"

Jenny was about to speak when the warm tones of her mother-in-law, Myah Brookes reached them, "Who is it, Jenny?" The figure of a graceful older woman came into view. She was drying her hands on a rough towel.

"If you please, Milady, I am seeking Nathaniel Brookes on a most urgent matter."

"And I see you are soaked to the skin on this foul day, Sir... Mr...?"

"Reeves, Samuel Reeves."

"Is that your horse out there?" asked Myah with a nod of her head.

"Indeed, Ma'am. It is."

"Come in out of the wet and I'll have Eric attend to your steed."

"Thank you," the stranger gratefully accepted the offer and stepped into the dry. His clothes dripped and he apologised profusely.

"Please, don't worry," said Jenny in her lilting Welsh, musical tones. "Let me take your cloak and hat, we have a roaring fire in the scullery and Edith will put them to dry on the fireguard. Edith! Take these for the gentlemen."

The kitchen maid, Edith, scurried to the hallway; she was an attractive girl of about eighteen, with burnished copper hair, and rosy pink cheeks. Her eyes widened as she took in the stranger and her glowing face blushed to a deeper hue. She hastily cast her eyes down from the man's engaging smile and stuttered, "Aye, of course, Miss Jenny." She curtseyed and fled to the back of the house carrying the saturated garments.

Jenny closed the door against the invading wind and driving rain as Eric was seen leading the stallion around the back to the stable yard.

"This way, Sir. Have you come far?"

"I have ridden for two days and nights from Devon."

"And your business?" asked Nathaniel's mother.

"If you please, I carry an urgent message for Mr Brookes. Do you know when he will be home?"

"He is attending to the birth of Fanny Jenkins' youngest child. It has been a trying time for her; she has been in labour longer than she should. But to answer your question, Mr Reeves, we never know when he will be back when dealing with such an emergency."

"Then if you don't mind, I'll wait."

Samuel Reeves followed the ladies through the house to the kitchen, where Edith had already laid out the gentleman's drenched garments, which were now drying in front of the roaring fire.

"Some refreshment, Sir? Some tea maybe?" asked Jenny.

"That would be lovely, thank you."

"Sit down, please." Jenny pulled out a chair and Samuel Reeves sat as Edith prepared a pot of tea. "I expect you need something hot inside you. Edith, get the gentleman a dish of cawl."

Soon there was the sound of dishes clattering. Edith served up some of the nourishing Welsh stew and a hunk of bread, which the man hungrily devoured, before expressing his pleasure, "That was more than delicious and more than welcome. I thank you."

Edith flushed with pleasure at the praise and scuttled back to the fire to turn the gentleman's cloak over again.

"So, Mr Reeves, you have travelled some distance?" enquired Myah.

"I have. If I'd known the weather was going to turn so drastically I would have deferred the trip until this shocking storm was done."

"Ah yes, these early summer months can be so fickle, the spring flowers bloom and fade as the summer ones begin to bud then sometimes instead of refreshing showers we receive a battalion of buckets to swamp us all. The rain has fair battered my remaining roses and the budding honeysuckle. Although they do say this summer should be better."

"Anything would be an improvement on the wet summer we suffered last year, so it would;" agreed Jenny.

Myah added, "I do pray this violent storm is but a temporary affliction, as the rest of the month has been unseasonably warm."

"It has indeed," confirmed the gentleman. "Folks in the country say to look to nature to predict our weather."

"I have done that since I was a little girl," smiled Jenny. Her eyes misted over, "Just like my father taught me to watch the spiders and their web building; to look at the blossom and berries on the trees; the flight of the birds. My dad was wise and knew it all."

Young Bartholomew tugged at his mother's skirts and whispered, "When is Daddy coming home?"

Jenny tenderly caressed her son's head, "He won't be long; I'm sure, my lovely. And look," she pointed through the window. "The sun is starting to peep through the clouds."

"Will the wind chase them all away?" he asked, his face crumpled in concern.

"I'm sure it will," laughed Jenny.

"Good, I want to go out on Minstrel. Daddy promised."

There was the sound of a door opening and footsteps striding down the corridor to the kitchen.

"Daddy!" cried young Bartholomew, his face creased in smiles as he ran to his father. Nathaniel Brookes scooped up his young son who protested vehemently, "Put me down… you're all wet."

"And do you know why?" asked Nathaniel seriously.

"No."

"Because it's been raining outside." Everyone laughed and then Nathaniel's eyes lit on the stranger, "What have we here? Visitors on a day like today?"

The man rose and locked Nathaniel's dark eyes with his own penetrating gaze. He extended his hand, "Samuel Reeves at your service. I come on a most urgent mission."

Nathaniel looked questioningly but said nothing. Samuel reached into his inside pocket and removed a letter bearing the red seal of the crown. Nathaniel turned it over in his hands and stared at it.

There was a pause.

"Aren't you going to open it?" asked his mother.

Nathaniel hesitated before breaking the seal and reading the contents. Both his wife and mother looked expectantly at him.

"I've been summoned to Ilfracombe in Devon."

"Whatever for?" asked his mother, Myah.

"They want me to ride again temporarily and patrol the South West Coast."

"But you can't," protested Jenny. "We need you here; the village needs you."

"It's signed by the King himself," said Nathaniel and he tossed the letter on the table for them all to see. Those in the room fell silent.

Eventually Jenny spoke in a small tight voice, "What are you going to do?"

"I don't know," sighed Nathaniel. "I really don't know."

2

Jamaica Four Weeks Earlier

THE SUN SHONE DOWN on the gentle slopes of the Blue Mountains some distance from the vibrant town of Kingston. A spectacular array of blooms decorated the land and the fragrance drifted on the southern breeze attracting armies of pollenating insects and birds. Close to the foot of the mountains was a small homestead with chickens running free. A washing line billowed with freshly laundered crisp cotton sheets and clothes drying freely in the fresh country air.

A handsome black and white working horse nibbled at a net of hay together with a toffee coloured mare and her foal in a small paddock. A brindle lurcher type mongrel lay asleep in the shade by an outbuilding. His head lifted up as he heard some unfamiliar sounds rolling on the breeze and caught the whiff of a scent. He whined softly in his throat and rose to his feet. There was a sudden bang and clatter further afield. The usually sociable dog laid back his ears and barked in frenzied agitation before disappearing around the back of the barn. He headed for a line of broken trees, which acted as camouflage. From this vantage point the dog watched, a soft rumbling coming from his throat.

Aleka stood at her table rolling out pastry dough and fashioning it into small patties. She was a tall, majestic looking woman with bronzed skin, high cheekbones, a neat nose and full sensual lips. Her beauty was striking, her tightly curled hair, braided and plaited with brightly coloured beads. She hummed happily as she worked when she heard the dog bark and then stop as suddenly. She shrugged and continued at her task but then there was a huge kerfuffle outside as the chickens ran squawking in the dusty yard.

Aleka wiped the flour off her hands and brushed them down her large white apron. She hastened to the door of her modest home to see what the ruckus was all about.

She was startled to see a band of about twelve men, some on horseback, ransacking her yard. One man had gathered freshly laid eggs, which he had in his hat whilst another was trying to catch the chickens. One ruffian had already caught two and snapped their necks. He swung them around his head in glee.

Another miscreant opened the gate to the paddock and tried to lead Samson away but he reared up and whinnied and seeing his chance bolted off into open country. The mare and foal were easily caught and their reins tied to one of the riders who cursed. "Leave the other. We'll pick him up on our return." His eyes lit on Aleka. "Well, well, what have we here?" Aleka stiffened and turned to run inside for a weapon. "Get her!" screamed the brute with tobacco stained rotting teeth.

One ginger-headed thug raced around to the back of the place with an evil leer on his face. Another, a fat, pot-bellied, bearded man dashed into the house after her. Minutes later he retreated with his arms raised as Aleka holding a loaded blunderbuss forced him out through the door back into the yard.

"You're on private property," she said calmly and clearly. "You have no business here. Leave, now." She spoke excellent English with only the hint of a Jamaican accent.

The leader of the rabble raised his hand, "We don't want no trouble. But my men are hungry. We've travelled a long distance. Just need a little sustenance and we'll be on our way."

Aleka didn't flinch, "Go or I'll shoot."

The leader played for time pretending to reason with her as the other men watched warily. They could see their ginger compatriot creeping up stealthily behind her. A quick shove from behind sent her sprawling and she lost the grip on her firearm. The other men were quick to pounce, snatching away her weapon and dragging her to her feet.

The leader, an arrogant man named Clive Bethell, screamed at his men, "Be careful! Don't mark her. She'll fetch a good price. Tie her hands and load her onto that mare. The rest of you take a good look around see what else you can find."

As soon as the dog saw his mistress being trussed up and dragged away he flew from his vantage point, hackles raised, growling fiercely. He barked and yapped at the feet of the horse where Clive Bethell sat. He roared, "Someone get rid of that cur now."

A brutish looking man, short with bandy legs, and an ugly lopsided face approached the animal brandishing a flintlock pistol. He took aim at the precise moment the dog leapt. Aleka cried out "Valiant! No!" The yell from the woman threw the shooter off guard and he let loose with his shot, which winged the dog in the shoulder. Valiant yelped, and urged by his mistress who shrieked, "Valiant, run!" the dog scrambled up and before another shot was fired he raced three-legged back to the woods.

One of the others lifted his weapon but Bethell called out, "Leave it. Don't waste your shot. He'll die anyway; probably in agony," he guffawed intending to inflict even more pain on the very striking woman he'd just captured.

Six of the looters dived into the house with a whoop, while Aleka was bound and tied and put on the horse. The men emerged with hessian sacks full of goods. These were hurriedly packed onto a mule. The criminals left quickly laughing raucously and headed for Kingston, formerly Santiago, and onto the docks to the slave ship that awaited them.

Once the mob of ruffians had left the place, the brindle lurcher came out of hiding and limped back into the yard. He looked around mournfully at the devastation, licked his injured shoulder and lay down. He raised his head to the cobalt blue sky and howled.

3

Goliath returns

IT WAS MANY HOURS later as the heat of the day had begun to cool into a warm and pleasant evening; a small cart pulled by another powerful working horse came trundling up the dusty track toward the house.

Goliath jumped down and stared in horror at his home, his yard littered with feathers and a dead chicken. He called out, panic filling his voice, "Aleka? Aleka?" He fled into the house shouting out his wife's name. He saw the interrupted baking, and that the house had been ransacked, grain and supplies had been stolen. He ran up the stairs, the mattresses had been ripped off the bed and shredded with a knife. His blood ran cold. He pulled up the rug and prised up a loose floorboard. The tin box was still there where Goliath and Aleka kept their money and valuables but that was little consolation to him for the loss of his wife. A roar of anguish erupted from his belly but as his bellow petered out he heard a strident whinny outside. Goliath ran to the yard where the magnificent Samson stood who shook his mane and whinnied again. Goliath crossed to him talking softly, soothingly and calming the anxious animal. There was another sound, a whimper, Goliath stopped and turned to see his injured dog, who limped pitifully toward him.

"Oh, Valiant. What have they done?"

Valiant sat and looked at his master putting his head on one side. He whimpered again.

Goliath carefully gathered up his dog and put him in the cart. He saddled Samson before tying him to the wagon and went back inside the house. He emerged soon after carrying a carpetbag, threw it on the seat next to him and urged the horse on. He set off along the dusty road in the direction of the town.

He passed few people, just a couple of weary workers footsore and tired.

He took a turning off the main track down a red earth and dusty lane. The cart rumbled on until he reached another homestead that belonged to his nearest neighbour.

Abraham Jacobs, a broad man with fire in his dark eyes, emerged with his musket levelled at what he considered was an intruder. As soon as he recognised Goliath he lowered his weapon. "Sorry, my friend. I didn't realise it was you." As he took in his neighbour's expression his tone became more serious, "What's happened?"

Goliath quickly explained, "My house has been looted. They've taken Aleka, my horses and shot my dog."

"Oh no, I'm sorry. There were rumours of slavers in the area. They have taken my farmhand's daughter, Abigail. I came home too late to stop them."

"I, too. I was late back from the plantation where I oversee the workers. They didn't come there."

"They wouldn't dare. White man owned property is taboo for them. They are seeking folks like us, but this time it's the women they're after, especially Mulattos, like Aleka."

"I hate that word."

"I, too… The white men consider them more attractive than Negroes like us but look down on them as half-breeds… What do you want me to do?"

"Can you take my horse and cart? And look after Valiant. He needs treatment."

"Bring him inside."

Goliath picked up his dog carefully that looked at him trustingly, whimpering softly and carried him into the house. Abraham quickly cleared the table of the few odd items and Valiant was set down.

Abraham examined the lurcher carefully. "It looks like the bullet has gone clean through. He's lucky it didn't hit any bone or major artery. I'll clean him up and pack it to stop the bleeding. It only seems to be oozing a little, now. I'll strap it up and with rest he should be all right."

"Thank you, Abraham. I knew you would help."

"I'm a bit rusty, it's some years since I treated animals, but I think Valiant will survive. The main thing is not for the wound to get infected. The strapping will stop the animal worrying the wound. How long will you be gone for?"

"I don't know. If I can catch the ship before it leaves port I'll rip it apart to find Aleka, if not…"

"If not?"

"I'll follow the vessel to whichever land it's headed. Samson will come with me."

"That'll cost."

"I have money."

"Don't let anyone hear you say that. Be careful how you bargain."

"I'll be fine," insisted Goliath but if I don't come back, the horse, cart and my property is yours."

Abraham nodded, "What about your job?"

"I'll have to send word to Mr Brannigan that I can no longer be there."

"I can do that for you, if you wish?"

"Have you writing equipment?"

"I have."

"Then I'll avail you of that while you tend to Valiant."

Abraham went to his cupboard and took out paper, pen and ink and as Abraham cleaned the dog's wound, Goliath wrote. He completed his missive and passed it to Abraham who took it and nodded, "I'll see Mr Brannigan gets this. Your animals and land will be safe with me. And if you see Abigail…"

"If I do, I will bring her back with me."

"Thank you."

The two men eyed each other, Goliath, a giant in men's terms standing at six feet seven inches, powerfully built and lithe like a cat; and Abraham short, stocky but none-the-less strong of stature with bulging muscles from years of working the land. They shook hands. Goliath bade goodbye to his beloved pet.

"Valiant… you have certainly lived up to your name." Valiant whined in his throat. "You be good now, stay with Abraham. Guard him as you would me."

It was if the animal understood his every word. He whined softly and licked Goliath's hand. "Good bye, my friend," and with that he strode out through the door, untied Samson, fixed his bag to the saddle and mounted. Goliath galloped off as the sun was beginning to set. It slipped down onto the horizon a flaming ball of glowing embers that set fire to the darkening sky.

It was a long ride to Kingston. Four hours later, he arrived, saddle sore and tired but the urgent need inside him forced him on. The ride would normally have taken longer but he had spurred Samson almost to his limits. He rode straight down to the docks, where merchants were clearing their wares that hadn't sold that day.

Three ships were moored up and Goliath pounded down to the first gangplank and accosted a sailor on duty. "Tell me, are any of these ships carrying slaves in its cargo?"

The sailor shook his head, "Not here. We're a merchant vessel, livestock and passenger ship bound for England. Next one along is headed to more of the Spice Islands before shipping off to America."

"What about a slaver?" persisted Goliath.

"There was one in port earlier. I don't like them or their kind but they left over four hours ago."

"Did they carry many?"

"Women; mainly women from what I could see, handsome ones, too, shackled and harnessed like cattle."

"Do you know where they've gone?"

"Rumour has it they're bound for Europe. England, I think. Someone mentioned Devon. Sorry, I can't tell you anymore."

"Thank you, my friend. You have been most helpful. What about the third ship?"

"Sets sail later tonight, stopping off at some places before going onto London."

"Does it take passengers?

"No. Goods only."

"Tell me when are you leaving?"

"The Lady Jane sails tomorrow afternoon, why?"

"Are there any spaces left?"

"I believe so, but you'll have to speak to the captain, Captain Heath."

"Where can I find him?"

"He'll be in the Coconut Shack next to the Tavern."

Goliath nodded, thanked the man again, strode off to Samson, mounted and trotted off the quayside into the less desirable part of town with its inns and whorehouses. He attracted some curious stares as he made his way through the busy port but the further he got into the less than salubrious neighbourhood, people went about their business and ignored him.

He tied up his horse outside the Coconut Shack famed for its rum and ale.

There was a water trough, next to the wooden veranda and Samson eagerly drank his fill. Goliath patted his loyal steed. "I'll have you settled soon," he assured Samson.

Goliath entered the shack, stooping to get through the door. His bulk filled the gap blocking the last of the fading sunlight. His eyes searched the bar as he looked for a seafaring man. He spotted one engaged in a game of cards and strode across, "Captain Heath?"

"Who wants to know?" growled the captain unhappy at being forced to look up from his hand.

"I do. I understand you have some passenger berths left on The Lady Jane. I require one and room below for my horse."

The captain folded his hand and stood up, "It'll cost."

"I can pay. How much?"

"Let's take this outside," said the captain as he noticed too many drunken ruffians taking an interest in the conversation. Heath, a good-sized man himself followed Goliath out onto the wooden veranda. They spoke in hushed tones; a deal was struck and they shook hands.

"Payment will be made before I board the ship tomorrow, you have my word." Goliath untied Samson and mounted. He encouraged Samson to trot quickly to a pleasanter part of town where there were better lodging houses and inns. He pulled up outside, 'The Dusky Maiden' and entered.

He was greeted cheerfully by the owner, a buxom, smiling woman in brightly coloured garb. "I must say I'm surprised to see you here," she smiled. "How is that lovely wife of yours?"

Goliath sighed heavily, "Let me see to Samson first and I'll tell you all. I need a room for the night, Rosie. Can you put me up?"

"Take your pick. Most of my residents left this morning all returning to their ships. I'll put you in number three, is that all right?"

Nathaniel inclined his head, "And have you paper and pen? I need to write a letter."

Rosie grinned toothily, "I'll put it in your room." Goliath nodded and Rosie went to prepare room three.

Goliath led Samson out to the backyard and stable where King, an amiable groomsman waited. "I'll groom him, if you can get some fresh water and hay. Here's something for your trouble." Goliath flicked a copper coin to the man and set about unsaddling his horse and giving him a good rub down. Satisfied he'd done his best, he bade his steed good night and returned to the house where Rosie had prepared a spicy fish stew served with flatbread.

Goliath bolted it down like a ravenous wolf; he'd forgotten how hungry he was; in between mouthfuls he explained what had happened. Rosie tutted in disapproval, her face puckered in a scowl; "Lordy me… Aleka – she a fine woman; refined and educated. Why they take her?"

"Abraham said the slavers were after Mulattos."

"Ah," nodded Rosie sagely. "They think they have prettier faces more to the white man's taste."

"Maybe."

"You should tell her father. He'd do something to get her back."

"Aleka's father has been sent to take over from the Governor in Sierra Leone. I'll send him word. Now I must write that letter. I have to catch that ship before it sails to take a message to my old friend in England."

"Friend?"

"Nathaniel Brookes. If anyone can help me; he can."

4

Decisions

THE WARRING CLOUDS HAD disbanded leaving a clutter free azure sky. Birds sang in joy at the departed storm and the air smelt sweet and fresh. Nathaniel and Samuel were walking on the sand at Mumbles. Nathaniel's horse, Jessie, had been tethered at the mouth of the cliff path with Samuel's stallion, Hunter.

They were deep in conversation as they strolled to the water's edge. Nathaniel picked up a flat stone and skimmed it across the surface of the now peaceful sea and watched as it skipped and bounced before sinking through the water to the sandy floor below.

"When do you need my answer?"

"We were hoping that you would return with me," replied Samuel. "Mr Bulled begged me to persuade you by any means, hence the order from the King. Our sovereign is not in good health and he doesn't want to see the seas plundered, ships wrecked and contraband filling the pockets of criminals. He needs to send a message to these rogues that we mean business. You did an excellent job on the Welsh coast. There hasn't been a man to match you since."

"I doubt that," said Nathaniel modestly. "I had help. My man Goliath was a huge part of that success. How many men do we have?"

"Sad to say but there's just me. Smugglers slaughtered my friend and colleague and now any would be volunteers have simply backed out. No one wants to be recruited as a Riding Officer these days. Their lives are short and difficult. The people ostracise us as if we are lepers."

"I know that feeling, but I have a job here. I am the only medical man around for miles. I have the respect of the people and I was about to start giving a helping hand to the newly formed local school. Lady Caroline Bevan was counting on me to educate the children in the rudiments of science."

"I understood it would be difficult but it is only temporary. I am told that we can supply a doctor in your place if that would sway you, Sir?"

"Please call me Nathaniel. Pray, tell me how you would do that?"

"We have ways and means and a man of the medical profession desperate to relocate."

"Why would that be?"

"Let's just say an indiscretion with a titled lady is proving more than problematical and he has a need to escape."

"I see... Let me think on it. I have no wish to return to riding even in the short term but the King's summons is hard to ignore... We have a room for you at the house. Stay with us and I will give you my answer in the morning... But tell me, what of the dragoons?"

"Few and far between. Most are tied up on the Cornish coast. There are many more coves and caves where a smuggler can hide his wares."

"My brother in law is a captain. He is shortly to be sent to the South West; Bude, I believe or Penzance. I will speak with him and see if there is anything that can be done. Meanwhile, let us get back to the house. I promised my son a pony ride before dinner. And as you have witnessed, the weather can change in an instant. Although your things should be dry by now, Mr Reeves."

Samuel nodded politely, "Yes and thank you for the loan of a coat. But, call me Sam, as my friends do."

"Sam it is, then." The two men walked back up the beach to their waiting steeds and began their ride back to the house.

Jenny was pacing the kitchen with a worried expression on her face. She was clutching a letter in a familiar hand addressed to Nathaniel. "That's Goliath's hand, we only heard from him two months ago. I have a very bad feeling about this, so I do, what with the King's message and all."

Myah lightly scolded her, "Come, come Jenny. You and your premonitions; it may not be bad news. Nathaniel won't be long and then your curiosity will be satisfied and your fears abated, I'm sure."

But Jenny continued to pace and her hand continued to shake. "But what if he decides to go? What will we do?"

"I'm sure it won't come to that. But let's wait and see, first. You may be worrying unnecessarily."

Edith turned over the heavy cloak on the guard. It was now almost dry. She kept quiet as she went about her work but it was clear that it upset her to see her mistress so distressed.

Jenny dropped into a seat at the kitchen table and her little boy snuggled up to her. The sound of the front door opening was heard and strong footsteps marched up the passageway into the kitchen.

Nathaniel felt the tension in the room and looked at his wife's face, her expression and demeanour, and then at his mother. "What's happened?"

"You've had another letter." Jenny passed Nathaniel the message.

"It's Goliath's writing," said Nathaniel curiously.

"I told you I recognised it," said Jenny to Myah. "What does it say?" she asked anxiously as Nathaniel ripped it open and began to read.

He looked up, "I must say his English has come on in leaps and bounds since his marriage to Aleka, no more Jamaican speak." The others waited quietly until he had finished reading. Nathaniel sighed, and tossed the missive on the table. "This changes everything."

"Why? What's happened?"

"Slavers have abducted Aleka supposedly to Devon. Goliath is following; if not already in the country, he will be shortly and Samson, too. Read for yourself. It's a sorry tale of woe." Myah picked up the letter and began to scour it. Nathaniel pounded his hand on the table. "My mind is made up." He turned to Sam. "Get word to your medical man to come here. I will return with you."

"But, Nathaniel…" interjected Jenny her face filled with concern. "What are we to do without you?"

"Goliath saved my life and yours. I cannot deny him my help in his time of need. I will meet with him, together we will find his wife and you, my sweet will look after our son until I return."

Myah passed the letter to Jenny, "I would expect nothing less of you, my son. It is a matter of honour. But I have to admit I'm afraid. These rogues you seek to control are vile and vicious."

"All the more reason why I must help him to find her."

"And I'm afraid of losing you," added Jenny quietly. "So, I will come with you."

"And who will look after Bart? You can't leave him, Jenny. Much as it pains me to say goodbye, you are his mother."

Jenny looked down and sighed, "I know you are right, but I just can't bear the thought of you riding again. It is a dangerous occupation. It nearly did for us all before."

"And one, I know well. Believe me, Cariad; I intend to stay alive. It would be different if I was to be alone but I won't be. I will have Sam here, and Goliath. He is coming back to find Aleka, together with Samson."

Jenny looked crestfallen. Myah slipped an arm around her daughter-in-law. "I know how hard it can be. Remember I, too, was married to a Riding Officer. We will weather this storm together. Our place is here."

Jenny turned away; her face expressed a mixture of confusion and love. She nodded, "I know what you're telling me is right but it is hard to take, so it is."

"Come, let's not be maudlin," said Nathaniel. "Let us make the most of the little time we have left."

"Aye," said Jenny and whispered almost to herself, "And pray it won't be our last."

5

Ready to ride

JENNY STOOD BY THE window of the spare room with her arms folded as if closing herself off from the pain of separation that was about to befall her. The sunlight refracted in golden rays around her, framing her against the leaded glass, which gave her the appearance of an angelic being while she watched Nathaniel laying out his long black cloak and cocked hat. He stuffed various essential clothing items into an almost full portmanteau.

The room was littered with garments, maps and other accoutrements. His easily recognisable black leather medical bag waited by the door. He stood up to his full height and rubbed at his back before indicating his packed cases and clothes, "I never thought I'd be donning these again." He stooped once more and rummaged in a cupboard and removed, a variety of maps detailing the North Devon coastline and those of Cornwall. They went into another bag along with a spyglass, compass and writing implements.

He turned to his wife; "I must do my duty for the King and help my friend. If it wasn't for Goliath we might never have been alive or together. It will not be forever."

Jenny's eyes filled with tears ready to flow and tumble down her cheek. Nathaniel crossed to her and took her in his arms and crushed her to him. "My love, believe me, I will return to you I promise. We have a life to live together."

"Oh, Nathaniel, I wanted to tell you that …"

They were interrupted by a crash of horse's hooves outside. Nathaniel looked out of the window and saw his old friend Goliath dismounting from the horse he, Nathaniel, had bought for him, which Goliath had taken back with him to Jamaica, Samson.

"Well, I'm blessed! Goliath is here," smiled Nathaniel. "Come let us greet him."

Jenny gave a wistful smile and followed her husband from the room. Myah was standing by the door. She gave Jenny's hand a small squeeze and encouraged her with her eyes. Jenny fiercely brushed away the burgeoning tears, set her face in a neutral expression and moved from the room along the corridor to the grand staircase.

Edith was already scuttling to the front door to open it. She fell back, her mouth shaped in an O of horror and wonder as she laid eyes on the giant Negro.

"It's all right, Edith. Let him in," called Nathaniel as he ran down the stairs to greet his friend.

The two men looked at each other a clear bond of understanding between them. Goliath extended his hand, which Nathaniel brushed aside and he clasped his friend in a bear hug. Samuel Reeves came out to the hall and his jaw dropped when he saw the huge man who towered over Nathaniel.

Goliath grinned at Jenny standing shyly at the foot of the stairs, "Miss Jenny." He paced toward her and bowed his head, "Thank you for allowing Nathaniel to help me. I know it must be hard after everything."

Jenny came forward, "Dear, Goliath. How can we ever thank you?"

"You thank me by helping me."

"You sly old dog," said Nathaniel. "What's happened to all your broken English? I hardly recognise your words."

"My Aleka, she has taught me much. It's all due to her."

"Come into the kitchen, Edith get my friend some refreshment and you, my friend, can tell me everything."

Goliath followed Nathaniel; Myah, Jenny and Sam all traipsed after them. Into the scullery they went where Edith scuttled to the range her eyes filled with fear. She busied herself preparing some soft bread rolls and buttered them generously. She went to the larder and took out some cheese from under its muslin cover together with some newly picked shallots and laid them out on the table.

Goliath murmured his thanks and barely remembering his manners fell onto the food. He was clearly hungry. Nathaniel watched him, "Eat your fill my friend. We will have dinner later and set off tomorrow morning. I dare say the Customs' Man, Bulled, will only be too glad to have you ride with me. And now, what do you know of where they have taken Aleka?"

Goliath grunted his mouth full. He managed to speak, "The slaver was headed for England to Devon, a place called Ilfracombe. They were to come into Rappery Cove and unload. From there, who knows? It could be Bristol or anywhere."

"Not likely," interrupted Sam. "If they were taking them to Bristol market they would have docked there. That's the obvious place. Maybe they're headed for the Cornish markets like Redruth and St. Austell. There are many there that lag behind the rest of the country in wanting to end this damnable trade."

"Or maybe they're a special consignment," said Nathaniel.

"Aye, destined for the whorehouses in the docklands and ports," said Sam and then apologised when he saw Goliath's expression. "Sorry, Goliath, no offence intended."

"None taken. I know the minds of these men."

"It sounds as if they want to offload them quickly. Maybe they have free men and women among their captives,"

"They have. Aleka is no slave. She was the illegitimate daughter of an English Governor. He refused to cut her off and brought her up with his other children. She was educated. She has worked hard to teach others. Now she is gone. This bitterly cruel trade must end. Aleka's father has been campaigning hard to outlaw this vile business." Goliath spoke with fierce passion. "I heard most of the cargo were women. Mulattos mainly."

"What are Mulattos?" asked Jenny innocently.

Goliath fixed her with his dark brooding eyes, "Mixed breed, Miss Jenny. It is frowned on, for black and white to mix, it's despised; and it is not a pleasant term. The ship came first from St. Lucia and then to Jamaica. There they raided our homestead, killed animals, stole supplies and my Aleka. I must find her." There was anguish in his voice.

Nathaniel placed his hand on Goliath's huge clenched fist. "I promise you, as I swore to avenge my father's death so I will help you to find her."

Goliath nodded, "I believe you, Nathaniel. But the slave trade is a bloody and brutal business and must be stopped in law."

"Yes, it should," agreed Nathaniel. "I believe there are moves afoot to bring in new laws for just such a purpose; just as your father-in-law is working to that same end. I believe it will happen. Public opinion is turning against them."

"But it will be hard to change the minds of these traders. It is easy money for them and brings great profits. Here is but one country, there are many more that deal in this cruel business that are not so far advanced in working to outlaw this industry."

Nathaniel nodded, "Come, let us forget our troubles for a moment and enjoy our last night. We will leave tomorrow at dawn. It is a lengthy ride to Devon. Fortunately, the weather looks as if it will be in our favour."

"Aye," said Sam. "For the moment this storm has abated but I believe we face worse in Devon. On the north coast it can be notoriously wet."

Dawn came all too soon for Jenny. She gazed out of her window as the sky burned with red fire while the sun rose up from the east. She gasped aloud at the sight such as she had never seen before as the flaming red ball crossed the horizon, the plumes of roaring crimson bled out across the water and into the sky, the flaming shape made on sky and sea looked exactly like a burning crucifix.

Nathaniel dressed only in his shirt crossed to his wife and saw the magnificent sight.

"It's a sign, I know it is," she whispered.

"But is it good or bad?" asked Nathaniel the hint of a twinkle in his eye.

"I don't know," murmured Jenny fearfully.

"Then I'll take it as good. That God is protecting us on our journey and our mission."

Jenny shuddered, "Or it could be a warning. Here take this." She unfastened the small cross that she always wore from around her neck. "Keep it with you at all times."

Nathaniel smiled at his sweet wife, "But your mother gave you that. You are never without it. Keep it to protect you and little Bart."

Bartholomew came in rubbing his eyes and yawning, "Daddy, I don't want you to go."

"I'll be back as soon as I can, I promise. I don't want to be away from either of you any longer than I can help it." He held them both close and was reluctant to release them.

"Now, we must get you dressed and Daddy must dress, too. Back to your room."

Bart turned solemnly and retreated from the room. Jenny turned to

Nathaniel; "I am very afraid; afraid for you, Goliath, for all of us. Please wear my cross."

"Very well, if it will make you feel better." He kissed the top of her head and pocketed the chain. "And you my sweet, will wear my Saint Christopher. Then we will both be safe." He took his medallion from his neck and fastened it around Jenny's neck. "Just like young lovers we exchange our love tokens."

Jenny blushed and smiled, "I will sleep easier now." There was a cry from Bart's room. "I must see to our son."

Nathaniel watched his wife fondly as she exited the room and murmured under his breath, "Dear sweet, Jenny."

Nathaniel donned his breeches and black leather, tall, riding boots. He slipped a waistcoat over his lace and cotton chemise, frouffing his lace jabot before putting on his jacket and cloak. Last was his cocked hat. He turned rapidly and his cape swirled about him. It was hard to admit but Nathaniel felt a tingle of excitement ripple through him at the thought of his quest. He picked up his old journal, which he was required to keep when he patrolled the coast, and stowed it safely in his bag.

Nathaniel swept from his room and dashed down the stairs where Sam and Goliath waited. They paraded to the kitchen for breakfast before their long ride. Edith had laid out a veritable feast. There was oatmeal with sweet cream, smoked herrings, sardines with mustard sauce, grilled trout with white butter sauce, cold veal pies, grilled kidneys, sausages with mashed potatoes, beef tongue with hot horseradish sauce and enough bacon to feed an army; three kinds of fresh bread, four types of rolls, with a choice of spreads including, butter, honey, orange marmalade, jams made from raspberries, cherries and apples. Beverages included French and Spanish brandies, fresh apple cider, tea and coffee.

"Why Edith you have surpassed yourself," observed Nathaniel.

"Under my instructions," said Myah entering the kitchen and overhearing. "Goodness knows when you will eat as well again."

"And goodness knows how Jessie would carry me if I sampled everything on offer," laughed Nathaniel.

Goliath helped himself, "It's a long time since I tasted anything as good as this."

"It's certainly grander fare than I'm used to, "said Sam as he reached for the teapot, which Edith hurriedly picked up for him. Their fingers touched and Edith flushed with colour and immediately glanced down. He smiled at the maid, "A more generous breakfast I've yet to see. I thank you for your hospitality Mrs Brookes and all your hard work, Edith."

Edith smiled in pleasure, "It's not all my doing, I had help from Mistress Jenny," the maid said quietly.

"None-the-less, you have served us well. That is, if we can move at all, after this lot," said Nathaniel.

Jenny beamed, "We have to give you a reason to hurry home to us."

The men ate their fill but their appetites were not big. There was anticipation and a clear sense of nervousness about them. They were anxious to be gone.

The sun was now climbing in the sky although it was still early morning. There was a fresh feel to the air. Eric, the groomsman, waited at the end of the path with the horses. Goliath was the first to give his thanks and bid farewell to the family who stood at the front door. He strode down the path, mounted Samson and waited for the others.

Samuel Reeves touched his hat, gave thanks and winked at Edith who blushed once more an even deeper shade of crimson and looked down shyly.

"Many thanks for your kind hospitality and I hope that I may see Edith again sometime," he said cheekily. This caused the maid to shrink behind Myah in acute embarrassment.

"Do you not have anyone at home, Mr Reeves," enquired Myah.

"No, Ma'am. There is no one. I have had little time to meet and make friends with anyone of the fair sex. In truth, I doubt I would have chance to meet someone with such skills, or as attractive as Edith so I really do hope to see her again, if she would wish it?"

"Edith?" asked Myah with a mischievous twinkle in her eyes. "May the gentleman write to you?"

Edith muttered, "That would be lovely but my skills in reading and writing are sadly lacking."

"That's not a problem, I will teach you. And I'm sure Jenny will help."

Sam's face broke into a grin, "Then that's settled," and he marched off to his steed, Hunter and sat astride him to wait for Nathaniel.

Nathaniel kissed his mother and son and turned to Jenny, "Let me look on you. Promise me you'll send word and let me have all of the news from home, especially how my successor fits into the community. I shall be keen to hear all and of course, the exploits of young Bart, here."

Jenny gazed at her husband, "Most certainly. You have my word."

Nathaniel held her close and kissed the top of her head. "Don't let us make this harder. I will carry you all in my heart until we are together again." He turned abruptly and stepped down the path to Jessie whose nostrils flared as she sensed the excitement in the atmosphere. As soon as Nathaniel was on her back she reared up and whinnied, her hooves playing in the air.

The three riders set off at a cracking pace and cantered to the road. They didn't look back and the family huddled together not knowing what was to happen to any of them.

6

Aleka

THE DINGY GREY SLAVER dipped and bowed in the churning leaden sea as land was sighted by the lookout in the crow's nest. The first mate, Albert Luxton, with a mouthful of broken, brown, nicotine stained teeth screeched out, "Land ahoy!" He gesticulated and pointed, his nails bitten down to the quick. A motley collection of crew members rushed on deck and scanned the vista; their faces wreathed in twisted grins at the thought of reaching land.

The turbulent treacherous waters around the rugged coastline with its many coves, dangerous rocks and reefs, swooped and dived like a bird of prey flexing its talons. The waves seemed to claw at the ship and the swell of the water carried with it the cry of mewling gulls and the rasping sigh of the spirit of the sea as it growled in anger at the invaders that dared to trespass.

Sometimes the waves towered so high that salt water swamped the deck and poured into the hold forcing the ship rats from their hiding places where they ran to fix their teeth onto anything that would keep them afloat.

Below deck stank. The acrid smell of ammonia and faecal matter stored in buckets slopped over the women chained together in the hold. One young girl barely fourteen years of age had collapsed in the flooded hold and drowned in the filth that swamped the prisoners.

Aleka looked on in sorrow at the child who now floated with the debris, her eyes lifeless and glazed with the everlasting mark of the terror she had endured. Four other women had also passed on this long voyage and their bodies bloated with gaseous air and bodily fluids had simply been tossed overboard to be devoured by whatever sea creatures lurked nearby.

There were now just forty of the original fifty women left, and twenty of the men that had boarded at another stop. They had been packed together in the hold with other cargo in cramped filthy conditions hardly seeing daylight and suffering the onslaught of hungry rats that came to gnaw in the night when they tried to sleep.

Aleka had woken many times from a rare sleep to the nips and bites of rodent sharp teeth. She would shout and flail her arms to try and scare the ever increasingly bold creatures and suffered bites not just from the vicious critters but from their parasitic fleas, too.

She let her head loll back and sighed. It was hard to maintain her dignity in such squalid conditions and circumstances. She was thankful that she had not been raped by any of the filthy crew that leered at her when they were occasionally allowed to take a little exercise on the top deck. Others, she knew, had not been so lucky.

The girl squashed next to her turned and painfully whispered, "Water, please, water."

Aleka tried to comfort the stricken female, who was severely dehydrated and disorientated. She patted the youngster's dry as parchment hand and their chains clanged together. She attempted to encourage the teenager to fight for survival, "Listen, Marjani, stay with me, fight to live. We will get out of this hell. We will." She said it with such fierce passion almost as if to convince herself more than her fellow captive. Marjani's eyes closed and Aleka shook her again. "Do not die! Do you hear me? We have to live."

As if with great effort Marjani managed to lift her eyelids. She murmured dryly, "Why? To be prostituted like common whores? I'd rather die. Leave me be," she whispered throatily.

It suddenly became very important to Aleka that Marjani should live and she spoke with urgency, "Who do you have in your life at home? Tell me. Who is important to you?"

Marjani's eyes fluttered and she whispered hoarsely, "My mother and father."

"Who else?"

"My little sisters and brothers."

"And?"

"There is Stefan…"

"Who is Stefan? What is he to you? How do you know him?"

A faint smile played on Marjani's full lips, now cracked with lack of moisture. A trickle of blood dripped as one crack split open. Almost gratefully

Marjani licked the blood from her mouth. Her eyes rested shut once more and she sighed.

Still, Aleka pressed, more urgently, "Tell me about Stefan."

"He is my friend. Two years older than me." She sighed again, "His mother was our teacher until she was stolen away. He and I…" she stopped.

"Go on."

"We hoped to be more than just friends. His father was a white man, Dutch, a sailor who looked after his family and came to visit, whenever he was in port. Stefan believed his father would come to live with them, when his sailing days were over. He and I…."

"Yes, go on."

"He and I… we hoped one day, when we finished our education, to marry and spread the word of God amongst our people."

"Then you, you love Stefan." Marjani nodded feebly and her head began to loll to one side.

There was a clatter from above and Aleka cried out, "Help us, please, in the name of God help us."

A face peered down into the hold, a redheaded man with a big bushy flame red beard and wearing a gold earring. He scanned the hold, where the women sat quietly, scarcely moving or breathing.

Aleka called again, "Please help us. My friend is dying. She needs water. Have pity, please."

The man with the rusty hair pulled back and Aleka's eyes closed in despair. She opened them as she heard another sound and saw the big burly sailor clambering down the rope ladder, carrying a bucket and ladle. He had pulled a scarf up over his nose and mouth to avoid the stench of death and filth that lay below from filling his lungs. He stepped across women who moaned and groaned, caught in the grip of fever, or some other ailment and moved toward Aleka and Marjani.

His voice was thick with a guttural accent that Aleka didn't recognise, "Here hold her head a wee bit for me. We've lost too many of ye already. Lift her head up, that's right." The man ladled some water to drip into Marjani's mouth. This revived her somewhat and she grabbed at the big spoon spilling it over her front. "Don't let her guzzle it. Slowly now, slowly." He guided some more water to her parched lips and gave her a little more to drink. He turned to Aleka, "You, too, Lassie. Drink." Aleka gratefully, supped from the spoon and drank more freely. The man continued, "Tomorrow, you'll be brought on deck, five at a time, to wash and be cleaned up. We'll soon be docking in port. You have to be clean and ready for transportation. You will need all your strength. You'll be dressed in something more than these rags. Here take this." He handed her a sponge soaked in the clean fresh water. "Squeeze a few drops into her mouth at regular intervals. It will help."

The man made to move away, "Wait!" cried Aleka. He stopped. "Tell me your name."

"It's Duncan, Duncan McLeish."

"Thank you, Duncan McLeish. May the Lord bless you."

For a moment the man looked dumbfounded as if he hadn't expected Christian words from one such as her. Duncan moved away and tended to some more women who cried out in their thirst before he returned to the top deck. Marjani looked more peaceful now, her head resting in Aleka's lap and a slight tinge of colour came back into her face as she slept.

The wind had dropped leaving an uncanny stillness. The slaver bobbed about in open water unable to draw fresh wind to power the sails to drive them across the bay and into harbour. The women had been brought aloft and doused with water and scrubbed with some kind of antiseptic soap.

Albert Luxton, first mate, strode up and down the line of female slaves passing around some scented pomade for them to oil and style their tangled hair. He also sprayed them with some sort of insecticide to delouse them once their clothes had been ripped from them and dumped overboard. Clean shapeless rough calico shift type garments were handed out for them to wear.

The men amongst the prisoners, who had been kept separate from the women, were oiled with something that made their burnished skin glisten, and made their muscles look more defined. They were without shirts and given breeches to cover their modesty.

They were all forced to line up before the captain who marched down the line as if inspecting his troops. He eyed the women appreciatively. He had what he believed was a good haul. The women now clean were reasonable looking, with firm flesh and unblemished skin. The men looked ready for work. In his eyes all was well. They just had to wait for the wind to pick up to blow them ashore. He yelled at his cook to bring out some grog for his men and gruel for his captives.

A haggard looking man with one eye and straggly hair emerged with his assistant, a young man who looked half-starved and just as terrified as the prisoners. The cook, Matthew Grimes, spat into the gruel, and served it up in small wooden bowls and handed them to the captives. His assistant ran around the members of the crew delivering their rations of rum. It seemed no one would be going ashore that day and the extra tot of rum would appease the men who were now yearning to set foot on dry land.

The constant bobbing of the boat on the sea did nothing to help the captives. Some were violently sick and forced to scrub the deck and clear away the vomit, others hung over the side of the ship groaning in despair. Aleka looked up at the seemingly innocent blue and as yet cloudless sky. But on the horizon thick cumulous nimbus clouds began to roll in toward the shore. The day was hot by English standards, the air moist and muggy.

As night fell there was still no sign of the wind needed to blow them toward land but cloud continued to build in the distance. The wizened boatswain proclaimed, "This unearthly calm happens before grave thunder storms. Best batten down goods and chattels, stop them slipping overboard."

Some of the crew laughed but others knew not to ignore the old man's warnings. Crates of supplies and contraband were tied down and harnessed together. The slaves were ordered to attach themselves to the thick chandlers' ropes that stretched around the sides of the ship's rails.

Aleka turned her face to the night sky, which twinkled with a myriad of stars. Things looked calm enough but Aleka knew the boatswain's words would come to fruition. She, too, could see the gathering army of clouds assembling on the horizon preparing to march over the currently deep still waters.

It wasn't long before the sky turned an ominous devil black and released its heavy load of soaking rain. Lightning split the heavens snaking down in a savage dance of forked fury as thunder crashed like discordant timpani drums. The sea churned and boiled with wrath, attacking the slave ship and sending its bows dipping into the water and swamping the decks. Women screamed above the shriek of the wind and men yelled at the wild tempest, cursing and invoking their Gods to save them from drowning. The slaver dipped and rolled in the swell. The anchor chain groaned and snapped like a weakened hammered piece of thin rusted metal and the boat was tossed about like a piece of driftwood on the waves.

Water poured over the bows, flooded the deck and gushed into the hold. Men too foolish or arrogant to hold on were swept overboard and others were prised from the partial safety of the rails, scooped up, and thrust out into the turbulent sea. Women screamed in the lashing rain and buffeting wind as the captain roared to the crew and slaves, ordering them to hang on tight.

Lightning sheeted and flashed, streaking through the bruised sky closely followed by the accompanying roaring growl of thunder that split and fractured the heavens. A splintering crack cleaved the ship's mast into two and the severed wood with its canvas sail flapping collapsed to the deck now awash with water. Shards of wood pierced the shoulder of one of the crew who screamed as the blood spouted from his punctured artery and showered Aleka sitting next to him. She gasped in horror and struggled to breathe.

There was nothing to be done. The man lost his hold on the rail, floated on the swirling water crashing into the far side of the ship. He shrieked in a final cry of pain before falling unconscious as he bled out, his blood mingling with the tempestuous sea.

Aleka closed her eyes against the driving rain. It was if God had deserted them, both captives and captors.

7

Back in the Saddle

THE SUNSHINE SMILED ON the unlikely trio as they cantered along the Welsh coast. Flint and quartz pebbles glinted in the morning light flashing like diamonds on the ground under the brilliant sapphire sky. They came across few people on the coast path. The ones they did meet stepped back warily recognising the traditional garb of Customs' Men and when they saw Goliath their mouths gaped in fear at the man's colour and size.

They rode solidly for three hours until their steeds shone with sweat. "We must rest. The horses need food, water and a good rub down, as do I," said Nathaniel with a grin.

They reined in their mounts and surveyed the scene below. They had already travelled from Mumbles, Swansea around the coastline of Glamorgan, through Cardiff and Newport. They picked their way down the cliff path that skirted the Bristol Channel to reach Gloucester before they could travel into the South West.

"Below we can see several farm houses and just beyond are Deerhurst and Apperley. There are alehouses in Deerhurst," said Sam.

"Aye, I seem to remember one down by the river not far from the priory. The Coalhouse I believe it's called," recalled Nathaniel.

"Yes, the other is the White Lion," confirmed Sam.

"Then what are we waiting for?" urged Goliath and gently heeled Samson in his sides. The loyal horse began to carefully step his way down the dry and difficult stone path. Sam and Nathaniel followed.

The sun was now fully up in the sky. There were men working in the fields surrounding the farms and Goliath frowned as he recognised men of his own colour and wondered aloud, "Do you think they're slaves?"

"It's hard to know for sure," said Nathaniel. "Although we may find out at the inn."

They continued down the cliff's side to the fields below and trotted on toward The Coalhouse. The horses clattered into the yard and a stable boy hurried from the back of the inn.

"See to your horses, Sir?" he asked and then gawped at Goliath as the man dismounted, "Cor, is he for real?" asked the boy without thinking.

"That he is," said Nathaniel handing the boy Jessie's reins. "Take all the horses, groom them, give them a good bed of straw and feed and water them. If you look after them well there will be a shilling in it for you."

"Yes, Sir," said the boy still looking at Goliath in trembling awe as he took Samson's reins.

The boy led the three horses to the stables and tripped as he gazed back over his shoulder at Goliath.

"I think you've frightened the wits out of the lad, Goliath," laughed Nathaniel.

They entered the hostelry. It was dark and dingy inside giving merit to its name. The small leaded windows were streaked with dirt and let in little light. The few customers playing cards at a table and supping ale, looked curiously at the arrivals. A black and white border collie sat asleep at one man's feet. One gambler with mouldy hay coloured hair spat on the floor and scraped back his chair. He muttered something about 'Customs' men' under his breath and left.

The trio approached the bar; "Three quarts of ale, Landlord and whatever vittles you have to offer," ordered Nathaniel.

The landlord sniffed and wiped his huge hand across his mouth, "And who might be asking? Let's see the colour of your money first."

Sam slapped coins on the counter. The noise echoed metallically in the dim, dank room. "Is that enough, Landlord?"

The burly man with a face scarred by fighting and ravaged by the weather sniffed again, "You look like Customs' men," he said accusingly.

"And what if we are? Our money is as good as any other," said Sam.

"I don't like Customs' men and neither do my customers. I'll thank you not to linger."

"And why would that be?" asked Goliath coming into view at the bar.

The landlord swore, "Jesus Christ," and crossed himself. "Where did that black devil come from?"

"I wouldn't annoy him, if I were you," said Nathaniel turning and winking at Goliath. "He's fond of the taste of white men."

The landlord immediately smartened up his service, "I got pork pies, ox and onion soup, bread and cheese."

"Then we'll have three bowls of soup with bread, and pork pies to follow," decided Nathaniel.

The landlord turned away and disappeared out back. They could just hear his growling tones giving the order to the kitchen maid.

The companions moved to a vacant table and sat to wait for their meal. The dog on the floor looked up at them with one ear cocked and whined softly in his throat. He was a scruffy looking shaggy border collie with loving brown eyes.

"Quiet, Trooper," hissed one man and the dog became silent but watched carefully its eyes following every move of the newcomers.

The landlord soon returned and began to pour their ale. Nathaniel rose and went to collect the frothing tankards on a tray. The dog got up and padded toward Nathaniel who stooped down to fuss the animal. Trooper licked Nathaniel's hand gratefully before being called back by his master. Nathaniel rose up to retrieve the tray.

"Here," said the landlord, "Don't I know you?"

"I doubt that very much," said Nathaniel picking up the tray.

"Yes, I do. It will come to me in a moment. You'll see." The landlord scratched his chin and sucked in a breath between his teeth, "Bloody hell, you're Brookes. You did for the smuggler Knight. Rumour had it you'd finished with riding," he said with twisted lips.

Other customers looked up inquisitively. Nathaniel looked back at the man behind the bar, "Then they got it wrong." He placed the tray on his table and turned. Eyes like knives pierced his back as the ruffians tried to memorise Nathaniel for future reference. He turned abruptly, "I'm looking for someone who deals in slaves? Can anyone help?"

The landlord chortled, "Don't think your man wants to be sold but he'd fetch a good price."

Goliath bristled at this but Nathaniel continued. "He's not for sale. No… I'm looking for women."

"Are you now?" scoffed the landlord in between picking his teeth.

The owner of the dog wearing drab dark clothes with an earring in his ear put his cards on the table and eyed Nathaniel. "I've heard there's a consignment due, a special order."

"And where might that be?" questioned Nathaniel crossing to him.

"What's it worth?"

"If the information you give me is good. I'll give you coin."

"How much?" rasped the man.

Nathaniel rubbed his chin as if in thought, "Shall we say half a crown?" He removed the coin from his money pouch and held it up tantalisingly for the ruffian to see. The fellow reached up to snatch it but Nathaniel closed his fist around it, "Ah, ah, ah," he said. "Information first, please."

The man licked his dry skin flaked lips that hinted at a life on the sea, "I have heard Captain Clive Bethell is on his way from here and to re-board for Ilfracombe down yonder."

"What else?"

"They are taking the women to Redruth in Cornwall and some to St. Austell."

"What day is the sale?"

"Scheduled for four weeks Tuesday."

"Thank you, my man. That wasn't so tough was it?" Nathaniel flicked the coin at the man who caught it eagerly. Nathaniel returned to his table.

It was then the kitchen maid brought out the soup and bread, which Nathaniel and his companions tucked into eagerly. Conversation forgotten the men filled their bellies. They didn't notice one of the men playing cards fold his hand and slip out of the back door.

Jonah Griggs left the inn swiftly and quietly. He hurried toward the other public house, The Red Lion. Jonah was a swarthy man with a strong physique who looked as if he could handle himself and judging by the scars on his face and his broken nose this had been put to the test many times.

He pushed open the heavy wooden door, which creaked eerily on its hinges. His eyes searched the now silent bar as everyone had stopped to see who had entered. As soon as they realised it was one of their own they resumed their raucous chatter.

Jonah spotted Richard Gosling immediately. There was no mistaking his blonde locks that waved and curled to his shoulders, his fine chiselled features, startling blue eyes and apparent gentle demeanour. Looking every inch the gentleman, he sat with a red headed doxy who attended on him as if he were the only man in the world. As Jonah approached he clicked his fingers and sent the wench away. She scowled angrily at Jonah's intrusion but none the less she left Richard's side albeit reluctantly.

Jonah sat and faced Richard. They made an odd looking couple one more suited to brawling, the other to the gentry.

"You have something for me?" His tone was soft and light. Richard Gosling was the epitome of respectability in his appearance but beneath the well-oiled charm there lurked something more sinister. Jonah nodded and wiped his grubby hand across his mouth removing a trail of spittle that lingered there. Richard didn't attempt to hide his distaste. "Use your handkerchief man." The words were soft but still Jonah flinched.

"I ain't got one," he apologised.

Richard sighed and waved his hand encouraging the man to continue. "What is it?"

"Customs' men, Riding Officers, three of them in The Coalhouse asking questions."

Richard's eyes narrowed, "What kind of questions?"

"About the slaver. Where the cargo of women are headed that sort of thing."

"What have they been told?'

"Alfred Challacombe took coin. He told of the slaver on its way to Ilfracombe then Redruth market and St. Austell."

"Did he now?" Richard's manner had become disturbingly chilling. "What else?"

"One of them's Nathaniel Brookes who did for the smuggler, Knight. Two others with him. One of them's a big buck nigger, a bloody giant, I tell you."

"Brookes…" he said the name slowly and savoured the sound. "The man was a legend. So, he's back, is he? And I suspect the giant is his man Friday."

"Dunno, didn't catch his name."

Richard curled his lip disdainfully at the man's ignorance, "If it is he would make a wonderful catch for us but it would be risky. Get back to the inn. Let me know what transpires. We may need to put them on watch. Tell the men to be prepared to move. On my say so." He dismissed Jonah with a wave of his hand and added, "Oh, and as for Alfred Challacombe…"

"Yes?"

"Kill him. There'll be coin in it for you."

Jonah rose to his feet and darted back out of the door. The wench who had been watching from the corner sashayed seductively back to Richard's side and continued to tease the man, taking his hand and leading him up the stairs.

Ruffians in the bar guffawed and shouted lewd comments, which Richard accepted, a bemused look on his face. He stopped midway on the stairs and called back with a hint of sarcasm in his address, "Gentlemen... I have a twitch and like an itch what better way to deal with it than to scratch it?"

One of the thugs drawled in his Gloucestershire twang, "Careful you don't get another itch from that harlot."

"Do you hear that my sweet? These men doubt your cleanliness. You are clean, aren't you? If not, you had better worry for your life."

The woman bristled, "I ain't no whore, not now. I keep m'self clean for one man and this is him."

The rogues below roared with laughter once more.

"You see," said Richard. "Give the lady some respect. She may have had a chequered past, but it's all thrust out of her now."

The villains howled in merriment once more and returned to their cards as Richard and his doxy reached the landing and disappeared inside one of the letting rooms where Richard threw the lusty wench down onto the bed. He whispered in her ear, nibbling at her lobe, "I don't care what they say, Molly, you are the best."

"I meant what I said, Rich. I don't work no more and I don't dally with any other man. Just you. You give me enough to get by, what with that and the kitchen work..."

Richard put his fingers on her lips and smothered her neck with kisses. He gently unlaced her bodice and lifted her skirts. She sighed and lay back as he groaned in pleasure of what was to come.

Jonah had made his way back to The Coalhouse. He slipped in silently through the back door and watched the Customs' men and his fellow gamblers, his eyes now threatening and dark.

"Jonah! Come and join us," called out one with a bushy black beard. Jonah grunted and headed to the bar where he ordered a quart of ale. He sipped slowly, the froth leaving a foamy moustache above his lips. His former companion called again.

"Nah, not got much left. Got a wife and kids to feed."

"By the looks of her you've fed her enough," chortled Alfred. "Come on man, you're my lucky charm. I always win big when you're in the game."

Jonah grunted in a surly fashion and turned his back on the men. He brooded on how he would stop Alfred's smug smile and began to enjoy thinking of how he would do it. If there was coin in it for him what was stopping him from relieving Alfred of his weighty purse as well? He cracked a grim humourless smile, which turned into a huge grin as he walked back to the gaming table. He sat next to Alfred, "I've not the brass to play but I'll be your amulet and drink your ale," he said with false cheeriness.

Nathaniel and friends had now finished their modest repast and Nathaniel ordered another round of drinks before requesting a room for the night.

"Two of you will have to share," the landlord chuntered gruffly.

"Goliath and I are used to that," said Nathaniel amiably.

"Very well. Two rooms, payment up front. Will you be wanting supper?"

"Whatever you can muster up will be good enough for us." Nathaniel fished in his money pouch and delivered four pence for the two rooms.

"And the grub?" groused the landlord. Nathaniel gave the man another three pence. Satisfied, the landlord called to the kitchen, "Gracie, show these gentlemen the rooms."

The kitchen maid hurried out and bobbed a courtesy before starting up the wooden staircase and leading them to their very basic rooms. Nathaniel and Goliath took the twin bedded room. It was basic but clean. Fresh water had been laid out in a jug with a clean bowl together with two rough towels and a bar of antiseptic soap.

Nathaniel turned to Sam Reeves, "I'm ready for forty winks; I'll see you downstairs at..." he turned to Gracie, "What time is supper?"

"From six to eight," she replied.

"Shall we say somewhere in the middle?" Sam nodded. "Expect us at seven." The girl bobbed again and fled downstairs. "Skittish that one," observed Nathaniel.

"But very pretty," said Sam.

"And I didn't think you'd noticed," laughed Nathaniel. "I thought our young maid Edith had caught your eye?"

"You're remarkably observant, Sir," mused Sam. "But I have sworn off women until our borders are under control."

"Never say never," chided Nathaniel. "Where the heart and fate lead may not fit with your timing, just accept it. And now, I'm overdue for a good rest." Nathaniel tossed his hat and cloak on one bed as Goliath stretched out on the other.

"See you at seven," smiled Sam and retreated into the other room.

Nathaniel flopped onto his cot. "I need a rest, it's a long time since I've ridden like this. My backside…"

"I know," agreed Goliath. "You have become soft using a wagon. You'll soon harden up."

"I hope," sighed Nathaniel and drifted off to sleep.

Jonah sat back in his chair supping his ale and watching the game. It was true he certainly seemed to be bringing Alfred luck. Alfred raked in the pot of money on the table, "Right, men. That's me done."

"I hope you'll give us chance to win our money back," whinged a rough looking fellow with a hairy wart on his face.

"Tomorrow, tomorrow will be time a plenty. I need to get home. Mary will be after me." Alfred rose and piled the money into his hat. He swaggered to the door followed by his collie dog.

Jonah scraped back his seat and followed, "Wait up, I'll walk with you."

The two left together in a seemingly jovial mood. The rest of their companions whinged and complained, while the landlord watched.

8

Blood and Thunder

JONAH AMBLED THROUGH THE village with Alfred, who boasted pompously about his winnings, his luck and his place in life. Jonah suffered the man's self-important crowing waiting for the right moment. They soon reached the edge of the village where they bade each other goodbye. Alfred lived at the edge of woodland outside the village and Jonah's abode was down by the river. They parted and Jonah ensured that the few people going about their daily business saw the two men saying a friendly farewell and going their separate ways.

Alfred ordered his dog, "Trooper, home now." The dog understood his master and trotted away as Alfred stopped to talk to a farmer herding some geese into his yard, while Jonah quickly slipped out of sight. He doubled back and around to avoid any villagers and thus remained invisible to any onlookers. He crept into the trees that edged the wood unnoticed, shinned up one by the path and waited. Jonah removed a weighty blade from its sheath, which he kept at his side and tested the metal. It was sharp, sharp enough to draw blood from his finger from even light pressure.

He heard Alfred before he saw him. The man was whistling cheerfully as if he hadn't a care in the world. Jonah smiled grimly and readied himself. 'Good, the dog wasn't with him.' That would have been something else to deal with.

Alfred swaggered into the copse; his hand jingled his money belt comfortingly, he whistled gratifyingly and began to stroll down the path. Jonah placed the knife carefully between his teeth and as Alfred passed, he dropped down stealthily as a cat onto the track behind him. Alfred was whistling so loudly he didn't hear a twig crack. Jonah was swift; he leapt on Alfred's back drawing his knife across the man's gullet, which spouted blood that gushed like a fountain. The man stood no chance, he gurgled in his throat as he tumbled to the floor, his eyes open wide in shock and horror. Jonah sliced through the money belt and removed the pouch. He stuffed it into his own pocket before swiftly searching the body for anything else that might be useful. He grabbed a silver watch fob and chain, which he secreted into his other pocket.

He was now shaking with the weight of the deed and fear of being caught. He looked cautiously around him and certain he had not been seen he gripped the man by his arms and dragged him off the forest path into the wood where he partially covered the body with rotting leaves, sticks and detritus, before slipping away.

Jonah, still trembling, hurried to a small brook that led to the river and washed his knife and hands cleaning them of blood. His shirt was drenched too; he determined to get rid of it and he noticed a few blood spots on his jacket, which he attempted to scrub clean. He removed his shirt stained with guilt and rolled it up into a small bundle before replacing his jacket, now clear of spatter and hastened to his humble dwelling. He slipped in quietly, unseen by anyone. He sighed in relief as he leaned against the door. His wife was out and would be until late visiting her sister in Gloucester.

Jonah placed the metal pin in the lock and hurried out the back where he dug in the old pigsty and buried his bloodied shirt. Once done, and now sweating profusely, he retreated to his scullery and washed himself thoroughly before foraging for a clean shirt to wear. He secreted the money pouch and watch into a small metal box, which he hid under a loose flagstone before covering it with a rag mat. He checked his jacket, still damp, and hung it up on the coat stand.

He knew he had to remain calm. He had no idea when the body would be found. He needed to keep a cool head and to collect payment from Richard Gosling. Jonah decided it was safer to stay home that night.

Nathaniel, Sam and Goliath sat in the bar enjoying their supper, when a big woman with enormous breasts pushed open the door. Her clothes strained against her bulk as she swept in like the prow of a ship in full sail. Her voice was thin and reedy, as she raucously demanded, "Where is he? Where's he hiding?"

She marched up to the table where the card game had been abandoned and the men left were merry from supping ale. "My Alfred, what have you done with him? Slipped out to the stables, has he?"

The landlord came out from behind the counter, "Now, Mary, stop this noise. Alfred left this afternoon. He said he was going home."

"And did he have brass?"

"Aye, he'd been lucky in cards."

"He'll be avoiding me, then. I can tell you that won't stay in his pocket; I'll be bound. Who was he with?"

"He left with Jonah Griggs."

"Did he now? Hm – 'spect they've gone to the Red Lion."

"I wouldn't know, Mary. You'd best get yourself back home. This ain't no place for a lady."

The men playing cards sniggered. One muttered under his breath, "Nothin' lady-like about her that's for sure!"

"I heard that, Basil Tufnell, don't you think I didn't and I shall be having words with your missus," snapped Mary as she spun around to face the men who fell quiet. With glaring eyes that would have withered the bravest of people, Mary flounced out. The men all heaved a sigh of relief.

The landlord tried to lighten the proceedings; "I don't envy Alfred when she gets hold of him."

"Nor me," said another, that's why I ain't never married."

"Ha! Who'd have you?" chortled Basil. The men fell into a good-natured banter over the pros and cons of taking a wife before they decided to drain their glasses and leave. They rolled out of the inn, laughing and joking as Nathaniel and his company ate.

"I suggest we get a good night's sleep. It's an early start for us tomorrow," advised Nathaniel as he stuffed the last piece of pie in his mouth. The others grunted in agreement and hurried to finish their meal before pushing their plates away.

They sat quietly for a moment, wondering what was to befall them on their journey. Sam suddenly rose, "One more drink and then I'll retire."

Sam moved to the bar when the door flew open and Mary fell in sobbing and wailing. "He's done for, gone, whatever will I do?"

The landlord looked genuinely concerned, "Come now, Mary. What do you mean?"

"It's Alfred, he's dead, murdered."

9

The Verdict

THE LANDLORD ATTEMPTED TO console the woman who continued to wail, "Mary, hush now. Tell me what happened."

"I don't know. He's dead, what matter how – he's gone."

"You need to tell the police, get a doctor."

"Fat lot of good that will do. And what am I to live on? He was robbed."

"How do you know?"

His money belt's gone and his silver watch from his father. Oh, what's to become of me? My poor, poor Alfred."

Nathaniel, unable to ignore the woman's pitiful state, stepped in to try and comfort the distraught female, "I may be able to help. I'm a medical man, show me."

"Only help I need now is an undertaker. You can't bring him back to life, can you?"

"No, but his body may tell us something about his attacker."

Samuel and Goliath listened with interest. They had finished their repast and rose flanking Nathaniel on either side. The woman crossed herself when she saw Goliath, "Lord have mercy. He's sent the devil himself."

Nathaniel reassured her, "No, you are mistaken. He is my right hand man so to speak and a good man. Come show us."

Mary with tears streaming down her cheeks dabbed at her eyes with a grubby handkerchief. She started for the door, "This way."

Nathaniel looked back at the landlord, "Don't shut up shop. We'll be back." The three followed the woman out of the bar and into the street. The sun was going down and the street outside filled with shadows. Mary walked on continually muttering and bemoaning her fate. Eventually they arrived at the edge of the wood by the river. There was quite a crowd standing around together with a village policeman speaking to the bystanders as possible witnesses. The man was clearly finding the whole experience very difficult. Alfred's dog was now lying at his master's side looking miserable.

Nathaniel stepped up, "May I be of assistance?"

"And who might you be?" asked the man with a hint of relief in his voice.

"Nathaniel Brookes at your service, Riding Officer and Doctor. I may be able to help you discover how and when he died."

The man's initial relief fled to disdain as he barked, "Anyone can see he had his throat cut."

"Yes, but I may be able to tell you something more."

"Go ahead," said the policeman.

Nathaniel stepped toward the body and brushed away the leaf litter. He made a quick examination, "He's still warm. Couldn't have been dead more than two to three hours. His throat's been slashed from behind with a sharp heavy serrated blade. Judging by the strike the killer was right handed. There would have been a lot of blood." Nathaniel surveyed the scene around him. "Whoever it was tried to hide the body. He wasn't killed here. Look." He pointed at marks made by feet leading to the copse. "He was dragged here."

Goliath shouted, "This way. The tracks lead into the trees." The onlookers caught sight of Goliath and a ripple of fear went through the crowd. Nathaniel followed Goliath to where the tracks began.

Nathaniel assessed the scene; he examined the surrounding trees. "Here, it's my belief someone climbed this tree, see how the bark has come away from the trunk. Then he dropped on the ground behind the man, attacked from the back ripping his throat before dragging the corpse into the woods to hide it. See." Nathaniel pointed at a blood spray on the bark of a birch and more blood that had pooled on the ground, blood mixed with mud that had a clear footprint in it. Nathaniel estimated the man's height and weight from the print and the size of his feet.

"Your killer is a stocky man about five foot eight or nine."

"That could be anyone. Fits the description of half the men in the village."

"Who saw him last?"

"I did," said the farmer that Alfred had stopped to chat to. "His friend Jonah bade him goodbye, he sent his dog home and we stopped and had a natter. I can't believe it. He promised to buy one of my geese at Christmas…"

"Where is Jonah?"

"Haven't seen him. At home I expect, someone should tell him."

"And the dog wasn't with him?"

"No, Trooper's an obedient dog. He just trotted home like I said."

"Pity. I expect he could lead us to the man's killer." Nathaniel turned to Mary, "Can I borrow your dog?"

"Borrow? You can keep him. The mutt won't do anything I say, was Alfred's through and through."

Nathaniel spoke softly to the dog, which lay forlornly at his master's side. "Trooper?" The dog pricked up his ears. "Come, Trooper. Help us find the man who did this." He continued to coax the dog.

Goliath crossed to them and dug in his pocket, "Try this." He took out a piece of beef jerky, "My dog Valiant loved this. Give him a treat and see if that will persuade him."

Nathaniel continued to soothe the animal, patting him and smoothing him down. Goliath tore off a bit of the dried strip of meat and offered it to the creature whose eyes were filled with sadness, but Trooper ignored him.

"Let me try," said Nathaniel. He began to talk softly and made small sounds in his throat. He sucked on a titbit of jerky and passed it to the dog, which eventually took it. "Good boy, good Trooper."

It was then the undertaker with his cart arrived to load the body and take it back to the village. As Alfred was hoisted on the wagon, the dog stood up as if he knew he wouldn't see his master again and this time he followed the men back to the site of the murder.

The dog immediately began sniffing around, "Good dog, good boy," urged Nathaniel, who had now picked up some prints leading through the forest. The dog followed and led them down to the river's edge. Nathaniel looked at the broken twigs and disturbed grassy bank. "Here's where our killer washed the blood off." There was another clear bloody footprint on the stones leading to the water.

Trooper barked suddenly and tore off down the path, the men and policeman followed. Every so often the dog would stop to see if they were coming and reassured that they were, continued on taking a circuitous route through the wood and back down toward the river. Twilight had now fully replaced the daylight and as they moved on dusk was turning to night.

The dog was growing ever more agitated and began to yap excitedly as he neared a poor tumbledown dwelling. Nathaniel raised his hand and turned to the policeman. "Do you know who lives here?"

"This here's Jonah's house."

Candles burnt behind the dirty cracked windowpanes and Nathaniel thought he detected a movement inside. "Someone's home."

The policeman marched up to the splintered wooden door and banged loudly. A sallow face peered out through the glass and they heard someone shuffle to the door. Jonah wrenched open the rickety door and looked out suspiciously. "Yes?"

"Jonah Griggs?"

"Who wants to know?"

Trooper dashed between the men's feet and began barking furiously.

"It seems you were one of the last people to see Alfred Challacombe alive."

"What do you mean? Is Alf dead?" said Jonah feigning surprise.

Nathaniel's eagle eye, swiftly took in the man's appearance. He looked reasonably clean but was sweating and there was a slight tremble in his hand. Nathaniel noticed some small rusty brown spots on one of his boots. His eyes narrowed. "No doubt you won't object to answering a few questions, Mr Griggs."

Jonah looked about him shiftily and blew through his teeth. "Don't suppose it can hurt."

"Can we come in?"

Grudgingly he opened the door but he was unable to stop Trooper who raced past Jonah and began sniffing all around the room, before pawing at the kitchen door. Nathaniel eyed the dog with interest. Jonah attempted to kick Trooper out of the way but the dog avoided the booted foot and Nathaniel caught sight of the sole of Jonah's boot that looked not only muddy but appeared to have blood splashes.

"Can we ask you about your movements today and when you left Alfred Challacombe?"

Griggs pretended to think, "Let's see. I was in The Coalhouse, played cards and supped a few ales. I got a little light headed so left to stretch my legs and stopped off at the Red Lion for a few minutes before going back to the Coalhouse."

"Then what?"

Jonah looked slyly at Nathaniel, "Well you should know, Mister. You were there. Alf called me over to the game; said I was his lucky mascot."

"I remember..." His tone was measured, "You left together, didn't you?"

"Yes. Parted company at Hicks' farm. Alf stopped to have a jaw with the farmer. I came on home."

"Did you now?" The dog was still frantically scrabbling at the door to the scullery.

"Mr Griggs, would you mind removing your boots?"

"Why? What for?" For the first time a flicker of fear entered Jonah's eyes."

Nathaniel pressed again backed by the policeman, "Do as he says, Mr Griggs." Reluctantly, Jonah removed his boots and kicked them across to them. Trooper went wild sniffing and jumping around the footwear. Nathaniel picked up the boots and examined them carefully. As he scraped at the blood spots on one boot Jonah visibly flinched.

Nathaniel turned the boots over revealing their bloody soles. "Can you explain this blood Mr Griggs?"

Jonah turned white and began to stammer. Suddenly he turned and made a bolt through the scullery door and out of the back. Trooper raced after Jonah as did the men. Trooper became distracted and raced into the pigsty where he began digging frantically.

Goliath grabbed one of the boots and lobbed it hard at the fleeing man who struggled without footwear on the stony path. It struck him firmly in his back and floored him. Goliath sprinted to the fallen man and held him tight for the officer to apprehend him.

It was then that Trooper finished his digging and unearthed Jonah's bloodied shirt. The dog dragged the garment to Nathaniel and wagged his tail. Nathaniel fussed and praised the dog before he retrieved the shirt. He showed it to the policeman. "I think this might be considered proof," said Nathaniel.

The officer took the shirt and forced Jonah to his feet. Trooper gave an excited bark and ran back into the house just as Jonah's wife, Alice, came marching in and hearing all the noise went out through the back. The woman looked about her horrified at the intrusion into her house.

"Whatever is going on here?" she demanded in a shrewish voice. "Where are you taking my Jonah? What's he done?"

Jonah hung his head in shame as he was forcibly propelled back through the yard. However, Nathaniel's attention was caught by Trooper whining and running around his feet in circles. "What is it?"

The dog tugged at Nathaniel's boot until Nathaniel followed Trooper back inside the house. The dog dashed to the scullery and began pawing at the rag mat. Nathaniel stooped down and pulled it back from the dusty flagstone floor. He gazed at a slate slab that appeared to be loose. He took a small pocketknife and prised up the tile to reveal a little metal box. Nathaniel opened it to reveal a money pouch and silver fob watch and chain. He snatched up the box, patted Trooper on the head and went out after the lawman, prisoner and his friends.

Trooper followed.

1 0

On the move

IT WAS SOON ESTABLISHED that the fob watch and chain belonged to Alfred. Those items together with the money he had won at cards went to his very grateful widow, Mary.

"I don't know how to thank you, Sir," she whispered.

"Your dog, Trooper had a lot to do with it. He uncovered Jonah's bloody shirt and your husband's belongings. He's a grand little chap."

"He was Alfred's dog not mine. Went everywhere with him. Don't know what to do about him now. I'm not good with animals." Mary looked sideways at Nathaniel, "If it please you, Sir; it seems the mutt has taken a liking to you. If you want him you can have him."

"Thank you but I have to ride onto Devon I don't think he could keep up with the horses. He's a real character and in other circumstances…"

"Please, Sir. He seems to have singled you out…"

"You should try your best with him. Dogs are tremendous companions."

"Yes, Sir. Thank you, Sir." Mary looked most disgruntled at the thought of keeping the animal but forced a smile to her lips.

Nathaniel's fellow riders waited for him to mount Jessie. They bade goodbye to the officer who had locked Jonah in a cell to await going before the magistrate. The policeman doffed his cap at Nathaniel, "God speed, and thank you."

The riders turned their horses and cantered off. Mary watched as they rode away and the scruffy collie whined softly in his throat. The woman indicated the disappearing riders and urged the dog, "Go. Go on." Trooper cocked his head on one side as if understanding her and licked her hand before racing off after the riders.

The news wasn't long in reaching Richard Gosling's ears. He set his handsome face in a harsh frown and pursed his lips. He turned to his companion and muttered, "Do we know what Jonah has said?"

"No, folks say he's clammed up as tight as a woman's corset."

"But we can't be sure he won't talk. If he spills his guts to save his own skin, I'll go down with him. I can't have that," murmured Richard as one of his men, Robbo looked about him to see if anyone was listening.

"Firstly, send my condolences to Alfred's widow and give her this." He passed Robbo a small velvet pouch containing coins and give this one," he took a leather drawstring bag, "To Jonah's wife. She'll need it to live with Jonah headed for the gallows."

"And Jonah?"

"Jonah needs to have an accident. We can't have him testifying for the Crown now, can we?"

"But how? He's locked up."

"I have an idea. We need to do bit of gardening, special gardening. There are some very dangerous plants around that can cause serious health problems even death," and he winked at Robbo. "If he talks it will lead back to us and I can't have that. There is too much at stake. Come." Richard rose from his seat, dropped his arm around Robbo's shoulders and they walked from the drawing room into the corridor toward the kitchen where the cook was feverishly preparing dinner and went out into the garden.

The two men strolled through the grounds of Richard Gosling's fine mansion and as they walked Richard pointed out some of the properties of various plants and shrubs. He indicated a flourishing Rhododendron bush, "Beautiful colour, isn't it? But beware. If the bush is pruned cover your face and mouth. Don't remain in an enclosed space with the cut branches."

"Why?"

"Because you will die. The fumes given off by the damaged plant are lethal. Cyanide, I believe…"

"But I can't get Rhododendron branches inside his cell."

"No, but there may be another way. The honey made from the pollen and nectar of the shrub is highly toxic. In the fourth century BC in Greece ten thousand soldiers were poisoned by such honey. I have a hive that makes this time bomb. It lowers blood pressure, shocks the body and often leads to death."

"But it's not guaranteed?"

"No," Richard paused. "But there are other things; you see that giant strapping plant over by the lake?" He pointed to an umbrella type plant with white umbelliferous flowers. "The sap from those giants is highly dangerous, even brushing against them can be deadly causing third degree burns when exposed to sunlight."

"How do you know all this?"

"Let's just say my mother is a wise woman. She came across it in the Caucasus and believing it to be a striking ornamental plant brought some seeds back with her from her merchant trip."

"But it sounds too difficult to harvest anything from that monstrosity."

"You could be right, but then we have foxgloves and monkshood, laburnum and more, Belladonna, Hemlock, Thorn Apple and of course all the fungi. We have a wealth of items right here in this garden. We just need the means to dispense them to our victim and in such a way that it cannot be traced back to us."

"How long have we got?"

"Time is something we are short of. We must plan carefully and quickly."

Nathaniel, Goliath and Sam had cantered off following the estuary and slowed to a trot on the stony path as they headed through Somerset toward Devon. Goliath stopped and surveyed the scene around him and called to the others to halt.

Some distance away on the path was a dog. Goliath dismounted and shaded his eyes. "Think we have a visitor," he murmured to Nathaniel.

Nathaniel narrowed his eyes to see the collie from the village scampering after them. "Oh no," he groaned.

"Looks like you have a friend," observed Samuel.

"How can I look after a dog when we ride?" asked Nathaniel.

"He might be useful," said Sam. "I mean, look how he rooted out his master's murderer."

Nathaniel looked back and for between his colleagues and heaved another sigh, "You think we should take him?"

"It's up to you," said Goliath. "But leaving him here could well be the end of him. It was clear that woman didn't want him."

By now the little dog was almost with them. They dismounted and the black and white collie sprinted joyfully to Nathaniel and danced around him in a frenzied greeting until he flopped on the floor panting with exhaustion.

"What now?"

"Looks like he's chosen you but the poor creature's worn out. He needs a rest."

Nathaniel turned to the others, "This is against my better judgement." He remounted Jessie. "Goliath, pass me the dog."

Goliath scooped up the longhaired, fluffy dog and gave him to Nathaniel, whereupon the mutt immediately began licking Nathaniel all over his face in absolute delight.

Nathaniel spoke sternly, "Now stop that! Let's get one thing straight, Trooper, if you're to ride with me you must be still." The dog seemed to understand and lay across the front of the saddle. Nathaniel kept one hand on his rein and the other on the dog. "We'll have to find something better than this. It's most awkward."

"Maybe in the next town or village we can pick up a basket to strap to Jessie. He can sit in that," suggested Sam.

Nathaniel grunted as if displeased but Goliath noted the merry twinkle in his friend's eyes and knew that Nathaniel was secretly delighted.

The trio and dog continued on their way until they reached the spreading village of Clevedon. Upon sight of it they winkled their way down the slope, treading carefully on the slippery path before them.

A lady inspected the consignment of female slaves imprisoned in the cellar of her mansion. She wore a highwayman's mask as if headed for a masquerade and breeches, like a man, with riding boots, a frilled chemise and rough leather jerkin. Only her hands betrayed her femininity as she walked around the group of women who sat on the stone floor in abject misery.

Clive Bethell prodded one woman roughly with a stick and ordered, "On your feet, all of you." The women scrambled up. Many were broken in spirit but Aleka stood in defiance. Her open hostility showed in her face and she stared distastefully at the woman.

"You! How dare you engage eyes with Milady? Show some humility. We will not stand for this kind of insolence."

Aleka glowered at her captors, "How dare you hold us against our will. I am a free woman and daughter of a British Governor."

"An illegitimate offspring, I'll be bound," spat Clive Bethell.

"I was taken into the family, raised and educated with them as an equal."

Clive snorted, "An equal? That will never be."

Aleka was undaunted and continued, "What woman would do this to another woman? You should be ashamed to treat your own sex in this manner."

The lady whispered in Bethell's ear and he stepped forward raising his baton. He cracked it behind Aleka's knees and she buckled to the floor. Bethell rasped, "Your impertinence will not be tolerated. If you can't hold your tongue maybe I'll cut it out and then we'll see how brave you are."

Bethell's harsh words had done the trick. A wave of fear ran through the other women. There were just forty female prisoners left. The men had been taken elsewhere. "Keep yourselves clean. You will be well fed and looked after as long as you obey us and submit to our will." The women had been shackled and straw bales had been placed in the dungeon on which they could sit. Fresh water was placed in buckets at strategic places allowing each woman access.

Bethell crossed to the stone steps and lifted a basket of bread and distributed it to all of the women who devoured it hungrily. "If you're quiet and respectful there will be something hot for you later," he grunted.

The woman turned without a word and went back up the steps to the next floor. Clive Bethell rattled his baton across the stony walls. The women remained silent and he followed the lady up the steps. The captives were stunned into silence and waited until they heard the stout wooden door shut and bolt. For a few minutes more they were hushed and then when believing it safe they began to talk amongst themselves.

Richard Gosling got off the bed and began to dress, "I'm late. I need to get back."

His doxy, Molly, pouted, "Not yet. Pleeeease." She drew out the word please in a pleading whine.

"Listen to me. Keep it warm. I'll be back. I have some business to attend to first."

"If I didn't know better I'd think you were a married man."

"Oh, no. Not me, not yet."

Richard buttoned up his shirt and donned his jacket and cloak. He tugged

Molly up from the bed and pulled her to him giving her a final kiss. She withdrew breathlessly, "I'll be waiting," she purred falling back onto the bed and suggestively played with her lips and forefinger before surrounding the entire digit with her mouth.

Richard laughed, "Oh, no you don't. You've caught me like that before." He swept out of the room, down the stairs and out into the afternoon air. His mount was waiting for him. He tossed the ostler a coin and cantered out of the yard.

His ride was swift, many people acknowledged him in the street with a friendly smile and wave. He rode on through the village to Clevedon Manor on Court Hill. He cantered down the magnificent drive to the West Wing where he was met by Sir Abraham Elton's valet, Guy Digby.

"Are we on track?"

"We are."

"Does his Lordship suspect?"

"Sir Abraham knows nothing. The women are in the dungeons of the West Wing out of sight and earshot."

"They need to be moved and quickly. Get Bethell to shift them back on the slaver and sail down to Ilfracombe as we first planned. Move them in the dead of night. It's too dangerous to transport them by road; too many curious people and too much to deal with. See that it's done."

"What about Milady? The women have seen her."

"But they won't recognise her. She wore a mask, I imagine?"

"She did, and men's clothes."

"Good. Now get this done as I command you."

Nathaniel and company had stopped at a recently opened church room, which appeared to cater for orphans in the parish. There they had purchased some food and drink and a small willow basket that had been strapped to Jessie believing it should provide a fine platform to carry the dog.

Nathaniel was more than used to listening to the chitchat around him and both he and Goliath had learned much of interest. One of the nuns from the Church rooms had let slip some of the rumours that were travelling down the coast. In fact, it seemed as if they were half expected to stop off there.

Sister Bridget had welcomed them in for some refreshment although she did look twice at Goliath as he dismounted from Samson and had hurriedly crossed herself. "You must be the Customs' men I've heard were travelling this way."

Nathaniel smiled at her disarmingly, "Well, what have you heard? I can then tell you whether or not the rumours are true. Sister Bridget had the good grace to blush and immediately began to apologise.

"If you please, Sir, I meant nothing by it. News travels fast along this coastline, especially when there has been a murder. We heard that you were instrumental in catching the man."

Nathaniel arched his eyebrow. "If you hear news and gossip this quickly perhaps you can help?"

Sister Bridget turned even pinker. "I doubt that, Sir. But I'll try."

Nathaniel questioned her closely but learned little, although it seemed there was a notable smuggling fraternity in the area that travelled between Bristol and Devon. "If you don't mind me saying so, Sir, you more or less cleaned up from Bristol to South Wales. Brought them to their knees I heard."

"Maybe." He paused, "In particular we are anxious to trace a consignment of women."

Sister Bridget shook her wimpled head, "All I know is that there's a lady involved in the enslavement of women. Rumour has it the gentry are in it up to their neck. But that's all I've heard and it is just gossip without any substance."

Nathaniel thanked her and the men bade her farewell.

Leaving Clevedon behind, the riders pressed on. Trooper sat looking forward to view the road ahead. They rode on with as much speed as they could toward Weston Super Mare and Burnham on Sea where they intended to rest awhile, before the last stretch through Somerset to Devon. They still had a fair way to go and if they were to stand any chance of finding Aleka they needed to move quickly.

Nathaniel kept mulling over the events on the journey so far and he believed folks knew more than they were saying. It wasn't easy for ordinary folk to confide in Customs' men. He knew he had lost loyal friends in Wales because of it. An image of Lily Pugh and her son Gwynfor came into his mind and he sighed sadly. Trooper sensing his master's sadness licked Nathaniel's hand consolingly bringing a smile to the officer's face. Nathaniel patted the mutt on his head and rode on.

11

Human Traffic

CLIVE BETHELL HAD ORGANISED three carts to take the captive women in the dead of night down to Portishead Docks where the slaver was masquerading as a merchant ship and trawler. Usually in a small fishing port it didn't attract the attention of the authorities. The port was quiet at night and he just needed to get them out safely and unobserved from the Manor.

Bethell stood on the worn stone steps leading to the dungeon and banged his stick on the iron door and across the wall. The women woke and looked up at their captor drowsily. Three of his men hurried down to the captives with ropes and gags and manhandled the women. They were unshackled so that they could walk but their hands were secured behind them and rags forced into their mouths and tied.

Aleka stood defiantly not wishing to comply but tensed her hands as they were roughly shoved behind her back and she was bound. A filthy rag was shoved in her mouth and knotted behind her head.

One of the crew took a length of rope and attached it to each woman so they were joined together. They were marched quietly from the dungeon and outside into the cool night air. Rough hands loaded them into the carts. Aleka shuddered as the man who lifted her up groped her with calloused hands, at the same time, obviously satisfying some lewd sexual craving.

The horses' hooves had been muffled with cloth as had the wheels of the cart to deaden the sound and they set off for the docks to the slaver that was readying to set sail.

Jonah Griggs was lamenting his capture and his actions and feeling very sorry for himself. He lay back on a hard wooden cot that hung from two chains in the wall. A coarse rough blanket was his only cover and an old cushion stuffed with horsehair served as a pillow. An iron bucket stood in one corner and a wooden pail and ladle filled with water.

Flies buzzed lazily around the slop bucket of urine and faeces. The stench in the cell was choking and Jonah tried to sleep but with thoughts racing in his head he was not going to be lucky enough to drift off into any kind of peaceful slumber.

The man in the next cell was full bearded with long straggly hair that hung in greasy strips to his shoulders. He was covered in scabs and every now and then he grunted as he scratched one of the many crusty lesions covering his suppurating sores. His shirt was filthy and ripped. His ribs could be clearly seen, as his frame was positively skeletal. His legs seemed withered and painfully thin. He coughed regularly and spat on the floor. The sputum mess was liberally flecked with blood but the man was beyond caring. He sat up, looking around wild eyed and manic as one of Jonah's wails penetrated his consciousness.

"Can't you shut your rattle?" the wild man griped. "What's the matter?"

"I'm done for," moaned Jonah. "I don't want to die," he whinged.

"You're done for in here anyway. If the gallows don't get you, the rats will."

Jonah shuddered, "It's not my fault. I was only obeying orders."

"I've heard that before. What do you want? To drag someone else down with you? Get your own back?" Jonah snivelled and sat trembling. He said nothing. The wild man shook his oily locks and pieces of scurf flew out showering his body with snow like flakes. "You do!" Jonah turned his face to the barbarian. "You want someone else to suffer. I can see it in your eyes. Remember those thoughts will not get you into heaven."

The man began rambling, quoting the Bible and throwing out nonsensical observations so Jonah turned away. He thought the prisoner was a raving lunatic.

Footsteps were heard clattering down the cold stone steps and a guard came down with a young woman carrying a basket. The guard smacked a baton against the bars of the wild man's cell who immediately stopped and ran to the corner of his lockup and cowered.

The guard announced, "Someone to see you, Jonah, bearing gifts."

Jonah looked up interested. He didn't recognise her and her face was in shadow as she wore a hood. The girl went to the bars. "Mary sent me. She couldn't come, couldn't face you, she said. Asked me to bring you some yeast buns. Said you liked them." The girl dipped her hand in the basket and lifted the cloth.

The guard, standing behind her, grabbed a bun, "I like yeast buns. I'll save one for later." He placed it on the bench where he then sat to watch the prisoners.

Jonah took the offered buns and called to the wild man, "Want one? There's plenty here." The man crawled from the corner and ventured to the bars. He took a bun and sniffed it, as would an animal before retreating back in the corner to nibble on it.

The girl hastened away quickly as Jonah called out, "Tell Mary, thank you." The girl nodded and hurried up the steps. The guard followed to see her out.

Jonah sat on his wooden cot and bit into his bun. The man in the next cell stuffed the food in his mouth before curling up in the corner. Jonah stretched out and looked up at the rocky ceiling marked with scratches where men had counted the passing days and he stolidly chewed his bun.

The guard returned and sat on the bench, picked up his bun and eagerly devoured it. "Tasty," he exclaimed and took a swig of water.

Some hours later another guard, Lucas, came to relieve the first who was slumped on the bench. "Come on. Time to wake up, George." He went to shake him but saw the man was face first in his own vomit. "George?" The guard listened to see if George was breathing. He wasn't. And he had no pulse.

The guard ran back up the steps to raise the alarm. More officers arrived together with a doctor, who checked George over before pronouncing, "He's dead. Did anyone here see anything?" He indicated the men in their cells seemingly asleep. Lucas rattled his baton across the bars, "Wakey, wakey!" There was no response. Lucas fished on George's body for the keys to open the cells.

The clunk and clang of the lock releasing was loud in the hushed atmosphere for no one dared to speak. The doctor went into one cell and then the other and shook his head. "I don't know what happened here, but they're all dead."

Aleka and her fellow captives had boarded the slaver and were now sailing around the coast toward the sleepy fishing harbour of Ilfracombe. The waters here were particularly dangerous and many boats had foundered on the rocks leaving the occupants and would be rescuers dead. The tragic loss of life in 1796 still weighed heavily on the people who lived there when all the slaves from one ship washed up dead on the beach in Rappery Cove.

Clive Bethell determined it would never happen again. His brother had lost his life on that ship. The water was much calmer than that day and he carefully steered the slaver across the bar and into the rocky cove where he dropped anchor. His cargo was ushered ashore in rowing boats where wagons awaited to transport their captives to Cornwall in preparation for the market at Redruth.

Aleka stood a clear head above the other women, her proud bearing set her apart and she wondered what she could do and how she could escape. For the moment she would watch and listen but she had no intention of being a slave to anyone. She looked around at her companions but saw no comfort there. For the most part the other women had, had their spirits broken.

Her friend Marjani had rallied physically but mentally she had withdrawn inside her mind and was now numb to all around her.

Nathaniel and his companions had long since left behind Clevedon and Nailsea. They continued on course, travelling the coastal path wherever possible and were on the outskirts of Somerset heading for the Devon border. The ride was hard and long, and neither Goliath nor Nathaniel had ridden in this way for a long time. Sam, however, was more used to it. He urged his travelling companions on.

"Hurry, and we might make the Devon coast by nightfall. You want to intercept that slaver, don't you?"

Nathaniel and Goliath repressed their groans and gripes about their aching backsides. They knew Sam was right so they swallowed down their protests and gritted their teeth following the young man without an audible complaint. Trooper sat in his basket lulled by the motion of the horse he closed his eyes and began to slumber.

The dusky twilight melded into the velvet black of night. A ceiling of stars pin pricked the sky and together with the silver moon lit their way. They were lucky no clouds were to be seen. The horses' hooves pounded along country lanes and roads sounding hollow on the stones and dirt as the men pressed their horses onward. They cantered through peaceful hillside hamlets and found the River Taw, which they followed to the estuary.

"Not far now," called Sam.

"I hope not. I'm ready for a hearty meal and bed," replied Nathaniel. "I bet Trooper is famished, too." At the mention of his name the dog looked up and cocked his head on one side. Nathaniel petted the animal behind his ear before urging Jessie onward, who had now slowed to a trot. Goliath grunted something unintelligible, which Nathaniel took to mean agreement. The three horsemen encouraged by the closeness of their destination spurred their steeds forward.

They skirted the riverbank and rural lanes, travelled past Barnstaple, Braunton, Ashford and came onto a more substantial road, which led to Ilfracombe. As they reached the top of a hill they looked down on the quiet town, harbour and quayside. Lights twinkled in cottages and houses, which tiered up the cliffs. The night air was still, almost brooding. There were a couple of big ships moored in the harbour and the only sound to be heard was the clang of a ship's bell.

Sam looked across at his companions, "We'll go to my lodgings and see if we can get you rooms there. Otherwise it will have to be the tavern. I'll take you to the Customs House first thing in the morning."

Nathaniel nodded, "Please. I'm tired and hungry. Will your landlady take a dog? And what about the horses?"

"The old coaching house has stables and a fine ostler. He will look after Jessie and Samson well. Hunter stables there. I wouldn't trust him anywhere else. Come."

Sam set off at a slow trot down the steep hills and into the town. The outlying houses were calm and serene but as they drew nearer the harbour and port, music assailed their ears. Someone was playing an accordion as drunken sailors tumbled out of the doors of the George and Dragon tavern and onto the quay. Ribald laughter could be heard inside while some men sang sea shanties and women pandered to their ego and needs.

"What's this?" asked Nathaniel.

"Where we can get a good meal. Don't worry; the women won't bother you if you avoid eye contact. The men are too interested in themselves to notice you."

"Maybe you're right but the garb of a riding officer can attract undue attention."

"Simply remove your hat," said Sam.

"But, I think they'll notice him," said Nathaniel jerking his thumb at Goliath. "Who wouldn't?"

"Ah yes… you have a point," said Sam with a grin. "He's difficult to hide."

Goliath chuckled, "Then let's do our worst, gentlemen."

The three dismounted, Trooper was lifted out of his basket and stayed close to Nathaniel. They led their horses to the stables where they were met by a trim and sprightly elderly gent. He was fit with a merry twinkle in his eye and looked at the arrivals, "So young, Mr Reeves, you've brought some friends with you this time?"

"That I have, Jim. Can you look after them as you would my Hunter?"

"Goes without saying, Mr Reeves."

Jim looked at the two new horses and assessed them, "It's a fine mare you have there, Sir. What's her name?"

"This is Jessie," said Nathaniel proudly.

"And the shire?"

"That would be Samson," said Goliath emerging from the shadows.

"Bloody hell," said the ostler taking a step back. "Are you real?" he asked, his eyes wide with fear.

"The last time I looked," said Goliath with a grin.

Jim swallowed hard and took the reins of the animals and led them away. He stopped at the stable doors and looked back taking in Goliath's stature and shook his head in disbelief.

Nathaniel slapped Goliath on his back. "It's good to see you can still put the fear of God into everyone you meet."

"With a little help from you I am turned into an unpredictable cannibal terror!" said Goliath with a laugh.

"It's true and I must apologise for those inferences but you have to admit those threats have served us well in the past," said Nathaniel with a twinkle in his eye.

"We can get a meal here and a room should my landlady have nothing available."

"How will we know?" asked Nathaniel.

"If you can get a table and order supper for three, I'll go and see Mrs Westaway and find out about the rooms. I'll not be long." Sam tipped his hat at them and strode up the quay toward some lodging houses on the higher road overlooking the harbour.

Nathaniel nodded and he and Goliath swept into the hostelry. The chatter was loud and uncouth. It took a while for the music to stop as the grinning accordionist with few teeth and spittle drooling from his lips was oblivious to their entry. He cast a careless eye over the usually bawdy company that one by one fell quiet then he, too, caught sight of the Negro giant, his jaw dropped and his legs almost gave way. The landlord came to the counter at the sudden hush. He was about to speak but then he saw Goliath.

Nathaniel broke the shocked silence, "A table good, Sir, if you please, and three quarts of ale. I have it on good authority you have food available. I'd like to order three meals. What do you have?"

The landlord gulped and licked his lips. By now the whole bar was straining to hear every word. The landlord broke the crushing silence that followed Nathaniel's request, "Got a good appetite, has he?" he said indicating Goliath.

Nathaniel clapped Goliath on the back, "Oh, indeed he has, Sir, but on this occasion the third meal is for another."

"Where? I don't see him."

"You will. He will be back shortly."

The landlord grunted and began serving the beer. "Food available is on the blackboard yonder."

The drinkers began to chat again and the accordionist struck up another tune but one man watched the duo closely. He was a large hulking beef of a man. Something stirred in his memory. He lumbered across from his corner and approached the two men. He tapped Goliath on the shoulder and stepped back as the giant turned.

"I know you," he said in his guttural tones. "You're that fighter from Jamaica. You were taken to be a slave," he said accusingly. "How did you escape? Cap'n thought you'd drowned."

Goliath's face furrowed in a frown, "I beat you fair and square and would do so again. You and your band of ruffians jumped me. I was a free man."

"And now?" growled the man. "Are you his lackey?" he said indicating Nathaniel.

Nathaniel turned abruptly, "He's his own man; hired by the Crown."

"And you owe me a purse of gold," added Goliath.

The man snorted in derision but at that moment Samuel Reeves entered the bar. The big man spat on the floor and muttered in disgust, "Riding Officers." He turned back to his gang of drinkers and gambling companions knocking shoulders with Sam.

"Harry Babb," said Sam. "Not causing any trouble, are you?"

Babb's demeanour changed to one of fawning servility, "No, Mr Reeves, most certainly not." He raised his huge hand and slapped Goliath on the back in a cursory manner. "Just reminiscing about a boxing bout, Sir." He smiled in an apparently friendly manner and moved back to his raucous compatriots.

Sam dropped his voice, "I don't recommend associating with him. He's a bad lot. Runs with Captain Tobias Stone's crew."

"I know Stone," said Goliath heavily. "He wanted me as his prize fighter, his puppet."

"Stone was a slave master. He's trying to be an above board merchant seaman but his past just won't let him go. However, I will say that Babb has helped us in the past for coin, but I wouldn't trust him."

"No?"

"Plays both sides to whatever suits him." He paused, "Lodgings are arranged, no worries there. So, what are we having to eat, Gentlemen?"

1 2

Aleka's Journey

ALEKA WOKE IN A cramped room on a mat on a hard floor. Her manacles had been removed but her feet were still shackled. She sat and looked about her in the gloom. The other women were similarly laid out on make shift beds. An older woman breezed in bringing two large jugs of something that steamed. A younger woman pushed a trolley with a tray of bowls, two more jugs and a ladle.

The younger woman distributed the bowls rousing those who still tried to sleep. As each woman grasped the bowl so a thin gruel type mixture was slopped into it. The women drank from the bowl, grateful for something warm in their stomachs.

The older woman with pinched cheeks and harsh looks reprimanded the younger more dough-faced female, "Not too much. It has to go round. You can always give them more later."

The younger one nodded, and apologised, "Sorry. I wasn't meaning anything by it." She looked around at the scrawny women, "I think they all look as if they could do with a good feed."

"You're not paid to think. Just do."

"Yes, Mrs Stone," mumbled the girl.

The captive women gratefully drank the watery mixture and were silent as they scrutinised their two women jailers. Deborah the plump younger female gathered up the clay bowls and stacked them back on the trolley while Mrs Stone ordered the women into groups. She explained quietly, "Some will be workers, others maid servants, and a select few for companionship and comfort, if you get my meaning."

Deborah nodded. She knew exactly what Mrs Stone intended for them and she shuddered. The strongest would be forced to act as slave workers in whatever capacity their owners wished. Those who looked presentable would be trained to take on staff duties in some of the finer houses and the others were destined to be the playthings of dissolute gentlemen.

Aleka struggled to stand. Her majestic frame and proud bearing set her apart from the others and she spoke perfect English, "What do you intend to with us? I am a free woman, daughter of the Governor of Sierra Leone."

Mrs Stone was taken aback at Aleka's nerve, "Woman, you are no longer free but my husband's property. You have been selected to serve gentlemen."

"You have no right. I am married and an educator."

Deborah looked concerned, she turned to Mrs Stone, "I didn't think anyone spoke English."

Mrs Stone looked surprised, "No, neither did I. Pidgin English, yes, but not like this."

"I demand to be given my freedom."

"You are in no position to demand anything," said Mrs Stone icily. "You will do as we tell you or I shall have you horsewhipped." She turned to Deborah, "Change her group. I had earmarked her for service in a good home but she is too free with her mouth. Put her over there with the whores. If she didn't need her tongue for her art I'd cut it out."

Deborah flinched at the thought but fearing for her own safety she tried to lead Aleka to the group indicated. Aleka whispered to the pasty-faced girl, "Why are you doing this? You know it's wrong. I feel it."

"If she speaks again, hit her. But not where it shows," ordered Mrs Stone.

"Please, just do as she asks or we'll both be for it," whispered Deborah.

"What's the problem?" called Mrs Stone.

"Nothing," said Deborah as she engineered Aleka into the other group.

Mrs Stone barked another order and Deborah hurried up. She gathered her trolley and pushed it out through the door, which clanged shut after them and a key was heard turning in the lock.

Aleka spoke out, "All of you, listen. We can stop this if we act together. They have no right to treat us like this." Many women looked confused as if they didn't understand her so she broke into the Jamaican patois they all knew.

And … Time passed.

Aleka had persuaded few women to fight back. Most were reconciled to their fate no matter how hard she tried to convince them. Britain, she knew from conversations with her father, was to pass laws to end the slave trade.

Questions were being asked in parliament and there were moves afoot to banish the slave trade throughout the British Empire. The injustice of their capture and enforced slavery made her so angry she wanted to smash something, anything, into a million pieces.

Time continued to eat into the daylight hours although incarcerated in a dungeon it was hard to know what time of day or night it was. Aleka tried to puzzle it out for herself. They had been given something resembling breakfast. Deborah had returned with bread, water and some pieces of salted meat, which she presumed was their lunch. No one had yet been around with supper and she felt sure it had been several hours since they were last inspected. Her stomach rumbled, growling to be fed.

Footsteps were heard coming down the well-trodden stone steps to the dungeon and keys rattled metallically in the lock. The huge door swung open. Deborah appeared with two scruffy looking men. Their hair curled to their shoulders and their clothes were stained and tattered. Behind the men stood Tobias Stone and Richard Gosling, who put handkerchiefs over their mouths to negate the smell of bodily functions and the stink of sweat from living in cramped unsanitary conditions.

"I thought they'd been cleaned and prepared," grumbled Gosling.

"There's only so much we can do, Sir," said Deborah.

"Well, it's not good enough," Stone complained. He spoke to the men, "Get them out of here as planned. I'll see they get cleaned up at the hostel in Redruth."

"Can we do that?" asked Gosling.

"We can," affirmed Stone. "Quickly now, get them out. We need to move them at night."

"It'll make it easier in the dark. No one will see them," said one of the ruffians as he guffawed.

The women were forced to their feet and they shuffled up the steps into the bright moonlight where covered wagons and horses waited. The men herded the three groups of women into the carts. Aleka tried to resist but being shackled it was not easy and she received a sharp stinging blow for her efforts.

The men each took a cart and Tobias Stone took the last. He bade farewell to Richard Gosling who called out, "Go carefully. We don't want any more mishaps. I'll see you in Redruth." He slapped the side of the covered dray for luck and the wain rattled off into the cool night air.

Richard Gosling rubbed his hands and made his way to where his horse was tethered. He mounted, kicked his heels into the horse's ribs and urged the animal forward.

Rider and horse galloped back to the Red Lion where Molly was waiting. She emerged from the kitchen a little hot and sweaty but her face creased into a grin when her eyes lit on Richard and she ran up to him. He lifted her up and swung her around. Molly giggled and then saw his serious expression. "What? What is it? You're off again, aren't you?"

"Sorry, Moll. I have to get back to the Manor and then onto Cornwall."

"When will you be back?"

"I'm not sure. When I do, you'll be the first person I'll call on, believe me."

Molly pouted before replying, "And what about your fine lady friend? Will she be going with you?"

"I've told you before you have no need to be jealous. It is purely business, nothing more. Come on, Moll. Give me a smile." The redhead forced one to her lips, which Richard immediately kissed. "And now, take me upstairs and I'll give you something to remember until I get back."

Molly chuckled and slipped out of his arms. She ran to the foot of the stairs and began to climb, glancing back at him provocatively over her shoulder. Richard chased after her and the two fell in through her door and onto the bed. He straddled her and poured kisses over her face and neck before unlacing her bodice and exposing her full, ripe breasts. Molly groaned in ecstasy as the two disrobed and pleasured each other yet again.

Richard left the hostelry with a satisfied smile on his face and cantered to the Manor, where he was met by his mother who sniffed his clothes imperiously. "You've been with that whore. You smell like a brothel. At least get her some decent perfume rather than that cheap scent she chooses to wear. The next consignment we get I'll put aside a bottle for her."

"You're not angry?"

"Why would I be? She keeps you satisfied and you remain a free man. A wife could have implications for the family business."

"I will refresh myself and be off. It's a long ride to Redruth."

"I understand Deborah and Mrs Stone have left with the wagons. They will make sure the women are presentable and alluring. They should fetch a most attractive price."

"Aren't you coming?"

"Maybe for the sale. I haven't decided yet. That should keep you on your toes." Lady Gosling stroked her son's face tenderly before catching his chin between her fingers. She kissed him and added, "Lest you forget…" Richard blushed but didn't pull away. "Go, now. Protect our investment." With that she glided out of the hall toward the staircase and smoothly mounted the stairs to her quarters.

Richard watched her go, a tight feeling knotting his stomach. He waited until she was out of sight before he twisted away and left the Manor, mounted his horse and galloped off into the dwindling light.

Aleka and the rest of the women had been housed during daylight hours at various stop off points. At each place they had been fed with a substantial meal. Deborah had explained that they needed to look their best and appear well fed. Folks were not interested in malnourished slaves who looked as if they might become ill or worse. The women were elated to be given some decent food for a change instead of the watery porridge slop mixture. They ate hungrily not knowing when they would have the opportunity of another meal.

Deborah checked all the women for lice or any other infestation. They were removed to a communal area with a stone floor where ten tin baths had been laid out. The women were given carbolic soap and told to strip and wash. Each bath of steaming water was used four times.

They had their hair plastered with some type of sulphur paste, which was cleaned off separately. Their coarse cotton garbs were removed to be cleaned and this time the females were presented with decent clothes, although not elaborate, the garments were clean and fitted far better than the loose cotton shifts they had worn previously.

A healthier bloom adorned their cheeks and they already looked more wholesome. Mrs Stone nodded approval when she arrived with her husband to inspect them. She instructed Deborah and two others to dress the women's hair. Aleka had no doubts. She knew that like pigs being fattened for market she and the others were being sanitized to make them more appealing to buyers. Fragrant pomade was passed around and patted onto their freshly washed hair. Deborah sprayed some type of cologne on their bodies to reduce the smell of sweat exacerbated by fear. This unexpected pampering did something to allay the captives' fears.

The women had been gathered in a large hall of yet another stately home. It was to this assembly that Richard Gosling arrived. He flung open the ornate double doors and stopped short at the sight of the young women. Some were very young and all were pretty but one woman caught Richard's eye. He was struck by the statuesque and proud bearing of Aleka with her fine features, high cheekbones, neat nose and perfect, sensual mouth. He singled her out and inspected her, nodding appreciatively at her scent and lithe body.

Aleka bridled at the way Richard Gosling stared at her. She disliked being ogled and was not used to being inspected as if she was a piece of meat and said so. Gosling laughed before taking her by the shoulders. She tried to shake off his hands, "Unhand me, now."

"Oh, a feisty one," he said with a smirk. "Don't worry your spirit will soon be broken. You will be bound to a new owner and made to do their bidding. In fact, I may buy you myself…"

Aleka bristled, "I belong to no man. I am my own person."

"Really? Then how come you are here?"

"I was stolen away from my home and husband."

"Oh? Then you are no stranger to men." He smiled lasciviously, "That will be a bonus."

Richard Gosling called out to the Stones, "This one, how much?"

Tobias Stone rubbed his chin, "She's a beauty. She'll fetch a good price. I don't know if we want to sell off our best prior to the sale."

Richard began to haggle. "Come on, surely there's some leeway here?"

Aleka rose up like a cobra about to strike and protested, "I am a free woman. You cannot do this to me."

"Oh, but we can," hissed Mrs Stone. "You had better keep quiet if you know what's good for you."

Aleka swallowed the retort ready to rise to her lips but inwardly she was planning her next move. She knew that in a sale she had no control over who bought her or where she would go. If she went before the sale she stood a better chance of escape. She remained silent.

"What? Nothing more to say? That's good. I think," said Richard. He eyed the Stones, "We'll discuss this upstairs." He turned to Aleka, "And you will pray that I succeed."

13

Starting work

NATHANIEL AND GOLIATH HAD settled in at Samuel Reeves' lodging house with Mrs Westaway. She was a homely woman and most accommodating once she got over her initial shock and fear of Goliath.

Breakfast had been a feast with fresh eggs, local ham and crusty bread. They had even tried the local delicacy of laver bread. Nathaniel had sampled it before in Wales and was keen to see the difference in recipes whilst Goliath was not so certain. He picked at the green sludge mixture on his plate.

"Go on, get it down you," urged Nathaniel. "It's full of vitamins to make you strong."

Goliath laughed before saying smugly, "Then, you my friend need it more than me. Here, have my share." So saying, he scraped his portion onto Nathaniel's plate with some glee.

Nathaniel shrugged and devoured it. "Aren't you afraid I'll beat you in an arm wrestle now?"

"We'll see!" replied the giant. "We'll see."

Trooper looked up hopefully from Nathaniel's feet wanting a small morsel from the plate and Nathaniel unable to resist the collie's pleading eyes slipped a small piece of bacon to the dog that gobbled it up.

Sam rose from his seat and took his plate out to Mrs Westaway in the kitchen. The others took his lead and followed suit as Trooper watched. Mrs Westaway flushed with pleasure before reprimanding them, "Now, now that's my job. What are you paying me for, else?" She turned to the dog, "And you, Trooper, can enjoy these scraps and she set down a plate of bacon bits and other titbits that the collie scoffed down in seconds. He licked his chops and wagged his tail as if it would drop off.

The men grinned before taking their leave with Trooper and departing their digs. It was a short walk to the harbour to check on their horses, which looked, calm, happy and well fed. Then Sam led the way around the harbour and they mounted the steps to the Customs' House. Reeves knocked respectfully before entering. Trooper stayed loyally at Nathaniel's side.

The men passed through the reception area to the inner office where Reeves knocked again. A voice filled with authority bade them to enter. They soon stood in front of a large mahogany desk before Daniel Bulled.

He was an older man with a florid complexion and wide girth. Never-the-less, there was an unmistakeable twinkle of good humour in his eyes. He rose to greet them.

"Mr Brookes and you must be Goliath. How fortunate you should be together. It is more than the crown or I could wish for." He glanced at the dog sitting respectfully at Nathaniel's feet. "Yours?" he asked Nathaniel.

"He is. He has proven to be very useful and could be again."

"Hmmm," his grunt was non-committal but he said no more. Trooper stayed quiet following the man's movements with his eyes.

He unrolled a number of maps and laid them out on a broad bench at the side of the room. These were flattened with the aid of paperweights and a couple of jam jars. "Here, Gentlemen; this is the coast you must ride. There are many different coves and beaches. Some are only accessible by water and therefore of no use to our enemies wishing to unload contraband and bring it ashore. Be vigilant. Don't waste your energy and time watching coves they don't use. It will be hard enough."

"And yet some of those places seemingly only accessible by water *can* be used as we both know," said Nathaniel nodding at Goliath and they both recalled their daring rescue across the cliff tops as they careered across the seemingly impenetrable cliffs, which hid the smugglers' caves at Pwll du.

"We have had several ships of late docking in Ilfracombe and dragoons have boarded and discovered contraband only to have it spirited away in the dead of night and the store house broken into. Rumours abound about a consignment of women meant for the slave trade, which as you know is on the wane." He sighed heavily, "No man should be subjugated by another and have his freedom and identity stolen. No woman either."

Nathaniel and Goliath exchanged a look. This was what they wanted to hear. "Do we know where they have gone?"

"My source tells me they were moved at night and have the protection of someone in the gentry. My man believes Redruth or St. Austell, maybe even Truro."

Nathaniel pursed his lips this was in accordance with what they believed. "Is your man to be trusted?"

"My informant has not let me down before," said Bulled.

"I believe the gentlemen are acquainted with the man. He and Goliath have crossed swords in the past," said Sam.

"Ah!" Daniel Bulled sighed. "He is something of a rogue but I believe he is serious about improving his life and status. One way he does this is by keeping his ear to the ground and tipping us off."

"And lining his own pockets whenever he can," added Sam.

"That remains to be seen… But back to the maps, Samuel will ride alone; the three of you will share the patrols between Devon and Cornwall. Samuel is at an advantage for he knows the land and beaches, which offer shelter to smugglers and the bays where wreckers practice. Samuel will start at the Devon Coast and you two, will cross the border into Cornwall. I will expect regular communications when you are away from base. Mail coaches travel the country roads from Cornwall to Devon. Samuel knows I get messages within two to three days and you all will be expected to return two monthly with a full report."

He passed one set of drawings to Daniel and a series of maps rolled and tied with a ribbon together with a dispatch bag to Nathaniel. "I expect to hear from you in three days, if not before, with monthly reports and we meet here two months from today. You two get to know the coastline. There are many places where smugglers can bring in their goods."

Bulled bent down and ruffled the dog behind his ears. Trooper stood sensing they were about to leave. Bulled shook hands with them, which was their signal to depart. They left with Samuel Reeves who apologised, "I had hoped we would have ridden together. But there, we have much ground to cover. I'll bid you farewell and good luck."

It was time to ride. Nathaniel and Goliath needed to retrieve their steeds and explore the coastline. They packed a few belongings and mounted their horses; Trooper was safely stashed in the willow basket.

They promised Mrs Westaway they would return but were not sure when. They paid their dues in advance and trotted out of the quaint seaside town.

They attracted a few stares and gasps from the locals who were not used to seeing two Customs Officers riding together, with a dog in a basket, or someone as distinctive as Goliath.

The officers intended to fully explore this part of the coast and needed to study the maps. So, they rode to the top of the town and back along the coast overlooking Hele Bay where they paused. Goliath turned to Nathaniel, "We have to find Aleka... head toward Redruth and St. Austell."

Nathaniel nodded in agreement, dismounted and removed the maps from the dispatch bag. He flattened one out. Goliath weighted the corners down with stones as it was stretched out on the grass. They studied the roads and position of Redruth in relation to where they were. "It's a hard ride over many miles. We'll have to move quickly and be prepared to report back."

"Then what are we waiting for?"

The maps were stowed away and they cantered off on their journey.

Aleka sat with the other women, her face furrowed in a frown. She attempted to listen to everything that was said around her and she had learned much. The Stones were the slavers who had sent Clive Bethell out on the rampage looking for women to steal. They were the ones organising the sale. Funding for the raiding parties had come from a titled woman who was linked to Richard Gosling. He was protecting the family investment. She had arranged the stopovers on route. Aleka suspected they were mother and son. She wondered how the titled woman would react if she knew her son was interested in the goods.

Just as she was thinking about her next move, Deborah returned with the same two scruffy men from before. The women were ordered to their feet, "Move it. Quickly now." The captives had lost their sparkle, their defiance, and the fight seemed to have been knocked out of them. "Not that one. That one stays." The chap with hair the colour of mouldy straw indicated Aleka. She started in surprise as Deborah came and unshackled her feet.

The women were herded out of the cellar and marched up the rocky steps to the ground floor. Aleka heard someone cry, "No more than ten to a wagon." She turned to Deborah crouched on the floor struggling to unlock the chains.

"What is to happen to me?"

"I reckon you's lucky. Sir Richard's taken a shine to you, he has. He's arranged a private sale. You's his property now." Aleka stiffened.

There was a clunking clank as the unlocked metal restraints fell to the floor. Aleka stretched down to rub her bruised sore ankles. "No time for that now. You're to come with me."

Aleka followed Deborah up the stone hewn steps that dipped in the middle through the tread of people from centuries past. They emerged into a hot kitchen, where cooks and maids worked. "Come on," urged Deborah.

They continued through the corridors to the great room, with doors that towered to the ceiling and made of mirror. Aleka caught her reflection and shuddered at her appearance. She looked unkempt and in spite of all her efforts dirty. Her braided hair with its bright beads was the only lively thing about her.

Deborah pushed open the huge doors and they entered. Richard Gosling sat comfortably in a fancy Louis XV chair upholstered in wine and cream satin stripes. He looked thoughtful and rose as the women entered the room. He strolled across and circled Aleka before ordering Deborah. "Wait by the door for my instructions, Deborah." He turned back to Aleka, all the while, eyeing her up and down.

"So, Missy. What do I call you?"

"My name is Aleka," she said proudly. "Aleka Herkenefer."

"Too much of a mouthful. From now on you will be known as Alice, Alice Hart." Aleka bit back the retort she was ready to spit at him. She stood there majestically looking impressive in spite of her ill-fitting clothes. "Nothing to say? You surprise me. I thought you would offer some comment."

Aleka took a deep breath, "Would it make any difference?"

"No. But an exchange of words might have been fun." He turned to Deborah, waiting patiently, "Take her upstairs and give her a proper bath. There is more serviceable and finer apparel waiting. Dress her and make her look presentable."

Deborah bobbed a curtsey and ushered Aleka out of the room. Aleka left with her head held high. She turned at the door, "This is not over."

"Oh, but it is. For you, it is." Richard Gosling watched Aleka as she left the room and smiled.

Goliath and Nathaniel had ridden hard. Night had fallen. Their way was lit by the stars and a crescent moon shining in the velvet night sky. Storm clouds began to roll in from the sea eclipsing the ethereal silver light from the heavens. They approached the cliff head and stared at the houses below.

The wind was gathering whipping up the sea below, which furiously lashed the craggy rocks, as would a stern schoolmaster punishing a trying child. They stared up the Valency valley and then out to Meachard Rock the island off Penally Point.

They had followed the coast road, passed through Trevalga, where it was rumoured that the inn there harboured smugglers and wreckers when the eyes of the law were not upon them. They were now looking down on a North Cornwall fishing village and harbour. Oxen were tethered patiently, with their carts, awaiting daybreak ready to transport goods from the cargo of merchant ships due into port at the quayside.

"I have heard of this place," murmured Nathaniel. "Sir Richard Grenville built these harbour walls in the 1500's. It is not an easy or safe place to enter."

"Ripe for wreckers and smugglers, then," said Goliath.

"Indeed. It would be foolish for a captain to try and enter these waters under their own sail. When a trader comes in sight, the harbour master sends out a boat with nine men, 'Hobblers', they're called, who would tow them safely into harbour."

Goliath nodded as his eagle eyes scoured the rocky tors. He spotted a blinking light moving on the cliff opposite them, "Over there. Look!"

Nathaniel focused his eyes on the far crag and once he'd adjusted to the fluctuating light he caught sight of a line of men, vagabonds, and ruffians by their attire. "Smugglers," he said under his breath. His eyes searched the horizon voraciously where a ship in full sail could just be seen dipping and rising on the surging water. He narrowed his eyes and looked closer at the rocky shore below where more men waited.

"This is the reason the carts are present. They're not waiting for legitimate cargo. By God, they're wreckers."

"What do we do? We are but two and there are many."

It was soon clear to them that the blinking light, a lantern waved at regular intervals, was attempting to draw the ship in to be breached on the treacherous rocks below. Men below waited to plunder and loot. This ship would find no safe harbour and survivors would have their throats slit or drown.

"I don't know," whispered Nathaniel not wishing his words to be carried on the wind. "We can't show our hand unprepared."

"And we can't let innocent men die," added Goliath.

"No."

"So, what do we do?"

As they spoke in hushed tones, Nathaniel took his spyglass from his saddlebag and trained it on the ship that lurched in the water. "She's coming about," said Nathaniel. "Headed for the rocks. There'll be no saving her. We must get down to the shoreline and stop them."

"How?"

Nathaniel shrugged, "We'll think as we ride." He clicked to Jessie who began negotiating the way down the steep road into the village of Boscastle along the rushing riverside where the water gurgled and swelled. Trooper remained alert in his basket as if he knew something was to happen.

Lights glowed behind the window drapes in the lines of terraced fishermen's cottages. Other houses lay in darkness while sounds of merriment emanated from The Napoleon Inn. The two riders slipped off their horses leaving them in the shrubbery close to the beach. Trooper safely out of his basket followed quietly.

They stepped onto the gritty sand and walked as quickly and quietly as possible and secreted themselves behind a crop of craggy rocks. Trooper gave a warning low rumbling growl in his throat and his ears went back. Nathaniel reassured and quietened the dog that sat at his side.

The salty wind ruffled through Nathaniel's thick dark hair as the sky was ripped apart by a jagged lightning strike. Thunder grumbled in the distance and ominous storm clouds rolled in eclipsing the moon and shrouding the starlight. The sound of the waves crashing on the shore rose to a crescendo as the bullying wind contorted the sea into turbulent white-capped breakers.

The light guided the boat away from the harbour toward the perilous rocks.

"What now?"

"We wait. There's no saving the ship. They wouldn't hear us above the noise of the storm but we can stop the brutes murdering the survivors."

Goliath nodded. The next few minutes were agonising as the stricken vessel splintered with a sickening crunch as it grounded on the jagged rocks, which pierced the boat's hull and ripped out the belly of the boat. The tortured screams of sailors as they were crushed by falling masts or fell into the turbulent waters rose above the howling wind that seemed engorged with unnatural fury. Men jumped into the violent sea to try and escape the cruel breakers that lashed the barnacled covered rocks and the wreckers waited.

There were six men on the beach waiting for the surf to fling its victims onto the sand. They moved forward in line drawing their vicious looking blades ready to slice the throat of any survivor. The first of the seamen floundered toward the shore gasping for air and pleading for help. Goliath stepped out drawing himself up to his towering height joined by Nathaniel who stood legs astride as he levelled his military flintlock light dragoon pistol.

"Stand down in the name of the King," shouted Nathaniel. The men turned and forgetting the drowning sailor they brandished their wicked knives and rushed toward the two officers. Trooper set off a ferocious barking, his hackles raised. Nathaniel fired; one man dropped to the sand, crying in agony, his kneecap broken. Three others moved toward Goliath trying to rush the giant. Goliath sidestepped one flipping him over avoiding the blade, which the man fell onto as he landed. It tore into his stomach and he screeched in pain. The second met Goliath's fist in a stomach-churning, fearsome blow loosening the man's teeth and breaking his nose. The third man hesitated and seeing the fate of his comrades began to run back up the sand. The deluging rain made the going tough. By this time Nathaniel had reloaded and the other two thugs hesitated. Nathaniel aimed again levelling his pistol at them.

The rain was swamping them in torrents as the storm gathered momentum. The two miscreants thought better of charging an armed man and fled up the beach raising the alarm trying to call above the cacophony of the savage storm. Goliath hastened along the sand, splashed through the surf and hauled out the distressed man.

In desperation other sailors jumped into the foaming wild sea. Nathaniel and Goliath managed to save another five men, before they attended to the wounds of the two wreckers who lay incapacitated on the grainy sand, their blood mingling with the driving rain.

By now some of the folks in the cottages had come out to see what was happening. Aid was on hand to help carry the injured and hurt to the Napoleon Inn. The men, who were on the cliffs seeing the activity below, like the cowards they were, fled.

Goliath had thrown his cloak's hood over his head. He managed to support two men, while Nathaniel lifted the miscreant with the knife wound. Trooper watched cautiously.

A few more villagers had emerged in the storm to see the events on the beach. They, too, came to help and two of them ran to carry the wrecker with the damaged kneecap. There was nothing to be done for the ship or others that had perished in the terrifying waters. All the locals could do now was to wait for the storm to abate and see what washed up on shore in the morning.

The inn was hushed as they entered, all music had stopped and people sat staring at the officers in blind accusation. The horses had been led to the stables and were being catered for by a groomsman. Nathaniel had retrieved his medicine bag and tended to the injured men.

The man with his belly ripped was a slight, slim chap with oily black hair and beard stubble. He had turned white under his sallow complexion through loss of blood.

Nathaniel ordered the landlord, "Hot water, plenty of it and quick. Oh, and we'll require a room for the night."

The landlord nodded, "You'll have the water but no room here. I'm full."

"Then we'll sleep in your bar."

The landlord grumbled, muttering obscenities under his breath and adding, "I want no truck with Riding Officers. Scum of the earth."

A woman sidled closer to Nathaniel, "Will he be all right?"

"He'll live as long as I can stop the bleeding and prevent infection. It needs stitching."

The woman looked concerned, "Save him and there'll be no floor for you. You'll both have a bed for the night... And your dog," she said, eyeing the collie who stayed valiantly at Nathaniel's side.

Nathaniel pressed a wad of muslin tight against the wound and glanced at her. "And you are?"

"Frances Wheelan," she jerked her thumb at the man. "Ross. I'm his wife. I warned him not to get involved with that lot. He said he had no choice. I know the tragedies families have suffered if the menfolk refuse to do as bid."

Nathaniel exchanged a glance with Goliath. They understood exactly what she meant. It was then Goliath chose to throw back his hood and the assembled company gasped. They had never seen anyone so big or black. "This is my man and fellow officer, Goliath. Treat him with respect and no harm will come to you." A few of the onlookers moved away muttering fearfully as the landlord returned with a pan of hot water, which he nearly dropped when he saw Goliath who was now standing up at his full height. The landlord hurriedly put down the water and retreated behind the bar. The man with the injured kneecap groaned.

"I'll be with you in a moment," affirmed Nathaniel. "Give him some whiskey to dull the pain," he said, as he made a hot poultice of herbs kept in his bag, a healing measure, which he had learned from Lily Pugh, the hard working Welsh woman who had lost her life because of smugglers. He gave the man some liquor to drink as he stitched the wound. Ross bellowed in pain. Nathaniel took the poultice and plastered it onto Ross' stomach. He strapped him up as best he could. "Where do you live?"

"The fishermen's cottages up yonder, third one in the row. I meant what I said. You can have a bed with us," said Mrs Wheelan.

Nathaniel nodded agreement. Goliath pulled on his hood and lifted the man up. He followed Mrs Wheelan out of the tavern while Nathaniel tended to the other man whose head was now lolling drunkenly. "What's his name?"

"He be Trevor Symons. Lost his wife last year."

"Does he live locally?"

"Back with his mother at Polruny farm. About two miles from here."

"He'll have to stay here. Landlord make a cot up here and someone get word to his mother. He'll need crutches. There'll be no more wrecking for him, not now."

The man's cracked kneecap was not impossible to fix even without the proper tools. Nathaniel removed the shot, cleaned up the wound and attempted to plaster it. Luckily for the man the patella had separated in just one place and if Nathaniel could line up the bones there was a chance the knee would mend and heal as long as he could get perfect alignment.

"He'll need to stay off his feet for six to eight weeks. No weight must be put on that leg. Do you understand?" he said to those watching, who nodded apprehensively. "Good. Now, something to eat and drink I think, Landlord." Nathaniel turned to the assembled company, "Nathaniel Brookes at your service."

One man on hearing the name left the tavern. The others just stared in shocked disbelief. Trooper gave a joyous bark as if emphasising Nathaniel's words.

14

Boscastle

THE DRIVING RAIN HAD ceased but the paths and roads were slippery and running with water. The three rivers that met in Boscastle were the Valency, Jordan and Paradise. They were swirling and rushing threatening to burst their banks and flood. Nathaniel made his way up the steep sloping track followed by the loyal Trooper. The moon had come out from its bank of cloud and stars were visible in the sky once more. He looked back at the beach. There were no signs of the wreckers or drowned sailors. He could see the ship breaking up on the reef and could just discern, wooden casks and chests bobbing on the squally surf. It would be at the turn of the tide when some of the cargo was likely to be washed ashore. He would deal with it then. Nathaniel turned back and continued his climb followed nimbly by the collie dog.

As he approached the line of fishermen's cottages someone came hurrying up behind him and rasped, "Mr Brookes."

Trooper growled.

Nathaniel turned and faced one of the men he recognised from the bar, "Yes?"

"I'm no snitch or turncoat but I know you and your reputation. I'm giving you a friendly warning and you didn't hear it from me." He looked around shiftily, "Some of my friends have disappeared, gone. Don't have to know what happened to them. There's a whole crew of wreckers all along this coast right down to Penzance… All in the employ of a titled lady… Word has it that whoever does for you will be well rewarded. There's a price on your head."

The hackles rose on Trooper's neck and he continued to warn the man by rumbling throatily. Nathaniel stopped and calmed the animal. Trooper sat close to Nathaniel's legs.

"And this lady is…?"

"I can't say. I don't want my throat cut like others before me. I'm just warning you that knives are out for you."

"And I will be careful, thank you. Is there anything else?"

The man spat on the ground and looked over his shoulder once more, "I've been told that if you can't be stopped. They'll make you."

"And how will they do that?"

The man dropped his vocal level so it was barely a whisper. The tone the man used sent shivers down Nathaniel's spine, "I'm told that as before they'll go after what's precious to you," he paused and licked his sea salt chapped lips. "Your wife and little un. Even your mam."

Nathaniel bristled at the warning, "I've been threatened before."

"They mean it. They know all about you. Word spread from the Bristol Channel you were coming. Your wife's name is Jenny. Your son's called Bart. They know where you live. And your sister… they know everything."

Nathaniel grabbed the man by the throat, "If anyone harms a hair on Jenny's head or that of my boy I'll not rest until I hunt them down and kill them. Go tell that to your masters."

The man winced, "Not me. Not my masters. It's just what I heard. I want no dealings with them. I just do what I have to, to stay alive. I came to warn you. I owe nothing to those bastards. I just keep my ear close to the ground, say little and hear a lot. I repeat, it's just what I've heard."

"Why should I believe you?"

"Can you afford not to?" The man glanced quickly about him again. "I best be gone. If I'm caught talking to you then I'll be done for, too." The man turned away ready to slink into the shadows of the inky black of night.

"Wait!" the man stopped. "What's your name?"

"Finlay, Finlay Sharman. And would I be telling you that if I was up to no good?" The man spat again and disappeared back down the track. Nathaniel watched him go. He ran back down the slippery track and entered a house close to the beach.

Nathaniel's mouth set in a grim hard line and a pulse twitched in his chiselled cheek. He leaned down to stroke and reassure Trooper before setting off again. He soon reached the outlying cottages, battling against the buffeting wind as he walked, and searched for the third dwelling. It was easy to spot; it was the only one with the muddy glow of oil lamps in the leaded windows.

Nathaniel walked up the tiny path and knocked on the brass horseshoe knocker. Footsteps were heard scurrying to the door, which opened a crack. Frances peered out. On seeing Nathaniel, she opened the door to admit him. A flurry of the still gusting wind almost blew him in. Trooper rushed past Nathaniel's feet and made for the fire where he set to cleaning his fur from mud and rain.

Nathaniel removed his Tricorne hat and still sodden cloak; which Frances took and shook gently on the slate floor before laying it out on a full size fireguard to dry. It was warm in the kitchen and although it was the beginning of summertime she had a fire on the range for cooking. His outer garments soon began to steam in the heat. Goliath's clothes already laid out were also drying well.

"I'll be giving you both some supper and scraps for your dog once you've checked on my Ross. He's in the parlour laid out on the couch."

"He'll be fine. He just needs to heal. I'm wondering why you've accepted us into your home. We're not well liked around here or anywhere."

"I've no call to have sympathy for wreckers. My pa died because of them and they forced Ross to join them, threatening me and my maid."

"Maid?"

"My daughter, Deborah. She's still missing."

"How so?"

"She's either dead or in bondage. They took our lass to make us behave. Put her in service we suspect. Threatened us. If we don't do as they ask they will take it out on Deborah. We had no choice."

"But if they know you have harboured us and taken us in – it could be worse for you."

"My Ross would be dead if it wasn't for your quick thinking and medical knowledge. He came after you not t'other way round. I can manage the gossip."

"Maybe so. But we had two wonderful friends in South Wales. They died because of our friendship."

Goliath remained silent but his eyes brightened with tears at the memory of Lily and Gwynfor. He swallowed in an attempt to suppress the emotion he felt and continued to listen. Trooper ventured from the spot he'd taken at the fireside and nuzzled Goliath's hand.

Frances weighed up what had been said and broke the silence. "I'm afraid no more," she said defiantly. "I refuse to be dictated to by those ruffians. And I want a favour." Nathaniel raised an eyebrow as he and Goliath became more alert. "I've heard that you are seeking a woman."

"How do you know that?"

"Word travels fast. Your arrival in the South West preceded you. We heard you were riding again. We know you were asking questions about a slave auction."

"And do you have answers?" asked Nathaniel.

"Anything you can tell us will help," added Goliath.

"No more than you already know. Auction planned for a market day in Redruth, maybe another in St. Austell."

"What can you tell us about these men, the slavers?"

"They're a tight knit group. The slave master who goes on the raiding parties is a foul man, Clive Bethell, as cruel as he is strong. He has his own crew. The bosses of him are the Stones, Tobias and his wife, Florence."

"And above them?"

"I have heard it's one of the gentry and a woman, a titled one at that. Something to do with that reprobate, Gosling. But that's all I know."

"Tell me about Gosling."

"A dissolute man with a penchant for women. He cares not how he gets his money. But..."

But?" prompted Nathaniel.

"I have heard he has a softer side... The man must have some conscience." Nathaniel looked questioningly so Frances explained, "If he loses a man through his actions or ruthlessness he will give a purse to those left behind."

"I see. Thank you, Frances. Tell me where is the nearest Custom House from here?"

"That would be Padstow, South Quay on the Camel Estuary. Others have gone, shut down. Dangerous job in this world, not one any man would want."

As if to emphasise her words the rain drummed a powerful tattoo on her windows and door, like a funeral march, as if heralding in a portent of doom. Frances shivered involuntarily. "I don't like this storm but I feel it's nothing compared to what is to come," she said cryptically and drew her thin shawl around her shoulders as if it would shield her from any malevolence.

Her husband Ross entered clutching his stomach and groaned. He struggled to keep his head up and stumbled toward them; "Keep your mouth shut, wench. You'll have us all murdered. Think of Deborah."

His wife turned, her eyes flashing angrily, "I am thinking of Deborah. That's if she is still alive. Selling our souls through blackmail and committing all sorts of atrocities does not sit well with me. It's time to make a stand. Starting now. This man saved your life. Would they have cared had you perished? No. Come to your senses, man." The anger in her voice began to turn tearful and she swallowed a sob. "You could be dead. What would I do?" She turned to Nathaniel, "You have beds here, both of you. Your dog can sleep in the kitchen. I'll help Ross back."

"Here, let me," said Goliath and he half carried the ailing man back into the other room. He placed the man onto the old fashioned cushioned settle and covered him with a patchwork cover. Ross' head lolled and he slipped into a sleep brought on by his exertions. Nathaniel with Trooper entered the room and he instructed Frances. "Keep the wound covered for three days. Then change the dressing. If it needs cleaning up use whatever you have to hand. Neat alcohol is good. It must be kept free of infection. The stitches can come out after ten days."

Frances nodded, "Into the kitchen all of you. Let's eat."

Trooper yapped as if he understood the conversation was about food making Nathaniel chuckle. "You, too, Trooper. Good boy!" The collie followed them out to the kitchen where they sat around the small beech wood table.

Frances set out some cooked chicken, bread, cheese and pickle, which they were happy to eat. Trooper had some chicken skin and scraps. Those around the table were quiet while they ate. Frances rose to clear away the debris. She wiped her hands on her apron and set aside some food for her husband. "I'll just see to Ross and then I'll be showing you your room." She nodded agreeably before leaving Nathaniel and Goliath.

"It's kind of her to do this," said Goliath.

"Yes," mused Nathaniel. "But I worry for her safety. And I know it's uncharitable but I also worry that while we are here, wreckers are on the sands gathering up the ship's cargo."

Goliath said nothing for a moment, "What time is high tide?"

"I'm not sure."

"You don't think they're back on the beach now? Surely not… and if they are they'll have to pass this way with their carts. Wouldn't we hear them?"

"We may do. But the night is unforgiving with the wind wild." Nathaniel was unusually subdued. "I don't like it. If this is a ruse to keep us out of the way, it's worked. If not, then Frances is putting her own life in danger. We know what the likes of the smugglers are capable of."

Goliath grunted and rose, "I'll take a look outside just in case…"

Nathaniel nodded, "I'll take a last look at Ross, give him some laudanum to help him sleep. If there is movement below let me know and don't go doing anything alone."

Goliath flashed one of his big smiles. "I'll not be taking on an army of cutthroats. I won't be long." He grabbed his hooded cloak, made for the door and unbarred it. The wind rushed in sending the oil lamp flames flickering and sputtering before he disappeared outside.

Nathaniel went to the sink and took a pan of water from the range to swill the crockery. He set the washed items on the drainer.

"And what do you think you're doing?" came the critical tones of Frances. "Where's the big man?"

"I'm just helping clear away before seeing to Ross before bed. Goliath has just stepped out."

Frances looked alarmed, "He's not going back to the beach?"

"No. He's just stepped outside. Why?"

"He'll not be safe. There's too many of them."

"What do you mean?"

"Turn of the tide they'll be there to scavenge and take away the loot. They'll murder him like they did my pa." She crossed herself, "Lord save us."

"Frances, we don't want to put you in any more danger so as soon as morning comes we will leave, but what of you and Ross?"

"He'll heal, thanks to you. Don't worry about us we'll get by. But if you do by chance come across our Deborah in your search try and get her back home to us."

"I will try."

At that moment Goliath returned. A blast of cold air came into the room with him. "It's stopped raining. No one's about. The tide looks as if it's on its way in. Any contraband that's escaped the ship will be floating on the water. It should get dumped on the sand. The rest can't be reclaimed until the sea has gone right out. The main cargo can't be reached until the tide is fully out. I could see in the starlight the ship's still grounded on the reef."

"Very well. We'll take to our beds and rise early. We can see what needs to be done then before moving on."

Frances nodded, "This way." She pulled back a curtain in the parlour hiding the twisted wooded stairs. She took a lamp from the window and led the way up to the bedrooms.

Trooper whined softly in his throat as he watched them go.

"Hush now," said Nathaniel. "Be a good boy. Stay."

The dog cocked his head on one side as if he understood and settled down on the floor by the stairs and listened.

The sound of the men's feet clumping above seemed to pacify the animal and he put his head on his paws and closed his eyes.

Upstairs, Frances ushered Nathaniel into a small but well-kept room. The bed was spotlessly clean with a quilted coverlet and pristine white pillow. A jug and bowl sat on the washstand and there was a chair for his clothes. Nathaniel nodded his approval. The adjoining room was for Goliath and was equally clean. They both bade Frances goodnight and settled into their rooms.

Nathaniel had just climbed into bed when there was a faint pitter-patter on the stairs and scratching on the door accompanied by a soft little whine.

Nathaniel got out and opened the door. Trooper scampered in wagging his tail. Nathaniel shook his head in amusement, sighed and closed the door. "All right, Trooper. Just for tonight. Come on." The black and white Border collie came in and lay on the floor next to the bed on an old rag mat. Nathaniel returned to his bed and tried to get to sleep. The wind outside although not as ferocious as in the storm was still battering the house and the windows rattled and whistled lifting the ragged curtains in a demented dance.

Nathaniel turned over and tried to get comfortable. He dropped his hand over the side of the bed only to have it eagerly licked by Trooper. Eventually, he turned again and rolled toward the window. With the lamp extinguished the room was an enveloping black. Heavy cloud outside ensured no moonlight or starlight penetrated the inkiness in the bedchamber and Nathaniel finally fell asleep.

He awoke some hours later to Trooper growling, his hackles raised. He set off a ferocious barking. Grogginess from sleep gone he was instantly awake. "What is it, boy? What have you heard?"

The wind had now dropped but Trooper continued to growl and bare his teeth. There were sounds of a disturbance downstairs and a door banging.

Footsteps were heard slowly mounting the stairs. Nathaniel crept out of bed and stood behind the door. Whoever it was appeared to pause outside his door. Trooper hurled himself at the entrance in a frenzy of barking.

Nathaniel whipped open the door as Goliath came out onto the landing as well as Frances Wheelan in her nightgown and wrap. A man in the shadows turned tail and fled back down the stairs followed by Trooper who tore at the man's ankles. He hurried back outside leaving the door banging behind him. There was a squeal and the collie came back inside limping.

Everyone was now awake and hurried downstairs. Goliath nodded at them, "I'll see what I can see," and he went out after the intruder.

Frances put her hand to her mouth and whispered, "Ross…"

They went into the parlour where the man lay. He was smothered in blood from other vicious wounds. His eyes rolled in his head and he groaned. Nathaniel rushed to his side, "Fetch a light and bring me hot water. I need to see what harm has been done."

Frances hurriedly brought a paraffin lamp and lit it, setting it on the table by the settle. "I'll get the water."

Nathaniel could see that the man had defensive wounds on his hands and arms, his neck had been slashed and another puncture wound was visible through his nightshirt above his stomach injury. Frances returned with a basin of hot water and fresh towels

Nathaniel barely glanced at her, "He's lucky, an inch closer to the left and it would have pierced his heart. We need to stop the bleeding." Nathaniel grabbed his bag still on the table and began to examine the stab wounds. "They're clean cuts, no arteries or major veins damaged."

"Can you save him?"

"I can try. But he's lost a lot of blood."

The bedding on the settle was saturated. Frances lifted her hand to her mouth in horror, "Lord save us. We could all be dead in our beds if it wasn't for your little dog."

"Aye, he's saved us all that's for sure. Here hold this muslin here and press hard." Frances did as she was asked while Nathaniel tended to the savage slash to Ross' neck. "A bit deeper and longer and we'd be calling the undertaker." He turned to Ross, "Do you know who did this, Ross? Who was it attacked you?"

The man rasped his reply the air rattling in his chest interspersed with cries

ods stacked on the quay into the cart and gathered the few items that
ed on the beach.

at about the ship? And the sailors who have drowned?"

can't help them now," said Nathaniel. We'll alert the authorities in
d they can deal with it plus take these two into custody. We need to
ng before the rest of the rabble return. I don't like the look of the odds
ger."

h nodded in agreement and mounted the front of the cart. He clicked
who began plodding up the steep hill toward the pub and the
house.

was now ablaze with the red fire of the sun and birds began their
s as gulls started to mewl and chatter at the break of day. They
eir horses from the hostelry stables, attached them to the cart and
the hill toward the fishermen's cottages.

tside Nathaniel pounded on the door. Frances was quick to
Trooper came hurtling out in delight at Nathaniel's return. He
up into the cart as Frances retrieved her bags. She stiffened
the two men trussed up like chickens and flashed a look of
iel.

one is unconscious and the other severely dazed. They'll take a
."

er knowing they couldn't see us," murmured Frances.
d her belongings and went inside to carry out Ross. He emerged
man and two coats, which he slung over the men's heads. He
back and covered him with a blanket, placing a cushion under
d Samson from the wagon and mounted him. Nathaniel did
while Frances sat at the front and took the reins.
d on up through the village and onto the main road, which
lves as they followed the road to Truro.

ached Truro the sun was truly up and people were bustling
ing about their business. The two prisoners were dropped
House together with the confiscated goods, which were
cell. Information was relayed regarding the wreck before
infirmary where Ross was admitted to one of the twenty
r rescuers farewell and her cart trundled on toward her

of pain. "I didn't get a good look, I woke with him atop of me." He coughed, "Your dog disturbed him. He was a big man and smelled of fish." He coughed again.

"Enough, no more talking." He turned to Frances; "I'll make him as comfortable as possible. Have you anywhere you can go?"

Frances shook her head, "I don't know… I have a cousin in Truro… She may help."

"You need to get yourself to a place of safety. If they think you're likely to talk they'll come after you again and I won't be here."

She nodded, "Looks like they wanted us all dead in our beds."

"Is there anything more you can tell me?"

Ross wheezed, "Keep your mouth shut woman. Think of our Deborah."

Nathaniel interrupted, "For heaven's sake man. You could be dead. We all could. What of Deborah then? These men owe you nothing, your loyalty is misplaced."

Frances whispered, "He's right, Ross. If we are to have any chance of getting her back we should do as Mr Brookes says."

The door opened as Goliath returned.

"Well?" asked Nathaniel as he continued to tend to Ross' wounds.

"I caught sight of the man heading along the river bank. He was making for a small crop of cottages, I'm sure."

"Would you know him again?"

Goliath shook his head. "He was a large man in height and stature. He had a full head of hair, from what I could see, it flowed to his shoulders. He limped a little." He grinned, "Trooper did a good job."

Nathaniel turned to Frances, "Do you know anyone like that?"

Frances nodded, "Ross said he stunk of fish. Sounds like one of the fishermen. The fellow who runs the Bonny Mermaid, a fishing vessel works from here."

"Do you have a name?"

Frances swallowed nervously and looked at her husband. Who nodded agreement, "Thomas, Thomas Nethercott. There I've said it."

"I'll see to Ross, I suggest you pack a bag for the two of you. Do you have transport?"

Frances nodded, "They take our horse and cart for ferrying goods from the ships. It'll still be down by the quay."

"Go and pack your belongings, Goliath will collect your cart and come back here. How will he know which one it is?"

"It's a shire that pulls it, brown and white with a white mane and tail. Answers to the name Bruno."

Nathaniel nodded to Goliath who left again, "I need to get Ross fit for travel. He shouldn't be moved really. I've heard there's a relatively new infirmary in Truro. We can get him there and you can stay at your sister's. We will travel with you. That should help."

Frances hesitated before speaking, "…Yes, Sir. Thank you, Sir. I'll get dressed and do as you ask." She left Nathaniel to continue ministering to Ross' wounds.

Nathaniel chatted as he worked attempting to reassure Ross and trying to get him to talk in the hope he might reveal something new, but the man was in severe pain and he had to give him some more laudanum to deal with it. This sedated him to such an extent he said little else.

The door opened again and Goliath strode in. "The horse and cart are on the quay but the tide is turning and goods are being washed ashore. What do we do?"

"We must secure them for the crown. We'll go down and gather what we can before returning for Frances and Ross. We need to collect Jessie and Samson."

"Will they be safe? We don't want the brutes returning to finish the job."

"I'll leave Trooper with them. He'll make enough noise to frighten them off."

Nathaniel covered Ross with a blanket and called up the stairs, "Frances. We're going to the Quay. Bar the door from the inside and lock the back door and windows. I'll leave Trooper with you. He'll alert you to any would be intruders. Do you have a gun?"

"I've my dad's old blunderbuss…"

"That'll do. Let's hope you don't have to use it." He instructed the dog, "Stay Trooper. I'll be back soon." Trooper whined softly in his throat and looked earnestly at Nathaniel who patted the animal. "Now, bolt the doors after us."

Frances nodded and followed them to the door. As soon as they exited she barred and bolted the door and did the same at the back before sitting in the parlour with the gun between her legs and watched over her sedated husband.

~ 94 ~

15

Wreckers and Sav

NATHANIEL AND GOLIATH STRODE dow
dim light they could see that already there we
not as many as before. They were scavenging
from the sand and loading it onto the quay. Th
of brandy, cheeses, bolts of silk, cotton a
spices and all manner of things.

The sky was turning pinker as dawn
broke the surface of the horizon it began to
that bled into the ever-lightening sky. Na
and the two men marched fearlessly tow
above the wind that had dropped drama

There was a momentary flurry
dropped their goods. Three ran off, s
of the beach leaving four thugs to fac

The adversaries eyed each other
on an unspoken command the four
who stood their ground. Nathaniel
seeing the firearm two dropped
wake of those who had run.
sidestepped and flipped them b
with the same result. Goliath
their heads together. They bo
the other was dazed.

Nathaniel put away his p
Goliath grabbed a rope to s

sister's house while Goliath, Trooper and Nathaniel rode onto Redruth after resting.

"Do you think they'll be safe?" asked Goliath.

"Who knows? These men can reach far and wide, further than we can ever imagine. We need to get to Redruth and ask about the slave sale but do it discretely. We don't want to trigger any alarm amongst them. But first things first, let's get there and find some where to stay."

They rode into the centre of Redruth and after numerous inquiries discovered that a Mrs Banfield had a farm on the outskirts of the town and was looking for someone to rent a small cottage on the side of the farm. They hoped that the lady wouldn't be prejudiced against them.

The riders broke into a trot as they left the town and travelled the country lanes in a jovial mood. They spoke little but their mood seemed elevated and was picked up in the jaunty stride of their mounts. Trooper sitting in the basket was more than content to doze.

The gentle sunshine warmed them denying the reality of the previous night's weather. Nathaniel knew that in the South West the conditions could change dramatically as could the wind and currents in the oceans. The summer meadows looked lush and green after the storm rain left them smelling fresh and sweet. Barley fields bowed their heads as they dried out in the all-enveloping blanket of warmth. Other abundant cereal crops were nearing their time for harvest, which promised to be generous. The countryside looked deceptively benevolent.

Nathaniel reined in Jessie and advised his friend, "That looks like a signpost ahead. It's so grown in it's difficult to tell."

Goliath heeled Samson and cantered to the four crossway ahead. He pushed away an intruding branch, which covered the sign and then cantered back. "Hayne Farm is off to the left."

"Time Trooper had a bit of a run," said Nathaniel looking at the dog who was now alert, sitting up and looking forward. Nathaniel dismounted and lifted the collie out of the basket. "Come on, Trooper." The animal looked at him before padding off and he began sniffing the grass bank at the side of the lane, before following the two men as the horses walked along the road.

After about a quarter of a mile they came to a turning where a sign reading Hayne Farm swung squeakily in the breeze. "This is the place. I suggest you stay here with Samson. I don't want to alarm Mrs Banfield or anyone who works with her. I'll go down and investigate. I'll come back once I know."

Goliath nodded, "I understand. Mustn't frighten the natives although the joke is wearing a little thin."

"I know and I'm not proud of it. Just shows people's lack of understanding."

"Hm! Ignorance and not tolerance."

Nathaniel shamefacedly agreed, "That's about the size of it." He spurred on Jessie and cantered down the farm lane. The field on his left housed some large saddleback pigs that appeared to cavort across the meadow at the sound of horse's hooves. On the right was a small herd of Friesian cows. Nathaniel continued until he came upon a courtyard in front of an old farmhouse, which stretched across the back of the yard. Just over a small wall through an archway were two stone cottages. Nathaniel dismounted and strode to the sturdy wooden door. He rapped smartly on the brass lion knocker and waited. He glanced about him as he waited. Trooper sat quietly at his feet.

There was obviously no one at home. Nathaniel walked around the back and saw a woman hanging out washing on a line between two trees. He crossed the grass and approached her, clearing his throat politely.

"Oh, dear Lord, what a fright you give me," she said jumping to one side and dropping a handful of clothes pegs.

Nathaniel stepped across to help pick them up. "Allow me."

"Thank you. And you are?"

"Nathaniel Brookes. You must be Mrs Banfield?"

"What if I am?"

"I understand you have a cottage to rent?"

"I may do."

"My colleague and I will need accommodation but I don't know for how long."

"Colleague?" she asked looking around.

"Oh, he'll be along in a moment. Do you have anything?"

"I do. It's just over yonder by the yard. There's stabling in the barn for your horses. What line of work are you in? You need to be able to pay," she said suspiciously.

Nathaniel took a deep breath, "We're Riding Officers, but I am also a medical man. We won't be here every day. We need somewhere as a base to work from."

Mrs Banfield sniffed, "Riding Officers. I won't be too popular sheltering your kind."

"Maybe not. But we can pay and it's good honest money."

She sniffed again as she mulled it over. "Two of you, you say? Horses and a dog?"

"Yes, a very well behaved dog."

There was another sniff before she gave her answer, "All right. Rent's payable two weeks in advance. You better come in and sort it out with me."

Mrs Banfield picked up her washing basket and walked to her back door, "Let the mutt stay outside. I got a cat with kittens in here."

Nathaniel ordered Trooper to stay and followed the woman indoors. They emerged again minutes later. Mrs Banfield carried a bunch of keys and led the way to the cottage. She opened up for Nathaniel to see.

Nathaniel nodded appreciatively, "This will do fine."

"Very well, don't let the dog on the furniture. Leave him in the porch when it's wet. I don't want mud showered all over my walls when he shakes his coat."

"Of course."

"This colleague of yours. He can be vouched for?"

"Indeed. He's a good honest man."

Mrs Banfield sniffed again and handed Nathaniel the keys, "Very well. I expect you've heard I'm a woman on my own. I do what I need to get by. You might see my farmhand about at times. That's Simon who works for me and lodges. Tell me, will you be needing any help? In the house, I mean."

"Thank you, yes. If there's someone you can recommend?"

"Maybe there is. I could take it on. That way I'll see the place is kept up to scratch. I'll think on't." She then followed with a list of instructions and other information. There were two wells on the property and a pump in the yard. Nathaniel listened carefully. "You don't say much, do you? Still maybe that's a good thing. Do you want help lighting the range? Kindling and wood's in the store next to the stabling barn. You'll be expected to chop more as you use it. There's not much coal but you can get some nutty slack from W.E. Johns in Redruth. Well, I think that's it." She extended her hand for Nathaniel to shake and disappeared back out of the door.

Nathaniel took a good look around. He went up the wooden twisted staircase. There were two bedrooms, one led into the other. Downstairs was a sitting room with an open fire and behind that a kitchen of sorts with a range. Although summer, the cottage needed airing and Nathaniel opened the windows before making his way back to Goliath, who was still waiting patiently. As he rode out of the yard Trooper loyally followed him.

"I'd almost given you up," grumbled Goliath.

"We have the cottage, but we need to buy some essentials and get the fire on the range lit."

"What do you suggest?"

"We'll go to the cottage and settle in. Once that's done I'll ride back to Redruth and pick up some food."

Goliath pulled up his hood and the two rode back to Hayne Farm.

It was late afternoon by the time Nathaniel had returned to Redruth and visited the market for some vegetables and fruit in season. He had left Trooper at the cottage and was able to use the basket to house his purchases. Having gathered some meat he needed one more item and that was bread. He learned that milk and eggs could be bought from his landlady, Mrs Banfield, who he discovered was indeed a widowed lady working hard to survive.

Nathaniel stepped into the bakery. There was a man at the counter, he was whispering to the baker. Nathaniel just caught the word 'slave' and listened more carefully whilst pretending to be occupied with his riding boot. The man who was respectably dressed and middle aged paid for his bread and left.

Nathaniel glanced back to see, which way he turned at the doorway. The man went left. Nathaniel ordered his bread and some pasties before broaching the delicate subject, "Excuse me, I couldn't help overhearing… the gentleman before me … I thought I recognised him…"

"Mr Weston?"

"Mr Weston, yes. Does he live close by?"

"He's over at West Trevarth House, why?"

"I wondered if he had anything to do with the sale?"

"Sale?"

"Slaves."

If the baker was rattled by Nathaniel's questions he certainly didn't show it and seemed perfectly willing to offer up information, "Oh yes. He's going to the auction."

"As am I," said Nathaniel.

"You after a woman, too?" The baker winked lasciviously.

"Me, no. Not for the bedroom. I need a maid."

"Good luck with that... I hear," said the baker leaning over the counter confidentially, "They are beautiful dusky maidens, ripe for your bed. I'd get one myself if I wasn't married already. Mr Weston's a widower. He wants company, someone to fulfil his needs. His last one died."

Nathaniel raised an eyebrow, "Really."

"Went down with something very nasty from bad water. Still it should be an entertaining event to watch."

"What time is it? The auction I mean."

"Eleven o'clock sharp, Thursday morning."

"That'll be where?"

"Fore Street by the town clock."

Nathaniel nodded his thanks, picked up his bread and pasties and left. He developed a jaunty stride pleased with what he had learned and aside from that the food smelled delicious.

He just needed to buy some butcher's scraps for Trooper and check out West Trevarth House before returning to Goliath.

16

Disappointment

NATHANIEL CANTERED BACK TO Hayne Farm with the needed items and tethered Jessie outside on the porch. He entered to a rapturous welcome from Trooper who wanted to lick him all over his face but then became more interested in the aromas coming from the cloth bag containing the bread and pasties.

"Not for you," said Nathaniel to the dog. "I have something else for you. I don't know what Jenny will say about the new addition to our family. But I think Bart will love him."

"What's not to like?" agreed Goliath. "Did you learn anything?"

"I did. I hope we have the means to buy back your wife should things prove difficult."

"I have money," said Goliath. "But it is an insult. She is a free woman."

"But these are bad times," sighed Nathaniel. "We will have to watch our backs." The men fell silent.

Nathaniel rose abruptly and foraged in the cupboard for plates and utensils before setting out the food he had bought. They were both hungry and the tantalising smell and sight of hot steak pasties made them grin. They had just begun to eat when Trooper ran to the door and began to growl, a soft low rumbling in his throat. Nathaniel went to the window and looked out, "I can't see anyone. What is it boy?" he returned to the table but Trooper continued to snarl and his hackles were raised. He stalked slowly toward the door before barking frenziedly.

Nathaniel exchanged a wary look with Goliath and rose again. This time he flung open the door and caught sight of a man running and leaping on a burnished black stallion with white fetlocks and a white tail at the farmyard entrance. Trooper streaked out after him yapping threateningly before Nathaniel called him back.

Nathaniel glanced about him and his eyes caught sight of something on the old rocking chair, which sat on the stoop. It was a small bucket, which contained a letter written in a bold hand on white parchment.

Nathaniel picked it up and turned it over in his hand. It was addressed to him. He broke the red wax seal and opened it up. The hand was a fine one, clearly educated with beautiful copperplate writing in black ink. There was no mistaking the threat for it boldly said, "Be warned. We are watching you and your family."

Nathaniel tossed the parchment onto the kitchen table. Goliath picked it up and read it, "Who is this? Did you see?"

Nathaniel shook his head, "I didn't see enough of the man, but I'd recognise his horse."

"That may be enough."

"I need to get a message home. I heard the mail coach stops in Truro, tomorrow." Goliath nodded, as Nathaniel continued. "We'll pay a visit to the Custom House, as well. The dragoons should be informed, too."

"And then there's the sale," said Goliath.

Nathaniel smiled grimly. "I hope your Aleka is there." Trooper seemed to recognise something in Nathaniel's tone and scampered to him his tail wagging low and fast and his head cocked on one side. Nathaniel leaned over and smoothed the animal that licked his hand.

"So do I." Goliath went to the small writing desk in the corner of the room he took out paper, and ink. "Write to your brother-in-law. Persuade him to find someone to watch over your family using whatever means he has."

Nathaniel nodded and marched to the desk dragging a wooden carver seat from the table. Trooper lay down at his feet and he began to write.

The market town of Truro was bustling and milling with people on that bright summer day. The sun shone benevolently. Goliath attracted many stares from the locals as they walked down Lemon Street but he was used to that by now and strode proudly next to Nathaniel.

Nathaniel had visited the Coach House and paid for his letter to be delivered. He wanted to ensure the letter made the postbag on the mail coach and they marched to the stopping point to wait.

Four passengers stood in line with their bags waiting to travel, a mother and her young son aged five or six, a portly gentleman with a beard and another older elegant lady dressed in silk carrying a portmanteau.

The coach came trundling across the cobbled street its wheel rims bumping over the stones. It pulled up at the coach stop and the driver and mailman alighted. The driver announced they would take a short break. Passengers could board, their bags would be safely stowed and the coach would leave again within the hour.

The driver busied himself with the bags while the mailman went to collect a bag of letters from the stop. Nathaniel crossed to him and passed him his missive, which was examined. Nathaniel gave him a tip and the mailman put it in his postbag.

Goliath looked questioningly, "What now?"

"Maybe, I'm too suspicious but I want to ensure the letter leaves safely. Wait here." Nathaniel followed by Trooper chased after the man into the inn. They sat at a corner table and watched him. The man kept his bag with him and collected letters from the landlord, which he also put in his bag, before ordering a drink and a bite to eat. There was nothing untoward in the man's behaviour and Nathaniel relaxed.

Satisfied that he had nothing to worry about he returned to Goliath, with Trooper at his feet, where his friend was studying a flyer that had been passed out to people on the street. The statuesque Negro was attracting the usual stares from men and women alike who, when Goliath returned the glaring looks, scurried by as fast as they could.

Nathaniel peered at the piece of paper, "Slave auction?"

"Yes, a different time from what we were told."

"And we shall be there. Come let's eat before we watch the coach leave." The two men swept back into the tavern. Trooper settled by Goliath's feet at Nathaniel's instruction to stay. His head was up, his manner alert as he watched Nathaniel walk to the counter.

The tavern was busy. There were few vacant tables. Travellers and merchants congregated at the bar. Talk was free and the two men listened closely, as they waited to order, hoping to learn any information that might help them. They took their drinks and sat to wait for their food. A young kitchen maid scurried across with two plates of stew.

A couple of Clive Bethell's men sauntered into the hostelry. They looked like rogues with their curling greasy hair and scarred faces. They pushed their way through to the bar and ordered ale. They glugged down a tankard each and wiped their mouths on their grimy sleeves before ordering another. This they supped less greedily and moved toward the entrance when one of them spotted Nathaniel and Goliath.

The swarthy man with a broken nose and angry raised scar across his right cheek whispered to his friend and the two approached their table. Trooper stood with hackles raised and began to growl.

"Keep that mutt under control," demanded the other miscreant with a shock of flame red oily hair and heavy beard. He nodded at Nathaniel, "Is that man yours?" he asked indicating Goliath.

Nathaniel spoke softly but firmly, "No, he is his own man and my friend. Why?"

"He looks remarkably like an escaped slave Tobias Stone had in custody a few years ago."

"Then you think wrong. This man is no slave."

Trooper growled again. This time he bared his teeth and the rumbling in his throat grew louder.

The flame haired man took a step back, "Is he safe?" he asked pointing at the dog.

"He is with me and my friends, as long as he doesn't smell fear. He ripped a hole in a man's leg once that tried to hurt his master," said Nathaniel looking to Goliath for support.

Goliath nodded and continued, "He has a thing about smugglers and wreckers. He doesn't like them."

"Or slavers," added Nathaniel.

Trooper moved fractionally closer to the men who took a step back.

"Keep him away from us. We ain't done nothing," said the swarthy man.

"Then you have nothing to worry about," said Nathaniel with a smile.

The two men backed off as others looked on curiously.

Nathaniel whispered to Goliath, "These men have long memories."

"So have I."

"No matter. They wouldn't dare to try anything at the moment. Too many witnesses, but we need to be on our guard. Eat up." They finished their food and ale and left the inn.

They waited at the roadside but were on the alert keeping a watchful eye out until they saw the Post Master with his bag clamber aboard the coach. The passengers took their seats, the driver settled in his place and the coach trundled off out of the town.

"I think we can consider our letters safe," said Nathaniel and they walked back to their horses with their provisions and set off for the farm. Trooper was safely stashed in his basket and enjoyed an ear scratch from Nathaniel as they trotted along the street.

Moments later the two thugs barrelled their way out from the hostelry and their eyes searched the road. The ginger man nudged his companion, "There, up ahead. They are headed for the outskirts of town." They barged through the milling crowds of people and mounted their waiting horses, following the officers at a discrete distance.

Aleka, dressed in the new clothes provided, surveyed her appearance in the mirror. She was kept in the West Wing of the house in an attic room and although grateful for a bath and fresh clothes she was agonising on how she could escape. There was a knock at the door. She stiffened not used to such niceties since being captured. The door opened and Deborah peered in timidly. "Er... Miss Alice..."

"My name is Aleka," said Aleka more fiercely than she intended.

"Um, sorry," said Deborah clearly confused.

"No, I apologise. It is not your fault. But I do not want this adopted name it is an insult."

"Yes, Miss. If you please, Miss Alice... I mean Aleka. You are wanted downstairs, by the master."

"And you are...?"

"Deborah..."

"You are his servant?"

"Not really. They took me from my parents to keep them in line."

"I don't understand..."

"Please, come. The master is waiting. I don't want to get into trouble."

Aleka sighed, "That is not my intention," she said graciously. "I will come," and she followed Deborah from the room.

Deborah scurried like a frightened mouse down the winding staircase and onto the landing and the grand staircase. She hurried downstairs and into the hall where she walked to a lavishly carved door and knocked timidly.

A voice boomed out that whoever it was should "Enter!"

Deborah gingerly opened the door and announced, "Miss Al...Alice, Sir, as requested."

"Thank you, Deborah," came the cool tones of Richard Gosling. She bobbed a curtsey and bowed her head, as Aleka walked in with her head held aloft.

Richard Gosling was with three other men. She felt their eyes on her, ogling, leering and undressing her. She faced her captor directly and eyed him coldly. "Why am I here?"

"My friends wish to make your acquaintance. In fact, if I tire of you one of them may want to buy you."

Aleka bristled but said nothing. The spark of fire in her eyes was enough. One man, Patrick Hamilton, wearing the garb of a clergyman smiled lasciviously and muttered, "She has spirit. I like that. It will be all the more amusing to break her." He grabbed her wrist and she shook it free her eyes blazing.

Richard wagged his finger at the minister, "Now, now. She is not yours yet and may not ever be.... Do not touch the goods. I warrant she will become more amenable in time."

"Pity," said the parson. "I rather like the fire in her eyes. It is more fun than having someone too compliant."

"That's where you and I differ," said Richard. "I prefer to pleasure my women as much as they pleasure me. I am not one to force my attentions on them."

Patrick Hamilton snorted and added, "We will see. If she is as feisty as she seems you may tire of non-reciprocation."

Aleka's nostrils flared, "I am not a piece of meat to be discussed as if bartering for the best deal. I am an educated woman."

"And that my dear, will be your downfall," sneered the pastor.

"Enough!" said Richard vehemently. "Alice. Return to your room. I will see you later."

Aleka swept from the room her head held high. She looked toward the front door but was alarmed to see a beefy male servant standing guard. There was a similar man barring the way to the downstairs' corridor and back entrance. She blew through her teeth in annoyance and climbed back up the stairs to her room, her mind working feverishly.

Nathaniel and Goliath rode back to the cottage with their provisions. Trooper sat in his basket and snoozed until the horses were tied up. "I'll see to Jessie and Samson," offered Goliath.

"And I'll get the maps out. We must start doing our job and ride."

Goliath nodded, "But we mustn't miss the sale."

"And we won't," affirmed Nathaniel. He scooped Trooper out of the basket and went inside, taking their purchases with him.

Goliath began to lead the horses to the stable block when he noticed a movement in the bushes at the end of the farm lane. He narrowed his eyes and frowned before walking apparently nonchalantly into the stable with the animals. Once inside he quickly unsaddled the pair and allowed them to feed from their nosebags. Murmuring that he would be back to rub them down he slipped out of the back of the barn and made his way around the back of the farm toward the gate and saw the two ruffians who had followed them.

Goliath crept stealthily until he was within earshot of their whispering.

The red headed man jerked his head toward the stable. "It'll take two or more of us to take the giant down. He'll be busy with the horses for another ten minutes or so, I reckon."

"Time enough then for us to take down Brookes and that dog. We have surprise on our side. Go, I'll keep a lookout and follow behind. No guns we don't want to alert that monster."

Goliath had heard enough he waited and watched as he saw the men remove steel blades and creep through the undergrowth toward the cottage. He slipped after them, careful not to attract any attention.

Nathaniel had put their shopping away and spread the maps out on the kitchen table. Trooper dozed on the rag mat but suddenly lifted up his head and whined.

"What is it, boy?"

Trooper padded to the cottage door and his hackles rose as he let out a warning growl. Nathaniel drew his flintlock pistol and moved cautiously toward the door where Trooper continued to growl the alarm. Nathaniel heard a faint scuffle outside.

Suddenly a shout went up, a bellow and a roar. Trooper barked frenetically and Nathaniel swept open the door. Outside on the path, Goliath held the two thugs, from the inn, by the back of their necks. He held one in each hand. Their knives had clattered to the ground. Trooper danced around the men in fevered excitement nipping at their ankles. Goliath strode forward and roughly shoved the two men inside.

Nathaniel took charge of one and Goliath the other. They each pushed one down in a kitchen chair and restrained them, tying their hands behind their backs to the chairs.

"What have we here?" said Nathaniel with a raised eyebrow.

"Our friends from the tavern were just discussing how to do away with us," grinned Goliath. "Their judgement was a little off."

"So, Gentlemen. What do you want?"

"I'm saying nothing," said the swarthy man.

"Really?" observed Nathaniel. "It looks to me as if you meant us harm. Now, we can't let you go. So, it looks as if we'll have to arrest you and take you to gaol. When you go before the magistrate in Truro you may change your mind about talking. I've heard Bodmin gaol is pretty harsh even for vermin like you."

The men said nothing and stared at the floor. Trooper stood threateningly baring his teeth and unmoving.

"What do you think Goliath? Should we bother to take them in or just do away with them here?"

"It would save the court's time," agreed Goliath.

The flame haired man looked up, "You can't do that?"

"Can't we? Who's to know?" asked Nathaniel walking slowly behind the man. He yanked back his head. "Think about it. Did anyone see you come here? Does anyone know you're here?" His question was greeted by silence. "I thought not."

"Tell me, Goliath are their knives sharper than ours? A blunt knife can make a hell of a mess."

Goliath picked up the blades and tested them. He smiled impishly at Nathaniel, "Oh, yes. Very sharp. Do you want me to dispatch them now?"

Nathaniel nodded curtly and Goliath stepped up to the swarthy man with a scar and set the knife at his throat. The brute began to babble, "No, no! Wait. You don't want to do this."

"And why not?" said Goliath removing the knife.

"Because we have information that will help you," the man gurgled.

"What do you think?" asked Nathaniel mischievously.

"I think it will be more fun to see how long it takes them to bleed out and die." Goliath raised the knife again.

The swarthy man rolled his eyes in terror and beads of sweat began to form on his brow. "I don't want to die."

Goliath made as if to draw the knife across the man's throat when Nathaniel stopped him. "Wait! Maybe they can be of use to us."

Goliath pretended to look crestfallen as he pulled the blade away. "But..." he protested.

Nathaniel folded his arms and stood in front of the two men. "If what you have to offer is worthwhile I'll let you go. If not, I'll let Goliath take you. Understand?" The man nodded his head furiously and Nathaniel drew up a chair, "Then let's hear it." He pointed at the flame haired man, "But you, I've heard nothing from you. What do you say?"

The ruffian blinked and rasped, "Talk to you and we're done for. Not talk to you and we're still dead men. Doesn't seem to be much choice."

"Ah, but that's if anyone discovers you've talked to us. We won't say anything if, as I've said, your information is useful." Nathaniel paused and stood up. I'll give you a minute to think about it." Nathaniel strode to the range and picked up the pan of water bubbling on the fire. The men flinched fearing to be scalded or worse.

"All right! All right, we'll talk."

"That's better. I think that's a very wise decision." Nathaniel returned to his seat and the men began to talk, answering their questions, almost feverishly. Once they had begun it was as if they couldn't get their words out fast enough.

17

Keeping the Home Fires Burning

"I JUST FEEL SO uneasy," said Jenny. "I had this awful feeling we were being watched. Edith felt it too."

"Imagination," said Myah trying to make light of Jenny's fears. "I'm sure it's nothing." Myah turned away and pretended to inspect the pot of stew that was simmering on the range. She hoped to hide the flash of uneasiness that had manifested in her eyes. Averting her gaze from Jenny she glanced out of the kitchen window and thought she spotted a movement in the shrubbery at the top of the garden and shivered. She turned back to Jenny smiling too broadly, "Goodness. You'll have me seeing bogeymen and boggarts everywhere!"

"Why what have you seen?" asked Jenny concerned.

"Where's Bart?"

"Playing outside. Why?"

"Call him in." There was an urgency in Myah's voice that could not be ignored.

Jenny fled to the kitchen door and flung it wide open. Her heart was beating wildly, "Bart! Bart."

Her young son tumbled out from the bushes and trotted back down the path to his mother. Jenny scooped him up and bundled him inside. Jenny leaned against the back door her face laced in worry.

"What's the matter, Mamma? Have I done something wrong?" asked Bart in his sweet baby tones. "You look cross."

"No, no… I just needed a big hug from my little boy."

"Not so little," said Bart with a pout and popped his thumb in his mouth.

"No, I know. You are growing big and strong. You'll be just like your father. I'm sure," she murmured.

"Can I go back outside and play, please?"

"No!" said Myah a little too quickly. "We will have some fun in the kitchen. I promised Edith we'd help her make Welsh cakes."

Bart puckered his lips, "But the man outside was going to play hide and seek with me," he protested.

"Man? What man?" asked Jenny wildly.

"A big man came to the end of the garden. He said we could play a game. It would be fun."

Jenny stooped down and took her small son by his shoulders, "Listen, Bart. You must never ever talk to strangers."

"What's a stranger?"

"People we don't know. You must always ask Mamma or Grandma first. Do you understand;" her tone was vehement and Bart began to cry.

Myah stepped in and whispered to Jenny, "Hush. You're frightening him," before she turned to Bart, "Listen, Bart. Don't cry. We can play lots of games inside."

"But I want to play hide and seek," he said sniffing back his tears.

"And so we shall. But, we must be careful about speaking to new people. Not everyone is as kind as they pretend to be."

"Why?"

"Some people are different, not so nice, and that's why you should always ask. After all you don't want to upset Mamma, or me. Do you?"

Bart solemnly shook his head, "No."

"Then that's grand. We just like to meet new friends first."

"Can I go and ask him in, then?" said Bart his face crumpling into a smile.

"Not today," smiled Myah. "Another time perhaps. Now, you run into the kitchen and see Edith. We'll be along in a minute."

Bart happily accepted this and ran off down the corridor to the kitchen. Myah turned to Jenny, "It seems your suspicions were right. We are being watched. We have to get word to Nathaniel. I feel it's something to do with him. Meanwhile we must lock and bolt all doors and windows. I don't like this. I don't like it at all."

Jenny turned away her face filled with confusion and concern, "I know he said we weren't to travel with him. But I'd feel safer if we were. We can't stay as prisoners in our own house. We have to do something."

"Maybe you're right. I have a cousin in Gloucester. I'll get word to her and ask if we can visit. Edith can look after the house here... No, on second thoughts, there is safety in numbers. I'll call Eric to bring the wagon. We will all travel into Swansea. I can send a message to my cousin, Moira. I'll write it now. Why don't you get a bag together for you and Bart? We can stay at The Cross Keys Swansea. Now, remember we need to try and load the bags without being observed. We may be lucky and get a boat from Swansea to Ilfracombe if the waters are calm." Myah swept off into her study to put pen to paper.

Jenny's hand flew to her throat, a habit she had acquired when nervous or worried. She went to the kitchen and saw that Bart was happily engaged with Edith and took the opportunity to slip upstairs and pack some clothes. She hesitated. How much should she take? How long would they be away? She decided to make sure there were enough and set about the task.

The late afternoon sun shone its spangled light through the casement, a leaded window with stained glass, which threw mottled patches of colour on the floor and furnishings. Myah stared anxiously out of one such window. She scoured the grounds around the house to detect any suspicious activity or movement. All seemed to be still.

She took her completed letter and secreted it into her portmanteau and took her newly packed leather travel bag from off the bed to take downstairs, ringing for Edith to come and help, before she dragged the bags to the landing outside her door.

The young maid ran up the stairs from the kitchen to attend her mistress. Myah pointed at the bags, "You take one and I'll manage the other."

Edith looked at the size of the luggage; "I could ask Eric to come and help?"

"Good idea. Ask him to bring the horse and carriage to the front gate. Tell him to do it quickly and as quietly as possible. We don't want to attract any undue attention."

"Yes, Ma'am." Edith dashed back down the stairs and out through the front door as Myah watched through the window. She saw Edith scurry down the path through the gate toward the stables and disappear inside.

A piercing scream ripped through the late warmth of the afternoon and Edith fled the stable block shrieking and crying. Birds fluttered up from the trees and shrubbery to escape the horror filled air.

Edith raced to the front door and pushed her way inside. She put the bar and locks on the inside, ran to the side door to ensure it was secured before hurtling to the kitchen and back door. She stared around wildly. The back door was ajar and there was no sign of Bart.

Edith screeched the child's name at the top of her voice. "Bart! Where are you?"

She heard a giggle behind her and spun around on her heels and noticed the pantry door slightly open. She flung back the door where Bart had hidden under a shelf. She pulled out the boy and hugged him tightly before hurrying to the back door and locking it securely.

Myah and Jenny hastened into the kitchen after hearing Edith's demented shrieks. Edith's face was white with shock and she trembled uncontrollably. Myah took one look at her and said gently, "Jenny, why don't you take Bart up to the playroom? I'll call you when we're ready."

Understanding her tone Jenny led Bart away promising them a fine game when they got upstairs. She tossed a worried glance at Myah before retreating along the corridor.

"All right, Edith. Take a deep breath. Tell me what has frightened you so much?"

"Oh, Ma'am," the words tumbled from Edith both in panic and relief, "It's Eric."

"What about him?"

"He's dead."

"Dead?"

"His throat was slit from here to here," she gestured with her hands. "I went to tell him about the carriage and called. There was no answer so I went into the stables and found him by the straw bales. Oh, Ma'am whatever will we do?" Edith descended into a weeping wail.

Myah stiffened. "This is clearly far more serious than I first thought. Edith, put your outside clothes on and go pack a bag. Bring it to the hall. Let me think."

Myah strode purposefully around the house. She checked all doors and windows and where possible closed the shutters against the encroaching twilight. She lit oil lamps in some rooms before going to the playroom where Jenny waited anxiously.

Myah stooped down to Bart. "We are going to play a wonderful game."

"Better than hide and seek?"

"Better than hide and seek," affirmed Myah. "We're going to pretend to be Riding Officers trying to escape from a band of bad men. We have to be very quiet and careful." She put her fingers to her lips. "We mustn't make a sound."

Bart clapped his hands in glee. "Oh, Mamma. It will be such fun."

Jenny managed a half smile and urged her son, "Run upstairs and I'll follow."

Bart dashed off happily as Jenny turned to her mother-in-law. "What is it?"

"Get the bags. We need to leave as soon as possible. I'll get the carriage. If I'm not out front in ten minutes, leave. Go out of the back door across the fields and get help in the village. Leave the oil lamps burning our enemies will believe we are inside. Now hurry."

Jenny nodded and ran upstairs to join her son while Myah put on her hat and cape. She went into the drawing room, unlocked the bureau and took out a set of duelling pistols and ammunition. She shoved one into the waistband of her dress, the other into her portmanteau and slipped out through a side door keeping a watchful eye out for any suspicious activity.

Myah's heart was beating wildly in her chest, thumping so loudly she feared someone would hear or even that it would leap out of her mouth. She swallowed hard and willed her trembling hands to stop shaking.

Myah hurried to the stables She placed her bag in the back of the carriage, stifling a cry when she espied the still, lifeless body of Eric by the bales. Steeling herself she led two horses from the stables and harnessed them to the carriage.

Myah took a deep breath and placed herself at the head of the horses standing between them so that she wasn't clearly visible and led the horses and wagon out into the waning light.

As soon as she arrived at the front gate, Jenny, Bart and Edith fled the house after locking the front door. They carried their bags, scuttled to the carriage and clambered aboard. Myah stepped up to the front seat and took the reins urging the horses on. The women sat tight lipped and afraid but Bart delighted in the "game" and beamed from ear to ear. As the day finally relinquished the last of its light to the inky blackness of night they made their way to the neighbouring well-populated town of Swansea and the safety of The Cross Keys Inn.

Myah pulled up the carriage outside the hostelry in St Mary Street. She turned to the others, "Wait here." Then slipped down and entered the Tudor fronted inn's smoky bar, which fell silent as she walked up to the landlord.

Curious glances turned to disinterest as she asked for lodging and the bar returned to its former ribald chatter. Myah agreed room rates and stabling for the horses and carriage. She handed over the cash and hurried back outside and the three women with Bart trooped in. Myah collected room keys and the unlikely foursome went upstairs. No one took any notice.

Myah assembled everyone in her room and spoke quietly, "We will be safe here for the night. I don't believe anyone knows who we are. I will send word to my cousin." She waved her prewritten letter. "I'll speak to the landlord about some reliable means of getting this to her. There must be a mail stop somewhere nearby."

"I don't like it, I don't like it at all," murmured Jenny.

"What's the matter, Mamma?" asked Bart his face puckered in worry.

"It's nothing, my lovely. It's all part of the game we're playing."

Bart's face creased in smiles, "It's a very exciting game but a bit scary."

Jenny hugged her small son tightly. "It won't be for much longer now, Cherub. We are going to see Grandma's cousin tomorrow. Won't that be grand?" Bart nodded and he snuggled into his mother's arms and his eyes began to droop. "That's enough playtime for today. I need to get you to bed." She laid her small son on one of the single beds in the room and covered him over. He popped his thumb in his mouth and fell asleep. Jenny sighed, "How I wish Nathaniel was here."

"I know, Jenny. I know. And I must inform the authorities about Eric. I'll do that by letter, too. We don't want to be delayed here."

Myah remained in her travelling clothes and bid the others goodbye before returning downstairs. She spoke quietly to the landlord, "Good Sir, do you know of anyone who could be trusted to deliver a letter to a mail post? Of course, I'll pay. I need to contact my cousin as a matter of urgency."

The landlord a burly man with a pale complexion and thick copper coloured hair licked his lips and leaned forward, "Where do you need to send your message?"

"Gloucester, but I don't know where the mail coach would travel from."

"I wouldn't trust anyone in here. Most would take your money and dump the missive. Let me think…" He looked at the heavy clock above the bar its pendulum swinging ponderously marking time. "There won't be anything doing tonight. Tell you what. My barman, Ivor, gets in here early tomorrow, around nine. He can clean up and mind the bar alone and I'll take you myself. You can ride with me if you like?"

"That's very kind Mr...?

"Lewis, Winston Lewis."

"Well, Mr Lewis I'll be downstairs on the dot of nine. Thank you. We shall all eat before I go."

"Just tell the kitchen maid, what you want for breakfast." Winston nodded to the scullery door. "You may just catch her now before she goes off duty."

Myah returned his nod and smiled, "Very well. Oh, and by the way, where is the local police station?"

Puzzled he replied, "We pass it on the way to the Post Office. I'll show you."

"Thank you. You are most kind." With that she walked to the scullery door and knocked quietly. She exchanged words with the serving wench and returned up the stairs and Winston Lewis looked admiringly after her.

18

Bartering and subterfuge

THE TWO RUFFIANS HELD by Goliath and Nathaniel had talked non-stop. The Riding Officers had learned much. They knew that they had been made targets and that the men at the top had given orders to hurt Nathaniel by going after those he loved. Who those men were, was unknown. Their identity was hinted at but not verified. It was a secret guarded as closely as had been the smuggler Knight who Nathaniel and Goliath had exposed and brought down when riding the Welsh coast.

Nathaniel tugged the hair of one thug and pulled his head back, "What you have told us had better be right or I will spread word about you in the taverns and on the docks that you really are the King's men in disguise and you know what that means. If I were you I would get back and lie low. Do you understand?"

The ruffian nodded, his eyes wild with fear. "We've spoken the truth. I swear."

Nathaniel turned to Goliath, "Cut them loose." He spoke to the brutes again. "Very well, I'm letting you go. If I were you I would get as far away from here as possible. Both of you."

Goliath cut their bonds and the two rubbed their wrists and fled. "Are you sure that was the right thing to do?" asked Goliath.

Nathaniel nodded, "They'll scarper. If they're wise they'll clear from the neighbourhood and find another place to dwell."

"Or they'll lie in wait somewhere and try to finish the job."

"Unlikely. We know their names, their current abode and where they are supposed to be headed next. We can soon fix a price on their heads as has been put on ours."

Goliath grunted clearly not convinced but he gave way to Nathaniel's wishes. "So, what's next?"

"We are going to a sale. Our money is as good as another. Let's see if your wife is on the list. But now, now we eat. I'm starved."

Goliath grinned and pulled out his knife, "I'll peel the onions!"

Myah accompanied by the landlord, Winston, had sent her letter by the mail coach and was now with the local policeman, a bold looking man with fierce eyes. Rather than leaving a letter Myah had decided it was better to speak with the police in case they thought the family had something to do with Eric's death.

"Where did you say this happened?" the officer asked in his broad Welsh accent.

"At home." Myah gave her address and told him the details of the attack and threat to her family.

"If after investigation this proves to be true I will need to interview you further and your maid Edith who discovered the body and anyone else involved in the matter."

"Most certainly, but we are leaving to travel to my cousin in Gloucester, where we will feel safer."

The policeman pursed his lips and frowned, "That's not ideal. You shouldn't be leaving the area…"

"But if her life is in danger, Percy," interjected the landlord. "You can't expect her to stick around. Anything could happen. You've not enough man-power to offer her any protection."

"Hmm…" The policeman considered Winston's words. "Very well, but I will need the address of this cousin and when you intend to return to your home, as I expect you will. I will need you to see me again on route. In fact, you will be required to check in at a police station wherever you settle. Here." He passed her a piece of paper on which he had scribbled notes. "Present this to the police when you arrive. It explains everything."

Myah nodded, "That is most agreeable and kind of you. I know this abhorrent matter must be dealt with lawfully and that you are taking a risk with this action."

"Action that would not normally be pursued if your son wasn't Nathaniel Brookes. We are aware of him and his loyalty to the service and the Crown. Indeed, he did much to improve the safety of the Welsh coast."

"Thank you, Officer. We will travel onto my cousin and rest assured I will let you know my whereabouts and when I shall be journeying back." She wrote down her cousin's address and passed it to him. "My grandson's pony Minstrel is still in the barn, unless he's been stolen and will need looking after. Can you help with that? I can pay."

"Of that I've no doubt. I will have the animal brought back to Swansea."

"Bring him to me. He will be looked after at the inn," offered Winston.

"Very well," The officer shook hands with her and Myah left with the landlord, Winston, thanking him profusely.

A smile of appreciation spread across his face, "My pleasure," he muttered almost indiscernibly as he accompanied her back to the inn.

The following morning the ladies left the inn after a hearty breakfast. Winston watched wistfully as he waved them goodbye. The wagon trundled off towards Gloucester. The mood amongst the women was tense but Jenny tried to maintain an aura of optimism for Bart's sake.

The carriage rolled off down the road. The warmth of the early morning sun that had started to peep through the clouds was welcoming to the travellers. It seemed to lift them to a brighter mood.

Bart snuggled up to his mother and began to nod off to sleep with the motion of the cart. Jenny whispered to Myah, "What of Eric?"

"The police are informing his family. They will remove the body for autopsy and study the scene of crime. I must check into the police station wherever we settle."

"Do you think we are safe?"

"For now. But we must be very careful and mindful of any strangers we meet."

Jenny nodded but a shiver ran through her body as a cloud passed over the smiling face of the sun. She turned her face heavenward to whisper a small prayer. "Dear Lord, please keep Nathaniel and Goliath safe and guard us all at this difficult time."

Myah patted Jenny's hand. "He will. I'm sure God will."

Nathaniel and Goliath readied themselves for the day. They saddled the horses to ride into Redruth and attend the slave auction. "What if Aleka is not there?" asked Goliath.

"She has to be. All the evidence points to her being there. If she isn't...
then we will deal with it and the search will go on;" reassured Nathaniel.

They mounted their steeds and set off from the cottage as Mrs Banfield
emerged from the farmhouse. She stepped back in shock as her eyes lit on
Goliath.

"Good day, Mrs Banfield," said Nathaniel politely and touched his hat
respectfully. Goliath nodded at the farmer's wife and smiled, revealing his
brilliantly perfect white teeth.

"G...G... Good day Mr Brookes." She stepped back warily and watched
them trot out of the yard followed by Trooper.

"I can see I will have some explaining to do upon my return," whispered
Nathaniel confidentially.

"Aye. Or we'll be evicted," mused Goliath, as he dug his heels into
Samson's flanks and they sprang into a canter in the leafy lane.

Redruth was buzzing. The square was bustling and alive with people who had
come to bid and others who wanted to watch the auction. Three covered
wagons were parked in the square where a platform and walkway had been
erected. A podium for the auctioneer stood at the side. On top of the dais
rested a large bullwhip.

A newly erected slave pen stood in the square where the male slaves stood
chained. They wore numbers around their necks and tar had been used to seal
their wounds of punishment struck on their journey. Prospective buyers
clustered around shouting their interest in individuals. People prodded them to
test their muscle strength. They were examined thoroughly as might a horse
trader inspect a stallion.

Snippets of vulgar conversation could be heard above the noise of excited
chatter and the mood was one of anticipation.

Nathaniel and Goliath walked to the back of the throng of people after
leaving their horses in the stables at a hostelry. Goliath towered over the tops
of the others in the crowd, who moved aside for him when they saw his
stature. Nathaniel climbed up on a seat for a better view with Trooper at his
feet and they waited for the start of the auction, which was heralded by the
banging of a drum and the crowd surged forward.

Six males dressed only in breeches, their torsos gleaming with oil, which
highlighted their muscles, earned through manual labour, were herded from

the pen out onto the platform. The chains were removed and the bullwhip cracked to make them turn around so that everyone could see their physique. One at a time they were forced to parade down the catwalk.

Clive Bethell, the slaver, forced open each individual's mouth to show healthy teeth and gums. The bidding started. Those farmers and households looking for good manual labour competed for the finest specimens, which were quickly sold.

Goliath was becoming more and more incensed at this brutal humiliation of strong men, who had been captured and subjugated. His fists clenched and unclenched at the thought of his Aleka being demeaned in this manner.

The men that had been sold were returned to the pen to await payment and collection. Another African man was pushed forward, prodded by a stick to make him move on the walkway. He was sweating profusely and the whites of his eyes showed as he rolled them in fear. Suddenly he leapt off the makeshift stage and pushed through the throng in a bid for freedom. People moved out of the way as he forged his way through. Clive Bethell bounded after him. He flicked the bullwhip, which cracked and caught the man around his ankle, flooring him.

The man tried to scramble up and flee but this time the curling tail of the weapon caught his back and opened a flesh wound on his already scarred back. The bidding stopped in spite of crude jokes made about the man's speed. No one wanted a rebel or troublemaker. Subservience was vital for a good sale.

The slave master was upon the man and he jerked his head in an unsaid order to two of his crew who came and dragged the now screaming man away leaving the crowd in uproar. There were shouts of disgust mixed with jeering and cries to get on with it. Clive Bethell attempted to silence the crowd. He yelled above the noise of the melee, "Do we continue? Or ….?"

The mass of people surged forward urging him to proceed. The last remaining men were pushed forward and quickly sold.

Nathaniel was sickened by what he had witnessed but was powerless to do anything. He felt for his friend Goliath who had witnessed some of the worst of human behaviour. Members of the crowd looked askance at the Negro giant, muttering at his presence in such a place at this time.

People waited impatiently while money changed hands and the slaves were led away to await collection by new masters, mainly farmers needing manual labourers. The noise and chatter rose in excitement and anticipation of the next part of the sale.

The murmurings ceased as Bethell announced the first batch of women to be auctioned. Women in the square turned away leaving men ready to leer at the scantily clad women being led out from one wagon and herded into the pen. Again, there was another free for all in accompaniment to the regular beat of the drum.

Goliath scoured the faces and bearing of the females. There was no sign of Aleka. He clambered up onto the seat where Nathaniel stood as one dusky maiden caught his eye.

"Do you see Aleka?" Nathaniel asked quietly.

"Goliath shook his head, "No. But I recognise one, number four. She is from my home village. Her name is Abigail, the daughter of a farmhand who works for a good friend of mine and I promised that if I found her I would bring her back."

"Then it looks like we shall be bidding for her," said Nathaniel.

"But it's wrong. She is a free woman."

"I know, I know but we are powerless to do anything here with this crowd. Leave this to me."

"Do we have enough money?"

Nathaniel nodded, "With what you brought and I have, then yes, I believe so. It is imperative that you remain calm."

Goliath nodded sadly. He could see the sense in Nathaniel's words. "I know you're right, but I really would like to rip these fiends' hearts out."

Bidding on the women was swift and the prices were high. The females were purchased quickly. It was now Abigail's turn. She stepped forward meekly as Bethell tore at her top revealing her adolescent pert breasts. She was a stunningly pretty girl and the price rose quickly. Two men remained in a bidding war rising from sixty pounds until one finally dropped out shaking his head as the bid reached one hundred and five pounds but before Bethell could bring down the hammer Nathaniel called out another bid. "One hundred and twenty pounds." There was a gasp from the crowd.

Clive Bethell searched for the person behind the voice who made the bid. Nathaniel raised his hand.

"Are there any more bids?" Bethell cried. No one murmured. "Sold to the gent at the back."

The sale continued and the last girl was sold. Goliath and Nathaniel waited for the final batch of girls to be herded into the pen and paraded. Goliath stared anxiously about him. "She's not here. Aleka's not here;" he said in despair.

"Maybe Abigail will be able to help us or maybe she's been sold already."

"I just pray she's still alive."

The crowd began to disperse and the folks who had bought slaves made their way down to the payment booth and to collect their property.

The men were brought out, one at a time as receipts for payment and paperwork exchanged hands. The men in restraints were led away by their owners and others waited for the females to be collected.

Nathaniel stood in line and took out a purse of gold. He slapped it on the bartering table, "Girl Four." Clive Bethell passed him his bill of sale and roughly pulled Abigail from the line. She kept her eyes downcast and allowed herself to be led away.

Soon the crowd dispersed. Nathaniel wrapped his cloak around the teenager and led her to the edge of the square where Goliath waited with Trooper. They hurried her away. She looked up as she saw strong black hands helping her down the road. She gasped in astonishment as her eyes lit on Goliath.

"But… how?" she gasped.

"No time for questions. All will be explained. We need to get away from here. Hurry."

They quickly made their way to the hostelry where they had left their horses and retrieved them. Goliath mounted Samson and Nathaniel lifted the girl up to him and onto the saddle before putting Trooper in his basket. They set off at a good pace toward their cottage. No one gave them a second glance believing that both companions were Nathaniel's purchases.

They rode in relative silence. All that could be heard were the horses' hooves and the sound of their panting breath as they cantered up the last lane to the farm. They quickly dismounted and Goliath helped Abigail from Samson. Trooper danced delightedly around the young girl, licking her hands in a huge show of affection.

"He really likes you," observed Nathaniel with a grin.

Abigail smiled shyly and followed Nathaniel inside the small cottage. He invited her to sit. "What's going to happen to me?"

Goliath assured her, "I'm going to do my best to get you home. You are not a slave but a free woman and I promised Abraham Jacobs that if I found you I would get you back to your father."

Abigail lowered her eyes, "Thank you."

"Abby, we need to talk to you, I have to know have you seen Aleka?"

"I'm sorry but I do not know Aleka, only you."

Goliath sighed, "It is true. Why would you know her? She is tall, statuesque, very striking, often wears beads in her hair."

Abigail raised her eyes. "I saw one such woman on the ship. There was no other like her but we were kept on different decks. Then on land I saw her again when we were taken to a big house where they treated us for lice and dressed us up."

"Where is she now?"

"We were split up. I heard she was taken by a man, one of the gentry."

"Do you have a name?"

Abigail shook her head, "I'm not sure. I only heard whispers and rumours, Richard someone. I'm sorry. What's going to happen to me?"

"I promised I'd get you home. And I will."

"But how? I may get taken again."

"That won't happen," said Nathaniel. "I have your papers and I will document you as a free person. We will ensure you a safe passage back to Jamaica. I will buy the ticket myself and we'll send word to your family."

"I will write to Abraham. I promise you he will ensure that you are met off the boat."

Abigail afforded them one of her rare smiles and murmured, "Thank you. Thank you so much."

"And now, you must be hungry," grinned Goliath. "I'll make you something to eat before we make preparations to take you to the docks and purchase your ticket. You will need clothes and a bag. The journey is long."

"I don't know what to say."

"Say nothing. Conserve your strength."

Goliath took a pan of stew that had been made and put it onto heat as Nathaniel took pen and paper to write to the girl's family. They were fulfilling their promises and soon the cottage was filled with the delicious aroma of meat and vegetables.

All the while, Trooper sat at Abigail's feet. He was beginning to drool at the luscious smell of good wholesome food. Abigail bent over and petted him, which sent the animal into a frenzy of excitement.

Nathaniel glanced up, "My, he's really taken to you."

Abigail smiled again and Trooper put his head on the girl's knee and whined softly in his throat. "He's lovely."

"Yes, he is and loyal, too." Nathaniel told the girl all about Trooper's past. She sat and listened enchanted with the tale.

"Will they take dogs on the ships?" asked Nathaniel.

"I expect so. They took Samson. And I believe dogs from this country are allowed in. Why?"

"I was just thinking maybe Trooper here would have a better home with Abigail. He will protect her on her journey."

"And maybe he won't want to leave you," said Goliath. "He did single you out, remember?"

"Yes, maybe you're right. It was just a thought."

"When the time comes. We will see. I am sure the dog will make his own choice."

"And now we have to eat and then ride."

Goliath served up the warming stew and they sat down to eat. Abigail was ravenous. She hadn't seen wholesome food in so long. "My this is good," she murmured as she took a spoonful. "I haven't eaten like this in I don't know how long."

There was a hearty silence as they filled their bellies and Trooper sat patiently waiting for his own meal, which Nathaniel gathered once he had cleared his dish. The collie lapped up what was given in relish, licking his bowl clean.

"Now," said Nathaniel seriously. "Will you be all right here alone?" Abigail looked frightened. "We have to ride. It's our job. I will leave Trooper here with you. Make yourself comfortable but I advise you not to go out and do not answer the door to anyone, not that anyone should come knocking. When we get back we will make arrangements for you to travel back home. Is that understood?" Abigail nodded and lowered her eyes. "Good. You should be safe enough. As I said, I will leave Trooper with you."

"Listen to Nathaniel. When we return I will take you to the docks myself to ensure your safety. Meanwhile lay low. Don't attract any attention to yourself. Trooper will give you fair warning if anyone is around the house."

"When will you be back?"

"I'm not sure. But there is food in the cupboard. It should be enough," said Goliath.

Nathaniel leaned over and ruffled Trooper's fur before rising from the table. "His grub is there." He pointed to a cupboard in the corner and you can give him any scraps you might have left.

Nathaniel stooped down and talked to the dog that tilted his head on one side and listened. It was as if he understood every word Nathaniel said. "Now you be a good boy, Trooper. Look after Abigail and keep her safe." The animal whined softly in his throat. His tail wagged softly and low before he settled at Abigail's feet. "Now bolt the door after us."

Abigail acknowledged them with a nod of her head before wrapping her arms around Goliath. Her eyes brimmed with tears, "Thank you. Thank you so much."

Nathaniel donned his cloak and hat. Goliath did likewise and the two left the cottage. Abigail quickly barred the door and leaned against it biting her lip.

19

Heroes   and   Villains

SILVER RIBBONS OF MOONLIGHT stretched along the path in front of the riders as they travelled the coastal path checking the small inlets and coves for any suspicious activity. They rode through the night hours with little to report until they skirted the track, which led down to the small fishing village of Porthallow. Alerted by sounds carried on the wind in the warm summer air and knowing they were so close to The Manacles, notorious for shipping disasters, they decided to investigate and picked their way carefully down the stony trail to the beach. They paused at the final bend in the track. The cottages alongside were shut up tight with the muddy glow from oil lamps seeping through the chinks in the curtains. The Five Pilchards Inn, which was situated close to the beach, was still open and two tough looking men stood outside talking freely and unaware of anyone listening. Odd words caught on the night air and drifted across to where Nathaniel and Goliath waited. They listened, trying to make complete sense of what was said.

"Draw them ……. Lights…… Women…… Brandy ……. Murder …"

Then there were some bawdy comments and the men retreated inside the tavern. Nathaniel put his fingers to his lips and they quietly led the horses back up the path and off to the left where a tumbledown abandoned cottage stood. They secured the horses behind it. The animals stayed still almost as if they had a sixth sense and knew the need not to shuffle or make a sound. Nathaniel crept back down the pebbled path trying not to dislodge any stones or crack any twigs. Behind them they heard the advance of horses' and donkeys' hooves. They tucked themselves away off the path and waited until the convoy of pack animals had passed and moved down onto the sandy beach, where their steps were muffled.

The moon was now shrouded in cloud and it was hard to see as thicker cloud tumbled across the night sky. Cold air met the humidity and promised a violent storm.

Needing a better view, the two officers slipped back down the path and avoiding the tavern they skirted around the top of the beach toward the other side of the cove where the sea crashed against the jagged rocks, gnawing ravenously as if greedily devouring the land. They knelt down and watched as a procession of people thronged on the beach with donkeys in tow. Some began building fires to lure the merchant ship travelling close to the coastline.

The weather was changing dramatically as it so often did in this part of the world. Evil thunderous clouds rolled across the sky as rain began to lash down with drops as big as pebbles. Lightning split the sky forking in white crooked spikes of nature's wrath. The choppy water changed into seething fury. The ocean boiled with anger tossing the merchant ship about on the water like matchwood.

Cries of sailors could be heard above the cacophony of the wailing wind that had sprung up as they struggled to cope in the churning waves. Walls of water grew and troughed sending the boat on a perilous death ride that tried to throw off its crew. Many hung on for their lives. Helplessly they watched as some of their shipmates were tossed into the foaming brine. Those that struck out for shore faced an army of wreckers waiting to slit their throats and more.

Goliath whispered to Nathaniel, "What do we do?"

Nathaniel sighed, "What can we do? We are but two and heavily outnumbered."

"Look! See how the ship is drawn to the wretched rocks."

"Aye, it's the cross currents and there it will founder and splinter. The weight of the water will crush the deck and sweep the goods into the sea."

"So, what is your plan?"

"We watch and wait. We will see where they take the cargo and sequester them for the king. If it is possible to help any of those poor lost mariners, we will try. But we must not show our hand too early. You are too noticeable. I may be able to divest myself of this hat and cloak. If I strip down to shirt and breeches I may pass for one of them."

"You can't. It's too dangerous," warned Goliath.

"Maybe, maybe not. Wait here." Nathaniel threw off his distinctive hat and cloak and his frock coat. He began to move from cover, down to the shingle and sand and scrambled over the rocks. The foul night helped hide his identity. The wreckers were intent on gathering what they could that floated to the shoreline like flotsam and jetsam as the ship broke up on the deadly rocks on the far side of the beach.

Nathaniel watched as one sailor floundered away from the stricken vessel and tried to head toward the shore but a beefy thug hauled him out of the water by the shoulders, wrenched his head back before slicing through the man's throat and shoving the body back into the crashing waves and onto the rocks.

Another brave soul began striking out for shore as the screams of other sailors being murdered by the wreckers shrieked on the wind. This man attempted to reach the far side of the bay where Goliath watched.

Thinking nothing for his own safety Nathaniel struck out to meet him. He grabbed at the terrified man who burbled in fear and exhaustion. Nathaniel hissed in his ear, "Quiet. I'm not here to hurt you. I'm trying to help." But the sailor flailed his arms, striking Nathaniel in the face. The man gulped for air and blubbered in terror. He kicked out with his legs catching Nathaniel in the stomach. The sailor was carried by the current and a wave threw the thrashing man onto the jagged rocks where he tried to scramble to safety.

Nathaniel was winded and now dazed he fell forward and floated face first in the stormy waters where the changing tides dragged him in and flushed him out in an almost continuous action. He snatched a mouthful of air but choked on the surging salt water and began to sink down into the murky depths, when two strong arms clasped him and pulled him to the foaming surface. Barely conscious he allowed himself to be hauled to safety. Goliath's herculean strength lifted Nathaniel up over his shoulder and back to cover.

Black clouds like a demon's shredded bat wings draped the moon and angry clouds shielded the starlight so it was almost impossible to see. Goliath took his chance and ran to their hiding place where he laid Nathaniel down on the long, tufted marram grass. There he rolled him over and compressed his back to release any residual seawater in his airways and lungs. He was rewarded with a cough and a splutter as Nathaniel spewed out the gagging salt water.

It was then the bold moon escaped its evil shroud and brought silver light to the beach of death. Too late Goliath saw the reeling sailor struggle up the sand to be met by three brutes who quickly dispatched him and threw his body back into the foaming brine, where his life force washed away with the ebbing tide.

As Nathaniel coughed up the remaining seawater Goliath watched the smugglers gather the goods and load them onto their donkeys and carts. There was an air of callous rejoicing amongst the wreckers who were not afraid to sing as they worked. Their sea shanties rose above the cacophony of the still murmuring wind, which had dropped from its deafening maelstrom to a whistling keen like a mother grieving for her lost child, unexpectedly snatched from her.

Goliath watched.

The horde of thieves gathered together and scrambled up the beach no longer hampered by lashing rain or buffeting wind. Goliath observed the path they took. His eyes followed the blurry glow of their oil lamps as they processed up the hill.

Nathaniel sat up trying to clear his ravaged throat scraped sore by the abrasive sea salt. He managed to rasp out, "What happened? The sailor…?" Goliath shook his head dismally and Nathaniel swore softly. "The contraband?"

"Being carried away as we speak."

"Then we must find out where. We need to sequester the goods for the King."

Goliath cautioned, "My friend you have had a brush with death. You need to rest."

Nathaniel stood to his feet groggily, "No, we must discover where they hide their goods. Come on." Nathaniel donned his discarded clothes once more over his wet body.

Reluctantly, Goliath stood and the two retraced their steps to their horses waiting for their return. Soft footed they made their way to the top of the beach and inched past the hostelry. Refrains of traditional songs crooned lightly on the wind and followed them up the cliff path as they warily tracked the fiends.

Nathaniel raised his fingers to his lips in caution and he willed Samson and Jessie to be as still and silent as snow. The band of smugglers had entered the small village of St. Keverne and trooped through the square taking the road down to Trythance farmhouse, which stood with a cottage and a number of stone outbuildings.

"There's too many of them to take the goods back now," whispered Nathaniel. "We'll check and see where they stash them."

They remained unobserved and watched as the donkeys were relieved of their burdens and the carts unloaded. All of the contraband was packed into one of the stone barns. There was much merriment and congratulatory slaps on the backs at a job well done. Nathaniel and Goliath quietly slipped away.

It was a long hard ride back to Redruth and they had reports to write, they would confiscate the goods in the morning.

Nathaniel and Goliath plodded into the yard. Jessie and Samson were as tired as their riders but before either of the men could relax they needed to attend to their loyal steeds. Both needed a good rub down, fresh water and feed. They led them into their stables and relieved their horses of their saddles.

"Tomorrow morning, we must get to the Custom House and inform them of the hidden contraband. They may be able to use local dragoons to requisition the goods.... I believe there is a military camp outside Truro and another at Penzance."

"We will have to get word."

"And I have promised to help Abigail. We have much to do."

The two friends made their way wearily to the cottage. An oil lamp burned dimly in the window behind dirt-streaked glass. Nathaniel knocked tentatively and Trooper could be heard whining on the other side of the door. Abigail opened it gingerly to admit them.

"Is everything all right?" asked Nathaniel seeing the look of consternation on her face.

"Some men came around and hammered on the door. They peered in through the windows. I hid in the bedroom trying to keep Trooper quiet."

"Good job we haven't cleaned them. They wouldn't have seen much," muttered Nathaniel.

"They sounded rough and were talking about you. When they saw your horses were gone they left. I haven't been outside the door. I was too afraid."

"Did you hear what they said?"

"Some of it. They mentioned a murder, your groomsman I think. And something about your family."

Nathaniel's expression swiftly changed from concern to one of fury. "Can you remember exactly what was said?"

Abigail shook her head, "Not really. I was frightened and trying hard not to be seen. I'm sorry... Oh, they did say they'd be back... I'm sorry."

"Then we'd best be ready for them."

"No sleep for us tonight, then," added Goliath.

"We'll watch in shifts. We won't be much good without sleep. Trooper here will warn us of any arrivals. How on earth did you keep him quiet?"

"It wasn't easy. He must have sensed I needed him not to bark, but he did growl. It was very strange."

"Strange or not it was the right thing to do. Next time we might not be so lucky."

The night was seemingly long and uneventful. Nathaniel filled his watch with preparing a report for the Custom's man, Daniel Bulled. He would take it to the Custom House in Truro to be dispatched to Ilfracombe. In it he detailed the information regarding the contraband and asked for the local dragoons to be sent to retrieve them for the King. He also took time to write to his brother in law, Philip who was a captain, explaining the situation just in case the local militia were not to be trusted as he had sadly discovered to his cost in Wales. Lastly, he penned a letter to Jenny and his family before falling asleep over his missive.

He awoke with a jerk as Goliath touched his shoulder, "Lie down, get some proper rest. I'll take over. We will wake Abigail at first light. I shall accompany her to the docks and see if we can get her home."

Nathaniel too tired for discussion rose wearily and made for his bed. Trooper scuttled at his feet and followed. No sooner did he lie on the bed that even without removing his boots and clothes he gave into his body's demand for sleep. Trooper curled up beside him and he, too, slept.

Morning came all too soon and as the first fingers of sunshine probed through the curtains' chink. Nathaniel awoke with a start. Trooper's head was up and he was growling. Nathaniel rose quietly and quickly. He splashed some water from the ewer on his face. He was now wide-awake as Goliath stepped into his room.

"What is it?" he asked his voice a whisper.

Goliath spoke in the same hushed way, "I think they're here."

"How many?"

"I'm not sure, three maybe four."

The low tones of men's voices filtered through the warm summer air. The words were barely discernible, a phrase here, a murmur there. Nothing tangible but both Nathaniel and Goliath were ready.

Abigail tiptoed in fully clothed, her face creased in concern. Her eyes bright with fear seemed to grow larger as her dark complexion began to look grey almost ashen. Although her breaths were snatched she remained silent, stroking Trooper for some form of comfort.

Nathaniel placed his sealed letters in his dispatch bag and picked up his flintlock pistol and cocked it in readiness. "What are we going to do?" asked Goliath in a hoarse whisper.

"You and Abigail go out the back. Get Samson and be careful. All being well I will meet you in back here in a few days. You will be able to see Abigail safely board a ship home. You have all your papers?"

Goliath nodded, "What about you? And Trooper?"

"I'll hold them off. Take Trooper with you. He will make a fine companion for Abigail on her journey."

"What if they won't let him travel with her?"

"Then keep him with you until we meet again. I'll miss the little chap." Nathaniel ruffled the dog's fur. He seemed to sense the severity of the situation and whined softly in his throat before licking Nathaniel's hand. "Quickly, go now."

Goliath and Abigail together with Trooper stealthily crept to the back of the cottage. Goliath looked around carefully. He could see no sign of the men and they slipped out into early morning light.

Nathaniel waited hoping his friend wouldn't be spotted. He knew he had to create some sort of diversion to give them a better chance of escape. He raised his pistol and began to slowly open the front leaded window.

20

On the road

GOLIATH AND ABIGAIL TOGETHER with brave Trooper travelled on the road from Redruth. Goliath had taken the willow basket and attached it so that Trooper could ride and rest for some of the journey. At that time of the morning there was no one to be seen and Goliath prayed that Nathaniel was safe and would come through any attack on the cottage unscathed. But his main fear was being seen and then marked by slavers. He knew he would cut an odd picture to those he passed in the sleepy Cornish villages. Towns he would avoid if it were at all possible. He would try and remain on the coastal paths. He did not want to attract undue attention. It would be a long hard ride to Bristol docks and even then, there was no guarantee he could gain passage for the girl.

But Goliath had the determination of a belligerent tiger stoically stalking its prey and as long as Samson could keep going he would press forward. Come nightfall he knew he would be forced to stop for rest, food and shelter and decided it was better and safer to stop at hostelries where he was known. He moved on and as the sun was beginning to set in the sapphire sky he approached Boscastle.

The blaze of fire slipped toward the horizon and its red embers glowed across the sea and sky as the light began to fade. The tangy smell of salt was fresh on the breeze and increased his appetite as they began to pick their way down the steep path to the cottage where he and Nathaniel had taken shelter before.

Goliath had no idea whether Frances Wheelan would be back at her cottage with her husband Ross but if not, he knew they could rest there for the night. Samson was sorely tired and needed bedding down with good straw and feed.

The row of cottages seemed devoid of people. Goliath dismounted and led the horse around the back to the small yard. He knocked quietly on the back door and waited. Nothing… taking a deep breath he carefully tried the handle and found it to be unlocked. He called out quietly, "Mrs Wheelan? Frances?"

A quick search revealed the place was indeed empty. He unloaded Trooper. The dog was glad of a moment to stretch his legs and relieve himself on the grass before following Goliath inside the cottage. Abigail slid off Samson and she too entered.

It seemed dark and dingy and had a mouldy damp smell from being empty and unlived in.

"The place is deserted. I suggest you stay here and settle down. Trooper will keep you company and be your eyes and ears should anyone come calling. It's best you stay out of sight. Even though we have your papers, we need to be wary."

Abigail nodded she was too tired to argue or question him.

"Have a look around and see if there is any food in the larder. There's a pump out back that we can draw water from for us to drink. Keep quiet. I'll not be long."

"Where are you going?" she asked her eyes wide with fear.

"Don't worry. I will see that Samson is treated properly and try and get us some grub at the inn. They'll believe I'm travelling with Nathaniel and that should keep us safe for the moment. Make sure the doors are shut securely behind me. You'll find oil lamps in the window and candles under the sink. I'll not be long."

Abigail nodded again and closed the door on the dwindling light. She peered through the window and watched Goliath's figure disappear around a bend in the track and muttered a small prayer before drawing the curtains and securing the doors. The front door was locked but she placed a chair under the handle of the back door and then began to look around for something, anything to eat.

She explored the cottage and refreshed herself with some water left in an ewer in a bedroom. She found clothes abandoned in a cupboard and wondered if she might borrow some as Abigail only had what she stood up in. She made up her mind to ask Goliath when he returned, if he returned. Abigail was none too sure. Still, she carried on doing as he had asked and took out candles from the cupboard under the sink and hunted for something to light them. She found some tapers in a drawer in the living room dresser together with a small tinder box with flint and yarn that smelled as if it had been soaked in something flammable.

Paraffin was discovered in a cubbyhole under the stairs. She filled the oil lamps and finally managed to light two of them. The rooms already seemed brighter and the musty damp smell that had pervaded her nose when she entered began to retreat. It would certainly improve with a fire in the range and she set about making one with paper, kindling and coal that was sitting on the hearth.

'Now, food,' she thought. Trooper whined softly, the little dog was hungry as well so she took a lit candle and searched the larder. There was some mouldering bread that was almost dust, which Abigail threw on the fire, a pot of pickles, pickled eggs, chutney and jams. Abigail hunted through the shelves and discovered dried peas and lentils, jars of fruit kept in honey. There was a wooden case that contained salted meat of some description and a bag of potatoes now just beginning to sprout.

Abigail took a pan and filled it with water to boil on the fire and tossed in some dried peas and lentils. She had just started to chop the best of the potatoes when the door rattled. Abigail froze uncertain what to do but Trooper trotted forward and wagged his tail. She looked cautiously out of the back window and saw Goliath standing there, removed the chair from under the handle to admit him.

Goliath was carrying something wrapped in a muslin cloth, which he placed on the table and unwrapped some pork, bread and cheese. He laid out two plates and set the food in the middle as Abigail stirred in the potatoes with the lentils before tossing in some shredded salted meat to make a fine stew.

Goliath inhaled the growing pleasing aroma with appreciation.

"What happened?" asked Abigail.

"As I thought the landlord believed I am travelling with Nathaniel and served me, albeit reluctantly. I kept my eyes and ears open and learned that dragoons had arrested several men from the village including our neighbours in the adjacent cottages. We won't be bothered. The Wheelans haven't returned although it's expected they'll come back when Ross has fully recovered from his injuries. It's rumoured that the gang have moved on from here further down the coast. That makes our stay here safer."

Goliath smelled the air again. "That smells good. We will eat well tonight."

"What of Samson?"

"Bedded down, watered and fed. We need to get something for Trooper. Poor mite must be starving."

Abigail nodded and took some of the shredded meat and placed it in a bowl. She took a ladleful of the broth she was stewing and added it to the meat setting it down for Trooper. The young collie sniffed it appreciatively and began wolfing it down. He licked the plate so hard it danced across the floor cutting a swathe through the dust that had settled in the owners' absence.

Abigail looked at Goliath and asked tentatively, "Upstairs there are some women's clothes. I have nothing but what I stand up in. Can I borrow some of the female items, if they fit?"

"I don't see why not. You'll need a bag with changes of clothes for your journey back. We had no time to kit you out. Go on. I will see Frances is reimbursed." He spread his lips in one of his rare smiles and nodded at her in encouragement.

Abigail handed him the spoon, "Here. Stir this while I put on something else. I'm sure this scratchy dress could walk away on its own if it tried." She wagged a finger at him, "Don't let it burn."

Goliath grunted and took the spoon while Abigail ascended the stairs clutching a candle. She returned to the bedroom and opened the wardrobe door. It was made of black carved mahogany with a double mirror on the outside. She noticed the silvering on the looking glass was flaking in one corner.

Abigail set down the candle, which fluttered and sputtered in complaint. The flame wavered at the draught of air that breathed through the window frame. She set out some clothes and selected some underwear from the drawer. She stripped off her clothes and tried on one of the dresses. It fitted as if it had been made for her.

For the first time in a long time Abigail smiled, *really* smiled. Her face was transformed from one of haggard worry to the youthful hue of hope and expectation. Her beauty was now plain to see.

She looked under the bed and pulled out a stout carpetbag and began to select some items to stuff into it. She only took what she thought she might need on the long journey home; enough for her to change when needed.

The aroma of the gently cooking stew wafted up the stairs and Abigail closed the bag, picked up the candle and hastened back down to the kitchen.

"I hope the owners won't mind but I have borrowed a bag and some clothes. I was beginning not to like my own company."

Goliath looked admiringly at her, "I don't believe the owners will be back any time soon and I am sure we can recompense them for any goods you have taken. I know where they are staying."

Abigail sighed in relief, "Good. I don't want to be called a thief."

"Don't worry. Now, let's eat. I'm starved."

They sat at the scrubbed pine table together and Goliath ladled out the hearty stew and placed the fresh bread onto the table. There was quiet while they ate. Goliath set down another plate for Trooper, which he attacked with relish, chasing the dish around the floor to lick up every morsel.

"Right. I'll clear up these dishes; you get some rest. We have a long way to travel tomorrow. The earlier we set off the further we can travel." Abigail rose from the table and mounted the stairs. Trooper started to pad after her. "Oh no, you don't. Out in the yard with you first and then you can slumber," warned Goliath.

The friendly collie went outside and did what was expected of him before scratching at the door to be let in. Goliath admitted the animal that dashed indoors, raced up the stairs and whined outside Abigail's bedroom door. She let him in and there was a peaceful hush in the air.

Goliath, however, was taking no chances. As soon as he had washed the dishes he checked the doors and windows, replacing the wooden chair under the back door handle. Finally, he snuffed out the oil lamp and took a flickering candle up to the bedchamber, where he hoped he would be able to rest. Morning would be upon them soon enough.

Nathaniel had stationed himself by the window and watched for any movement in the approaching country lane. He half wished he had the little dog Trooper with him. He also worried about the fate of his family as well as that of Goliath and Abigail. The fading light had begun to play tricks on his eyes and he was seeing intruders in the shrubbery where there were none, but then softly on the whispering breeze the soft footfalls of horses could be heard. There was also the murmur of conspiratorial voices, which seemed to get louder. Nathaniel shook his head as if to clear it and rubbed his eyes. At the gateway to the farm stood four horses with riders who looked none too savoury even at that distance. Nathaniel waited.

One rider began to walk along the farm track toward the cottage when to everyone's surprise Mrs Banfield emerged from the back of the farmhouse and confronted the intruder. Nathaniel listened as the words carried to him.

"And just what business do you have here? You're trespassing on my land." Her voice was aggressive, her tone assertive.

The ruffian touched his hat in mock respect, "Sorry to alarm you, Ma'am. Our business is with the men yon." He jerked his head toward the cottage, where Nathaniel waited. "We understand that they reside there."

"Are they expecting you?"

"Well, no."

"Then I suggest you take you and your men off my property until Mr Brookes and his man are home."

The man appeared to consider her words and spat on the ground. "Well, see here it's like this… I don't take orders from no woman. And whether it please you or not I'll be knocking at the door and if they ain't home then I'll wait."

"Then I shall have to call my husband to make sure you leave." Mrs Banfield backed away from the men.

"Got wed overnight, did you? I understood you were a widow woman. I don't think you'll be calling anyone." The ruffian dismounted and moved menacingly toward Mrs Banfield who had shrunk back in horror.

Nathaniel had seen and heard enough. He opened the cottage door his pistol in his hand and walked toward the men.

"Do I know you?"

"Just paying our respects, Mr Brookes. We heard you were after information."

"Did you indeed? And where from might I ask?"

"Word has it in town you're looking for a woman."

Nathaniel moved closer to his landlady. "Mrs Banfield. Why don't you go back indoors? I'll deal with this."

"Aye. And I'll help you," said a man stepping out from the house. He was tall for a Cornishman with a strong frame and brawny muscles. He had a thick head of chestnut hair, which reached to his shoulders. The man sided with Nathaniel as they faced the thugs. "Go on, Mabel," urged the man.

Mrs Banfield needed no further bidding and retreated back inside her house. Her face appeared at the window as she watched the proceedings.

Nathaniel glanced at his newfound aid and supposed that this must be

Simon. The horses shifted their feet nervously in the fading light as the men looked uncertainly at each other. They were further interrupted by the arrival of another rider.

Nathaniel looked up in surprise and relief at Samuel Reeves who trotted into the yard. Sam looked curiously at the apparent standoff between his colleague and the ruffians before him. "Is everything all right, Officer Brookes?"

Nathaniel nodded, "Nothing that we can't handle." He included Simon with a jerk of his head.

"Good. The dragoons will be glad to hear that. They are on their way."

At the mention of the dragoons the men became nervous and remounted. The spokesman of the group cleared his throat, "We'll be away. Our business can wait." They turned tail and spurred their horses on out of the farmyard and back to the lane.

Nathaniel, Simon and Sam watched them go, as did Mabel Banfield who emerged from the farmhouse wiping her hands on her apron.

"Thank goodness, they've gone. They looked an unsavoury lot."

"We'll have to be careful. They could return. Did you recognise them?"

Mabel Banfield shook her head, "No, but if I see any of them again I'll give them a wide berth. I'm uncomfortable that they know where I live. I don't want any trouble, Mr Brookes."

"And I don't want to make any trouble for you." He turned to Simon, "Thank you. Simon, is it?" The man nodded. "I don't think we'd have come out of that confrontation unscathed if it weren't for you."

Simon smiled; "I don't like slavers or smugglers. They did for my pa when he refused to help them. Glad to be of service. If you need me again, call. I'd best go and see Mrs Banfield." He nodded at Sam, "Looks like you have important business to attend to."

Nathaniel inclined his head and watched the man walk away before turning to Sam, "What are you doing here? What's happened?"

Sam indicated Nathaniel's cottage, "Shall we go inside and I'll explain everything."

Sam dismounted and led Hunter to the cottage. He secured him to the porch post and they went inside. Nathaniel filled and set a black cast iron kettle onto the glowing range, which he replenished with fuel before taking a brown clay teapot and setting it on the table.

"You read my mind. This is just what I could do with after a long ride," said Sam.

"Tea is good at any time," grinned Nathaniel. "Now tell me, what brings you here?"

Samuel Reeves licked his lips, dry from the wind through his long ride. "Your home was attacked."

The colour drained from Nathaniel's face, "What happened? Is Jenny all right? Bart? Mamma?" his words gushed out like water breeching a dam.

"Yes, yes. The family felt uncomfortable that they were being watched and unsafe. A strange man had approached Bart so they decided to leave. While they were getting their things together they discovered that Eric your groomsman had been murdered."

"What?" Nathaniel felt his legs give way as if they had turned to sand. He steadied himself on the back of the chair before sinking into the seat.

"They left for Swansea before moving onto Gloucester to stay with your mother's cousin, Moira. For the moment they are safe, but in your absence the house was ransacked. Whoever it was must have been searching for evidence of your whereabouts or where the family had fled to."

"Then it won't take them long to find me. Word spreads like wildfire. You saw those men. If they can find me they can find my family. There would be information enough in my mother's bureau with correspondence between her and her cousin. It's just a matter of time."

Sam sighed, "Which is why they are not staying long at your relative's house. They don't want to endanger them."

"Then where are they going?"

Sam shrugged, "They were discussing that when I left." He paused, "Either to London or they were talking of following you here to Cornwall."

Nathaniel interrupted, "That's madness. They'll be walking straight into the direst danger here. I won't be able to keep them safe. You saw those men."

"I know but I believe they may have plumped for the third option."

"Third option?"

"Jenny was adamant that Bart should be kept safe at all costs. She suggested that Myah and Bart should seek sanctuary in London."

"And Jenny?"

"Jenny felt she should travel with Edith to find you."

Nathaniel rubbed his hand wearily over his forehead. The kettle on the range began to steam and Nathaniel busied himself making a brew of tea. It was the distraction he needed to allow him to think. Sam sat pensively without speaking. Nathaniel poured them both a cup of tea. He took a long draught almost burning his mouth before murmuring, "So, we don't know where they are or what they will do?"

"Not quite."

"Well, out with it, man. Don't keep me in suspense."

"Word has been sent to the Military Camp at Bude. I believe your brother-in-law is on his way there. A platoon of dragoons will be dispatched and should have the information you require." Sam looked around, "Where is Goliath?"

"Bristol. He rescued a girl from his home country and is getting her safe passage back to Jamaica. Then he will return. We still have to find Aleka."

The two men sat in the heavy silence that had descended and sipped their tea.

21

Saying Goodbye

THE SKY WAS A bleak oppressive grey. Sailors and crew worked on the dockside loading luggage onto a passenger ship bound for the Ivory Coast, Ghana, Haiti and Jamaica. People milled around on the quay, saying farewell to family and friends before boarding the East India passenger ship. A motherly looking woman with three young children stood to one side waiting patiently.

Goliath smiled down at Abigail, "It is a long journey home. I have sent word on the naval ship, HMS York. They left for Jamaica yesterday and my letter will reach your family before you land. There will be someone there to meet you. I have asked them to confirm your safe arrival, as the ship is due to return as an escort to a convoy of one hundred and fifty five merchant ships. You will be safe here and this lady has agreed to watch over you on the voyage." He nodded at the pleasant faced woman trying to control one of her sons who was running around mischievously.

Abigail bowed her head, "Thank you so much for all you have done for me. I know my father will reimburse the money you have spent and loaned me. If it were not for you and Mr Brookes I would have died here. I would have rather taken my own life than be a sex slave to anyone."

She threw her arms around the giant and hugged him. Goliath stroked her head, "What are we going to do about Trooper?"

The little collie sat at their feet and cocked his head on one side as if he understood what they were saying and whined softly in his throat.

"I would love to have him with me but I worry about the journey and whether he will survive the heat at home. That's if I can even take him into the country."

Goliath nodded. "I understand. The little chap will be company for me on the way back. Will you be all right?"

Abigail stooped down and ruffled Trooper's fur. He licked her hand lovingly. The woman who had been listening carefully to the conversation stepped forward. "She will be fine and a great help to me with these three." She indicated the three children, one of whom was still skipping around families and baggage on the dockside. She caught him by the back of his collar. "Perhaps, Abigail, you would like to help me with this one?" The little boy squirmed in her grip.

Abigail smiled and took the little chap's hand. "I know a grand game we can play once we're aboard. Interested?"

The little boy nodded brightly. He grinned at his siblings, "Are you coming?"

"Can we, Mamma?" asked the little girl with golden curls.

Her mother nodded, "Remember we are in cabin ten." She extended her hand to Goliath and shook it. "Abigail will be safe with us. I promise."

Goliath nodded courteously and bade her farewell. Satisfied he left the quay without looking back and Trooper followed dutifully.

Aleka was working in the kitchen of Richard Gosling's Manor House. Deborah was alongside her preparing vegetables for the cook, Ethel Grice. Aleka eyed the young girl, "Why do you stand for this? Why don't you leave?"

Deborah mumbled, "I can't. It's better this way."

"But why? I'm sure you could get a better position elsewhere."

"It's not just me. It's my mam and dad."

"Oh?"

"They use me to keep them in line and to make sure I behave."

"That's disgusting. It makes you no better than a slave."

Deborah bowed her head in shame. "I know."

Just then the cook, Ethel Grice, approached the two of them. "Stop talking. Plenty of time for chat when you've finished your chores," she said grumpily. The cook was a large woman with a small mealy mouth. She was emphatic about the running of her kitchen. Although not unpleasant she was a hard taskmaster. She insisted on running her kitchen with a tight rein.

Aleka and Deborah stopped talking as the cook had ordered them and the door opened. Richard Gosling marched up to the women, "Have they finished their tasks, Cook?"

The cook sniffed imperiously, "Almost."

"Then you'll not mind if I whisk this one away?" Without waiting for a response, he took Aleka's wrist and pulled her to him. His hot breath steamed in her face and she flinched at the closeness of the encounter. "Now, now. Don't resist; that is unless you want to be sold."

Aleka knew that she was better off with the Goslings than in an open slave market where anything might happen to her. She hurriedly palmed the small knife she was using, secreted it in her apron pocket and allowed herself to be led away. She called over her shoulder, "We will talk further, Deborah." But Deborah remained silent and fearful as Aleka followed Sir Richard from the room.

Richard ran lightly up the ornate staircase, which led to a landing from the hall. He marched purposefully down a corridor to a set of back stairs and began to mount them. Aleka followed her mind working rapidly overtime.

He stopped outside Aleka's bedroom door, "I believe this is your room, is it not?" She nodded and he opened the door and entered the sparsely furnished room. "It would please me if you would be kind to your master. You could have so much, if you so desired."

Aleka tried to suppress her anger and managed to speak politely, "I know you treat me well here and that I would fare far worse in another household but I pray you to listen to me."

Richard Gosling stood askance his hands on his hips and cocked his head to one side. "Go ahead." There was a small spark of something in his eyes; quite what it was Aleka could not determine. "I was born a free woman, daughter to a British Governor who now is in office in Sierra Leone. I have been educated to a high standard and I am a married woman. I was abducted by a band of slavers and all I want is to return to my home." She dropped her head and lowered her voice, "I am not someone's plaything."

Richard pursed his lips and eyed Aleka up and down. "It is true you have the bearing of a free woman. I respect your honesty but I am a man and I have paid good money for you. Whatever your life was before it is gone; so, forget it. You are mine and right now I desire you."

Richard Gosling pulled Aleka into the room and closed the door firmly. The room fell into shadow as the sun passed behind a cloud and the light in the sky diminished. Aleka fingered the small knife in her hand as she felt in her pocket. He threw her down on the bed and she turned her face away feeling hot stinging tears rise to her eyes.

Richard stared at her, "I can't do this." Aleka turned her face back to him and released her hold on the blade. "Yes, I find you maddeningly desirable and exotic but I cannot enjoy coupling with a non-compliant woman. It is important to me that you are as pleasured as I am."

Aleka sat up and held Gosling's gaze. "Then what are we to do?"

Gosling rubbed his chin, "I don't know. I have a business to run. I suppose I could throw you back in the pool of slave women but that idea pleases me little."

"Then what?"

Gosling sighed as he paraded around the small room. He opened the casement window and looked out across his land to the woods and countryside beyond the gardens. The sun was beginning to emerge from the heavy cloud that had suffocated the warmth and light and the rogue grey puffball gradually moved across the land to the trees, which seemed unusually unwelcoming in the enforced drab lack of light. But, then the sun seemed to smile and extend its rays to the woods, which began to appear more benign.

"I'll tell you what I'll do," said Sir Richard. "I will give you three months. You will spend time with me, get to know me and by then I hope you will have taken a liking to me and will change your mind. You are an accomplished woman, I will have you read to me and entertain me. If at the end of the three months you still want no part of me then I will sell you on. I will have no conscience in this. The parson, Patrick Hamilton expressed an interest in you. He will have you. I cannot promise you how he will treat you."

Aleka lowered her eyes; three months would give her time, "I remember the parson. He seemed a cold, cruel man."

Gosling nodded, "Then we have a deal? We understand each other?"

Aleka rose from the bed and nodded, "We do." Gosling stepped to the door when she stopped him, "May I ask you something?"

He turned quizzically, "Yes?"

"To prove my usefulness in other ways, may I have permission to teach Deborah to read?"

Gosling studied Aleka's face thoughtfully, "You know I prefer this civility you're displaying. Why not? I see no harm in it."

"I will require access to books, paper and pen," added Aleka.

"Fine," said Gosling. "I will see to it. And now return to your duties, any teaching will have to be done in your own time." He turned abruptly and left the room.

Aleka smiled. It was a small battle but a fight that she had won. She removed the knife and hid it in the drawer of her nightstand before following the master back down the stairs and corridors to the kitchen.

Richard Gosling addressed the kitchen staff, "Well, well it seems we have a learned woman among us and one who would teach you to read, Deborah. But in your own time." He glanced at Aleka. "I will send materials across for you." With a parting look at the amazed staff he nodded to Aleka and left.

As soon as he was out of earshot the cook, Deborah and the kitchen maid set to whispering and questioning Aleka about what had just transpired. Aleka smiled inscrutably and responded, "That is between me and the master but he understands that I am a free woman."

The cook snorted, "Huh, if milady hears that she'll knock it out of you," she paused, "and him." She gestured over her shoulder where Richard Gosling had left and bristling with an indignation that Aleka couldn't fathom the cook returned to her work.

2 2

Waiting to ride

NATHANIEL AND SAM SAT at the kitchen table each stoically eating a bowl of oatmeal prepared in a big iron pan sitting on the range.

"So, what's the plan?" asked Nathaniel between mouthfuls.

"I have my instructions. We have to report back after we ride. Bulled is anxious over lack of reports from us and alarmed at the increased activity in my area. One man alone cannot do the work that you and Goliath have done both in Wales and here."

"Maybe so. But, it's a tough coastline with all the coves and caves. We can't always rely on the help of informants. We need more dragoons and not those in cahoots with the smugglers."

"I believe your brother–in–law has a new posting to back you up."

"Philip? That would be wonderful. It was suggested he was joining a camp in the South West."

"But nothing's certain. We've been promised before."

"But this time surely the King has ordered it?" said Nathaniel.

"There is that. We can but hope."

"So, what's next?"

"We have to meet with local dragoons to hand over the impounded merchandise that you have captured. Further to that we are to keep watch over the coastline from here stretching down to the Lizard. It will be a long day and night. There are two French merchant ships passing through these waters carrying a considerable number of goods. Our informants have told us that wreckers plan to attack the vessels. The weather should turn this evening and aid them in their murderous quest and we have to stop them."

"Just the two of us?"

"I had hoped your man, Goliath would be here."

"That only makes three against a whole band of cutthroats."

"I think we can safely say that Goliath is worth two men, maybe more."

"There is that."

"Also, if they can be persuaded, the dragoons we meet with this morning may be able to assist us, as well."

"Then we had better finish our breakfast and get moving." Nathaniel studied Sam's face, "Was there anything else?"

"Yes, if I am right after listening to your family's discussion I believe Jenny and Edith will make their way here."

"To Redruth?" gasped Nathaniel. "I know you said they might but I hardly dared believe it. It's too dangerous. What about mother and Bart?"

"I told you. Safe. Staying in London."

"Why didn't they all stay?"

"You try telling your wife to stay put! She has a will and mind of her own."

"There is that," agreed Nathaniel.

The colleagues finished their breakfast and cleared away. Sam put on his cloak, "I'll see to the horses and bring them around."

Nathaniel nodded. His mind was working overtime. By his reckoning Goliath should be back by nightfall, if not, then Nathaniel believed he had cause to worry.

He donned his cap and signature hat, took a last look around the cottage before he exited the front door where Sam was waiting.

He jumped onto Jessie's back and pulled her reins up short, as she seemed unusually skittish. Nathaniel's eyes narrowed, what had caught his horse's attention? Sam was about to speak but Nathaniel put his finger to his lips and cocked his ear to one side to listen. In the distance on the breeze there was the faint sound of a horse's hooves. He gestured to Sam and the two men manoeuvred their steeds around to the back of the cottage where they waited. Jessie was eager to be off. She bowed her head and pawed at the ground, while Samuel removed his hat and covered Hunter's eyes with it.

The soft thudding footfalls of another animal could clearly be heard approaching. To Nathaniel's ears it appeared to be just one but there was also the rumbling sound of cartwheels following in its wake with another heavier animal's plodding stride.

Nathaniel waited as whoever had approached dismounted and stepped onto the rickety wooden veranda and tried the door. Nathaniel removed his flintlock pistol and released the hammer as he spurred Jessie forward to the front of the house. To his delight he pulled up short at the familiar figure of Goliath trying the front door and dismounted immediately.

The two men embraced each other in a warm hug as a furious squealing was heard from the basket carried by Samson. Trooper was desperate to get out and be welcomed by Nathaniel. Nathaniel walked to the basket and let the collie down onto the floor, where the dog went into a frenzied race around the yard in absolute pleasure, as another cart turned into the gate and proceeded toward the men and the cottage.

Trooper began to bark at the rumbling wagon until Nathaniel called him back. Obediently the dog padded back to Nathaniel who lovingly scratched the animal behind his ears.

Nathaniel's face was wreathed in smiles as he saw the lovely face of his wife, Jenny. But with the joy of seeing her he also felt a wave of fear knowing the danger she would be in just by association. Swallowing his concerns, he opened his arms and Jenny scrambled down from the cart and flung herself into his embrace. Edith sat shyly on the cart's seat and waited. Trooper danced around the couple with little excited yaps.

"I've missed you so much," whispered Jenny. Nathaniel crushed her closer to him. Trooper jumped up waving his paws.

"Jenny meet Trooper."

Jenny looked down at the collie, now sitting with his head cocked on one side, making small noises in the back of his throat. She stooped down and ruffled the dog's fur. "Hello, Trooper."

"He has been a great companion and help," said Nathaniel.

"As long as he doesn't replace me," mused Jenny as she looked around. "And what of Aleka?"

"No sign. Not yet."

"I'm sorry, Goliath," said Jenny. "You remember Edith, don't you?"

"I most certainly do," interrupted Sam stepping forward and offering his hand to the maid to help her down from the cart.

"I suggest we go inside before we have to take off and ride;" said Nathaniel.

They entered the small cottage and Nathaniel set the big black kettle on the fire, which he stoked up. "I believe a cup of tea will be more than welcome after your long ride."

Jenny nodded and Edith murmured, "Please, Mr Brookes. I should be doing that."

"We are not at home now, Edith. This is our domain so you just take a seat." Edith flushed with colour but did as she was asked and sat silently next to Jenny at the table. "The teacups are not as you're used to but they serve us well. No matching china here," said Nathaniel with a grin.

"They're perfectly serviceable," replied Jenny. "As long as it's hot and warm it will refresh us fine."

There was a clattering of cups as Nathaniel busied himself warming the brown clay teapot in readiness for the scoops of fresh tea. Samuel's eyes feasted on Edith causing the poor girl to blush even more. Her eyes caught his and he winked cheekily at her. She immediately cast her glance down to the table uncertain where to look and unable to look the gentleman in the face. Samuel laughed kindly and suggested; "Once we have had our tea I will take Miss Edith outside for a short walk around the farm and leave you two to chat. You will have much to say to each other, I am sure, and things will be better said between the two of you than in company."

Nathaniel nodded, "I would be grateful for that. Thank you."

"And I will take Trooper for a walk," offered Goliath. At the mention of the word 'walk' the little collie cocked his on one side and thumped his tail on the floor before rising and nudging Goliath's hand with his muzzle.

A heavy silence hung in the air while they drank their tea. Samuel drained his cup, declined a second and stretched his hand out to Edith, "Come, Edith. Let us leave man and wife together." Edith rose uncertainly and glanced at her mistress who encouraged her with her eyes. She allowed herself to be led outside. Goliath, too stood up and called the gentle collie to his side and exited the cottage. Samuel's voice could be heard saying as he closed the door. "You can explain all that has been happening and I will do the same but first I want to learn more about you."

Nathaniel laughed inwardly at Sam's obvious and clumsy attempts at courtship but he didn't speak until the door was firmly closed. He placed his hand over Jenny's and explained events as they had happened. Jenny listened attentively her expression turning to one of horror as she heard of the terrible fate of the sailors who were wrecked and murdered in the Cornish Cove.

~ 152 ~

Then it was Nathaniel's turn to look shocked as Jenny recounted happenings at the family home, the death of Eric their groomsman; and how Bart was in such danger playing in the garden. Nathaniel's grip on Jenny's hand grew tighter and his knuckles turned white. He stifled the strong language that threatened to escape his lips. Silence pressed heavily, suspended in the room like hanging doom.

"What of mother and Bart, now?" he asked eventually trying to control the quaver in his voice.

"Safe, for now," said Jenny. "They first went to your mother's cousin Moira in Gloucester."

"That's what I heard."

"Your mother is clever, Nathaniel. She knew she could be tracked down through family and acquaintances and so they travelled to London, taking the late coach. From there she was moving to the east coast taking residence in a hotel before finding suitable accommodation for them both until the danger has passed."

Nathaniel nodded, "I understand that but these ruffians have links far and wide. How are we expected to get in touch with her or her with us should the need arise?"

"She knows where we are and both she and Bart are safe."

"I cannot believe there is no contingency should we need to speak to her."

"But there is," Jenny smiled inscrutably. Nathaniel looked questioningly. "Fear not. Your mother has an admirer. It's someone who will go the extra mile to protect her. If we need to get word to her, we have a point of contact to get a message through to her."

"And who pray is this protector?"

"Mr Lewis, Winston Lewis landlord of the Cross Keys Inn in Swansea. He was most helpful to us and is someone I believe we can trust. Your mother is keeping in touch with him. They have developed some sort of code between them when writing and he is in a position to drop everything, if need be, and accompany her home."

Nathaniel shook his head, "I trust no man, only Goliath. But if you say he's worthy I have to believe."

"He helped us get word to Moira and the police about Eric's death."

"About that... has anyone given anything to his widow? She will need help."

"Your mother sent her some money to pay for the funeral and see her through these few months. We didn't go to the funeral, didn't dare."

Nathaniel squeezed Jenny's hand. "When we have found Aleka, finished riding and it's safe to come home I will visit her and see what help our family can afford her. What of my successor?"

"I know not. We have been in touch with no one since we left; too afraid we might be traced."

"Very wise. And now, let me look at you."

Nathaniel took Jenny's hand and lifted her up. His eyes caressed her face; her beauty and he crushed her to him. She melded with his body in a passionate embrace as he whispered, "My love, my dear sweet love; how I have missed you."

"And I you," she murmured.

"I don't know how but you are even more beautiful than I remember; you have a glow about you. Your eyes sparkle with fire."

Jenny was about to respond when there was a scratching and whine at the door. Nathaniel released his wife with a chuckle. "Trooper wonders what is going on." He stepped to the door and opened it and the collie dashed in fussing and running around them. "I wonder what Bart will make of him?" mused Nathaniel.

"He will love him, I'm sure," replied Jenny. "It is good for a child to have a pet, good for his character."

"I owe this little fellow my life on more than one occasion." Nathaniel stooped down and scratched the collie behind his lazy ear, which sent him into a frenzy of licking Nathaniel's hand as Goliath stepped back through the door.

"Then Trooper will be an important family member when we can finally get home," said Jenny.

"And when might that be?" asked Goliath as he pulled up a chair.

"When we have found Aleka and put those responsible behind bars. But now we must decide what is safest for you, my sweet. Word spreads rapidly amongst those that would do us harm. You and Edith are not safe here. These vicious brutes know where we are. I can't let you face the same terrors that you did before."

Jenny shuddered at the memory of the ruffians who humiliated, assaulted and demeaned her in Wales and she sighed heavily, pleading, "But I want to be with you."

"As lovely as that would be, it is impossible. You know in your heart that it's the truth."

Jenny lowered her head and nodded silently before saying, "You do have one thing on your side."

Nathaniel looked questioningly at her, "And what might that be?"

"Your brother-in-law Philip is, as we speak, on his way here to help you in your quest. He has been granted permission by the King and his company to assist you in this terrible fight. I am surprised he is not already here."

"And when were you going to tell us that? We had hoped but dared not believe... This is wonderful news."

"What's wonderful news?" asked Samuel as he and Edith arrived back from their walk.

Nathaniel explained and the mood of the company lifted immediately. "We must make enquiries as to where they can stay. There is no room for everyone here at the cottage; Mrs Banfield would have a fit!"

Jenny hesitated before speaking, "And I have something else to tell you but I need to tell Nathaniel first, if you will excuse us."

Jenny vacated the room and stepped outside with the little dog at her heels. Puzzled, Nathaniel joined her. Goliath watched them walk down the farm track a small way when Nathaniel whooped picked up his wife and swung her around in a display of pure joy.

Goliath nodded as he observed them through the open door and smiled knowingly as the two returned to the cottage. "May I be the first to congratulate you on your good news?"

Jenny smiled sweetly and asked, "What do you know, Goliath?"

"It is obvious. I knew as soon as I saw you. You have that shining health that radiates out. How far along are you?"

Samuel and Edith looked up in surprise. Sam turned to Edith, "You didn't know?"

"No. I had no idea," said Edith turning pink.

Jenny smiled shyly, "I wanted to tell Nathaniel before he left but it was never the right moment. By my calculations I am twelve or thirteen weeks gone. We are to be parents again."

Congratulations flew around the room like a murmuration of starlings with waves of backslapping and smiles. To any onlooker they all looked the epitome of carefree happiness. No one noticed the shriek of a disturbed pheasant that broke cover and fluttered with tail feathers trembling as it took wing; no one except Trooper who padded to the open door and growled softly.

Nathaniel spotted Trooper's hackles rising and raised his hand for quiet. One by one the assembled company fell silent. Nathaniel listened. There in the distance was the soft footfall of horses' hooves, belonging to seven or eight horses or so Nathaniel thought. He called Trooper inside and barred the door watching warily through the window.

No one dared to speak and they waited until the approach became louder and a small platoon of Dragoons entered the farm gate and trotted down the track led by Captain Philip Chapman who had risen through the ranks from Second Lieutenant and was Nathaniel's brother-in-law.

Beaming brightly Nathaniel unbarred the door and strode out to meet him, "Captain Chapman, my dear friend, welcome. Tell me, how is that sister of mine?"

Philip Chapman dismounted handing the reins of his horse to his subaltern. He grinned from ear to ear and embraced Nathaniel.

"Naomi is fine, thank you. She is safe and well, as is Sarah- Jane. They are staying with my mother at the moment. Better she is there than at home. We have all received notification warning us of the dire threat to you, your family and anyone associated with you. That's why I'm here to help commandeer the confiscated goods and to let you do what you do best. Ride."

Nathaniel nodded, "Then where are you billeted?"

"We are to be stationed at the camp in Penzance, just for the time being. There are plans to move us further afield to Bude once everything is secured. Penzance is just temporary."

"Then you still have quite a ride. Come inside and I'll go through what we know and where we have goods under lock and key that you can collect." He turned to Goliath, "And you my friend can tell me how you managed to get here so quickly and where the wagon and horses came from."

Goliath laughed, "Bought and paid for and I bought a cattle box, now sold, to transport Samson so as not to tire him. Easily explained."

The group trooped into the cottage to make their plans.

23

Getting to know you

ALEKA SAT ON THE window seat of her attic room with Deborah who was struggling to focus on the letters of the alphabet that Aleka had drawn on a slate. The girl pronounced them hesitantly before copying the same symbols on her own chalkboard. Aleka smiled broadly revealing her startlingly white teeth. "That's it! Well done, Deborah. You have the letters and the sound combinations so now we can move onto the written text."

Deborah flushed with pleasure, delighted at the praise. "Do you really think you can learn me to read?"

"*Teach* you to read, not learn. You learn and I teach. Do you understand?" Deborah nodded, twisting her mouth awkwardly. "Good. You can do this, Deborah. You'll see. Now, let us look at this book together." Aleka rose and took a child's book from the box called The Parent's Assistant or Stories for Children by Maria Edgeworth. She turned to the first story, "The Orphans."

"Now this will be somewhat difficult for you, but I don't have any proper teaching aids yet so we will have to improvise. I will read some to you and you will follow. I will select some of the simpler sentences for you to read and we'll see how we go. Is that all right?" Deborah nodded agreement with her lips pursed tightly. "What's the matter?" asked Aleka with concern catching Deborah's pained expression.

"I'm really nervous," Deborah blurted out. "I'm afraid of making mistakes and then you won't want to teach me."

"That's not going to happen," reassured Aleka. "Ready?" she asked nodding her head and Deborah's response was an inclination of her head in agreement. Psychologically Deborah was ready to learn.

Aleka launched into the story of the Orphans and Deborah was soon drawn into the moral tale of the children brought up to be industrious and honest and the fate that befell them. She stopped at simple words and let Deborah read the easier sentences. So keen was Deborah to hear the rest of the story she insisted on reading to the end albeit hesitantly in parts. Aleka questioned her understanding and found Deborah to be a bright and willing pupil and more than eager to move onto the next story called Lazy Lawrence.

Richard Gosling was snuggling up to his doxy, Molly. She arched her back expectantly and sighed, "Oh, how I have missed you."

"And I you," murmured Richard kissing her neck and travelling down toward her décolletage and breasts. They fell backward onto the bed and with fevered urgency Molly flipped over Richard to straddle him and began to explore her lover's body with her tongue. Richard groaned in pleasure. He was transported to another place, at another time and his imagination took flight. He had a vision of Aleka, her proud bearing, braided hair and dusky smooth skin. He felt her perfect pouty lips glide over his torso following the line of his body hair down past his navel and unable to help himself sighed, "Oh, Alice."

Molly stopped. Her yielding body turned rigid and she sat up abruptly, "What did you call me?"

Dazed between fantasy and reality Richard didn't realise she had heard his involuntary words. He looked confused. "What? I didn't say anything. I just sighed that it was nice," he murmured.

"Alice. You called me Alice. Who is Alice?" persisted Molly petulantly.

"I said it was nice," insisted Richard. "I have not been with anyone called Alice." Richard attempted to return to the previous moment when he was about to enjoy Molly's lips on his naked body. Come on, Moll. You know I've not been with anyone else. How could I keep anyone else happy? You suck all my sap and energy. Fair exhausting it is."

Molly was not really convinced but for fear of losing her love appeared to accept his words endeavouring to do some investigation of her own later. She fell upon him again determining she would beat any other woman where it mattered and that was in bed. Richard groaned in ecstasy.

Time passed pleasurably until both were sated and they flopped back on the bed their brows glistening with an earned sheen from steamy sex. Richard kissed the tip of Molly's nose and exclaimed, "You are mine, Moll and mine alone. There is no other." The words tripped off his tongue with ease. He wasn't lying. There was no one else… yet, he thought, as Aleka's face filled his mind.

He rose quickly and began dressing, "I have to go. My mother will be expecting me. We have to prepare plans for our next venture. I'll see you tomorrow."

Molly pouted. "You promise?"

"I promise," he assured her bending forward to give her a quick kiss before leaving the chamber.

Molly watched the door close softly behind him before she, too, began to dress. She picked up the money that Richard had left and stuffed it inside her bodice. It was time she paid her mother a visit to find out what was really going on at the Manor.

Across the water in Sierra Leone Governor Zachary Macaulay had received Goliath's letter. He stared at the envelope for some time puzzling why it was Goliath's handwriting and not that of his daughter's. He placed it on his desk before sighing to himself. "Open it or you'll never know." He just hoped that his daughter Aleka was all right.

With trembling hands, he tore open the missive and began to read. His eyes widened in horror as he read the stark truth of his daughter's abduction. He abhorred the Slave Trade after his experiences in Jamaica where he witnessed first-hand the barbaric brutality and suppression of African men and women. He had constantly fought hard for the abolition of all slavery advocating the value of Christianity and his intention to spread the word of God. He had worked tirelessly with William Wilberforce to change the laws. For partly this reason he had been made Governor of Sierra Leone, which was a haven for emancipated slaves.

The thought of his daughter becoming a sex slave or worse filled him with anger and he determined to do whatever he could to track her down. He tossed down the letter in disgust and thumped his desk in fury.

His aide, George Bartram, on hearing what he perceived to be a disturbance knocked politely on the Governor's door. Zachary Macaulay's voice boomed out, "Enter."

"Is everything all right, Sir?" asked the aide.

"No." He pointed to the letter on his desk. "My daughter, Aleka has been abducted from her home in Jamaica, taken on a slaver to England." George Bartram looked aghast he couldn't get any words out.

"I will have to go to England. What information do we have on the active slavers in operation? I need everything we can discover. Bring in the files and send someone down to the docks to see if any ships are headed for England."

The aide finally found his voice and acknowledged the Governor, "Yes, Sir." He left the office to search through his documents and files while Zachary paced around his office. He paused at the window and gazed outside, his brow furrowed in concern.

George tapped on the open door, a hefty pile of files under his arm. He crossed to the desk and deposited them. Zachary indicated a chair, "Here, George, you can help me go through these. Two heads are better than one."

"I'll just send someone on your errand to the docks first, Sir."

Zachary nodded and sat behind his desk. He divided up the folders and pushed one pile to the other side of the desk, picked up a sheet of paper and pencil and began to peruse the documents in front of him. He sighed knowing this would be a long and arduous task.

His aide stepped back quietly into the office and he, too, began to scrutinise the files in front of him.

Molly had dressed discreetly looking more modest than she did in her usual flamboyant outfits, which emphasised her curves. She donned a cloak and bonnet before making her way toward the Manor, where Richard Gosling resided with his mother. Fortunately, the day was good and the sun shone. It was a good hour's walk but Molly was determined to get her much needed answers. She plodded on doggedly.

In the distance she could see two riders. Not wanting to be observed she hurried towards a small copse and hid. She watched carefully as the riders approached. It was no one she recognised. She squinted her eyes and could just make out a uniform. "Dragoons," she whispered under her breath.

Feeling uneasy Molly looked around the small copse as the riders were cantering toward her. She spied an oak tree with many spreading leafy branches, hitched up her skirt and scrambled up into the canopy. Not wanting to be seen she settled herself and waited in the hope they would pass her by. Molly had experienced being caught by soldiers in the past and didn't want to suffer at their hands again.

It seemed an interminable wait for them to pass, when to her horror the two riders approached the thicket and dismounted. They tied up their horses and Molly stayed very still hardly daring to breathe while one of the men relieved himself behind a tree.

Snippets of conversation drifted up to her and her attention was alerted when she heard the name of Richard Gosling. She strained to listen to every word.

"They say a dusky maiden has taken his fancy."

"Yes, and she is well educated."

"In the carnal arts?" laughed one.

"Some say she's the daughter of a Governor."

"Bit dangerous, then?"

"Too right. Especially when that Riding Officer, Brookes, is looking for one such woman. She's married to his man, Goliath. They are searching for her. I understand a purse of gold has been set as a reward."

"Then what's stopping us from claiming it?"

"Anyone that fingers Gosling is a dead man. Mark my word."

"Even so. A purse of gold."

Molly shifted uneasily in her precarious perch and the leaf canopy trembled. One of the dragoons glanced up and caught sight of a feminine foot. He shaded his eyes from the sunshine and gazed up at the spreading branches.

"Hello…. What have we here? Just what do you think you're up to, young lady?"

Molly froze uncertain whether to speak or not.

"What is it? Cat got your tongue?" rasped the other dragoon who was now also looking up.

"I'm not coming down lest I know your intentions," Molly said with a pout.

"Oh, she does speak," said the first with a laugh.

"Intentions? Does she think we are dishonourable then?" smirked the second.

"She'll have to come down to find out…."

"Or we could climb up and get her."

"Don't you dare. I'll scream and scream."

"And just who will hear you?"

"My screaming will shatter your eardrums, so it will!"

"Look, Missy. Neither of us is going to hurt you. Come down before you fall down. Where are you going, anyway?"

Molly sniffed, "To the Manor to see my mother. She's the cook there, so she is. She's expecting me."

"Come on down. We won't bite."

Molly eyed the two soldiers uncertainly. They looked friendly enough but as she well knew looks could be deceiving.

"Think I'll sit here awhile."

"Suit yourself."

"Can I ask a question?" asked Molly.

"Go ahead. It's a free country."

"You were talking about a man, a Riding Officer."

"So, you were listening?"

"Couldn't help it."

"What do you want to know? Or is it the reward that interests you?"

"Not really, I'm just curious. How can a free woman be taken as a slave?"

"That's how they do it. All slaves were free once. It will be a good job when that law is passed in Parliament and the foul practice stopped."

Molly had heard enough. The last sentence led her to believe that these dragoons were good men and not a threat. She began to ease herself out from the tree. She slithered down the last few feet and one of the soldiers caught her before she tumbled to the ground. He stood her up and steadied her before helping her brush bark and twigs from her clothes.

"Did you say you were headed to the Manor?" asked one.

"Yes, to see my mother."

"You don't work there then?"

"No, I am a kitchen maid in a local inn," she replied shyly.

Now she was face to face with them she could see they were both pleasant featured. In fact, one was quite handsome. He was tall, trim and strikingly good-looking. The other had a kindness and gentleness about him. He was the one to click his heels and address her politely. "King's First Dragoon Guard William Soper at your service."

The other took her hand and gently brushed his lips across the back of it, "King's first Dragoon Guard, Algernon Bexley at your service and you are?"

Molly hesitated, "Molly, Molly Grice."

"So, Molly you are on your way to the Manor? Could you do with a lift? You can ride behind me, if you so wish."

Molly blushed, "Why thank you. Yes."

Algernon mounted his steed, stretched out his hand and helped her into the saddle behind him and they set off toward the Manor.

As they rode Algernon chatted freely and learned that Richard Gosling resided there with his mother and heard more about the cook, Molly's mother. In turn, Molly gleaned what she could about the Riding Officer and his partner and their search for Goliath's wife.

"Is it possible your mother would give us some refreshments to see us on our way?" asked Algernon as they approached the big house.

"I don't see why not," replied Molly. "But we need to go to the back. She will get into trouble if you go to the main entrance."

"Then you tell me where we should ride."

Molly directed him along the gravel driveway toward the stables and the servants' quarters. They arrived at the back door and scullery of the Manor and tied up their horses close to the outside pump, where Algernon pumped water into a trough for their mounts to drink freely as Molly knocked tentatively on the back door.

One of the manservants, Jacob answered the door. If he was surprised to see Molly there he didn't show it. "Miss Molly, how can I help?"

"I need to see my mother, please. And these two soldiers require some refreshment before moving on."

"Then you'd better come in." He opened the door to admit her and nodded toward the dragoons. "Welcome."

They trooped into the kitchen. Molly's mother turned in surprise, "Moll, whatever are you doing here?" She crossed to her daughter and hugged her.

"I needed to see you. These gents were kind enough to give me a ride here. I said you'd give them some refreshment for their journey. We can talk later."

Molly's mother welcomed them all to the table. She fussed around the men, who thanked her appreciatively before rising to say their goodbyes. Algernon took Molly's hand and kissed it, "And you dear lady, may I write to you? Where would I send the mail?"

Molly blushed. Something of a new experience for her and bowed her head coquettishly, "Yes, Sir you may. Send any missive care of my mother, here at the Manor. If that's all right?" Her mother nodded her agreement but said nothing and the two men bade them both farewell, clicked their heels and left.

Once the door had closed the cook set about chastising Molly, "Whatever are you thinking of girl? What will Sir Richard say?"

"He can say what he likes. I'm not his property;" Molly said feistily. "There's something going on with him and I need to find out what it is. I'm a free woman I can choose who I want to be my friends. Besides, I can't read. I'll need you to help me with that. I wasn't going to admit to such ignorance."

"Then you'd better sit down again and tell me why it is that you have come."

Molly sat down with a flounce and a stubborn look on her face. She blurted out, "He's been good to me and to you; helped me change my life but I feel he's tiring of me. He called me by another name when we were… you know."

"What name would that be?" questioned her mother.

"Alice."

"Alice? Well, I never."

"What, what is it?"

"You'd best prepare yourself." Molly's mother was just about to inform her daughter of the new arrival at the Manor when the door opened. Deborah followed by Aleka entered the kitchen.

Deborah was filled with excitement, "My lessons are going so well. I can't believe what a good teacher Alice is," she gushed.

"Alice?" murmured Molly in shock her face paling.

"Molly, meet Alice," her mother said slowly.

Molly's first instinct was to rise and fly at the black beauty with her hands clawed like that of a bear. Her mother dragged her back and Deborah stepped in front of Aleka to protect her. "Just what is going on?" screamed Molly now totally distraught.

Jacob decided to make himself scarce and ventured down to the wine cellar leaving the women staring at each other in icy silence. It was Molly's mother who attempted to calm the festering mood belying the quiet and bade them all sit down.

As the cook attempted to chair the proceedings, Molly clenched and unclenched her fists at the story, which emerged. When completed, Molly passed a weary hand over her brow in an attempt to stifle the range of emotions flooding through her. She was sick to her stomach that was taut with fear and trepidation. Her breathing was laboured as she tried to digest all she had heard. Then just as suddenly as she had risen to fury she became inexplicably calm. She had come to a decision.

"Enough is enough. It is time to right the wrongs that have been made and I am just the person to do it," she sighed.

"Molly…" warned her mother. "Just what do you intend to do?"

"I am going to help Alice or Aleka, whatever she's called and help myself in the process."

"But, I have no way of paying you," said Aleka.

"Don't worry. I will be paid, as you will see and you can teach me to read."

"I don't understand…"

"You will. Here's what I plan to do."

2 4

Finding Nathaniel

MOLLY HAD PACKED A small valise. Dressed modestly she waited patiently for the coach that would take her to Redruth. She avoided all eye contact with the other waiting passengers. But her quick mind had already observed her travelling companions. She had immediately ascertained the class and type of people they were, none of whom she recognised, thankfully. Her mood was not the best after a row with the landlord of the inn but Molly knew that if she had been told the truth about the large reward in revealing Aleka's whereabouts then she would have no need to worry financially. If not, she could soon get another placement and at worst she could return to her old ways although that was not something she relished.

The coach was running late and speculation was rife amongst the passengers who were worried that the notorious highwayman who had moved from Salisbury and Bath was now attacking wealthy travellers to the South West of England through Exeter and beyond. They chattered about safety and precautions to prevent robbery should they be stopped.

A large gentleman who was sweating profusely and constantly mopping his face with a lace handkerchief announced he had sent all of his luggage with valuables on ahead to await his arrival in Liskeard. He carried only a small leather bag with overnight essentials. Another prim woman with a pinched face and wasp waist boasted of a secret compartment in her case, which hid her valuables. Molly thought it stupid of the woman to say anything, as she couldn't possibly know who might be listening. She felt inclined to say so but thought better of it. She was not prepared to get involved in a wrangle of words.

Molly wisely kept her head down and said nothing. She listened carefully to everything that was said. Her mother had always told her that was why she had two ears and one mouth. If you listened more than you talked you would learn much more.

A sigh of relief went around the assembled waiting passengers as the coach could be heard in the distance. The sound of rumbling wheels and clip-clop of horses' hooves travelled to them on the morning air. Soon it came into view.

A smart team of four chestnuts trotted in pulling an elegant stagecoach. The driver pulled up at the coach stop. A lad beside him hopped down and helped the coachman unload some of the bags from the roof before stacking the waiting baggage and roping it down. Four people alighted and the boy raced away to prepare nets of hay, oats and water for the horses. They needed to rest so a fresh team would be brought in for the next part of the journey.

The coachman checked his passenger list against the names of those waiting like a sergeant major taking roll call. The ostler's boy led the tired steeds away to the stables as the ostler brought out the fresh team to harness up.

Molly sighed, preparing herself for the journey ahead and wondering how she would fare in finding Nathaniel Brookes and his man. But find them, she would and collect her prize. There would be no more kitchen maid work for her or anything else. She would begin a new life that wasn't reliant on any man. On that her mind was set.

There was one man who after his comfort break on arrival had already settled back on the coach. Zachary Macaulay looked uncomfortable. He, too, was a man on a mission. He barely glanced up as the other passengers settled in beside him. He wasn't in the mood for pleasantries and did not want to engage in conversation with the other travellers.

The coach rocked as the other customers found their seats in the carriage. Zachary Macaulay sighed heavily. His demeanour was sad and depressed. He glanced at his pocket watch and sighed again.

"Wishing the time away won't get us there any faster," said the woman with the pinched face.

Macaulay was not so rude as to ignore her but merely muttered, "Quite. Quite."

"Have you come far?" the woman persisted.

"Far enough," said Macaulay in a noncommittal tone designed to end the conversation.

The woman sniffed imperiously, "I see." But of course, she didn't. She eyed up the man's attire and decided he was some kind of toff who wouldn't converse with ordinary folk and so turned her attention to Molly. "And you, Miss. Are you local?"

Molly wanted to tell her to shut up and mind her own business. She certainly didn't want anyone to know her reasons for travelling but she forced a smile, gestured to her throat and whispered, "Sorry, I have little voice and it pains me to talk. Please forgive me, Ma'am." She gave a small cough as if to verify her words. The woman nodded and began to regale the man she had conversed with earlier. Molly decided there and then that it would be a long journey and she deliberately closed her eyes signalling an end to any future communication.

Redruth was bustling with people. Nathaniel and Goliath plodded through the streets on their steeds. Heads turned and folks stared as they picked their way across the cobbles. They had, had a tough but successful week. Wreckers had been stopped and smugglers' caches of goods confiscated. The dragoons had loaded the contraband and were ferrying it to a place of safety where it was to be collected. Word was spreading that Brookes and his man meant business and already the price that had been placed on their and their families' heads had been increased.

They arrived at the post stop in the town. Nathaniel dismounted and went inside to collect further orders and mail. Amongst the letters was one from Sierra Leone addressed to Goliath. He turned the letter over in his hand with its official red seal and went out to his friend.

"Goliath, this is for you. It's official and from Sierra Leone."

Goliath broke the seal and opened the missive, "It's from Governor Macaulay. He's coming to England. In fact, he is probably here now."

"What's he going to do?"

"He's coming to find us and proposes to lobby Parliament to try to speed up the law making process, in the abolition of the trade. He wants all the information we have to try and find Aleka and the perpetrators who stole her from her home."

"That's good news. We have new orders from Bulled. I suggest we get back and see how we can arrange to get Jenny and Edith to safety."

"At least Trooper will be on the alert and Sam is with them until he joins his dragoons in Penzance."

Molly had never been further than Bristol. She was nervous and apprehensive but had the drive and determination of a woman hurt by love. Although she didn't want to be drawn into conversation she kept her head down and listened. Molly was used to listening it had served her well in the past. She learned a lot but not much of any specific use to her until the gentleman to her left commented on the pleasant seasonal weather of a temperate climate. It seems he had travelled from abroad from an overseas colony. The man did not want to be drawn into conversation and had only commented in order to silence the very curious woman who seemed to want to know why everyone was travelling. Molly closed her eyes.

"How far be you travelling?" she asked in a broad Cornish accent.

Not wishing to appear rude the gentleman finally responded with, "Redruth."

This was enough to set the woman off into a monologue. "Redruth? I know it well. Pleasing little market town. Me, I'm off to Truro. That's where my mam lives. It's lovely and mild there all year round. Beautiful flowers. They can grow palms there, too, like in the tropics. Dare say, you have palms where you come from." She nodded at the gent who smiled benignly but said nothing. "Course, we don't have no coconuts or fancy fruit down there, just the usual but I dare say in some of the manor houses' gardens and hothouses they could grow some exotic stuff. We got figs. They're quite fancy, really."

Molly switched off as the woman droned on extolling the virtue of figs and what could be done with them. So, Molly closed her eyes feigning sleep but not before she had taken a sidelong look at the gentleman alighting at Redruth. He looked a man of substance with his pristine clothes and silk embroidered waistcoat. He also wore a large gold signet ring as if he was someone of great importance. Molly drifted away in her imagination inventing the scenario behind the man. He looked impressive and Molly wondered if he was a politician or something more than a very wealthy man.

At Hayne Farm cottage Nathaniel was trying to reason with Jenny again, "Cariad, it is not safe for you here, especially now." He patted her tummy lovingly.

"But I want to be with you."

"And I would love you to be."

"Then why not?"

"I've told you. It's not practical. Jenny, you know what can happen. You know what happened last time. Can we risk little Bart and whoever is in there?" he patted her tummy again.

Jenny looked crestfallen, her mouth turned down, "In my heart I know you're right but…"

"But nothing. We have to be responsible. I need to help Goliath find Aleka. I have to finish this job for the king. Have you forgotten I was commanded to do this?"

"Of course not. It's just… oh, I don't know. Everything has been turned upside down. It's not safe to go home. The family is torn apart and I… I…" she broke down in tears.

Nathaniel pulled her close, "There, there, Cariad. It won't be forever. Our home will be safe, I promise you. We have many friends. I don't intend riding forever. We were promised that it's only temporary. Lord knows I want my life back, too."

Jenny snuggled into his strong arms and tried to suppress her hiccupping sobs. "So, what do we do?"

"You and Edith should leave at first light and get yourselves away from the treacherous coast. You need to get to a big city; lose yourselves in the crowds. You will be safer there. Send word to my mother and together you need to wait this out, please."

Jenny nodded sadly. She knew he was right. "How will you know where to find me?"

"You know where I am and I swear by all that's holy, I will find you. We have friends that will help. You can telegraph me at the office in Redruth and keep me abreast of all the news. You are not safe here, especially now." He patted her tummy lovingly again.

"But I so want to be with you," she protested.

"You are a stubborn woman but we have to be sensible. If anything were to happen to you. I would never forgive myself. I would be desolate without you."

"And I you." Jenny held Nathaniel in a tight embrace as he stroked her lustrous hair. She pulled away and stared earnestly into his eyes. "I know you're right and I so miss Bart. I will do as you bid. We have a long way to travel. It will be better to leave after a good night's rest. It is a long way back."

Trooper sat at their feet with his head on one side as if listening sympathetically. Jenny stooped and rubbed the collie behind his ears and he licked her hand gratefully. "And you will have Trooper. He will look after you."

Nathaniel nodded, relieved that she had finally agreed. "I have. He is a bold dog with a brave heart and has warned us of danger many times. He is a good friend to have." Nathaniel continued, "We will plan your journey back together. There are places on route where we have friends; places to stay that will be safer than just taking potluck. Word will have spread that you are here with me and I am sure that those that plot against me would be only too pleased to take you prisoner, or worse, just to get back at me."

Jenny's eyes were now bright with unshed tears and she sighed heavily, "Again, I know what we must do but I don't like it. I don't like it at all."

The conversation was at an end. Nathaniel continued to hold Jenny close. He kissed the top of her head before moving her away from him, tilting her chin and clasping her once more in a powerfully passionate embrace before murmuring, "Come, I'll get the maps."

At the next stop all the remaining passengers left the coach except for Molly and the impressive looking gentleman. No new passengers boarded and once the team of horses were changed the driver and his groom refreshed themselves with something to eat and drink.

Molly and the gentleman remained on the coach. He afforded her a cursory nod. "How far are you travelling?" he enquired politely.

"Redruth and you?" she asked.

"The same. It's a long time since I have been in the West Country."

They travelled on and occasionally commented on the beautiful scenery and lush countryside. Molly was bursting to say more but restrained herself. She would learn more from listening and observing.

The coach eventually trundled into Redruth with its two remaining passengers. They retrieved their luggage and walked into the Post House. Molly stood aside for the gentleman of means to address the clerk behind the counter first. He waited while the elderly clerk wearing spectacles shuffled to the counter. He peered up at the expensively dressed gentleman who had an aura of authority around him.

"Yes? Can I help you?"

"I'm looking for one Nathaniel Brookes. I understand that he and his man lodge somewhere near here. I have important business with them."

The old man sniffed, "You mean, the Riding Officer?"

Molly's ears pricked up.

"Yes."

The clerk sniffed again, "Don't have much truck with them but yes, I know where they are."

Zachary Macaulay leaned forward a hint of impatience in his voice. "Then can you tell me where?" The clerk hesitated. "Then can you tell me where?" Governor Macaulay pressed again.

The clerk took his time before taking a piece of paper. He picked up a pen, "Important business, you say?" in a tone that intended to elicit some more information.

"Yes. For the Crown," he added intending to shut the man up in hope he would smarten up his act.

The man scrawled an address on the paper and passed it to him. "There. They're renting from Mrs Banfield." He passed Governor Macaulay the slip of paper with the address of Hayne Farm.

Molly took note of the name and continued to listen.

"How, pray, can I get to this place?"

The clerk scratched his balding head, "Short of hiring a horse and riding there yourself?"

"I have luggage. So that would be impossible."

"You may be able to persuade Vernon Grimshaw to take you in his gig. For a price, of course."

"Of course," said Zachary sarcastically.

"How far is this place?"

"Hm, let me see…" he scratched his head again. "Must be about five or six miles out."

"Then tell me, is there a decent hotel I could check into and leave my baggage? Who would I hire a horse from then?"

"On the outskirts of town is Parkanal; top notch place. They sometimes take in quality guests. I would try there first. Or if you want somewhere closer there's Tabbs Hotel in Fore Street. Then you can come back to town to see Vernon Grimshaw. He's the only one around here to hire any form of transport. You'll find him further down this street with his yard and stables."

Zachary Macaulay took the proffered piece of paper and gave the clerk a shilling for his trouble and began to walk away.

The clerk began to address Molly, "And what can I do for you, young lady?" But, Molly turned and sped after the gentleman. She called back over her shoulder, "Nothing, thank you." She caught the man by his tail coat, "Sir, Sir…. If you please…"

Macaulay stopped and looked curiously at the wench, "Yes?"

"Excuse me, Sir but I think we can be helping each other."

"I hardly think so, Miss… Miss?"

"Grice. Molly Grice and I think you'll be very interested in what I have to say. Very interested," she emphasised looking him straight in the eyes.

Zachary Macaulay raised an eyebrow and finally said, "Very well, what have you to tell me?"

"You are looking for Mr Brookes and his man Goliath." It wasn't a question. "Would it be something to do with … Aleka?"

Zachary Macaulay's mouth dropped open, "What do you know of Aleka?"

"Let me travel with you and I'll explain on the way. I know there is a reward for information that will lead to finding her."

Zachary Macaulay nodded agreement and the two set off from the post stop together.

Nathaniel had spread the maps out on the kitchen table. He had marked one with several crosses and drawn a line on the route that Jenny and Edith should take. He pointed at the crosses, "These are places you can stop off on route; the ones I have marked in red are safe houses with people that know me. If Samuel rides with you, then you should be protected. You need to get back to mother as soon as possible. I will send word that you are on your way. I suspect you will have to move around quickly and often, as the tentacles of this network are far reaching. Nowhere will be safe for long. As soon as we find Aleka I will relinquish the cape and hat and return home."

"What about the King?"

"I will have done my bit. The service knows I won't ride permanently. The problem the Crown has, is with recruitment. There are not enough of us but I have some ideas to help with that. It is hard to find good honest men."

Jenny nodded, accepting what he said but still nonetheless worried.

Zachary Macaulay and Molly had walked to Fore Street and settled in at Tabbs Hotel. The concierge had sent a porter to collect their luggage from the Post Stop. They had adjourned to the lounge area to enjoy some refreshment while Molly continued to inform Governor Macaulay of what she knew.

"Where is this Manor House? And what is this 'supposed' gentleman's name?"

"That I'll not say until I have assurances that he will not be punished."

"You know I can't guarantee that," he chided.

"Maybe, but I don't see why you just can't get your daughter back and leave him alone?"

"My dear, it's not as simple as that. The trade he is involved in is a damnable one. For someone to be subjugated to another and forced to work against their will purely because of the colour of their skin is not only vile but against all Christian principles."

A gleam appeared in Molly's eye, "What if the person in the trade was coerced into it by another family member, one who is morally far worse than him."

Governor Macaulay considered this for a moment and rubbed his chin thoughtfully. There was a lengthy pause before he finally spoke, "In that case I think something might be done."

Molly beamed, "Then I want your word as a gentleman that he will suffer no blame. Then and only then will I strike a deal."

"If what you say is true…"

"It is. I promise you. Many's the time he has helped others anonymously. Why, when one of his workmen died he helped out financially from his own pocket to help the poor man's family who had no means. He is not a bad man."

Governor Macaulay thought some more and extended his hand, "If we find my daughter, I will do what I can."

"Then I will tell you when we get to Brookes and his man. Can you ride?"

"I used to but I am out of practice. Perhaps it is best for me to hire a gig to take us to the address the Postmaster gave us. I will speak to the porter when he returns with our bags."

"I am not someone of means, Sir. I cannot share in the hire costs."

"That will not be a problem. I have money enough. In fact, I will cover the cost of your room here, too, if you can lead me to my daughter. If successful the reward you spoke of will set you up for life. Until then I will take care of all expenses."

Molly bowed her head, "That is most kind and much appreciated... May I ask a question?"

"Go ahead."

"Please don't consider me to be impertinent, I do not wish to cause offence but you are white where as Aleka."

Governor Macaulay interrupted her. "Yes, you are right. I strayed from my wife when I was in the colonies for over a year. A man gets lonely. Aleka was the result of my affair. My wife was surprisingly understanding and allowed me to raise Aleka with our own daughters. I know my wife was relieved when Aleka married and thus was no longer reminded of my infidelity. Sad to say, my wife passed away five years ago or maybe this mission would have been impossible to fulfil."

Molly nodded her head, shyly. "I know it can be hard for a man on his own. Especially for those with less understanding wives ..."

Governor Macaulay looked curiously at Molly, "You speak with some authority on the subject. I would like to hear more. I do not believe you are what you seem. Are you?"

Molly did something she hadn't done for years. She blushed, profusely.

The sun was just rising up from the horizon and stained the gently lightening sky a bloody red, which seeped into the few, low smoky clouds and bled across the land. Birds began their morning ritual as they woke from slumber and sang to herald in the start of another day. Blackbirds and song thrushes warbled and chirruped a joyful song that was joined by many other songbirds.

Jenny and Edith were dressed in travelling clothes, their bags stowed carefully in the cart. Samuel Reeves was ready and prepared as Nathaniel and Goliath were saying their goodbyes.

"No more, my love," said Nathaniel. "You have your maps. It is time to leave and make haste to a place of safety. Sam will accompany you. Be careful where you stop and stay. Only send me word when you reach Mamma. I will be waiting."

Jenny inclined her head in agreement and bade Nathaniel a final farewell.

Their tones were hushed as they whispered a final but loving adieu to each other. Jenny picked up her cloth bag, put on her bonnet and retreated to the waiting cart.

Edith was already seated as Jenny clambered up and took the reins. Nathaniel watched as the wagon trundled out of the yard to the country lane. Samuel Reeves joked, "If this doesn't give me a chance to get to know Edith better then, nothing will!"

Trooper trotted to Nathaniel's side wagging his tail and gave a small friendly bark.

Nathaniel waited until he could no longer hear the wagon and then slipped back inside the cottage where Goliath had made a huge pot of porridge.

2 5

The arrival

NATHANIEL PASSED A WEARY hand over his brow as he finished the oatmeal Goliath had prepared. "I don't know what to say, Goliath. I have sworn to help you find your wife but I really don't know what we need to do next. People aren't talking, we have no leads."

"I know things look bleak," Goliath replied. "But if she is not in a sale then she must have been bought privately."

Nathaniel covered his friend's hand with his own, "We will not give up. Someone must know something. Our biggest problem is discovering the area where she has been taken. Once that is established it should not be a problem. Aleka sounds like someone it would be extremely hard to hide."

"We must speak to our informants," urged Goliath.

"What informants? I know of none here. In Wales we have friends, but in this place…"

Goliath raised his fingers to his lips as Trooper began to growl with his hackles raised. "I hear a wagon, horses… something…"

Nathaniel tried to quieten the suspicious dog before going to the window and peering out.

A gig with two passengers driven by Vernon Grimshaw was travelling into the yard. Nathaniel recognised the portly driver, "It's Vernon from the stables in town. He has two people with him, neither of whom I recognise. Wait here and I will go and see what they want."

Nathaniel opened the cottage door and stood on the veranda with Trooper at his side who kept up the deep rumbling in his throat. The gig pulled up.

"Can I help you?" queried Nathaniel.

"I certainly hope so, Mr Brookes. It is Mr Brookes, isn't it?"

"At your service, Sir. And you are?"

Goliath burst out of the door, "Governor Macaulay, Sir."

Nathaniel raised his eyebrow as Goliath joined him on the veranda. "You got my letter?"

"I did and I came as quickly as I could," said Zachary Macaulay as he stepped down off the gig and helped Molly down. "This is Molly Grice. She knows where to find Aleka."

"Then you'd best come in."

Trooper warmly welcomed the arrivals and ran around their feet expecting a fuss but he stopped his antics as Vernon Grimshaw moved in his seat and eyed the man before growling again.

Zachary Macaulay turned to Vernon Grimshaw, "Please wait here. As soon as my business is finished I will require you to take us back to town."

Vernon Grimshaw touched his cap respectfully but a sly look entered his eyes. "I would appreciate some refreshment for myself and my horse."

"Indeed," nodded Nathaniel. "There is a water trough at the back of the cottage outside the stable where you will also find hay. I'll put a seat out on the porch and fetch you a drink. What would you like? Tea... water... cider?"

"It's a warm day. I would prefer a cold drink. Cider will be fine."

Nathaniel nodded and bid the Governor and Molly enter the cottage. Trooper bounded in after them. Vernon Grimshaw took the gig around the back and let the horse drink from the trough, before fetching some hay and tossing it down. He secured the animal to a post by the stable before returning to the front of the cottage where there was a seat outside and a tankard of cool cider. He manoeuvred the chair close to the open window, sat under the veranda canopy and supped his cider keeping alert as he strained to hear what was being said inside. His eyes almost popped as he eavesdropped on the meeting and learned information that he decided would be valuable to him, extremely valuable.

Governor Macaulay sighed, "All you have said is very worrying. What you have explained leads me to say that we must act fast. Not only that it seems your family, too, are in grave danger."

"I know they are," replied Nathaniel. "I have been targeted before in this way. They have their safe houses on route as I have told you. But we mustn't be complacent. I am fully aware of the threats these criminals pose against me and Goliath."

"Because you are good at your job and the pressure from the King forces your hand."

Nathaniel's response was measured, "Yes, but once we have found Aleka I am returning to my old life as a medical man."

"What about your replacement at home? The King? And what of your riding?" quizzed Macaulay.

"I hear the new doctor is a bit of a bounder but for the most part is doing a splendid job. However, there is room enough in the area for another medical practitioner. My rounds cover a vast area. It will be good to share the load, so to speak."

"And the King?"

"Will understand. He is aware I only took the job as a temporary measure."

"But, will he see it like that? You are, after all, getting results."

"I have many ideas. The problem lies with recruitment. Men are afraid to ride. There is not enough military support for them. Men just won't come forward."

"Because of the threats to their person and property?"

Goliath interrupted, "This discussion is academic. Let Nathaniel proceed as he sees fit. We are losing valuable time."

Macaulay deferred, "You are quite right to bring the matter back to hand. So, if what young Molly is saying is correct, then Aleka is with this Gosling fellow?"

"Yes, in his house, but his mother is the one behind the slaving. She forces him to do his work. I'm sure he would get out if he could," said Molly.

"And pray what is your interest in all this?"

Molly blushed, "Richard looks after me and I him. He is my man. If his love is taken by another I will be forced into drudgery by giving men… what they desire."

"A doxy?" Macaulay didn't mince his words.

Molly took a deep breath and raised her head up high. I admit I was once, but I am no longer as I have Richard taking care of me. I do not intend to return to that life again."

Macaulay grunted approval, "Well, said. As you know I am no stranger to the sins of the flesh but I have tried to make recompense." There was a pause as he considered his next words, rubbing his chin in the characteristic way he had when deep in thought. "We must move and move now."

Goliath sighed in relief, "Then let's go."

"First things first. Nathaniel, send word to your family. I will return with Molly to the hotel and write to the King on your behalf. My missive will be tempered with the promise of fruitful discussion and plans to increase recruitment. Then we will head for Gosling's residence. Young Molly will show us the way."

"We would be quicker on horseback. Can you not send your luggage on the coach and hire or buy a steed?" He turned to Molly; "I take it you can ride?"

"I can," she beamed. "It has been sometime since I was in the saddle but yes, I can manage a horse."

"Then that's settled, you return with Vernon Grimshaw and attend to matters. We will await you here. I shall see Mrs Banfield," said Nathaniel.

Macaulay levered himself up and scraped back his chair. As he opened the cottage door Vernon Grimshaw stood rapidly his face flushing with guilt.

"Mr Grimshaw, back to town. You can guide us to purchase two good mounts."

Grimshaw touched his forelock servilely and began to chat in a garrulous manner about finding decent horses and went to fetch his own. He returned leading them, still gabbling idly about nothing. Once the animals were harnessed Molly boarded the wagon and the gig trundled out of the yard. Nathaniel's eyes narrowed, "A trifle chatty don't you think, for one usually so silent."

Goliath nodded agreement, "The sooner we are gone from this place, the better. How much do you think he heard?"

"Enough. Loose tongues can broker misery. We must watch our backs and get word to Jenny."

Nathaniel fetched some paper, a pen and ink and began to write. It was short and to the point, warning Jenny of possible retribution and informing her with the facts as he knew them. It was as well to be prepared. He signed with a flourish and sealed the letter.

"How do we get it to the post when we have to wait for the Governor's and Molly's return?"

"I warrant it will take them some time to find horses capable of the journey. I can go into town now."

"And tire Jessie before we ride? That's a mistake, Nathaniel."

Trooper sat at Nathaniel's feet and whined as if in agreement. He sighed, "Yes, I suppose you're right." He thought for a moment before adding; "I'll go and see Mrs Banfield. Keep Trooper here with you. I don't want him scaring the cats."

Goliath nodded his acknowledgement and watched Nathaniel walk away from the yard to Mrs Banfield's farmhouse.

He strode to the back door a knocked politely. Mrs Banfield answered the door her hair awry and flour on her hands. "Mr Brookes. How can I help you?"

"I am sorry to say that my man and I have to leave. I am not sure if or when we will be back."

"I see. What of your lodgings?"

"I will send word. That I promise you. But if you don't hear before the tenancy runs out then please feel free to re-let the cottage."

Mrs Banfield, nodded before wiping a stray hair from her face with her hand as the wind gusted through the yard. "I understand. I wish you well in whatever it is you have to do."

Nathaniel clicked his heels as an officer would and turned away.

"Mr Brookes?" Nathaniel stopped. "Good luck." Nathaniel raised his hand in acknowledgement and continued walking.

Having pointed Zachary Macaulay and Molly in the right direction to purchase two horses Vernon Grimshaw was eager to get to the local hostelry where he knew he could get paid for valuable information and he believed he had extremely worthwhile information. With a spring in his step and a whistle on his lips he strode jauntily to the less salubrious part of town. He was headed for The Golden Lion in Caleneck Street an infamous hostelry, which provided more services than just beer. Other nefarious activities took place there from prostitution and cock fighting to badger baiting, all considered to be fine sport and entertainment.

The crude chatter from customers could be heard as he turned the corner where a drunken brawl spilled out through the doors into the middle of the street. Men jeered and urged the men on who surrounded the bare-knuckle fighters. Bets were being placed and taken by a grossly overweight ruffian who sported a straggly, unkempt beard and gold earring in his ear. Grimshaw stopped. He had no desire to become involved in a fight. He carefully skirted the derisive, shouting crowd and edged his way along the front of the inn to the entrance and slipped in away from the jostling throng.

As he stepped through the threshold a woman in a tight red corset, which undercut her bust in a shabby calico frock, accosted him. "Want a good time, Dearie?" She was close enough for him to smell her gin sodden breath. He grimaced in distaste and waved her away before ducking under the archway and moving to the left 'ale' side of the pub rather than to the right where women of lax morals posed and sat on the stairs waiting for clients.

Smoke clouded over the heavy wooden tables in the dingy public bar, which smelt of spilled beer and the unhealthy odour of unwashed flesh. Vernon Grimshaw's nose twitched and he removed a handkerchief to cover his nose as he scoured the room.

In the corner by the bar swigging from a pewter tankard sat Clive Bethell. His cruel baton lay on the table in front of him. His arrogance was apparent in the way he sat with his legs splayed. He spat on the floor and wiped his nose across his sleeve. His voice was raucous and rough as he banged his tankard on the table and shouted to the landlord, "Fill her up again, Landlord."

"Ye'd better bring it here. I'm not waiting on ye."

Bethell glowered, his beetling brows meeting in a thunderous frown shrouding his face in anger. He rose clumsily, picked up his baton and slammed it on the table. "I shouldn't rile me if I was you," and he patted the pistol stuffed in his belt.

Vernon cleared his throat and stepped forward struggling to keep the hesitancy from his voice. "It's all right. I'll take it." He grasped Bethell's proffered mug and took it to the bar for the landlord to fill. Bethell took his seat again with a grunt. Vernon fished in his pocket for money to pay for the liquor. He carried the vessel to the slave master and pulled up a chair. "Here. Sup this."

Bethell looked suspiciously at Grimshaw, "What is it you want? You don't bring me ale for nothing."

Vernon licked his lips, "On the contrary… it's what I may do for you."

Bethell took a swig and wiped his mouth with his sleeve. He eyed the man before him, "Ain't you the fellow with horses and a gig?" Grimshaw nodded and Bethell continued; "I got horses, I got transport. What on earth could you possibly have that would interest me?"

Grimshaw licked his lips again, pulled up a chair and sat. He glanced about him. No one else appeared to be listening. As soon as the altercation between Bethell and the landlord had been averted they had all returned to their previous pastimes of lewd chatter, gambling and drinking. Grimshaw leaned forward and hissed, "Nathaniel Brookes"

Bethell's mean eyes gazed deep into those of Vernon Grimshaw, who felt as if he was staring at the very devil, himself. It was as much as he could do to resist crossing himself.

"And what do you know of Brookes?" he asked mockingly with a distinct sneer. "That I don't already know? I know where he lodges, what else is there?"

"I know his plans and where his wife and family are to be."

There was a lengthy pause as Bethell considered Grimshaw's words. "And why would you be telling me this?"

"Let's say, I have a financial interest and just maybe a need for one of your women."

"Now we get to the truth." Bethell spat on the floor. "It's money you're after."

Grimshaw acknowledged with a nod of his head, "But for valuable information or maybe one of your women." He licked his lips lasciviously.

"My girls fetch a high price. How did you come by this knowledge?" He took another gulp of his drink.

Grimshaw continued, "Straight from their own mouths," and he explained how he had come to overhear the discussion between Brookes, Goliath and his visitors.

Bethell rubbed his bristly chin before spitting again. "Come back here in an hour and I'll have your answer."

"You may have left it too late by then. They will have had too much of a start.

"Listen!" rasped Bethell slamming the crude baton on the table. "You'll do as I ask. Now leave."

Reluctantly Vernon Grimshaw rose from his seat and left the tavern to make his way back to his stables. Bethell pulled at his bristly chin deep in thought, before draining his tankard. He glanced about him eyeing up the men in his employ either gambling, drinking or otherwise engaged with women. He staggered to his feet and lurched toward the next table and grabbed a roughneck with a balding head by the arm. "Get the men together. We need to move."

"But, Sir. The men are having their fun. You promised us a week off."

"Well, not no more," growled Bethell. "We've got a job on. One that will see us rid of a dangerous man for good and net us a large prize in the process."

"Who? Who are you talking about?" demanded the ruffian.

"Brookes. We'll get rid of him once and for all."

Jenny, Edith and Samuel Reeves trundled along the minor Cornish country lanes and roads heading for their first stop, which was Bodmin, twenty-six miles away. The clouds were beginning to gather and roll in from the west, darkening the sky. The smell of newly cut grass was sweet on the air belying the mood of the company, who travelled on in solemn silence.

Sam tried to lighten the atmosphere by initiating conversation but when met with monosyllabic answers closing all avenues of communication he eventually gave up and the band moved on in an uncomfortable suppressed hush. Only the clip clop of the horses' hooves and reverberating wagon wheels strived to break the painful quiet.

There was a rumble in the distance, which Sam recognised as an approaching storm. He urged his horse, Hunter, onward calling out, "We'll have to pick up the pace if we want to outrun the storm. Pull your hoods up. It looks like we'll be getting wet."

Jenny and Edith dutifully obliged.

As the cart turned along a twist in the lane, a jagged lightning bolt forked down striking a slender birch tree, splitting its trunk to its heart. The sound of the cracking wood and igniting sap competed with the crash of violent thunder, which in turn initiated a vicious wind that threatened to pull the hoods from their heads and rip their capes from their bodies. The burgeoning black clouds began to release their soaking load and the rain lashed down.

Samuel tried to shout above nature's cacophony. "We must keep moving. Don't pause for a moment. You saw what happened to that tree."

"Surely, if we see shelter it will be safer to stop and wait for the storm to pass?" said Jenny.

"Or we will bring the storm upon us. Trees are magnets for lightning."

"I'm not such a fool as to seek refuge in a wood. But maybe there's a barn or outbuilding that we could wait in and get dry," continued Jenny. "Like there, over there!" She pointed at a ramshackle building with a slated roof that stood in the next field.

Sam nodded, "I'll check it out." He urged his horse on and galloped toward the field entrance and dismounted at the old barn. He opened the barred door and ventured inside with Hunter. Moments later he reappeared and signalled to Jenny to drive the cart toward the building just as another streak of lightning slashed across the sky.

Jenny coaxed the now frightened horses on and into the meadow. Sam had opened the barn door and Jenny was able to safely drive the wagon and animals inside. Sam held fast to the door in the buffeting wind and managed to secure it from the inside.

Inside the barn there was straw a plenty on which to sit and lay out their sodden clothes. The horses seemed calmer in spite of the fierce whistling wind that shook the old building. Hunter soon found some hay to nibble and Sam took some fodder to the other horses. A bucket of meal leaned against a wooden strut. Jenny emptied the contents on the dirt floor for the animals. "They'll need water. I'm sure I saw a pump at the side of the building, if it works."

"You're not going anywhere in this." Sam remonstrated. "Nathaniel would never forgive me. I'll venture out to see when the worst has passed."

Jenny nodded in agreement, "We'd better make ourselves comfortable. Who knows how long we will have to wait."

The trio settled down on the straw saying little as the storm raged about them. Edith's face was white and pinched in fear. She said nothing even though Sam tried to reassure her. She was just too frightened to speak.

2 6

Villains and Rogues

CLIVE BETHELL SAT IN the tavern with members of his motley crew, cleared his throat and, as was his habit, spat on the floor. He wiped some of the dribbling spittle from his mouth and turned to his men eyeing each of them in turn. His voice was chilling and rasping where moonshine liquor had burnt his throat, "Well, me boys... we have a chance to rid ourselves of that nuisance, Brookes. What do you say? Are we agreed?"

There was a chorus of approval of 'Ayes' and 'Let's get him.'

"There may, of course be some sport in it for ourselves. We go after his little wifey then it will be a simple matter to hold Brookes to ransom. Give up the riding or else...." This was greeted by loud guffaws and jeers coupled with vulgar gestures.

"When do we go?" asked another ruffian.

"As soon as this storm has abated. I don't expect they'll be out on the road in this. It should be easy to spot where they're sheltering. Especially as we know their route." Bethell parted his lips cruelly into a sly, knowing grin, revealing his decaying teeth like those of a rancid shark. His men cheered. "Finish your grog, eat and get your things together. Be ready to leave in an hour."

A passingly handsome rogue screeched, "Just time enough to get laid before our trip." he laughed humourlessly.

Another called out, "Why waste your money when there will be a clean woman to satisfy your lust?"

"Then I'll just have a second helping," mused the scoundrel. The men chortled in glee once more as Bethell moved to the tavern entrance. "Remember, one hour!"

He pulled on his hat, donned his cape, moved into the street and into the driving rain. He turned a corner and met Vernon Grimshaw scurrying toward him in the direction of the tavern.

Bethell pulled him to one side in a doorway, "Now, give me all the details."

Vernon Grimshaw sniffed imperiously, "Do you think I'm stupid? Let's see the colour of your money first."

Bethell took out a purse of gold coins and selected five guineas and six half guineas, which he counted out into Grimshaw's hand. Grimshaw remained holding his hand open to receive more and reluctantly Bethell counted out a further two guineas. Grimshaw's fist closed about them and he stuffed them into his money belt before starting to talk. There they stayed until Bethell was satisfied. They shook hands and Grimshaw walked back the way he had come with a distinctive arrogance in his stride in spite of the rain.

Bethell watched him go, his mouth curved in a cruel grin and he spat on the ground, his phlegmy sputum mixing with the dust and rain. He smirked and then guffawed loudly, throwing back his head in unbridled glee allowing the rain to drench his face. He shook his dripping locks and retreated toward the tavern, where he called his men to order.

"You have fifteen minutes and then we must be off. Be saddled up and ready to leave or you'll not be paid." He chortled again, this time holding his belly in a deep guttural cackling laugh.

Samuel Reeves opened the barn door. The rain was still falling in torrents. He sighed and turned back to the women. "At least the horses will have a bit of a rest. We can't wait for too long or we won't make it to Bodmin in the light. If it hasn't eased off soon we will still have to get going."

Jenny nodded, anxious to be off, "The sooner the better. I don't have a good feeling. I certainly don't feel safe. There's just something…" Her words tailed off.

The three sat in silence and listened to the wind rattling the barn doors and the rain pounding against the roof. Samuel attempted to lighten the mood and chatted to Edith keen to learn all he could about the pretty maid. "So, Edith is there anyone special in your life?"

Edith blushed a deep crimson, "Why no, Sir. My life is with Miss Jenny, Bart and Mrs Brookes."

"Surely you must have time for yourself away from work? Family? Siblings?"

"My Mam and Dad are dead."

"I'm sorry… How? If you don't mind me asking."

"Brought down by the speckled monster. I was away at the time visiting my cousin and not allowed back. The contents and house had to be burned. Small pox is a terrible thing. Sad to say my little brothers and sisters went the same way. I have no one excepting one cousin and aunty. Even my Uncle Dai succumbed… so you see, Sir. I have no one really."

"That's a sad tale," commiserated Samuel. "How old were you?"

"I was just twelve, Sir. Mrs Brookes kindly took me in and I have stayed with her, and moved on to help with chores for Dr Brookes and his family. They are the nearest ones to family I've got."

"But what about your cousin and Aunty?"

"Moved away, Sir. Took themselves off to the Midlands. I believe they are both in service somewhere."

There was a lull in conversation punctuated by the rain playing a metronome-tapping tune on the barn roof, which was gradually slowing.

"I think the worst is over," said Samuel. "Do you want to risk it?"

Jenny nodded, "Let's go. I will feel happier on the road. At least we'll be doing something."

Samuel rose from the bale of straw he was sitting on. "Right then, we'll make a move."

He opened the barn doors. The wind was still blustery and blew the doors shut, once more. Samuel pushed them open again and propped up the door. The sombre rain clouds had moved on and although still grey it was certainly drier. They clambered back into the cart in order to go on their way.

"One consolation," said Samuel, "If we *are* being followed then the villains in pursuit will also have been held up."

Jenny shivered. "Come on, let's go."

Bethell's men rode the same roads through the driving rain. He urged his men on, "They can't have got far. More than likely they'll stop and then we'll have them. Come on!" He kicked at the flanks of his horse and the stallion broke from a canter to a gallop, quickly followed by the rest.

They splashed through puddles and mud, the relentless rain making their hats and coats sodden. A few swore and spat into the gusting wind. Others kept their heads down and travelled on in the wake of their leaders.

The cutthroats cantered on. Bethell spotted the hoof prints and cartwheel tracks in the mud. They looked fresh. A grim, surly grin played on his lips. "We're on the right course, lads," he shouted.

The coarse crew cheered and hurtled on through the now weakening rain. Storm clouds were clearing and a hint of blue could be seen in the previously monotone grey sky. They passed the gambrel barn where their targets had been holed up during the worst of the weather and continued.

Jenny, Edith and Sam arrived on the outskirts of Bodmin. They had travelled across the desolate moor deserted even by the ponies in the atrocious weather but now the rain had ceased and the declining sun flirted with the diminishing cloud cover that had been blown across the wild heath.

The cart rattled on through the lanes toward the town, which seemed to be particularly busy considering the approaching roads had been so quiet. Crowds filled the street on the grim approach to the sinister granite-built gaol, which stood forbidding and stark in Berrycoombe Lane. Sam halted on Hunter and put his hand up to stop the cart continuing. "There must be a hanging. A mob is gathering around the prison entrance and some are thronging to Five Ways and climbing the hill."

Jenny shivered, "I don't want to witness someone being hung."

"No. It is not a pleasant sight to see someone do the dance of death on the three-legged mare."

"Three- legged mare?" asked Edith puzzled.

"The name given to the gibbet. But we will have a bigger problem."

"What's that?"

"The hotels and guesthouses will be filled with people from outside. They come from miles around to see such a spectacle."

"What about our safe house?"

"It may be compromised. I suggest we push on, bypass the town and make our way to Jamaica Inn."

A poster torn from its mount by the now dying wind flew along their path. Sam dismounted to pick it up. It showed a picture of one, Richard Andrews found guilty of forgery and fraud. The date was clear it was today outside the Southern gate.

The trio continued on their way although the horses were tired. They walked at a quiet pace, avoiding the town and trundled down the road to Bolventor Church.

They met with many jubilant people eager to reach Bodmin in time for the hanging. Sam knew Bodmin would be bursting at the seams. Jenny shuddered, "How can people think a hanging is entertainment? It's beyond me, so it is."

"Some would say he deserved it," said Sam.

"A life for a life is one thing but some are hanged for stealing a loaf of bread to feed their family. That's not justice."

"No, to say it's harsh is true. But how else do we keep people in order? It acts as a deterrent not to do wrong."

"But the spectacle of hanging feeds on the worst characteristics of human nature," said Jenny. "People who do wrong should be punished but each case taken on its own merit. Murder is different. No one has the right to take another's life. I've seen enough of that in my time."

"What do you say, Edith?" asked Sam enjoying the debate.

"Who me?" Edith said blushing a deep crimson.

"Yes, your voice is just as valid in this discussion. Anyway, it helps to pass the time."

"Then, I can tell you that I agree with Miss Jenny. In the Bible it says an eye for an eye and a tooth for a tooth. Murder is different."

"And what about theft?"

Edith shrugged, "It depends. If someone is struggling to look after their family and they are forced into that predicament then they should be helped not punished."

"Fine sentiments," said Sam. "But what about smugglers and those who steal from the Crown?"

Edith dropped her head, "I don't know enough about it, Sir."

Sam nodded, "I understand. It's a rum business. There are those who think it is all right to avoid taxes by bringing in goods for the locals, or to plunder wrecks. But, those who deliberately draw in a merchant ship to founder on rocks in a storm then slit the throats of the surviving crew... what of them?"

"I know not, Sir."

It was then Jenny interrupted, "I know enough of murdering smugglers and thieves to know it is a hard job that you do. I lost my own father to such men and if it hadn't been for Nathaniel and Goliath I, too, would have died."

Silence fell on the threesome with this admission. It seemed there was nothing more to be discussed.

The clouds bowled away across the afternoon sky revealing the warm face of the sun.

Bethell and his crew were tracking across the moor passing stragglers hastening to Bodmin for the hanging. He shouted back, ""Is some poor beef head to dangle in the Sheriff's frame?"

"Aye," replied one. "He's for the deadly nevergreen."

"Anyone I know?" Bethell asked.

"Not an honest thief;" came the reply. "A cheater and a fraudster."

"No one I know then," he guffawed. "It'll be good entertainment to see him dance on the end of a rope."

The man waved his hand and hurried on. Bethell urged his men to press on. "No time to lose. We must catch up with that raven-haired beauty. Once we have her we can control Brookes." He cackled loudly in cruel glee. "And we will have some fun ourselves." His remark was greeted by cheers and whoops from his men.

The afternoon light dwindled into dusk. The earlier rain had freshened the grasses and heathers on the moor. Sam took a big lungful of air, "I love the smell of the countryside after a shower. It fair lifts my spirits."

"Shower?" laughed Jenny. "Storm more like."

"You know what I mean," said Sam. "Everything looks clean and shiny, the raindrops on the grass glistening like crystal treasures, the smell of the earth and that unmistakeable freshness that only comes with the morning dew or after a cloudburst."

"My, my;" said Jenny cheekily. "You are sounding just like a poet, so you are. Like William Hopkin's, Bugeilio'r Gwenith Gwyn."

"What's that?" asked Sam puzzled. "It's a fair mouthful!"

"The English call it, 'Watching the White Wheat'. Oh, it is a lovely song and well known for its tragic love story."

"Then that's a tale you must tell us after supper. I'm sure Edith will enjoy it, too." Edith looked down and blushed much to Sam's amusement. "See, the Inn is just ahead." He pointed along the track and the shape of the hostelry came into view.

Spurred on by the thought of a bed for the night and a decent meal Sam urged Hunter forward and Jenny shook the reins of the horses biting on their bits and salivating for they, too, were tired and hungry.

The inn sign swung in the remnants of the wind that had coursed through the moors and swept up country. Jenny drove the cart into the yard and Sam called for the ostler to take charge of the weary, hungry horses. Sam helped Jenny and Edith down and retrieved their baggage.

The ostler came to take the horses away and the trio stepped to the main door of the tavern and entered. Edith scurried in with her head bowed behind Jenny, as Sam followed.

Men in the bar turned to stare at the new arrivals and eyed up the two women. As soon as they saw the figure of Sam following them they lost interest and returned to their tankards and card games.

Sam strode up to the bar and addressed the landlord, "We require two rooms for the night, and whatever repast you have to offer us."

The landlord grunted and sniffed, "Two rooms you say?"

Sam nodded, "One for me and one for the ladies."

"I'll take payment up front," prompted the landlord.

Sam revealed his money belt and removed some coins, which he passed to the grumpy landlord.

"My daughter will show you up." He shouted to the kitchen, "Mary! Get out here now."

A mousey haired teenager emerged from the kitchen. She shoved the straggling strands of her hair back under her mop cap. She moved quickly in a fluttering fashion and in obedience to her father. "Yes, Papa?"

"Show these travellers to their rooms. He removed two heavy iron keys from behind the bar. Room four for the gent and six for the ladies. Then back to the kitchen to prepare their evening meal."

"Yes, Papa," twittered the youngster. She turned to the guests, "Follow me." She led them to the back of the bar to a wood panelled room, pulled back a heavy brocade curtain and opened the door behind it hiding a twisting staircase. She chirruped as she walked, "Come far, have you? Been a foul day for getting across the moor, I'll be bound. Old Barnabus, his horse almost got stuck in a bog. His own fault really," she chirped. "Horses know a thing or two about the moors and unsafe ground. He didn't want to budge when Barnie spurred him on. Luckily the horse threw him and he landed on the edge of the quagmire. A few steps more and he would have been stuck good and proper." She continued to peep in this manner until they reached the landing and crossed to the letting rooms. "There we are. I'll go and get your supper on. It's beef, gravy and suet pudding with potatoes and carrots. Will that do you?"

The weary trio assented and took the keys from Mary who scurried away. Sam doffed his hat to the ladies, I will knock on your door when I'm settled and we can go downstairs together." Jenny nodded and they each entered their rooms.

Clive Bethell and his band of ruffians urged their horses on excited by the thrill of what they thought was to come. Bethell was convinced that he was close to his quarry. "They will soon be in our sights," he shouted out. Adrenalin filled their veins and all remnants of fatigue disappeared. "Headed for Jamaica Inn I'll bet. Well, Mrs Brookes, my men and I will be joining you." He raised his arm as if charging and the men sniggered fervently in sadistic delight and raced on across the desolate moor.

The moon had risen leaving a looping silver ribbon tract along the stone and grass path. Lanterns from the inn could be seen glowing dimly in the distance. Bethell and his men slowed to a trot as their prospective resting place came into view.

The newly painted sign blew in the softly sighing night breeze and the wind whispered through the trees as Bethell and his crew trotted into the yard. The ostler came out to see the new arrivals and shrank away as he recognised Bethell. Used to such a reception Bethell didn't seem to notice or study the man's face. The ostler kept his head down and away from the gaze of the band of villains.

The men dismounted and tied their horses to a wooden strut next to the stables, leaving them in the ostler's care as they swaggered toward the entrance of the bar. Bethell thrust the reins of his mount to the man, "Tell me have you seen a female traveller with her maid, would have arrived not long before us maybe half an hour or more?"

The ostler didn't speak but shook his head vigorously. Bethell snorted in disgust, "I'd get more sense from a flea." He snapped, "Take care of the horses," and spat on the ground before following his men into the bar. The ostler took Bethell's horse into the stables and shook awake a sleeping boy lying on a bale of straw. "Henry! Wake up. Take this horse and put him in the far stable. Then collect the rest of them tied to the post outside. You will have to deal with this crew and collect the cash due."

"Why, father?" asked the lad.

"It's best you don't know too much but these men are evil. The leader of the vermin hasn't recognised me yet but he will in daylight, of that I'm sure. I'll help you bed the animals down but you must stay with them and see to them in the morning for if he sees me, as sure as my heart beats he'll slit my throat from ear to ear."

The boy shivered. "What'll you do?"

"Once the work is done I'll get back to mother. They don't know you and if any of them ask your name just give them your first name."

"What if they ask my surname?"

"Use your grandmother's maiden name, Pengelly. He won't know her." The boy nodded but was filled with questions. His father silenced him, "As I said the less you know now the better, but once these rogues have gone I'll answer all your queries, I promise."

With that the boy had to be satisfied. He knew when not to press his father and the two concentrated on seeing to the tired horses.

Bethell's crew filled the bar with their raucous laughter and chatter. Their drinking was out of control for all except Bethell who growled a word of warning, "Steady men. We don't need our merriment to overtake our mission."

Two rolled their eyes in disdain whilst another studied his ale before drinking it down in one go, wiping his mouth on his hand and asking the landlord for another as he banged his tankard on the bar. The others looked suitably chastised and dropped their heads shame-facedly before retreating to a corner of the bar with Bethell.

They sat, watched and waited, supping their ale slowly. The other three members of their crew were drinking themselves to oblivion. Bethell snorted and muttered to the others. "They shall be left to their own devices. I want no truck with men that can't obey orders."

"Will there be enough of us?" asked one.

"Ample. We are five, they are but three. If we can separate them out we should be able to get the woman on her own. She's the only one we need."

"How do we know they're here?"

"We don't. Not for definite. I'll ask a few questions and see what I can learn."

As Bethell finished speaking the door at the far end of the bar, which led upstairs opened and two women came in and sat at a quiet table on the other side of the bar. They were soon followed by Sam's tall figure, who joined them and sat.

All the while Bethell observed. He watched carefully straining his ears to hear any conversation or words that passed between them. They spoke in low tones and he was unable to catch anything that was said.

"Which is which?" asked one of his men.

"I don't know," rasped Bethell. "They're both dark and both pretty. It's hard to tell."

Bethell rose and wandered to the far end of the bar under the pretence of ordering food when he saw the landlord's daughter Mary emerge from the kitchen carrying a tray to them. He turned to survey the bar in the hope of catching what was being said but he was unlucky. He placed his order and meandered back to his table.

"Well?" asked a man with crooked teeth.

"Couldn't hear a thing. What's your guess?" replied Bethell.

"They both have lovely apple dumpling shops."

Bethell snorted in derision, "You, you're obsessed with breasts…. And?"

"And why not? But take a closer look I think that one is poisoned. Look at her belly."

"You think she's pregnant?"

"I do. I've a nose for these things."

"Well, there are a lot of young 'uns running around of your doing that's for sure."

"Mind you, Brookes already has one brat. Would they be wanting double trouble so soon?"

"I know not. We'd best find out."

"Or take them both." Bethell rubbed his grizzled chin thoughtfully.

2 7

No Way Out

BETHELL SWIGGED DOWN HIS ale and scraped his chair away from the table. "I'll check on the horses. We need to have them ready to leave at dawn. I'll try and find out when that brood is intending to be off. Get me another ale and order me a meal." He flipped a coin to a bow-legged rogue, who grinned revealing his broken teeth.

Bethell slipped out and made his way to the stables. He spotted the stable boy, "Hey, you, boy! Where's the ostler?"

The ostler recognised Bethell's tones and hid behind the bales of straw.

"Gone home for his tea, I think," said Henry.

"When there's horses to look after?"

"He won't be long," said the boy.

"I dare say. Maybe you can help me…"

"If I can, Sir."

"There's a gent and two ladies staying at the inn. Do you know who they are?" The boy shook his head. "What time have they asked for the horses in the morning?"

"I'm not sure. I think they said after breakfast. I believe the man's called Reeves but don't know the ladies."

Bethell spat into the dirt floor. He heard a rustling at the back of the stables, "Who's back there?"

"No one, Sir. Maybe a rat."

"Sounds like a big rat," said Bethell suspiciously.

The boy's eyes flitted toward the straw. Bethell aware of this feigned disinterest and started for the stable entrance, popping a piece of chewing tobacco into his mouth. "Just make sure our horses are ready to ride at dawn."

"Yes, Sir."

Bethell sauntered forward as if returning to the bar and ducked out of sight along the side of the hostelry to watch. He didn't have long to wait. The figure of the ostler emerged nervously looking anxiously about him. There was something familiar in the man's gait and Bethell narrowed his eyes.

Bethell spat again and came out from hiding walking at a distance as he shadowed the man. As soon as the man was clear of the pub grounds Bethell moved swiftly behind him. "So, Ostler you off for your tea, now? Then, why did the boy lie?"

The ostler froze momentarily before making a run for it. Bethell chased after the man and tackled him to the ground in a flying leap, "Well, well, well. Just who have we here?" He scrambled off the man and rolled him over. The man put his arms up to cover his face. "As I live and breathe, if it isn't Wilfred Tanner. And the lad… is he yours?"

The ostler's breath came in short sharp gasps as he struggled to hold his water. "No, Mr. Bethell, Sir. Just a lad from the village."

"And, are you with my Charlotte? Stole her away from me you did, together with a fat purse of gold, if I remember correctly."

The ostler began to bluster and fuss, his eyes roaming wildly over Bethell's grinning face. Bethell stood and hauled the man to his feet. "That was a long time ago, Wilfred. Water under the bridge now. Best let bygones be bygones, eh?"

Wilfred stood there his head bowed stuttering his thanks.

Bethell's grin turned cruelly evil. He watched the ostler walk away and removed a sharp highly engraved, decorated knife from the scabbard at his belt. He tested the point and satisfied at the sharpness of the blade, which produced fresh blood from his thumb he moved after Wilfred. He waited until his quarry had turned the corner and moved swiftly and stealthily after him.

Before Wilfred could escape, Bethell leapt on his back and drew his blade across Wilfred's throat and rasped in his ear, "That's for taking the woman I loved and stealing my gold."

Wilfred dropped to the ground his body twitching as his life force fled his body. Bethell watched in pitiless satisfaction, as the light in his victim's eyes shrunk to a glazed dull stare. Bethell grabbed the ostler by his arms and dragged him over and behind the drystone wall before covering the fresh corpse with debris and rotting vegetation in an attempt to hide his wicked deed. He vaulted back over the wall and swaggered back along the path carelessly stepping in the pool of sticky congealing blood, his gory footprints betraying his vindictive, merciless slaughter as did the blood spatter staining his front. Bethell spat out his brown tobacco juice, threw back his head and laughed raucously before walking brazenly back inside the inn.

Trooper was hoisted into his willow basket on Jessie and Nathaniel mounted. Goliath, on Samson, waited by the farm entrance to the country lane. They could hear the sound of horses approaching and were pleased to see Molly and Zachary Macaulay trotting toward them. The unlikely quartet travelled the roads, skirting puddles and headed for the main route through Cornwall to Wadebridge. They knew they wouldn't reach the Ship Inn before nightfall unless they spurred their horses on.

Macaulay called out; "I'm not used to this! Reckon I'll need a good long soak when we get to the inn."

Nathaniel laughed as he replied, "I was just as bad when I started riding again... the first week is the worst!"

Conversation dwindled to nothing as they continued their trek to Wadebridge. The evening sun was diminishing into twilight and shadows flourished amongst the trees by the track as they steadily trotted onward. Travelling at the pace set was manageable by the horses when interspersed with breaks of comfortable walking; allowing the animals a breather before setting off at a trot again. They could manage between eight and twelve miles an hour and expected to complete the thirty-mile journey in three hours.

Time marched on and as dusk evaporated into night the muddy, twinkling lights of the town could be seen in the distance as they passed through a number of small villages with their streets deserted.

"How much further?" enquired Molly. "I'm tired, so is my horse."

"As are we all;" answered Zachary.

"Not long now," reassured Nathaniel.

By the time they reached the outskirts of Wadebridge the clock was striking nine. Nathaniel rode on confidently toward the Ship Inn where sounds of merriment could be heard drifting into the street. Governor Macaulay dismounted and sighed in relief as he stretched his body and rubbed his rump. Molly slipped off her mount in similar discomfort and yawned loudly. "I'd give a shilling for a good foot rub and a bath."

Nathaniel grinned, "If you and Governor Macaulay step inside and arrange our rooms Goliath and I will see to the horses. I suggest Molly poses as your daughter, Sir. There will be less questions."

Macaulay acknowledged with a mock salute and extended his arm to Molly. "Come my dear, let us investigate what the inn has to offer." The two walked into the hostelry together.

The following morning, while Sam, Jenny and Edith were having their breakfast, Bethell emerged with his men and sent them to retrieve their now well rested horses. He had ascertained the route that Samuel Reeves and the women were to take and ordered his men to wait at strategic points along the route.

Bethell watched his men ride away and went to take the reins of his own horse from the stable lad. His eyes narrowed, "Hey, lad. Tell me, what's your name?"

The stable lad shivered, "Henry, Sir."

"Henry what?" asked Bethell.

The lad screwed up his face before responding, "Pengelly, Sir."

"Pengelly?"

"Aye, Sir."

"No relation to Wilfred Tanner, then?"

Henry hesitated slightly before answering, "No, Sir. None, Sir."

"And where is Tanner this morning?"

"Don't know, Sir. He didn't come home last night."

"Thought you weren't related?"

"I'm not. I just lodge with them."

"Then you best tell Mrs Tanner that Wilfred won't be back." He guffawed loudly.

The boy looked distressed and tears welled up in his eyes.

Suddenly, there was an ear-splitting scream that reverberated across the moor. One of the kitchen maids came screaming along the track, "Murder! Murder! Help, someone please."

Bethell started nervously, his previous arrogance slipping away. He began to mount his horse, as the kitchen maid yelled, "Tis Wilfred. Wilfred Tanner the ostler. Help, help!"

People inside the inn began to filter outside as the maid raised the alarm. In an act of bravery Henry caught hold of the reins of Bethell's steed. Bethell took his riding crop and began lashing at the boy, who was now yelling, "It's him! It's him. He said he wouldn't be coming back."

Bethell cracked the boy's knuckles hard until he let go of the reins. With that he brought the horse around and galloped out of the yard to shouts of the folks from the inn.

The kitchen maid collapsed on the ground in an outpouring of grief. Her skirt hem was covered in congealed, sticky blood as were her hands. She knelt and wailed. "He's dead, dead."

Henry ran to the maid rubbing his knuckles that were bleeding and sore. "Where? Where? Where's my father?"

She pointed up the path and sobbed, "Over the wall."

Henry sprinted up the stone path and spotted the pool of blood on the ground near the wall. He saw the bloody footprints leading back to Jamaica Inn and leaped over the wall. Feverishly, he dug off the remaining leaf litter and debris from around his father's head. Henry sobbed uncontrollably as he gazed at his father's face now frozen in an expression of horror and the viciously slashed throat.

People staying at the Inn came out with the landlord to see what was happening, among them were Samuel Reeves, Jenny and Edith dressed in their travelling clothes. Jenny looked aghast at the scene as people crowded round to stare.

"This is terrible. Someone should get the law; a murderer is on the loose," said one bystander.

"It would mean going back to Bodmin. Contacting the constabulary," said Jenny.

The folks standing around and shook their heads. No one was prepared to travel to Bodmin and no one wanted to get involved. They muttered under their breath and walked away. Jenny looked at the landlord.

"Don't look at me! I don't want the law out here. It's not good for business."

Henry stepped forward, "I'll go. He's my father."

"And who will tend to the horses?" asked the landlord. "I'd have to get someone else and you could lose your job. Then who would look after you and your mam?"

"That sounds like blackmail;" said Jenny.

"That may be so, but he has to think of his future. What if the swine who did this, then did for him? Then where would his mother be? And her with another mouth to feed."

Jenny looked crestfallen, "I have to admit that I understand what you are saying." She thought for a moment, "Then I'll go." Samuel and Edith protested but she silenced them raising her hand. And turned to Sam, "You go on. Take Edith and I'll meet you later, so I will. Wait for me at the next stop." Jenny turned to Henry, "You have a horse I can hire?"

Henry nodded, "Yes. Come this way."

"Now wait a minute," said Sam. "This is not a good idea. We should not split up. It's too dangerous."

Jenny's eyes flashed, "And it's not safe to have a killer running free to commit more murders. I will be fine. I'll see you at the next stop, as we discussed at breakfast. No arguments. Look after Edith."

Samuel Reeves stamped his foot in annoyance. He knew there was no arguing with Jenny when her mind was made up. "Why don't I go? You and Edith go on."

"Now that would be silly. No man to ride with us. No, I will be quicker and safer on my own. Stick to my plan." Without waiting for any further discussion, she followed Henry to the stables emerging moments later on a striking black stallion. Jenny kicked into the animal's flanks and headed back the way they had come. Fortunately, it was a better day and Jenny hoped she would be able to travel the ten miles to Bodmin without a hitch. She waved goodbye and set off back along the track through the moor.

Edith looked anxiously at Sam, "Do you think she will be all right?"

"I hope so," he said grimly. "Nathaniel would never forgive me if anything happened to her. But, I know she is a strong-willed woman. Nathaniel has said so on many occasions. She is not someone to be ruled by others. Come on. We'd best get on our way. Jenny will be a day behind us now. I hope she will be able to change her horse in Bodmin."

Sam and Edith returned to the inn to fetch their bags. They settled up with the landlord and waited for Henry to bring out the horses and cart. The day looked friendly enough with the warm, smiling face of the sun and the few trees beckoning gently in the soft breeze. The air smelt fresh with dew but Edith shivered.

"I can't get the image of that poor man out of my mind. What a terrible way to die;" she observed.

"I've seen worse," said Sam. "At least he died quickly. He didn't suffer like some."

"I don't know how you can live with the memories. If I saw everything you've witnessed I would be a screaming wreck."

Sam smiled at Edith, "You have a good heart, I'll grant you that," and Edith smiled shyly.

They travelled along the track in silence leaving the inn behind them. Pheasants flew from the hedgerows and cried in alarm as rumbling cartwheels disturbed them from their foraging. The morning sun smiled down but behind its benevolent smile was something else. The air was unnervingly still after the ravages of the previous day's storm. The trees stood strongly defiant as if in silent judgement of all they had witnessed through the centuries and although the top notes of the air were sweetly fragrant and fresh, there was an underlining odour of horses, which mingled with old leather and men's sweat that crept up Sam's nostrils putting him on his guard.

Ahead he could see the moorland seeping into woodland and an uneasy serpentine twisting began to coil and writhe in his stomach. He could feel his hearty breakfast rising in his throat and he didn't know why. His eyes shifted about as they searched for some hidden danger or threat.

Jenny had eventually reached Bodmin. She had marched into the local constabulary reporting what she had witnessed and seen at Jamaica Inn.

The lean, miserable looking red-cheeked constable on duty looked at her suspiciously. "And what might you be doing at the inn, a single woman on her own, Miss...?"

"Brookes, Mrs Brookes." She emphasised the word Mrs, before continuing, "I was not alone, I was with some travelling companions."

"And they are... where?"

"I left them to come here. I will catch up with them at the next stop."

The constable, a thin ferret faced man, with a drooping moustache and red thread veined cheeks, sniffed imperiously in disapproval. "Women travelling alone around here. It's not safe. Especially near that inn. We get some unsavoury characters around there."

"It seemed fine to us. It is relatively new and they looked after us well."

"Then you're one of the lucky ones." He sniffed again. "Rumour has it a gang of cutthroats are headed that way. Smugglers and slavers, I heard."

"Well, I didn't see anyone like that but there again I wasn't looking. But if what you are saying is true then maybe they are responsible for that poor man's death, so they are."

"It was the ostler, you say?" Jenny nodded. "Pity, Wilfred Tanner was a good sort, leaves a loving wife and family. Who'll look after them now? And what could poor Wilf have done to warrant such a foul and bloody act?"

Jenny shook her head, "I know not. Now, I'd best be on my way. I've done my duty."

The constable's demeanour changed rapidly and his expression became more accommodating, "If you hold on a minute, Miss... er.. Madame. I expect you'll be needing to change your horse. I'll take you to Austin Richards. He's the chap in business with the inn. I'll come back with you. At least you won't be riding alone."

Jenny hesitated before smiling broadly, "Why thank you, Constable ....?"

"Ley, Ma'am. Brookes you say? No relation to Riding Officer Brookes?"

"You've heard of him?"

The policeman nodded, "Who hasn't? Made quite a name for himself, he has. Him and his man, Friday."

"You mean Goliath?"

"Is that his name? I can see why. Thundering great man. You related?"

"I'm Nathaniel's wife."

"In that case I most definitely will accompany you as far as the inn, where we can begin our investigations." He called through a door, "Tom, you come with me and Basil, you can come and man the desk."

A jovial looking man with a balding head came through from the back of the building. "Right you are, Edward." He beamed at Jenny, "Ma'am," and went behind the desk.

Jenny smiled back and another younger policeman came through buttoning his coat. "Coming!"

"Right. Let's get going, we need to get horses," ordered Ley as he followed Jenny out of the door. "Don't forget to lock up safely tonight, Basil for we won't be back in time."

They walked out into the midday sunshine just as a cloud eclipsed its warmth. Jenny looked up and watched a buzzard circle overhead, which was being chased and bullied by two crows that cawed threateningly. Jenny wiped her hand across her brow. She felt more than uneasy. It was a feeling she just couldn't shake off.

28

Dangerous Liaisons

NATHANIEL AND GOLIATH HAD settled comfortably into their rooms. Trooper, as always, refused to leave Nathaniel's side. He lay at his feet but his ears were pricked and he was alert. They awaited the arrival of Molly and the Governor to join them for dinner and to set their future travelling plans.

In the corner of the bar were a group of odd-looking men playing cards and Trooper watched them carefully. The door opened and a familiar hulking figure lumbered in to sit with the men. Trooper growled softly in his throat.

"Well, I never," murmured Goliath. "Harry Babb as I live and breathe."

"Nathaniel glanced across at the new arrival, "A little away from his usual territory, isn't he?"

"I wonder why…?"

The two officers tried to watch and listen without attracting too much attention, but the men kept their voices low and hushed. Their faces were in profile so it was difficult to see their lips, which would have helped the officers decipher some of what was being said.

Nathaniel and Goliath were interrupted by the arrival of Molly and Governor Macaulay. "Is something wrong?" asked the Governor.

Nathaniel kept his voice low, "Just those men over there… We know a couple…"

"Involved in the slave trade," added Goliath. "We can't hear what they're saying. It can't be good."

"Perhaps, I can help?" said Molly as she studied the men before she ducked her head down. "But, no! I recognise one. He mustn't see me… if he does, he'll tell Richard. I can't take that risk. I'm going back to my room."

"What about your supper?"

"I'll take it upstairs. Tell them I have a headache." She rose quickly from the table and turned away bowing her head.

One ruffian, Abel Swinton, who was sitting at the table looked up and glanced her way. He rubbed his grizzled chin, a puzzled expression on his face, which turned to one of knowing and he gave a barely perceptible nod.

He turned to Harry Babb, "If I'm not mistaken, that's Sir Richard's doxy. What's her name?" Harry shrugged and shook his head. "No matter, it will come to me." He snapped his fingers, "Molly, Molly Grice as I live and breathe. How interesting. What would she be doing with Riding Officers and the gentry?" he furrowed his brow as he thought some more. "I take it you don't know the whore?"

Babb shook his head, "Not me. But, she's a pretty wench. Do you think she's here on Gosling's bidding?"

"Checking up on us you mean? I very much doubt it. I believe she has other things on her mind. Maybe you could rekindle your acquaintanceship with Brookes and his man."

"Why would I do that?"

"See what you could learn. Perhaps you could offer them some titbit of information; something not too damaging that would win their confidence, find out what she's up to. I'll make it worth your while." He laughed raucously, "They probably will pay you, too."

"What? What would I tell them?"

"Tell them... tell them, you know where there's a stash of contraband stored. Something the King's men can't ignore."

"But, I don't know of any such place."

"No. But I will tell you after we've moved the most valuable items, of course. That should be enough to win them across, especially if they think you've been fingered as a traitor. Why, they may even let you ride with them and be your saviour." The ruffian laughed uproariously. "This could be very good for us indeed, very good."

Harry Babb looked totally confused and scratched his ear uncertain where this conversation was headed. The two men huddled together talking in low tones, not wishing to attract any more attention than necessary.

Jenny and the constable rode back to the Inn where the body of the Ostler still lay on the ground although the landlord and Henry had covered him with a blanket and put a pillow under his head. The constable checked his pulse. He was definitely dead.

"I'll be needing witness statements from those that are here. Best take this inside and I will need a wagon to remove the body and take it to the undertakers."

Henry nodded, "I can help you with that. And anything else you need to know. We are almost certain we know who's responsible."

The constable frowned, "We have to be certain and not just make a random guess;" he said sternly.

Charlotte, Henry's mother, red-eyed from weeping spoke up in a tremulous voice, "Oh, we know all right. It is that swine Bethell who made my life a misery with his controlling, cruel ways. Always free with his fists I suffered too many black eyes. It was my Wilfred that saved me from him, a kinder man you couldn't wish to meet. And now he's gone." She began to weep again. "You can write in your book that it was Clive Bethell, rogue, smuggler, thief, slaver and now he can add murder to his misdeeds."

Jenny bit her lip knowing exactly the sort of man Charlotte Tanner was talking about. She had experienced first-hand the cruelty to herself and her father from smuggling cutthroats.

Jenny ventured toward the constable, Edward Ley; "You have heard all I had to say. There is nothing new or more that I can remember. Do I have your permission to continue my journey?"

Edward inclined his head, "Of course, Mrs Brookes. Please do. But are you sure you will be safe riding by yourself? With murderers and robbers in the area I do not like the thought of you travelling alone."

The landlord stepped forward and interrupted, "I agree. Knowing those miscreants, as I do, I feel you'd be safer with company."

Edward nodded, "Are you offering?"

"Well, I can't leave the inn but my wife's cousin has to travel to Liskeard later today. He would ride with you, I'm sure. There should be room at The Crow's Nest Inn for you to stop off."

Jenny was not so foolish as to turn down the offer of a riding companion and said so. The landlord took her back inside to wait for the man who would travel with her.

Sam and Edith were halfway through the thick woodland. All the while Sam tried to keep his wits about him, constantly on the alert for any movement in the trees. His horse, Hunter, could sense his master's tension and trod his way warily across the stony track, his ears pricked.

Farther ahead, Bethell and his thuggish band were lying in wait. They had hidden amongst the trees and had the path covered from both sides. Bethell carefully removed his flintlock pistol from his belt and waited hardly daring to breathe.

The cartwheels rumbled closer when Hunter sensitive to the smell of other horses and the sweat of man became skittish. He reared up on his hind legs and whinnied loudly. Sam tried to calm him when from the forest five men burst onto the path. Bethell fired and nicked Sam in the shoulder and his horse bolted. There was nothing he could do.

The ruffians leapt aboard the wagon, snatched the reins of the horses and Edith was grabbed by the waist and pulled from her seat. She screamed shrilly, was struck across the face before being thrown over the back of a horse.

The men searched the wagon for Jenny, who was nowhere to be seen but never-the-less delighted with their prize they rode off down the path. Three riders went after Sam while the others took the wagon and veered off the track toward St. Cleer.

Sam sped away on Hunter who galloped as if his life depended on it. He travelled back down the track and careered off into the woodland. Such was Sam's riding skills he evaded low branches and managed to weave his way through the forest path and out onto moorland, where he followed an old bridle path, which led back to the road. Once there he decided to return to the Inn. He had to warn Jenny and report Edith's abduction and the theft of the wagon and horses.

Anger filled him that brutes such as these would prey on such an innocent, sweet young woman. He determined he would find her and rescue her from the ensuing danger, but knew he would need help.

Sam ploughed on not knowing whether the ruffians were still in pursuit. He glanced back over his shoulder but could see no one. Little did he know that his evasion tactics had worked and two of the thugs had been knocked off their mounts by low branches. The third had slowed and he could only manage to pick his way along the leaf littered path. Sam was now well ahead and he believed the miscreants had little hope of catching up with him.

Jenny was resting uneasily upstairs in Jamaica Inn. She knew her travelling companion was expected within the hour and decided to go back downstairs. Her thoughts were running riot making her feel nervous and jumpy. She made her way to the bar and was surprised when she saw Sam propping up the counter with a tankard of ale in his hand. He slammed down the pewter mug and strode toward Jenny in a distressed state.

Jenny took one look at his anguished face and was immediately on the alert, "Whatever has happened? Sam?"

Sam stared intently at her before bursting out with his story. Jenny's face turned white as he explained the ambush and what had occurred. "Believe me, Mrs Brookes … Jenny. There was nothing I could do. I was just one man against five and I was lucky to escape."

"No one blames you, Sam. I know the likes of these vermin. They were after me, I know it and now, poor Edith is taken. I fear for her life and sanity. We must make plans to rescue her."

"But, how? We don't know where they took her and we will need help."

"I will try to get word to my brother-in-law, Captain Philip Chapman. He will have men at his disposal. He has helped Nathaniel in the past. I know he is somewhere in the South West. Or maybe the landlord or his cousin will help point us in the direction of a military camp. They would be forced to help us." Jenny's hand fingered her throat. "We must try and contact Nathaniel and Goliath."

"But, we have no idea where Nathaniel is, either." He hung his head, "It's a mess and it's all my fault."

"Come, come, Sam don't be so defeatist. There must be something we can do. We need to think like them and form a plan."

Sam took a long draught of his ale and sunk into a seat by the bar. Jenny's eyes gleamed, "I have an idea."

Nathaniel and his party of travellers had escaped the attentions of Harry Babb and friends. The rogue's attempts at 'friendly' conversation had been ignored. Nathaniel was keen to move on quickly leaving the motley crew behind who had been thwarted in their intentions. They had moved on safely and were now in the area of Boscastle. They made their way to the sixteenth century Napoleon Inn in the high street. They sat in the bar and studied their maps for the quickest route to Richard Gosling's Manor.

Trooper sat faithfully at Nathaniel's feet and waited for him to pet and smooth him down. He rewarded Nathaniel by lovingly licking his hand. Governor Macaulay traced his finger across the proposed route, "How long do you think it will take us to get there?"

"Once rested up, I would say, we have three days riding ahead of us," said Nathaniel.

"As long as we travel at a trot interspersed with periods of walking, yes, that is possible," agreed Goliath folding up the map.

The bar door opened and a group of strong looking young men entered. One spotted Nathaniel and Goliath and he nudged another of the men, who looked surprised. They whispered between themselves before settling across the bar ensuring they could see Nathaniel and his companions.

Goliath kept a wary eye on the men. He had a talent for lip reading learnt from his days on the slaver and without scrutinising them too closely he was able to pick up something of what was being said.

"Don't look now but they are talking about us. They know who we are."

Nathaniel took a swig of his drink and peered over the top of his mug. "My, my, word spreads fast in this part of the world. No sooner do we leave one band of rogues behind than there is another to take their place. What are they saying?"

"Something about a price on our heads and about Jenny."

Nathaniel looked up sharply, "Jenny?"

"They've turned away. I can't see their lips now."

"Well, keep looking, in case you can pick up anything else."

Goliath nodded and kept a discreet eye on the thugs.

Jenny and Sam had left Jamaica Inn and were on the road that would take them to the nearest military stronghold. They were pushing their horses to the limits to try and get there before nightfall.

Conversation was impossible. Their words were lost in the wind. All Jenny could hear was the thunder of the horses' hooves and their panting breaths, see their nostrils streaming and huffing with a smoke like vapour in the cooling air and hear her own pounding heart.

Sam slowed Hunter to a walk and Jenny stopped cantering to come alongside him. Hardly catching her breath, she managed to gulp out, "Why have we stopped?"

"The horses need rest and we are nearing the coastal camp at Bude. I only hope the landlord's cousin was right, Jenny."

"He was. He mentioned him by name. He said the captain had moved there from Penzance. There can't be two with the same name. It has to be where Captain Philip Chapman is currently based. I am sure of it. I feel it. He will help, I know he will."

"Then, let's get to it." Sam dismounted and allowed Hunter to nibble at some grass on the verge of the track they were following and removed a map from his saddlebag. He spread it out as best he could in the surging breeze coming off the sea. Jenny, jumped off her mount and held onto the fluttering map for Sam to trace his finger along the route they would take.

"Where are we?" asked Jenny.

Sam tapped the weathered map, "By my reckoning we are here."

"So, how long?"

"We will have to walk. If we lead them we should be there inside the hour."

"They need water."

"There are two small rivers." Sam pointed at the map again. "The rivers Neet & Strat. These two watercourses rise from the farmlands of North Cornwall before meeting at Marhamchurch, then flowing northwards, over Summerleaze beach and into the sea. We can pause there for them to drink, unless we find some clean ditch water on the way."

Jenny nodded as she patted her horse, steaming with sweat from the hard ride. "These animals have done us proud. We must have already travelled some thirty miles."

"More than is expected that is certain. They deserve a rest," said Sam. "Come on. Let's get them to water."

A terrified Edith sat silent and still next to the commandeered wagon in a temporary camp on Bodmin Moor. She dared not move or speak for fear of attracting attention. She had suffered the rough pawing and mauling of smugglers' hands on her body and was steeling herself for much worse. For the moment, they would leave her alone but as soon as they reached the next village where some of the men resided, she knew her purity would be savagely tarnished. The thought of what they threatened to do to her, filled her with horror.

She kept her eyes and ears open and tried to listen to the ruffians who had been joined by more thugs at the safe house. She heard their future plans and knew they were eventually headed for the public houses in Boscastle where they had previously gathered. Boscastle was a wrecker's paradise. Many merchant ships passed that way and the men were adept at drawing them into the notoriously craggy bay with its dangerous rocks, when the weather and night skies would mask their cruel deeds. It was now time for them to return. But, first they were to travel to another house on the moor and await instructions.

Clive Bethell had warned his men off Edith temporarily. Her wrists were bound behind her back and a filthy rag had been shoved in her mouth and tied. But it seemed some of the thugs were not in the mood to listen to orders.

Bethell took a hefty swig of rum as he sat by the peat fuelled camp fire. He allowed his eyes to roam over Edith's young firm body with its pert breasts and wasp waist. Her hair had come loose from her bonnet and was draped alluringly over her shoulders and her milk white skin looked soft and inviting. Bethell imagined what he was going to do to her, once he could claim Jenny Brookes in her place, or better still have Nathaniel's head on a platter like a sacrificial John the Baptist. His mind filled with torrid images and in his opinion, he was to be the first to sample this maid. After that his men could take their turn. Their needs would have to be satisfied but not before he had had his fill.

Bethell took another long draught. The rum both warmed and burnt his throat. He wiped his mouth on his sleeve as a dribble of spittle hung on his lips. He groaned pleasurably as his fantasies about Edith filled his mind and he felt a stirring twitch. His mental ramblings stopped abruptly as one of his men, Abe Newton, tottered drunkenly to where Edith sat in fear. He almost fell down beside her as he towered over her leering lewdly. He eased himself down beside her and began to unbutton her bodice.

Edith tried to scream but the gag muffled the small sounds she was able to make. She squirmed and wriggled away from his probing fingers and scrambled up beside the wagon. Bethell was having none of it. He roared Abe's name and yelled, "Hands off her!"

Abe turned with a snort of derision. "You said she was for us! I want my piece of her, now."

Bethell stood up and drew himself up to his full height. He corked his rum and set it down. "I said, leave her be."

"Why? What's the difference, whether it's here or there?" snarled Abe challengingly.

"She's collateral. Our security to get what we want. We await our orders from Tobias. We need Brookes and his man off our backs. She's our bargaining chip."

Abe rose swaying ominously and spat on the ground. "I say, she's ours and I want mine, now."

Bethell drew his musket and aimed at the drunken sot. "Don't make me fire Abe. I don't want to lose a good man but I will shoot if I have to."

By now the other ruffians had all eyes glued to the unfolding scene, watching with interest as to who would win this battle of wills.

Abe glared at Bethell, who believed his man was going to give way and stop his lecherous advances but Abe threw up his arms in disdain and stumbled back down to continue pawing at Edith.

Bethell warned the rogue once more, "Move away, Abe or…"

Abe staggered up again, "Or you'll what?"

"It's the drink talking," said Bethell trying to placate the man, who it seemed was having none of it as he started to unlace his breeches. He gave Edith a push, her bonnet flew off under the cart and he thrust her on her back, lifted her skirts ready to fall upon her, when the shot rang out. Abe's bellow died on his lips as he tumbled forward and landed on the terrified maid. She struggled to crawl out from underneath him. Bethell hauled Abe's body off Edith and he pushed it away with his booted foot before turning to his motley crew.

"Let that be a lesson to all of you. The woman is not to be touched until I say so. Understood?"

Bethell's words and what they had just witnessed was more sobering than anything else. They backed off and returned silently to sitting around the fire. Bethell rasped at two of his men, "Parker, Trevelyan get rid of Abe's body, now." The thugs hurried across to Abe's lifeless body and each took an arm and dragged him off toward the peat bog that was on the moor and threw the man into it. They watched and waited until the corpse finally sank into the murky sludge and disappeared.

When they returned the mood of frivolity had truly broken. The gang turned in for the night and Bethell attended to Edith whose face was white with shock and fear. He helped her to her feet and lifted her into the back of the wagon, leaving her traumatised and quaking with dread.

Nothing more was said that night. The only sounds to be heard were the men snoring and the unworldly call of the nightjars as they foraged for moths and insects under the cover of darkness.

29

Aleka's trials

ALEKA HAD BEEN SUMMONED to the drawing room in the manor where Richard Gosling was entertaining the parson, Patrick Hamilton. He was not Richard's favourite companion of choice. In truth he disliked the man intensely for his cruel and savage treatment of women.

"So, have you thought anymore about my proposition? Regarding Alice?"

"I have told you, she is not for sale. Not yet."

"Methinks, you might change your mind when you hear my news."

Richard turned away from the drinks table where he was pouring the reverend a large glass of port. He raised one eyebrow quizzically, "And pray what might that be?"

"Rumour has it that men are on their way from the West Country to retrieve the woman. Some say they have your name and are coming for you. The wench is indeed someone of note. A Governor's daughter, they say."

"Do they now? And pray just where did you get this information?" replied Richard.

The parson was tight lipped. It seemed to amuse him that he possessed more knowledge than Sir Richard. He finally responded with a trite, "Oh, ways and means, ways and means."

Sir Richard passed the drink to the parson sitting comfortably on a beautifully upholstered plum velvet Georgian chair. "Many rumours abound and I am sure that this is merely another." Sir Richard was dismissive in his response.

"Have you not questioned her education? Her refinement? She is a cut above the rest of those you bring back from Africa and the West Indies."

"I know what she has claimed but…"

"Don't doubt it. Dare you take the risk?"

"Just what are you saying?"

"Forget your three months. And your promise to the wench. Sell her to me. She will disappear without a trace." A cruel gleam had lit in the parson's eye.

Richard tusselled with his feelings and the reverend's words. It was clear from his expression that he found the parson's suggestion distasteful. He paused reflectively.

"Reverend, I thank you for your offer but in spite of the business I am involved in I do keep my word. I shall ensure Alice is well hidden should we be surprised by any unwelcome visitors."

The parson's facial expression changed to one of cold anger. He tipped back his drink and stood as there was a knock on the door.

"Enter," called Richard.

Aleka opened the door and Richard held back a gasp at her elegance and beauty. She was truly majestic in stature.

"You sent for me?" Her tone was cultured and refined.

"Yes, the reverend here is looking to buy you. But I have told him there is to be no sale as I keep my promises. What say you?"

Aleka bristled at the suggestion, "I have told you I am a free woman. I am also married." She glanced at the parson who stood there ogling her and shuddered. "If I may be so bold, if the reverend was to take me I cannot guarantee his manhood would remain intact."

The parson crossed to her and took her chin between his fingers, "Insolent wench. Threaten me, would you?" He dealt her a stinging blow and pushed her away.

Aleka fell back. Her cheek bearing the mark of his hand. Richard stepped forward and intervened. "You have your answer, Reverend Hamilton and now I suggest you leave."

The parson grabbed his hat and strode to the door, "You will regret this, Sir Richard." He turned back and cast a lustful eye on Aleka, "And you, madam will discover what it is to be a slave. I promise you that." He flung open the door and left.

Sir Richard stepped toward Aleka, "You see what other men are like? I cannot protect you forever. You will have to submit to my will or be let loose for someone else to break your spirit."

Aleka paused before regaining her full composure, "If you think that this exchange would endear you to me then you are sadly mistaken. I am no man's property. I am my own woman. And by my reckoning I still have three weeks left before you receive your answer."

Sir Richard nodded, "Yes, my dear, you are correct. I still have time to win you over. Now, I pray you, come with me."

"But I have a reading lesson with Deborah."

"That can wait." Richard turned to the door as his mother entered the room.

"Richard, my dear, what is this I hear about you refusing a sale from the Reverend Hamilton?"

"It's true. We can discuss it later." Sir Richard's tone was brusque and his mother turned a cursory eye on Aleka.

"I cannot have you ruining the business in this way. You will send for the reverend and tell him he can have the woman. She will be more trouble than she's worth. You need to knock these silly notions out of your head. If you don't recall him. Then I will."

Sir Richard looked aghast at his mother and pleaded, "Mother, please. We will discuss this later as I promised. Alice will be more use to us than to be sold on."

"The parson is offering a lot of money. It is not to be discounted."

"Yes, and how long will she live in his care? It is a waste when we can use her to do much good in the community."

"And maybe warm your bed," she said wryly, before turning away disdainfully.

Richard bit back the retort ready to spring to his tongue. He took Aleka's arm, which she didn't shake off. "Come with me. Come with me now if you want to save your skin."

Aleka then disentangled herself from his protective grasp, "I can walk well enough myself. Thank you." But Richard insisted on steering her out of the door and to the back stairs.

"This way, there is not much time. If I know my mother she will have that fiend back in a flash. This is the only way. Trust me."

Aleka didn't need reminding and allowed herself to be propelled down the stairs to the cellars and basement. The smell below was uninviting and earthy and the stone steps and floor were permeated with dampness. They entered a store of a type with old furniture and other cast aside items. Richard lit one of the stout candles that graced a shelf. He moved to the back of the subterranean room and felt along the wall before finding a protuberance, which he pressed. There was a grinding noise of rock against stone that clearly hadn't been touched for years. A portion of the wall opened noisily to reveal an underground room.

"Here, you'll be safe. Few know of its existence, not even my mother. I found it by accident when playing as a child. Here you can hide until the danger is past."

Aleka stepped into the cold damp space. Richard rescued a dilapidated chair and some sackcloth from the pile of stacked curios in the anti-room along with a pair of thick motheaten velvet curtains. He placed them in the room and grabbed a candelabra with half spent candles. "Only light them one at a time when needed. Here." He passed her his tinderbox with spills and flint. "You know how to use this?"

Aleka nodded, "Yes, I have used something similar at home."

"I will return when I can, but stay out of sight and if you hear any sounds out here; ignore them. We don't want you getting caught."

"But…"

"No buts. I will bring you something to pass the time away and some warm clothing as soon as I am able. Now, not a word. If I know my mother, Reverend Hamilton will be returning very soon, expecting to claim you as his prize."

Aleka knew not to argue. She did not want to be trafficked to the hideously cruel man, so she remained quiet and allowed herself to be closeted into this gloomy, dismal room. She settled herself on the rickety chair and waited. She did not have to wait long.

Lady Sarah Gosling had indeed caught up with the parson and made a private deal. She went to the wing where Aleka slept and examined her room. She was followed throughout her search by the now extremely irate parson. Lady Gosling descended the stairs calling for her son before disappearing to the kitchen where the cook and Deborah were at work and demanded, "Alice… where is she?"

The cook apologised profusely and Deborah shook her head. "She was summoned to see the young master," stuttered Deborah.

"And, where is he?" Lady Gosling roared.

Receiving no satisfactory answer, she flounced out of the kitchen and called her footman and other workers to search the house. Lady Gosling descended into the cellar and stared around the murky chamber. No matter where they went or looked there was no sign of Aleka or indeed her son, Richard.

Lady Gosling thrust the purse of gold she had taken from the parson back at him. "I am sorry, Reverend. I have no idea where my son has taken the woman; probably to one of the local hostelries, I'll be bound. Rest assured that when I find him and her I will complete our deal.

The reverend bowed and took his leave while Lady Gosling shook with fury at the actions of her reprobate son.

Parson Hamilton got onto the seat of his horse and trap and spurred the horse toward his home. He was travelling on a narrow track when he was met by four on horseback. He pulled up his animal to allow them to pass when he spotted Goliath on Samson. He hastily surmised who they were and who they had come for and decided to make some mischief for the Goslings, which he thought, would put them in their place.

"Good day, Sirs, and Madam," said the parson effusively polite. "May I ask which way you are headed?"

"Nathaniel deferentially touched his hat, "Good day to you, too. Are we on the right road to the manor of Sir Richard Gosling?"

Trooper sitting in his basket growled in alarm.

Ignoring the dog, the parson continued, "Indeed, you are, Sir. Are you looking for anyone in particular?"

Goliath threw back his hood. "Yes, my wife," replied Goliath.

"Who is also my daughter," added Governor Macaulay.

The parson rubbed his chin, "I see. Rumour has it that there is a woman incarcerated there, a female slave. Would that be her?"

"Quite possibly. Thank you."

"Not at all," grinned the parson. "Good luck." He urged his horse on as Trooper let out a bark of warning as the group cantered past to the brow of the hill when he let out a roar of laughter. 'How amusing,' he thought. This would be something to tell his likeminded friends. He hoped Gosling got what he deserved.

Nathaniel and his party had travelled many miles toward Sir Richard Gosling's manor unaware that word of their travels had reached the ears of the traders and the element of surprise had been taken from them. The news imparted by the reverend was welcomed and they hurried on. Only Molly slowed and held back. The Governor stopped until she came alongside. "That man, he didn't recognise me. He is a foul brute, a wicked man who betrays his cloth. And the cross"

"You know him?"

Molly snorted, "A man free with his fists when he wants his pleasure. I have heard most women he buys end up dead. Come on." She kicked her horse's flanks and galloped to catch up with Nathaniel and Goliath.

They reduced to a trot as they approached the long path and carriageway that led to the Manor, before pulling up outside the impressive entrance. They were startled by a number of servants racing around the outside of the building with calls of "Miss Alice."

Governor Macaulay dismounted, "Leave this to me." He strode somewhat painfully, after his long ride, to the heavy carved wooden doors and used the bell pull. Nathaniel slipped off Jessie and stopped one of the young men running around outside.

"Tell me young sir, what is amiss?"

"One of our maidservants is missing. Milady has sent us all to find her."

"And her name is Alice?"

"Yes, Sir."

Nathaniel let the lad go who ran around the back of the Manor. As he did so the heavily ornate door opened and Lady Gosling stood there looking harassed.

"Yes? Can I help you?"

"I sincerely hope so," gushed Governor Macaulay. "Let me introduce myself, I am Governor Zachary Macaulay and I am in search of my daughter."

"I'm sorry," said Lady Gosling. "I know nothing of your daughter."

Goliath dismounted to stand shoulder to shoulder with the Governor. Lady Gosling's eyes filled with shock and horror as she took in Goliath's muscled bulk and huge stature. "If you please, the lady who was stolen from her home is my wife."

Lady Gosling was completely taken aback and attempted to change tack. "Why don't you come in and we can discuss this further? Stolen you say? How shocking. Step this way"

The four secured their horses, which glad of the rest began nibbling some grass by the lake that ran adjacent to the property. Molly tugged at Nathaniel's sleeve as he removed Trooper from the basket.

"That's Lady Gosling. She's not to be trusted. Rumour has it she's the head of all this murky business."

The four weary travellers followed her ladyship into the drawing room, where they were invited to sit. Lady Gosling rang the bell to summon Deborah.

"Deborah, some tea and refreshments for our travellers, if you please." She looked disagreeably at Trooper who sat close to Nathaniel's feet. "And a bowl of water for the dog." She forced a smile and studied the people before her.

Nathaniel's attention was caught as he heard the name, Deborah and he wondered how he could get the girl alone to speak with her. From what he had learned previously he hoped it might be the missing girl from Boscastle.

Lady Gosling continued scrutinising each of them in turn and a flicker of alarm entered her eyes when she saw Molly. She couldn't be certain as this female looked half respectable but the woman bore a strong resemblance to her son's doxy.

"Have I seen you somewhere before miss…er…?"

"Grice. Molly Grice. I am Ethel Grice's daughter."

"Ethel…?" said Lady Gosling vaguely.

"Your cook."

"Ah, then that must be it. I knew you looked familiar."

"Well, Gentlemen, I don't see how I could possibly help you."

"Please bear with us, Milady;" continued Macaulay as he attempted to flatter and cajole her. "I am sure you have nothing to do with this infamous deed. After all it was slavers that abducted her from her home and brought her to this country. Ruffians that have led us a merry dance but have led us here. Is it possible that someone in your employ could have hidden her away somewhere. After all, this house is very well proportioned. Could someone have abused your hospitality and secreted someone here without your knowledge?"

Lady Gosling's cheeks began to turn pink and she rose and walked to the window, as if to look out. "My, it's warm in here," she exclaimed. She turned back to the Governor, "Why, Sir, anything is possible. I am away a great deal so something could have happened in my absence, I suppose."

"Then, would you allow us to look around your property? Just in case? I'm sure that you are innocent of any wrongdoing and would not object to us satisfying ourselves of the fact and then you will not be troubled by us again."

If Lady Gosling was flustered she didn't show it. The door opened and Deborah entered with a trolley of tea items and set them down.

She placed a bowl of water at Nathaniel's feet. Trooper lapped greedily and gratefully. Lady Gosling grimaced at the noise and the water that dripped from the mutt's mouth but she hastily changed her expression into a smile.

"Deborah, would you open the window a fraction. It is a trifle warm in here."

"Yes, Milady."

Deborah dutifully curtseyed and tried to do as she was bid.

Nathaniel rose to help the young maid who was struggling with the window catch. "Here, let me." He smiled gently before whispering to her, "Are you Deborah Wheelan from Boscastle?"

Deborah started in surprise and her hand flew to her mouth. It gave Nathaniel the answer he needed. "There we go, the latch just needed a little more force;" he said as the sash was pushed up allowing the summer air to enter.

Trooper padded across to his master and put his paws on the sill to look out of the window. He gave a small woof as he watched an invading rabbit hop onto the lawn outside.

Nathaniel called him back. Dutifully the collie returned to his master's feet.

"So, Lady Gosling, do we have your permission to look around the manor?"

Lady Gosling, appeared to consider her options and concluded after a small pause, "Why not? If you do find anything I will have whoever's responsible horse whipped." She smiled dazzlingly at them. "Please, Deborah show these gentlemen back into the hall." She turned to Molly, "And I dare say you will want to see your mother? You may go to the kitchen. You know where it is."

The group left the drawing room. The agreeable smile left Lady Gosling's face and turned into a snarl of fury. She could hardly suppress an angry shout. But knew now was not the time. She rang her call bell and one of her male servants came rushing in. "Follow them and watch them. Report back to me. Keep your ears and eyes open. Do you understand?"

3 0

The Search

NATHANIEL WAS QUICK TO move, he addressed Deborah. "I am a friend of your parents. I promised that if I found you I would return you to their care."

Deborah's eyes filled with tears of gratitude. "But, they'll find me again and bring me back. I know they will."

"No, they won't. You have my word. Now, where are we likely to find Aleka?"

"Aleka? You mean Alice? I can take you to her bedroom."

"That's a start."

They followed Deborah to the back stairs. Nathaniel turned to Governor Macaulay, "I'm sure Lady Gosling has sent someone to follow us. Perhaps you could distract him and get him to show you the rooms down stairs. That will give us more of a free hand in our search with Deborah."

Zachary Macaulay nodded in agreement, "Of course. I'll tell the young man that we have split up to take less time." Zachary pretended to attend to his boots and waited for the young servant to catch up with him, while Nathaniel and Goliath hurried after Deborah.

She led them to a small attic room, "There. That's where Alice sleeps and where she teaches me to read."

"She's teaching you?" said Goliath.

Deborah nodded, "I couldn't read a word until she began to help me." She knocked lightly on the door, "Miss Alice?"

There was no answer, so Goliath tried the door and entered the room followed by Trooper and Nathaniel.

Goliath stared around the neatly ordered room. He saw her brightly coloured beads that she used to braid her hair and picked up some hand written notes. "This is Aleka's writing. The girl is telling the truth. Now what?"

"I have an idea," said Nathaniel. He opened a drawer containing clothing. "This is no good. It's all freshly laundered."

"What do you need?" asked Deborah.

"Something that she has worn. Something that would have her scent."

Deborah closed the door. Hanging on the hook on the back was a night-gown. "Will this do?"

"Perfect," said Nathaniel. He took the gown and stooped down to Trooper. "Here, Trooper. Smell this."

The collie cocked his head on one side and looked at Nathaniel, who thrust the garment at the little dog. Goliath realising what Nathaniel was attempting, coaxed the dog, too. "Come on, Trooper find Aleka."

The collie sniffed the nightgown and dashed around the room smelling every corner. He searched under the bed before excitedly running to the door and pawing it. They opened it and Trooper raced off and descended the stairs quickly followed by Nathaniel, Goliath and Deborah.

The faithful collie ran from the wing they were in and darted along the corridor to the stone steps that led to the dungeon where the slaves had been kept and Deborah had taken them food. They plunged into the depths of the manor. There was little light. Deborah stopped and picked up a large wax candle, which Goliath was able to ignite from his tinder box. He shone the candle around the damp musty room, which appeared to have been empty for some time. There were buckets in the corner and some mouldy crusts of bread. Trooper became really excited and began to whine.

"What is it, boy?" Trooper continued to whine.

"She was here. I know it," said Goliath.

Behind the wall in the secret room Aleka waited. She hardly dared breathe. She could hear voices in the cellar and tried to listen.

"It's no good. She's not here. Let's go," said Nathaniel but Trooper stubbornly refused to move. He whined some more and began sniffing the back wall.

"Trooper, come;" ordered Nathaniel. But still the dog refused to follow and continued to patrol the wall.

"Wait," said Goliath. "The dog knows something we don't." He called at the top of his voice, "Aleka! Aleka are you here?"

Aleka heard her name and listened more closely. There was something very familiar about the tone and accent."

"Aleka!"

"Lord save me, Goliath, is it you?" She cried out at the top of her voice and hammered on the stone wall.

Trooper frenziedly began to dig at the base of the wall.

"Did you hear that?" said Deborah. "I'm sure I heard a woman's voice."

"Hush," said Nathaniel and tapped on the wall again. There was an answering rap.

"Aleka," yelled Goliath.

"Yes, yes. It's me," she shouted. Her voice was muffled and it was difficult to discern what she was saying.

"She's behind this wall. How do we get to her?"

Deborah shrugged, "I have no idea. I thought this was the only chamber down here."

"There must be a secret way in. Feel the walls." Goliath held up the candle as Nathaniel felt along the stone work. Trooper continued to dig.

"Look!" At the base of the wall where Trooper had continued to dig there was a narrow band of faint flickering light. "Aleka!" Goliath was becoming desperate.

Aleka shrieked with all her might, "There's a stone that sticks out. You have to press it and the wall will open. I don't know where the mechanism is in here."

Goliath and Nathaniel ran their hands along the patch of wall where the light trickled through. They were meticulous in their search. Deborah watched in disbelief and Trooper continued to whine.

"There's something here," said Goliath. "Here where the rock bulges." He pressed it hard and there was a ratcheting, grinding sound. The rock wall began to move and opened to reveal the hidden chamber. Aleka flew sobbing into the strong arms of her husband. He held her close and Trooper danced excitedly around them.

"Are you hurt? Have they touched you?"

"No. The master has been good to me. He hid me here from the parson who wanted to buy me." The words tumbled from her.

"We must get out of here. Hurry now. Deborah you will come with us and I will return you to your parents;" said Nathaniel. "Close this place up again. It may come in useful for someone else."

Goliath hit the protuberance and the wall sealed itself. He nuzzled Aleka's hair and drank in her scent. "I cannot believe we have found you. We have been searching for so long." They started for the stairs and made their way up to the main house.

"Do you need to get anything, Deborah?" asked Nathaniel gently.

"There's nothing here I want," she said. "I just want to go home."

"Right, let's call the Governor and get out of here."

"The Governor?" asked Aleka. "Do you mean my father?"

Goliath nodded, "He received my letter telling of your abduction and came across to search for you. We joined forces in Cornwall."

Aleka wiped the fresh tears that sprouted from her eyes. "I can't believe it."

Nathaniel urged them on. "Hurry. We need to get out now. This must all be documented with the police and Custom House. They will need statements from both of you."

Deborah urged them on, "Follow me. There is another way out of here avoiding the main house." She preceded them and led them through a labyrinth of corridors until they reached the back of the manor. They hurried toward the lawn where they had left their horses. Trooper sat at Jessie's feet and waited to be put in his basket.

"Take Aleka. Let Deborah ride Molly's horse and I'll meet you at the Custom House."

"What about you?"

"I'll get the Governor and we'll be away. No need to alarm her ladyship. She will find out soon enough what will be in store for her."

Goliath nodded. He didn't need telling twice. He helped Deborah onto Molly's horse. She protested, "But I can't ride."

"Don't worry. I will lead you. Just hang on tight." He pulled Aleka up behind him in the saddle and they took off.

Nathaniel strode to the house and tugged the bell pull. The door was opened by a servant. Nathaniel spoke commandingly, "Where is Governor Macaulay?"

"I believe he's in the kitchen, Sir."

"Take me there." He ordered the man. "Oh, and thank her ladyship for her help. Tell her we will be in touch."

"Yes, Sir. This way."

Nathaniel marched on toward the kitchen where Molly sat at the scrubbed pine table with her mother. Governor Macaulay stood at the back door.

"Ah, Governor. Our business here is done. We must leave and continue our search." He tried to inflect some meaning to his words by the expression in his eyes, which Zachary finally realised what was intended. "Molly are you coming with us?"

Molly shook her head, "Thank you, no."

"As you wish." Nathaniel turned smartly on his heel and left by the back door followed by the Governor leaving the cook and servants looking puzzled.

'We must hurry, Sir. Before they realise the game is up;" said Nathaniel quietly.

"And Aleka?"

"Safe."

They reached the horses, and mounted. "I don't feel like riding again for another minute I'm so saddle sore. But, I'm sure we will be safer away from this place." Nathaniel leapt on Jessie's back and began to trot away as Lady Gosling appeared at the door. Her face creased in a frown. Nathaniel gave a cheeky wave and the two burst into a canter.

"Time to get out of here," urged Nathaniel and they followed the path the others had taken.

Jenny stood before Major Charles Watson with Sam at her side. He was an imposing figure in his red jacket and cream breeches with a gold sash.

"Captain, Chapman you say?"

"Yes, he's my brother-in-law and we need his and your help most urgently."

Major Watson summoned his adjutant with a ring of the brass bell on his desk. "Clive, fetch Captain Chapman from his barracks. There is someone to see him." The young aide nodded and left the room "Now, tell me the whole sorry story again," said the major.

Together, Jenny and Sam proceeded to tell the major again of all that had passed in the last few days. They were interrupted by a knock on the door.

"Come," ordered Major Watson and Philip Chapman entered. His face registered alarm when he saw Jenny standing there.

"Is everything all right? Whatever has happened? Is Naomi all right?"

"Naomi is fine. We need your help."

Philip listened carefully to their tale of woe, "I know Bethell, the scourge of the land. He and his crew are the dregs of human kind. I am concerned that young Edith will have suffered lamentably and may not even be alive."

"Then we must hurry. Can you get your men together?"

"As long as Major Watson agrees."

The major acquiesced, "But of course. Take who you need."

Relieved Philip seemed to grow in stature, "Have you your maps? Can you show me where she was taken?"

Sam nodded his head. He opened his dispatch bag that was strung around his neck and retrieved a chart. He spread it out and traced the route they had taken from Jamaica Inn and approximately where the ambush had occurred.

Major Watson peered over their shoulders at the area indicated, "We know of a few places these criminals like to camp. Often near peat bogs where they can get rid of anyone who pays them undue attention. He took a pencil from his desk and marked the map in three places. "I suggest you search here first and if they are not lodged here then there is a house on the moors where we have found contraband before. It is a known hideout of these criminals. Finally, there is a whore house at Bolventor where these ruffians frequent to pleasure themselves. They may have information there."

Captain Chapman nodded assertively, "Thank you, Sir. I suggest, Mrs Brookes stays here until our return." He turned to Jenny, "No disrespect, Jenny, but if you put yourself in danger, who knows what will happen. I, for one, refuse to answer to Nathaniel. He would never forgive me."

Jenny nodded reluctantly, "I know what you're saying is right but I feel duty bound to come with you."

Sam was in total agreement with the captain and adamant, "No. Not now I know you are with child. We have to think of your unborn baby. Stay here, please."

"I have to say I concur with the captain," said Major Watson. "You have been through enough. I am surprised with all the riding that you haven't miscarried already."

Jenny defended herself, "Most of the time I have driven a cart. It is only in the last couple of days I have been forced to ride. But, I see the sense in your words and although I will remain anxious until Edith is safe I will let you do what you need to, so I will."

The men all breathed a sigh of relief. Major Watson offered Jenny his arm, "Let me show you to a place where you can rest. It is where my wife attends me on the occasions she comes to visit."

Jenny turned to Sam before taking the major's arm, "God speed, Sam. Be safe and please find Edith."

Sam acknowledged with an encouraging smile, "I'll bring her back or die trying," he said.

"No one wants anyone to lose their life," said Jenny with an anxious expression on her face. "Good luck." With that she took the major's arm and left the office.

Sam donned his cap and patted Philip on the back, "Come, Captain. We have a hard ride ahead of us."

31

Finding Edith

SAM, CAPTAIN CHAPMAN AND twelve dragoons had been travelling through the day and night. Desperately trying to spare their horses, their trek back to Bodmin Moor was taking longer than expected. They had made camp near Camelford where the horses and men gained a well-deserved rest.

The moon shone brightly in the velvet night sky and a lone owl hooted eerily at the edge of the woods. The men had settled around the camp fire and slumbered leaving Sam and another dragoon on watch. Sam heard someone stir and felt a tap on his shoulder. He stretched up his arms and stifled a yawn. Captain Chapman whispered, "We leave at first light. Your turn to snooze now. Get some rest."

Sam murmured his thanks and lay down to catch some much needed sleep as time ticked on. He knew it would soon be dawn. In spite of the snoring grunts of the men around him he managed to block out all the extraneous sounds quite quickly and drifted into a dreamless sleep.

Time passed.

A magpie called and chattered excitedly as crows began to caw. Sparrows and dunnocks started to chirrup. Dragoons stirred and Sam came to; his back ached from sleeping on the hard ground and for a moment he wondered where he was and then he remembered. He took a lungful of the early morning air and looked about him.

The heavy mist on the edge of the small town that skirted the moor hung low but promised to be vanquished by the rising sun. The dragoons awoke and shook their heads groggily. They cleared the camp and saw to their horses, before preparing to ride. The captain promised they would stop off on route for something to eat and fill their rumbling stomachs. They headed for the market where traders would be up early to set up their wares. There they would find street food to purchase before veering off toward Rough Tor and the moors. Rumour had it that brigands and other unsavoury characters were given to stay on ground near Hawks Tor considered a safe place for them to hide out. Philip Chapman was banking on this, as the moor was a large area to search and not always as benign as it appeared in daylight. Bogs and marshland masqueraded as solid ground and many a poor person had been trapped and died in the sinking mud from straying from the recognised paths.

Clive Bethell and his ruffian gang had moved onto a tumbledown neglected farmstead near Dozmary Pool. It was there they knew to wait until word reached them from their bosses, the Stones. They believed they had leverage with Edith as their captive. She would be instrumental in helping to stop Brookes ruining their illicit trade. As soon as they knew how to proceed they would then use Edith as they liked. There was no honour amongst them. To Bethell women were only good for one thing and that was to be used by men in any way they wished.

Bethell and his men had left their camp in a hurry and not bothered to clear up any evidence of their stay. Wagon wheel tracks and horses' hoof prints were in abundance in the mud and grass, which led all the way to their new hideout.

The rundown farm had been vacated for some two years when the owners had moved onto better land. Robbers and vagabonds were quick to use it to evade the law and Bethell was no exception. The nearby pool was a useful water source and housed many types of different water birds. Game like deer and rabbits would come there to drink so a constant food source was available for the taking.

Bethell sat in a rickety wooden carver chair and rubbed his bristly chin. He refrained from spitting on the floor as was his usual habit but instead used a chipped enamel mug for the purpose. He stared at Edith who cowered uncomfortably in the corner, her hands still tightly bound and ordered one of his men to undo her bonds.

"Get the wench up. We might as well make use of her while we can. She can cook and serve us just as she did for the Brookes." He laughed nastily enjoying the terrified girl's expression. "Now, you can get busy. There's a brace of pheasants there to pluck. You can cook for us all. There's half a sack of potatoes in the pantry and other items. See what you can do. Some good wholesome grub is what we're after. Do well and I'll keep you safe from my men who as you know are desperate to taste your flesh."

Edith flinched in horror at his words as she rubbed her bruised wrists to try and get the circulation back into her hands that tingled in complaint with fizzing pins and needles. Although feeling better to have something to do and to be free of her restraints her anxiety continued to manifest in her shaking hands. She eventually found her voice, "I'll need pans and a knife to clean the birds and peel the potatoes."

"You'll find all you need in the cupboards," growled Bethell.

"And water?"

"Get it from the pump outside."

Edith nodded timidly. She took a rag and wiped down the dusty splintered table before placing the pheasants down. She opened an old battered drawer in the dilapidated dresser and searched through the selection of kitchen implements and selected one knife, which she carefully secreted in her pocket before picking up another blade and turning back to the table.

Edith's hands were shaking as she dragged a shabby stool across the kitchen floor leaving track marks in the grime and dust. She sat and began to pluck the feathers from the first bird. Clive Bethell watched. Edith could feel his eyes on her and it sent her flesh crawling. However, she continued to clean the bird divesting it of its innards before quartering it and then starting on the next.

The silence in the room was unbearable. All that could be heard was the soft sound of feathers being ripped from the body of the creature. She looked up from her task, "I need to get water to clean the bird."

Bethell grunted, "Use the pan by the range and leave the knife on the table. We don't want any accidents now, do we?"

Edith placed the implement down and rubbed her sweating hands down her skirt. She took the jug indicated by Bethell and moved to the door. Bethell rose from his seat with a swagger and followed her to the door. He opened it to let her through and watched from the doorway picking his teeth with a pin kept in his coat lapel.

Edith walked to the pump trying to get an idea of her surroundings as much as she was able and to count the number of men in view. As she pumped the handle she gazed across the moor from whence they had come. She noted the position of the wagon and the horses nibbling on the grass. There was no great area of cover apart from a clump of trees on a small mound. The land was open and anyone would be seen trying to escape or enter the homestead. Her eyes pricked with tears as she believed her chance of escape was non-existent but she was comforted by the feel of the blade hidden in her skirt pocket. She refused to be violated by any of these thugs and would prefer to plunge the knife into her own heart if necessary.

As the water began to gush into her jug she was aware of the attention the criminal gang afforded her and hastened back inside to continue with her chores keen to be away from the leering eyes. She sighed in despair desperately willing herself not to cry.

The Dragoons together with Sam had arrived at the suspect area near Hawks Tor. Sam swore softly. There was no one to be seen and no evidence of anyone staying there recently. Captain Philip Chapman scratched his head. He dismounted and took out his map of the moor. Sam joined him.

"Where did you say you were ambushed?" Sam pointed it out on the map.

"I wonder...."

"What? What do you wonder?"

"I marked three likely spots on the map but it's my guess, they know that we know of their usual haunts. It's a risk but let us take the lesser used trail. I feel they would want to be near water if they were to hide out for any length of time. We'll move on. Go to the body of water near here and if there is nothing move onto Colliford and Dozmary pool."

Sam replied, "I'm in your hands, Captain. I just hope you're right."

Captain Chapman gave the order to mount and the platoon continued onward. The horses moved slowly as the ground they were travelling was less well known.

They had been travelling for about three miles when the lead dragoon gave a shout, "Over here, Sir." Sam and the Captain raced to his side and dismounted. Near to the water and a dangerous peat bog was a small thicket with the remains of a camp fire. In the marshy ground were many hoof prints and wheel tracks of a cart, which led away from the thicket taking a route north east.

"This has to be them," said Sam excitedly.

"It maybe or it may lead us to a place where they have stashed goods. Either way it's all we have at the moment. Come."

The dragoons were now charged with hope and determination. They began to follow the trail doggedly riding where others had ridden before.

They had hardly gone more than a few yards when Sam gave a shout, "Here, look! It can barely be seen." He jumped off Hunter and wrested a piece of material clagged in mud and half buried. "It's Edith's. I'm sure of it. Her bonnet. Look!" He lifted up the item for all to see.

Captain Chapman grinned broadly, "Then we are right. Dragoons forward!"

The men moved onward with enthusiasm and they continued to follow the tracks ahead of them for a further two miles. In the distance they could see a small spiral of smoke drifting up into the sky from a near derelict cottage close to Dozmary pool. The Captain held up his hand and ordered his men to halt.

"We have the element of surprise on our hands. We cannot let them see us. I suggest we wait until the cover of night and then make our move. We will camp here."

"But anything could happen to Edith between now and then," protested Sam.

"If they see us coming, they could pick us off one by one. Maybe even kill poor Edith so there is no witness to their misdeeds."

"What do you suggest?" said Sam subdued.

"We wait until dark and stealthily make our way to the house and take them by surprise. Six men around the back with you and six to the front with me. We will wait until they're off guard or sleeping." He added, "I know you are keen to find Edith. You will have to be patient and trust me."

Sam grimaced. He knew Captain Chapman was right. He would have to wait and bide his time. He sucked in a mouthful of air and murmured, "It's going to be a long night."

Captain Chapman patted him on his back before calling his men to settle and get some rest. Knowing Clive Bethell, as he did, he knew the rescue operation would be tough. Philip took his musket and checked over the firing mechanism to ensure it was in good working order. He noted Sam was watching him and advised, "I suggest you do the same as should all the men. We need our firearms in good working order."

At the Long Room in the Custom House Mr Thomas Anderson, the Excise Officer and Collector, together with the local chief constable, William Colling, sat and listened to the dramatic tale imparted to them. Anderson was a large man with a florid complexion who had a habit of mopping his brow with cotton cloth. He looked shocked especially at Deborah's testimony that clearly implicated Lady Gosling as the head of the criminal gang of rogues.

Chief Constable Colling rubbed his hands in glee, "This is astonishing news. With Deborah Wheelan's testimony and Aleka's statement we have enough to round up the whole band of criminals."

"All the same, I would be loath to enter the manor to arrest the gentry without more proof," exclaimed Anderson turning to Colling.

"What more proof do you need, man?" remonstrated Governor Macaulay. "I think you should know that I can bring the full weight of the Crown whose unequivocal support is behind me regarding this arrest and prosecution. I have been instructed by his Majesty to speak in the final debate on repealing the Slave Trade, a debate put on hold until I had recovered my daughter. As you appreciate this cause is close to my heart and on arrival in England I met with the King and you will be following his instructions through me."

Colling grinned, "I will be delighted to follow through, Sir. I have no loyalty to the gentry, whatsoever. Lady Gosling and her haughty manner looks down on the rest of the community." He rubbed his hands again. "I can hardly wait!"

Anderson mopped his brow that had sprouted more beads of sweat. He blustered, "I beg your pardon, I did not mean to question the evidence. I just don't relish the task in front of me."

"We are not in these jobs for popularity," asserted Governor Macaulay. "I for one would be happy to accompany the constabulary and witness the proceedings."

Anderson hastily responded, "There will be no need, Sir. I shall see that it is done."

"There is no time like the present," insisted Macaulay. He turned to Aleka, "Can you complete your statement and help Deborah compose hers?"

Aleka assented, "Of course, father."

"And then," interrupted Nathaniel turning to Deborah; "We must get you back to your parents."

"But haven't they left home?" asked Deborah.

"Temporarily," said Nathaniel. "They have gone to a relative in Truro."

"My mother's cousin lives there."

"Once these rogues are imprisoned it will be safe to return to your home. We will get you on the coach to Truro. Do you know where to go in Truro?"

Deborah nodded, "I visited there when I was a little girl. I can remember the place."

"That's good. You know, Deborah, you will have done an immense amount of good. You should be very proud of yourself."

"I don't feel it. I am really scared but if Alice... I mean Aleka can stand against them, then so can I."

Governor Macaulay beamed, "That's the spirit. You will both make a difference and now I suggest, Aleka travels with me to London where I can highlight her case in order to back Sir William Grenville and his anti-slavery bill."

"But father..."

Goliath interrupted, "Your father is right, Aleka. It will aid in the abolition of this abhorrent trade. Nathaniel and I have to find Miss Jenny and secure his home so that the family can return. Once your business is concluded then we can move on."

Aleka bowed her head and said quietly, "I am not sure I want to return home. I would be afraid something like that could happen again. Britain may be leading the way in abolishing the slave trade throughout its empire but that is not the case with other countries."

"Then you could both come to Sierra Leone where those who were once slaves walk free under my protection. But, there is much to discuss. This can be dealt with later. First things first."

3 2

R e s o l u t i o n s

NIGHT HAD FALLEN. THE moon, although bright, was now on the wane and when covered by cloud the darkness was all enveloping. Samuel Reeves, Captain Chapman and the dragoons had made their way quietly and slowly along the track following the route of the smuggling cutthroats. Copying the trick, the rogues used, the soldiers had wrapped cloth around the feet of the horses to muffle the sound of their approach.

They had reached the thicket close to the tumbledown farmhouse and dismounted praying that no one had heard their arrival and waited. They knew they had to time their attack perfectly or there would be deaths.

Edith had made an excellent meal from what was available and the men were well fed. After consuming a quantity of rum from the cellar the brigands were somewhat drunk and feeling sleepy. Edith set about quietly clearing up. She tried not to make too much noise but was shaking with nerves. She knew that men's eyes were watching her, mentally undressing her and she shivered.

She went outside followed by Bethell to collect water. He carried a lamp and watched while she pumped. The flickering light did not go unnoticed by the dragoons waiting in the thicket. Captain Chapman alerted Sam and pointed out the wavering lamp glow.

Edith carried the pail of water into the dwelling and filled the cauldron on the range to boil in readiness to wash the crockery and pans. She looked anxiously about her. Most of the ruffians had dozed off sated by a surfeit of good food and rum. Only one on watch and Bethell remained awake, but both were taking more than an idle interest in Edith.

Bethell sidled up beside Edith and stroked her cheek. She flinched and then froze. He spat on the floor and hissed, "Once you are done with the chores then I reckon it's time you and I got better acquainted." Edith choked back a sob. "I expect old Fletcher here will be entertained enough to want a taste, too." He chortled to himself careful not to wake his slumbering men.

He dragged a fractured chair away from the table and sat astride it and watched Edith lasciviously. He allowed himself to fantasise about the young maid to the exclusion of all other thoughts. Fletcher moved away from the window and perched on the table behind Bethell and began to make lewd suggestions. The two men engaged in lecherous banter and Edith grew pink in the face with embarrassment and fear at the lustful crude language used by both men.

Suddenly the doors burst open both front and back and the dragoons poured in. The groggy men came to and went for their pistols. Shots were fired and fighting broke out. Edith screamed before ducking down and she crawled into the space under the sink pulling the rough cloth that hid the space underneath to hide. She could just see through a tiny hole and watched nervously.

The ruffians struggled against the dragoons and brawled like the thugs they were breaking the already damaged furniture and using broken chair legs as weapons against the well-armed dragoons.

Two dragoons fell.

There was little light and the fighting spilled out onto the moorland and into the all-enveloping night. One of Bethell's men, fatally wounded, slipped inside and slid down by the sink dropping his double barrel flintlock pistol, which clattered to the floor. Edith saw the weapon fall. She saw the opportunity and amidst the mayhem she managed to grab the weapon and returned to her hidey-hole.

Bethell and Fletcher, free with their fists and weapons, were tussling with the soldiers. In the weak light it was hard to see which group had the upper hand. Outside two of Bethell's men had been subdued and secured. Captain Chapman ran back inside to help Sam who was struggling with Bethell. Chapman levelled his pistol at Bethell and ordered him to stand down.

Fletcher and the other ruffians inside the farmhouse and the dragoons fell silent becoming still. Bethell appeared to release Sam and it looked as if he was about to raise his hands in surrender but he surprised everyone with a swift flip of his wrists and manoeuvred Sam into a headlock. He pulled him in front of him as a human shield and levelled his pistol at Sam's head. "So, what's it to be, Captain? Shoot your own man to reach me? He's dead anyway." There was silence. Bethell continued, "Or maybe you could get off a head shot and still risk killing him? Either way you lose. And I will retaliate and kill him then you. Your call." He spat onto the floor.

Edith listened and saw all from her hidden place under the sink. She heard the click of a pistol hammer being drawn back. Filled with anger at her situation and the threat to Samuel Reeves something inside her snapped. Edith carefully pulled back the cloth, she stood up quietly and stepped out into the room behind Bethell. She had never touched a firearm before but raised the flintlock pistol levelling it at Bethell's back and fired.

The smell of cordite filled her nose and she shivered in shock as Bethell released his grip on Sam and his pistol tumbled to the floor. As if in slow motion the shock registered on the slaver's face before he dropped to his knees on the floor. His eyes glazed over and he fell face forward, dead.

The stunned dragoons gave a collective gasp. Fletcher grimaced and reached for his knife when Edith found her voice and called, "STOP! Stop fighting all of you." She turned to Fletcher still pointing the pistol and aimed it at his chest, "Drop the knife or I'll shoot."

Fletcher wiped his mouth on his sleeve and not liking the odds stooped and placed the blade on the floor, raising his hands. Captain Chapman took charge and ordered his men to secure the rest of the gang, who one by one surrendered to the dragoons.

Sam went to Edith's side and took the weapon from her. He looked admiringly at the young maid. "Well, aren't you a surprise? You saved my life. Thank you, Edith." Edith blushed. Sam wrapped his arms around her and she leaned into him shaking uncontrollably and trying hard not to cry. "You are a brave woman, Edith. I owe you my life." He tilted her chin and gently kissed her trembling lips.

Deborah had arrived by coach in Truro. Her testimony together with that of Aleka and Governor Macaulay had proved instrumental in the arrest and capture of the Stones. Lady Gosling and her son Richard were under investigation. If need be Deborah was prepared to travel back once more to testify again on the prosecution of the gentry that had subjugated her for so long.

Deborah was full of both apprehension and hope as the coach hit the outskirts of Truro and made its way to the coach stop. Advance word had been sent to her parents and her mother was there to greet her.

"Oh, my dear Lord," exclaimed Frances on seeing her daughter alight. They fell into each other's arms unable to stop the flow of tears of relief and happiness. "Here, let me look at you," said Frances once she had stopped hugging her daughter. She stepped back from Deborah. "My, you have matured and lost a little weight, I fancy."

Deborah laughed, "I think I needed to. I was always too fond of your cooking and puddings."

Francis Wheelan smiled in gratitude, "We have to give thanks to Nathaniel Brookes and his man. If it weren't for them I know you would still be enslaved by the Goslings and made to do their bidding and your father most certainly would be dead. It doesn't bear thinking about."

Frances Wheelan tucked her arm in her daughter's and they walked to Lemon Quay where the wagon waited. Her father sat holding the reins, a look of expectation on his face. He was now fully recovered from his hideous injuries. His joy was apparent as his eyes lit on the face of his daughter. "Well, well. Thanks be to God that he has seen fit to return you to us. We didn't know if you were alive or dead."

"Very much alive thanks to Nathaniel Brookes and I am eager to learn and improve. Miss Aleka has been teaching me to read."

"Reading, indeed? That will improve your chances of work and a good position," said Ross.

"Maybe here, in Truro, but not in Boscastle and that is after all our home," replied Deborah.

"Yes, as soon as it is safe to return Nathaniel has promised to let us know," added Frances.

"But maybe we won't want to go," said Ross. "We have made a good life here. I never expected it but it's true."

"We can relax and take our time," said Frances. "We must celebrate not only your homecoming but I have secured a job as a seamstress and Ross has work in one of the local tin mines. No more worrying about wrecking and smuggling. Not anymore."

"And I should find it easy to gain employment here. There is more work around here. As long as I am free, I feel as if I can do anything."

"That's my girl," said Ross as he urged the horse onto the small cottage they were renting. "We can retrieve all our belongings when the time is right. Now we must look to the future."

Captain Chapman with what was left of his dragoons and the rabble they had arrested made their way back to the military camp at Bude where Jenny waited to greet Sam and Edith. It was a joyous reunion.

"Are we safe, then, to return home?" asked Jenny in her sweet lilting Welsh tones. "I am tired of running away. Now that these cutthroats will get what they deserve, surely we can go home and live our lives?"

Captain Chapman responded, "Although this band is captured there are far more involved in these nefarious activities. You should wait until Nathaniel sends confirmation."

"And when will that be?" sighed Jenny disconsolately. "And where do we go from here? I thought slavery was already abolished."

"It was deemed in 1772 that any slave setting foot on English soil would be freed but pockets of the country have ignored this. This custom needs to be abolished throughout the colonies. Besides the original wording is ambiguous and the law needs to make it clear that the act of dealing in this abhorrent practice is outlawed completely. The trade has gone underground and must be stamped out;" said Major Watson explaining the country's current position. "My instructions are to take you to their lodgings in Redruth. Governor Macaulay is to speak in Parliament. His daughter, Goliath and Nathaniel are to be present and will be called on if needed to lobby those members of parliament reluctant to accept the truth of this hideous trade. Wilberforce's movement to ban it completely must be supported."

"Then what?" asked Jenny.

Nathaniel has already sent for his mother, Bart, Sarah-Jane and Naomi. He hopes to accompany them home and then he will return for you."

Jenny pursed her lips stubbornly in that way she had when she disagreed with having to accept choices made for her. She tossed her head defiantly and sighed through her words, "Very well, but don't expect me to like it."

Captain Chapman smiled, "I wouldn't have assumed anything different. We will set off at first light tomorrow."

With that Jenny had to be satisfied. She rubbed her growing tummy tenderly. "I hope that that will be an end to riding. Nathaniel promised me."

"If Nathaniel promised then I know he will keep his word," said Sam. "Come, get some rest. We have an early start tomorrow."

Gosling Manor was now being subjected to a surprise raid by the local constabulary. Six police officers burst into the manor house led by their staff sergeant who ordered an immediate search of the premises. Lady Gosling emerged from her drawing room where she was enjoying afternoon tea with the Reverend Hamilton.

"What is the meaning of this interruption?" she demanded.

"I have an arrest warrant for you, your ladyship and another authorising a full search of the manor."

Lady Gosling bristled, "And what pray am I supposed to have done?"

"Trading in Slaves and kidnapping."

"This is outrageous. I shall have you horsewhipped and demoted to a mere constable for these ridiculous accusations," Lady Gosling protested vehemently.

Reverend Hamilton came out from the drawing room. "I couldn't help overhearing. Is there anything I can do?"

"Yes, find my son. I am a victim in all this," cried Lady Gosling as she was led away.

In spite of her declarations she was ushered away to be transported to a waiting carriage and ferried to the gaol at Gloucester Castle to await trial. Rumour had it that if she was found guilty she could be taken to a prison hulk like HMS Captivity in Gosport or even to Portchester Castle.

Lady Gosling was adamant that her son was the mastermind behind these criminal activities and that she was innocent and being made a scapegoat by association.

Sir Richard watched the arrival of the police from an upstairs window. His mouth set in a hard line. He knew why they were here and left his room. He crept down the back stairs to the cellars and underground corridors. He hurriedly found the stone that opened the same underground room where he had hidden Aleka and slipped inside. He heard clearly the thudding feet of the police as they searched the subterranean corridors and the shouts from his mother placing responsibility squarely on his shoulders and frowned.

He waited. He dare not light any candles just in case the light seeped into the passageway. He sat in the same rickety chair where Aleka had sat and he thought hard. He would wait until the constabulary had left and then go to see Molly at the inn. From the information he had received he knew she had something to do with the involvement of the police and the disappearance of Aleka and Deborah and vowed, with grim certainty, he would get to the truth of the matter.

He heard movement outside the hidden chamber and gulped a mouthful of air. He didn't move and he didn't breathe until the footsteps faded away. His heart was pounding. He began to understand how many of his captives must have felt when being confined against their will.

Richard Gosling waited and waited.

It was two hours later when Richard emerged from his underground prison. He stealthily crept through the passages, made his way up the back stairs without seeing anyone and slipped out into the cool evening air. He soon mounted his steed and began to make his way to the tavern where Molly worked.

He heard the music and laughter as he approached the hostelry and dismounted calling the Ostler to take charge of his steed before striding in through the doors to the public bar but Molly was nowhere to be seen.

Richard went to the bar, "Is Moll in?"

The landlord scratched his chin, "The wench is in London, pleading the case for someone to be exonerated of kidnap, so I understand. Word has it that you are the man she is so desperate to clear." Gosling looked shocked at the information. The landlord continued, "She's fighting your battle for you with some bigwig Governor from Sierra Leone. She's capitalised on your kind heartedness in helping others down on their luck. Even got some dusky maiden to join her in the plea. You're a lucky man, Sir Richard."

Richard Gosling was stuck for words. He finally blurted out, "Any idea when she'll be back?"

The landlord shook his head, "Not a notion. I could certainly do with her, getting to my busy time of year."

Richard Gosling sighed, uncertain what to do or say. "I'll have an ale," he finally pronounced putting his money on the counter before turning away from the bar to survey the occupants in the tavern. There were those that he knew and some other not so familiar faces at the tables. He turned back to the bar, "Newcomers to the area?" he asked in a low voice.

"Men up from Cornwall. Members of Stone's gang. Did you hear Tobias and his wife have been arrested? They are both singing a pretty song to get a lesser sentence. Reckon that's where the word came from about your mother, Lady Gosling. From them and young Deborah Wheelan. I tell you, the good days are gone."

Richard supped his ale thoughtfully.

In Redruth Jenny had made the acquaintance of Mrs Banfield. She and Edith had set up the cottage to make it as homely as they could. With Nathaniel and Goliath in London Sam was under pressure to ride the Cornish coast but after some frantic messaging with his boss, Daniel Bulled, he was given permission to wait for the return of Brookes and his man in order to keep the two women safe. Even though Bethell was gone, there were many other dangerous rogues who would have liked to get their hands on Brookes' wife and with a bounty on her head it was not a safe place to be.

Jenny turned restlessly in her sleep. Something was niggling her and invading her dreams. She awoke with a start, certain she had heard a noise outside. Jenny rose quietly, careful not to disturb Edith in the next bed. She crept to the window and was staggered to see a light at the end of the lane in the shrubbery. It appeared to be signalling to someone close to the house. Jenny donned a robe over her nightclothes. She put her hand over Edith's mouth and woke her, instilling her to be quiet with her eyes.

Edith immediately sat up in bed. "Put something on, dress as quickly and quietly as you can. I think we have company."

Edith didn't need telling twice. Now wide awake she did as she was bid. "Who are they? What do they want?"

"I fear it is us," replied Jenny. "We must get out of here and fast." Jenny, too, began to dress.

"What about Sam?"

"He must still be sleeping. Hurry now. They mustn't know we are awake."

Jenny grabbed her coat and the two slipped quietly from the room. She knocked tentatively on Sam's door but his bed was empty.

The two women crept down the stairs and into the kitchen, where Sam was standing watching hidden from view from the window. He spoke in hushed tones, "From what I can see there's about eight of them."

"What do we do?"

"I will try and hold them off while you get out the back."

"No, they may be watching the back, too. You can't hold them off alone. It's madness," said Jenny.

"We have to do something. We can't be sitting targets," said Sam.

In the shrubbery, the men were using rags soaked in whale oil and animal fat. There was a sadistic glee running through the foul mouthed group as they prepared to storm the cottage and set it alight. But their flickering lights and covert mutterings had alerted Mable Banfield and her man, Simon who appeared at their back door holding a firearm.

Mabel Banfield shouted to the intruders, "Get off my property or it will be the worse for you." She waved the rifle at them but they were more intent on storming the cottage than taking her threat seriously.

Jenny and Edith saw this diversion as their opportunity and crept to the back door. Jenny tentatively started to open the door when it was barred shut from the outside. There was a hideous crackling outside as flames began to lick and devour the wood of the back porch. Smoke began to wisp under the door and plume up the wall. Shouts went up from outside as the glass in the kitchen window imploded sending shards of flying glass to the stone floor.

They both ran back to Sam who was preparing to fire on the men he could see.

"We can't get out of the back the fire is spreading."

"Go upstairs."

"But that won't be safe. How do we get out?"

"The fire will take a while to reach the upstairs' rooms. Soak some linen in water, put it over your faces." Jenny went to argue but Sam yelled, "Just do it!" The women who had begun to cough ran up the twisting stairs while Sam prepared to take on the thugs who were intent on burning down the cottage.

Jenny's heart was racing as she and Edith dashed to the front bedroom and peered out of the window and watched the unfolding drama below.

Simon had fired on one brute brandishing a burning torch. He fell, wounded to the floor. His screams went up in the night air as his clothes caught fire. He ran to the water trough and jumped in to douse the flames as his skin began to blister and shrivel.

A nightjar shrieked and birds flew up from the shrubbery awoken by the hullaballoo and fire. They flew off to the safety of the fields. Sam took aim and felled another ruffian who was attempting to set fire to the front of the cottage.

It was to this scene that a platoon of dragoons arrived with Captain Chapman, Nathaniel, Goliath and Trooper.

The dragoons charged.

The criminals that survived the bayonetting were rounded up and tied together as Trooper jumped around, nipping their ankles and barking fiercely.

"Where's Jenny?" shouted Nathaniel in anguish. His voice boomed up to the rooftop.

Hearing her husband's voice, Jenny opened the casement window, "Up here with Edith."

The flames had taken hold of the back of the house. The front was now beginning to burn and choking smoke billowed up. One of the scoundrels struggled against his bonds and jeered, "Your missus is done for Brookes. There'll be no saving her." He was rewarded with a solid bite from Trooper and the man tried to kick the dog, but the canine was too agile and clever to be caught. He sank his teeth into the thug's ankles again.

The soldiers took buckets, pans, any vessel that could hold water as Simon pumped and filled them. The containers were passed down the row of dragoons and the first in line threw the water on the ever engulfing flames.

Goliath roared, "They'll have to jump. Do we have a blanket? Anything?"

Mabel ran inside and returned with a patchwork bed spread and looked questioningly.

Nathaniel understood what Goliath intended and they each took a corner. "Here, Philip take one end. Simon?"

Simon stopped pumping water, a dragoon took over from him and Mabel replaced a soldier in the line. The Riding Officers and men stood underneath the casement window holding out the coverlet to break the fall.

Jenny urged Edith, "Go on Edith, jump."

Edith protested, "No, Miss Jenny. It's you who must be saved first, for the sake of the baby."

"Don't argue. Do as I bid. Please."

"But I am afraid of heights," whimpered Edith.

Just then, Sam came thundering up the stairs. "It's no good we can't get out the front the flames are too strong and hot. You must jump."

"I can't," said Edith. "I'm afraid."

"If you don't, you'll burn to death. Is that what you want? I'll lift you up. Close your eyes and leap."

Reluctantly, Edith clambered onto the window sill, shut her eyes and taking a deep breath jumped. The men moved to catch her and she scrambled out of the life saving counterpane. "Come on Miss Jenny. You must be next."

Jenny scrambled up. She crossed herself and said a quick prayer and with her hands firmly placed protectively on her stomach she jumped. A freak gust of wind blew the hungry flames toward her as she hurtled to the ground and her cotton nightshirt caught alight. As she landed, Nathaniel grabbed her and smothered the flames with his own body before crushing her to him. He stroked her hair tenderly when Trooper alerted him by barking and Goliath called, "Nathaniel, hurry. Sam!"

Nathaniel retrieved his corner of the bedcover and the men all held it out for Sam who waited at the window. Wracked with coughing from the deadly smoke, as the searing flames continued to greedily devour all in its path, Sam leapt from the window, his arms flapping like a bird struggling to fly. The men holding the bedspread braced themselves. He landed with a thump and scrambled off, "I thought I was a goner, then. I really did," he muttered.

Nathaniel embraced the man he had come to regard as his friend before Jenny alerted them to those trying to kill the fire. They hurried to help Mrs Banfield and the others to get the fire under control.

Exhausted and sweaty it was over two hours before the dragoons and the others finally stopped the spread of the fire. The cottage was a mess, a smouldering mass of embers. Mrs Banfield was totally distraught.

"This property is one of my main sources of income. What am I to do?"

Simon put his arm around the weeping woman, "I'll get help. We'll rebuild. I promise."

"And we will help," said Captain Chapman; "Once we have put the survivors of this rabble in prison."

Mable sniffed back her tears, "Thank you, Captain but I fear I do not have the money to afford a rebuild."

"That won't be a problem," said Nathaniel. "My family will help." He turned to Philip, "Let me know what you need."

Captain Chapman nodded and assured Mabel Banfield, "Nathaniel Brookes is a man of his word. You can count on it."

"Come inside, Gentlemen. The least I can do is give you some repast. We all need sustenance and rest after the night we have had;" said Mabel. She went inside with Simon and the men trooped after her. They were grubby with smuts and very weary.

"What now?" asked Jenny her face crumpled in concern.

"We, my love are going home."

"Is it safe?"

"It is as safe as it can be. My mother will join us there with young Bart. I believe Aleka and her father will meet with Goliath at our home. Now, let us follow the others inside and get something to eat. You are eating for two now."

Jenny snuggled up to her husband and arm in arm they entered the Banfield's farmhouse.

33

What next?

JENNY HUGGED HER SMALL son to her, before greeting her mother-in-law, Myah. Tears streamed down her face at the joy of the reunion. "There, there, all is well. No one is hurt."

"Except for poor Eric."

"That was awful. What about his family?"

"Taken care of. He lived with his mother in the village. No one else."

Bart came running out of the house followed by Trooper, "Mamma, is it all right if I play with Trooper? He is so much fun. I really love him."

Jenny and Nathaniel laughed at their son's antics, "Go ahead! Trooper will look after you," said Nathaniel and as if to re-enforce what was said Trooper gave an excited woof. Bart whooped and the two raced around the garden joyfully.

Jenny and Nathaniel smiled at their son's enthusiasm, before Jenny became more serious, "At least if Bart is occupied it will give me a chance to continue to get the house sorted out. It was so badly ransacked and I never felt it would look like home again. Who knew it would get so dusty in our absence?"

"You, my love, worry too much," said Nathaniel.

"Do you think it is really over? Are we safe in our own home?"

"I believe so. As I said before we are as safe as we can be. With the gang rounded up we should be. I can't say for all the top dogs in this wretched business. We don't know how many there are and their reach is wide."

Jenny looked unconvinced and went into the house with Nathaniel where Goliath was enjoying a hot drink with Sam in the kitchen. Edith stood preparing vegetables for the next meal.

"Here, let me help you," Jenny said addressing Edith. "Aleka and her father are expected on the four o' clock coach. We have much to do."

"And I will work with you," said Myah breezing into the kitchen. "Once the men are out from under our feet we can carry on."

Sam hastily gulped down the last of his drink and scraped back his chair. "I know when we're not wanted. Come, Goliath. Let us take our horses out." Goliath grunted and followed Sam from the kitchen to the front door where Nathaniel stood watching his small son throwing a stick for Trooper who happily retrieved it and waited for him to throw again.

"What say you, Bart? Our friends are going to ride along the beach. Do you want to come?"

"I'd rather play with Trooper," said Bart.

"He can come, too, if you wish?"

Bart gave a shout of joy and Nathaniel turned to his friends. "You go on, ahead. We will follow and meet you on the beach." He turned to Bart, "Run in and tell your mother what we are doing, while I get Jessie and Minstrel ready." Bart flew in through the door with Trooper at his heels leaving Nathaniel laughing at his young son's exuberance.

In Portchester Castle, Richard Gosling sat brooding in his cell. He gazed around at the filthy state of his prison and the indignities he had been forced to suffer. Some small spark of conscience gave him further insight to what his captive slaves had suffered. He grimaced. The place reeked of urine and other body waste.

There was a clang of keys as the gaoler approached his cell and unlocked the door. Gosling looked up in surprise as he was urged out of his dungeon. He was released from his chains. "What's happening?"

"You are free to go, for the time being," said the guard.

Gosling was not one to question this decision. He was anxious to get out into the fresh air and see the sky and outside world.

He was under no illusion. His woman, Molly had brokered some sort of deal for his release but he still felt betrayed. He would let a suitable amount of time pass and then he would search for her. What he would do when he found her was anyone's guess. But Gosling had plans and retribution filled his mind.

34

Is it goodbye?

GOLIATH STOOD AT THE coach stop with Nathaniel. He was both excited and apprehensive. He looked at the large clock hanging outside the watchmaker's shop. "Looking at the clock won't make the coach arrive any sooner," said Nathaniel with a chuckle.

"I know, I know," said Goliath sheepishly but still gazing anxiously down the approach road. He shaded his eyes from the bright afternoon sun and stared into the distance. He could see a dust cloud in the distance. "That's it! I'm sure of it," he said enthusiastically.

"I think you're right," said Nathaniel looking into the distance.

It soon became clear that it was indeed the four o' clock coach. And both men waited anxiously for its arrival. They had been joined by several other people also keen to meet the travellers from the coach.

The wagon trundled to a stop and the first people off were a mother and child who were greeted happily by a waiting family. Next to alight was Governor Macaulay. He held out his hand to his daughter, Aleka, and helped her off the coach. Goliath took her in his arms and held her close. Governor Macaulay looked on in approval. The coachman and his man took the luggage from off the roof when Nathaniel gasped in amazement as Molly stepped down behind Aleka. She stood there looking nervous and embarrassed.

"Molly! Whatever brings you to Swansea?" said Nathaniel before he could contain himself.

"I will explain all to you in due course. Is there room for us to lodge with you tonight?" asked the Governor.

"Why certainly," replied Nathaniel. "Come let us gather your bags and take them to the wagon. We can talk on the way. We have enough space to accommodate everyone."

Nathaniel picked up two cases and Goliath took a portmanteau. They led the way to the waiting cart. Goliath and Aleka made themselves comfortable in the back whilst the Governor and Molly sat up front with Nathaniel and they began their trek back to the house.

"I don't understand," said Nathaniel to Molly. "I thought you were staying close to Sir Richard?" He turned to Governor Macaulay, "Wasn't there a plea for clemency for the man who was a victim of his mother?"

Molly sighed and her face turned white, "It wasn't quite like that. There is a price on my head now. Even though I have more than enough money at the present, I can't go home or stay at the Manor with my mother."

"Then what are you to do?"

"I was praying, as I helped you, you may be able to help me." She looked across hopefully at Nathaniel.

Nathaniel blew through his lips in a non-committable fashion. "We'll talk further when we get back. For now, I must think."

Nathaniel and company had all arrived safely back at their home in Mumbles. He had talked extensively with Molly and the others on the journey back and was happy to be greeted by his mother, wife and young son. All was as it should be in the Brookes' household.

"This way, Molly. Follow me." Nathaniel led the way to the kitchen where Edith was busy preparing the evening meal. He ushered her to the table as his mother and wife looked on curiously. No conversation could be made until Trooper had stopped jumping around Nathaniel in a fit of ecstasy on seeing his master's return. "Bart, take Trooper outside and play. We have much to discuss and I can't think with his excited yapping."

Bart called the dog and ran out through the back door to the garden with Trooper at his heels and Nathaniel spoke carefully, "Molly, you have indeed helped us all. No one knows that better than Aleka and Goliath and we know what it's like to have a price on our heads. I have a suggestion." He turned to his mother, "Did you say we had guests tonight?"

"Why, yes. Philip and Naomi are coming together with two of his dragoons and Lady Caroline Bevan and her maid in waiting. In fact, Lady Caroline will be here earlier as she told me she has much to discuss with you."

"She has indeed. So, Molly…"

Molly leaned forward eager to hear what Nathaniel had to say. He turned to Aleka, "What say you Aleka? Are you prepared to continue to teach young Molly here to read?"

"Indeed, I am. She is a quick learner. Why? What do you have in mind?"

"I cannot promise anything yet. First, I must speak to Lady Caroline Bevan."

"Nathaniel!" reprimanded Myah. "You cannot leave young Molly hanging like that."

"Nor do I intend to," said Nathaniel inscrutably with a twinkle in his eye. "At least not for too long. Tell me, Molly, what are your feelings towards learning and school?"

"School?" said Molly sharply.

"It's not as frightening as it sounds," said Nathaniel laughingly trying to calm her. "As I said on the way, if you can learn to read and write well, then there will be many more avenues open to you. We will speak more after I have spoken with Lady Caroline." He turned to his mother, "What news of Sam? Is he to join us, too? Edith?"

Edith blushed to her ears and her bonnet, "I know not, Sir. He has promised to write when he can."

"I believe Samuel Reeves has been summoned to Mr. Bulled. He has to take your final reports and has much to explain, especially with your resignations."

The doorbell clanged at the front of the house.

"That will be Lady Bevan. I'll take her into the drawing room," said Myah.

"No need. I'll go. I'll ring when we've finished. Then the others can join us and we may have some announcements to make." Nathaniel swept up from the table and strode down the passageway.

In the drawing room, Lady Bevan stood looking out of the window at Bart chasing around the garden with Trooper. She smiled in delight as she watched the lad laughing and playing rough and tumble.

"You have a fine son, Nathaniel."

"He can be a handful but he's a good boy."

"Looking forward to school?"

"He is indeed…. And that's what I wanted to talk to you about."

"About Bart?"

"No, school."

"As you know my friend Goliath and his wife are looking to settle here, temporarily until all slaving is outlawed. It is not safe for them at their home and they do not want to relocate to Sierra Leone."

"Ah, where all slaves are given their freedom as on English soil."

"Except here the slave trade has gone underground. Soon though our country will be completely safe from such cruelty."

"So, what do you want, Nathaniel?"

"I was hoping with Aleka's skills that she would make a fine teacher for you to employ. And more than that I have another young woman who has surrendered into our protection. She is willing to learn and could be a useful assistant and help with the children."

"That would be more than welcome. There is only Iris and me and, of course, you to organise the science programme."

"Indeed. I am more than happy to help. Perhaps you would like to meet the women concerned?"

"We are all to have dinner, are we not?"

"Yes."

"Then, by all means. I shall be delighted to make their acquaintance."

"As I thought, Lady Caroline. I knew you would not let me down."

Nathaniel stepped to the bell pull and rang. Moments later the door opened and Aleka glided majestically in followed by Molly with her head bowed. Nathaniel made the introductions and announced, "I will leave you all to talk. We will convene in the dining room in say," he glanced at his fob watch, "In ten minutes?" he nodded at the ladies and left closing the door quietly.

The dining room was buzzing with animated conversation as guests and family mingled before Myah invited everyone to sit. Two seats remained empty. "What has happened to your Dragoons, Mother?"

"They will be here. They are on their way to join the military camp in Glamorgan."

Before Myah had finished speaking the bell clanged again. Nathaniel rose to admit them. He returned seconds later with two uniformed men who clicked their heels in greeting.

"First Dragoon Guards, Algernon Bexley and William Soper at your service."

Nathaniel completed the introductions, when Algernon spotted Molly, "Well, I never. If it isn't the cook's daughter from the manor, Molly, isn't it?"

"I believe so," added William, "Molly Grice."

Molly turned quite pink and nodded as the soldiers took their seats. She eventually found her voice and murmured, "Although I believe for safety reasons I will need to change my name. Grice links me with the Goslings and I need a completely fresh start."

The evening progressed well as the sun slipped down leaving the sky a blaze of crimson fire. It seemed that new friendships were beginning and future plans were being made that would ensure they would all have a secure future. Duty done for King and country they now had to look to their own lives and family. That is until the tide would turn again.

Author's Acknowledgements

THIS BOOK IS DEDICATED to all those who support and encourage me, especially my loving husband, Andrew Spear who persuaded me to write full time.

I must mention my lovely son, Ben Fielder who shares my passion for writing and thanks for all the excellent discussions and ideas we share together.

To my commissioning editor Sarah Luddington who is a tower of strength and valuable mentor.

Thanks to some special people in my life, Pamela Hamer, Dawn Wheeler, Sue Taylor, Barbara Davis, Gail Angove and Karen Gulliford.

My lovely FB friends from around the world, who have bought all my books, read them and wanted more.

Future titles will hopefully include, a brand new thriller, the sequel to The Electra Conspiracy and a sixth in the Detective Inspector Allison series. Please feel free to contact me on my Facebook Author's page: https://www.facebook.com/Elizabeth-Revill-221311591283258
If you like my books please click 'Like'. Thank you.

Other books by the author

The terrifying Inspector Allison
psychological thrillers:
Killing me Softly,
Prayer for the Dying
God only Knows
Would I Lie To You
Windows for the Dead

Llewellyn Family Saga:
Whispers on the Wind
Shadows on the Moon
Rainbows in the Clouds
Thunder in the Sun

Against the Tide
Turn of the Tide

Stand alone novels:
The Electra Conspiracy
Sanjukta and the Box of Souls
The Forsaken and the Damned